Julie Miller is an award-winning *USA TODAY* best-selling author of breathtaking romantic suspense—with a National Readers' Choice Award and a Daphne du Maurier Award, among other prizes. She has also earned an *RT Book Reviews* Career Achievement Award. For a complete list of her books, monthly newsletter and more, go to juliemiller.org

Jane Godman is a 2019 Romantic Novelists' Award and National Readers' Choice Award winner and double Daphne du Maurier Award finalist. She writes thrillers for Mills & Boon and also writes paranormal romance. When she isn't reading or writing romance, Jane enjoys cooking, spending time with her family and watching the antics of her dogs, Gravy and Vera.

Discover more at millsandboon.co.uk

K-9 PROTECTOR

JULIE MILLER

COLTON 911: SUSPECT UNDER SIEGE

JANE GODMAN

MILLS & BOON

First Published in Great Britain 2020
by Mills & Boon, an imprint of HarperCollins*Publishers*
1 London Bridge Street, London, SE1 9GF

K-9 Protector © 2020 Julie Miller
Colton 911: Suspect Under Siege © 2020 Harlequin Books S.A.

Special thanks and acknowledgement are given to Jane Godman
for her contribution to the *Colton 911: Grand Rapids* series

ISBN: 978-0-263-28043-2

0820

MIX
Paper from
responsible sources
FSC˙ C007454

FSC
www.fsc.org

Printed and bound in Spain
by CPI, Barcelona

K-9 PROTECTOR

JULIE MILLER

For Dr. Missy and the staff at
Animal Medical Clinic in Grand Island, NE.

You've taken such good care of many of our pets.
And you've supported us when we've lost
our furry loved ones. Thank you.

Chapter One

"He was totally flirting with you, Mom."

Dr. Hazel Cooper startled as her older daughter opened the door to the examination room. She crumpled the disturbing note she'd been reading in her fist and stuffed it into the pocket of her scrubs jacket before fixing a smile on her face and turning around. "You mean Sergeant Burke? I was up to my elbows in dead ear mites and cleaning goop. He brought Gunny in so I could clean his ears and make sure the medication is clearing up the yeast infection he had. He helped me hold the dog and we discussed updating Gunny's leptospirosis vaccine. None of that is flirting."

Ashley Cooper pulled on a pair of sterile gloves before sweeping the pile of soiled gauze and cotton swabs off the stainless steel table into the trash. "I was here to hold the dog. Burke didn't have to."

"Gunny is his boy. Burke is a hands-on kind of owner."

"I can tell he's *hands-on*," Ashley teased. "When Burke moved around the table, he brushed against you. By the way, *you* didn't move away."

Hazel shook her head at that silly reasoning. "Practicality. Not evidence. I wanted to show him that the infection had cleared up."

"Methinks she doth protest too much." Ashley pulled aside the blinds on the exam room's window, giving Hazel a clear view of the parking lot and the man in the black KCPD uniform loading his Czech shepherd, Gunny, into the back of his K-9 unit truck. "He's a bachelor, right? I bet all kinds of women are throwing themselves at him. And yet he brings his dog here to trade quips and rub shoulders with you."

Jedediah Burke opened the back door and issued a sharp command, and the black-and-tan brindle dog, built like a sturdier German shepherd, jumped inside. The muscular dog was strong and moved his powerful body with a fluid grace. Not unlike his partner and handler. As commander of KCPD's K-9 unit, Burke oversaw the ongoing training of the twelve dogs and handlers working for the department, in addition to his own duties as a patrol officer. The material of Burke's fitted black T-shirt stretched tautly across his broad shoulders and tapered down to the thick leather utility belt at his waist and the gun holstered to the thigh of his black cargo pants.

She tamped down the little frissons of awareness that hummed inside her blood as Burke leaned into the truck, pulling other parts of his uniform taut across another well-defined part of his body. The man was fit and interesting and aging like a fine wine. And she really did appreciate a good merlot.

Hazel shook her head at the analogy that sprang to mind. Her daughter's fantasies must be rubbing off on her. She pulled the curtain and turned away from the window. Yes, Jedediah Burke was an attractive man, but she wasn't in the market for romance. Or whatever sort of relationship her daughter was imagining for her.

She'd done just fine without a man for sixteen years.

Many of those years had been difficult. All of them had been lonely. But after that blindingly stellar mistake she'd made in saying "I do" to her ex-husband, could she really trust herself to handle anything more than a few frissons of sexual awareness? Could she ever know a man well enough to give in to her hormones and risk her heart again?

"He's not a bachelor," Hazel corrected, needing to inject some logic and common sense into this conversation. "Burke is divorced." She disposed of the syringe in the sharps container and peeled off her gloves.

"What a coincidence. So are you." Ashley held up the trash can for Hazel to toss her gloves. "You have that in common. I bet that gives you plenty to talk about besides vet care and police work. Failed marriages. Broken hearts. Have you ever comforted each other? I bet he's good in the sack, too."

"Ashley Marie Cooper! I am not just your mother—I'm your boss." She glanced toward the door, confirming it was closed and that no one was overhearing this mother-daughter conversation. "You will not be discussing me being in the sack with anyone. Especially here at work, where another employee could overhear."

"Did I mention you specifically?" she teased. "Or have you been thinking the same thing?"

"Give it a rest." Hazel pulled up the computer screen on the workstation beside the sink to update Gunny's records. "Sergeant Burke doesn't flirt. And neither do I."

Ashley was messing with the curtains again. "Then why is he coming back in here?"

"What?" Hazel spun around to look through the window. Burke was striding across the parking lot, jogging up the concrete steps to the clinic's front door.

"Got you. You just fluffed your hair."

Hazel pulled her fingers down to her side. "My bangs were in my eyes."

Ashley touched her mouth. "A little lip gloss wouldn't hurt, either. You should keep a tube in your pocket." She reached into the pocket of her own scrubs and pulled out a small compact of pink raspberry balm. "Here. Borrow mine."

Hazel backed away from the offer. "You should find a nice young man your own age and focus on him instead of creating a love life for me." She turned her attention back to the computer. "Burke and I work together. He runs KCPD's K-9 unit, and I manage the dogs' health concerns. We're friends. Colleagues. Period."

Ashley pulled the disinfectant spray from the cabinet beside Hazel and spritzed the examination table. "Then you are woefully out of practice in reading men. He was eyeing your butt when you bent over to pick up the cotton swab you dropped. When was the last time you went out on a date?"

"Why are we having this conversation?"

"Because you were just looking at his butt, too. Or is it the square jaw or those deep brown eyes you like?"

"Why are you sizing up Jedediah Burke's attributes? He's old enough to be your father."

"He's not old enough to be yours." Ashley came up beside Hazel and draped her arm around her shoulders. "Besides, hot is hot at any age."

Although Hazel absolutely loved having Ashley working with her at the clinic as a vet tech, they were going to have to set some ground rules about conversations getting too personal here at work. Especially around the rest of the staff, who might not be familiar with her daughters Ashley and Polly's lifelong quest to play matchmaker for their single mother ever since she divorced their father after he went to prison to serve a fifteen-year sentence.

Ashley and Polly had been children then, ages six and four. If only they knew the whole reason for that divorce—and why an eight-year sentence had been extended to fifteen. They'd already been traumatized enough, and Hazel had done everything in her power to protect them. There were some secrets that no child needed to know about her father.

Hazel turned and pressed a kiss to Ashley's cheek. "Just for that remark, you get to finish cleaning up in here. I believe Mrs. Stinson's corgis are waiting for me in room one."

"That's not all that's waiting out there."

A soft knock at the exam room door mercifully ended the conversation. Before Hazel could reach it, the door swung open and Jedediah Burke filled the door frame.

"Hey, Dr. Coop." His low-pitched drawl skittered across her eardrums and made various nerve endings prick to attention throughout her body. He removed his black KCPD ball cap in a politely deferential gesture that spoke to long-ignored feminine appreciations inside her. "One of your receptionists out front said you were still back here. That it was all right to come in."

Good grief, Ashley was right. He did have a square jaw, dusted by an intriguing mix of dark brown stubble salted with silver, which echoed the military-short cut that framed his handsome face.

Why had Ashley put these thoughts in her head? Not that a normal, healthy woman of any age wouldn't notice that Jedediah Burke was an attractive man. But she'd never allowed herself to react to the masculinity oozing from every pore and that air of natural authority he carried on those broad shoulders. And now she was…reacting. Former Army sergeant turned veteran KCPD cop Jedediah Burke was… Burke. A longtime acquaintance. A colleague. A friend.

He wasn't potential dating material any more than the author of those sickly personal letters she'd been receiving was.

Remembering the disturbing notes effectively put the kibosh on these uncomfortable feelings that had surfaced, allowing her to once again bury her attraction to Burke under a friendly facade. "That's fine." She could even get past the staring and offer him a genuine smile. "Did you forget something?"

"Two things. I think I left Gunny's chew toy in the exam room. That dog is all about play. If I lose his favorite toy, he won't work for me."

Ashley picked it up from beneath a chair and handed it to him. "Here."

"Thanks." He smiled and nodded before turning those whiskey-brown eyes back to Hazel. "Plus, I forgot to tell you that I'll be in training sessions with a couple of new recruits all morning tomorrow. The rest of my team and their dogs are coming in to have lunch before you run the monthly checkups on the canine crew. Ed's Barbecue is catering the meal as a thank-you for Pike Taylor and K-9 Hans stopping those teenagers who tried to rob him last month. You're welcome to join us."

"Ed's Barbecue?" She didn't need to fake her enthusiasm at the mention of her favorite hole-in-the-wall barbecue joint. "Are you getting the scalloped barbecue potatoes?"

Burke grinned. "Can't have the pulled pork without the potatoes."

"I can't pass those up." She'd walk an extra mile to

keep the carbs from settling on her already round hips for a chance to indulge in Ed's creamy, yummy potato dish. "I'll get there are soon as I can tomorrow. Make sure you save me some."

"Will do. See you tomorrow." He put his hat back on and tipped the brim of it to her and then to Ashley. "Dr. Coop. Ash."

"Burke." Ashley's squee of excitement burst from her lips the moment the door closed behind him. She threw her arms around Hazel and hugged her. "See? That's flirting. He asked you out to lunch."

"Down, girl." Hazel patted her daughter's arm before pulling away. "The men and women on his team and all their dogs will be there, too. Nothing says romance like routine checkups on slobbery canines and updating vaccinations."

Ashley rolled her green eyes toward the ceiling in a dramatic gesture. "You're killin' me here, Mom. Burke's a stud. And a nice guy. You two share interests and don't have any trouble communicating with each other. Isn't that what you want in a relationship?" Hazel returned to the computer to finish her updates. Ashley followed, her tone sounding more mature, less giddy. "You are an attractive, intelligent, funny, desirable woman who shouldn't be alone as much as you are. Dad hasn't been a part of our lives for sixteen years now. Yes, he's been out of prison for a few months—but we've made it abundantly clear that we don't need his kind of trouble in our lives anymore. Polly and I are grown-up now. You don't have to be the stalwart single mom who provides for us and protects us 24-7. It's okay to move on and fall in love again." She shrugged as though any kind of protest would be a nonstarter. "Polly and I agree—

Jedediah Burke is a prime candidate for you to date. Or have a fling with."

"You dragged your sister into discussing my love life?" Two years younger than Ashley, and a junior in nursing at Saint Luke's, Polly Cooper might be the quieter of her two daughters, but there was no denying that she could be just as stubborn about a cause as the outgoing Ashley. "Of course you have." With a weary sigh, she faced the younger version of herself. "First of all, I'm your mother and I love you both, and I will never *not* want to protect you in any way I can. Secondly, I know it's in good fun, but this matchmaking has to stop. If Burke gets wind of this conversation, it might embarrass him. Not to mention embarrass me if anyone else overhears this grand design you have for us."

There was another soft knock at the door, and for a split second Hazel held her breath, half expecting, perhaps half hoping, that Burke had come back for some reason.

Instead, Todd Mizner, another of the three vet techs who worked for her, stepped into the room, reminding her of just how busy the clinic could get this time of the afternoon. Todd was a few years older than Ashley and was attractive in a nerdy-professor kind of way, with his dark-rimmed glasses and longish hair that he pulled back into a ponytail. The young man was driven to achieve, commuting twice a week to Manhattan, Kansas, to pursue his DVM degree while holding down this job, and he had a real knack for handling animals. Her daughter could do worse than a hardworking cutie like Todd.

Hazel turned to give Ashley a meaningful glance. "Speaking of grand designs…"

But her daughter shook her blond ponytail down her

back, dismissing the matchmaking role reversal, and left the room.

Right. Much to Hazel's chagrin, Todd Mizner wasn't bad boy enough to suit Ashley's adventurous taste in men. Although Ashley had thankfully left her wild-child teenage years behind her, it was another lingering by-product in how the Cooper women dealt with the rest of the world after those long years of uncertainty surrounding Aaron Cooper's betrayal and the subsequent divorce, trial and incarceration.

"It's not so comfortable when the shoe's on the other foot, is it?" she called after Ashley before the door closed.

Todd joined Hazel at the counter while she printed off the notes for Gunny's file. "What was that about?"

"Nothing. Some girl talk."

He reached around her to click the computer mouse. "I've got the X-rays ready on that poodle with the herniated disk. Looks like there is a fracture in the pelvis."

"Oh, damn." That could mean surgery instead of the laser therapy she'd been planning on using to reduce the inflammation making the dog drag its right hind leg. She took her reading glasses from her chest pocket and waited for him to pull the film up on the screen.

Todd muttered a curse against her ear, reminding Hazel that he was standing right behind her. "This computer is doing its own thing again. I can't get the pictures I took to load."

Whether it was a problem with the software or the compatibility of the hardware, Hazel didn't know. And with patients waiting, she didn't have time to figure it out, either. "All right. I'll go look at the film in the X-ray room. You go on to exam three and sit with Maggie's owner. I know she's stressing about the accident.

Make sure there's a box of tissues in the room and see if you can pull up the X-rays on the computer screen in there. I'll want to show her pictures to explain what's going on."

"Can't Ashley do that?"

"She's doing the prelim intake on Cassie and Reggie." Mrs. Stinson's corgis would have to wait until Hazel assessed the poodle's injuries and started treatment. "With the dog's age, Mrs. Miller may be thinking there's nothing we can do for Maggie. I don't want her alone in there." She tipped her chin up to Todd and smiled. "Go use some of that Mizner charm on her to keep her distracted until I can get there."

"But you promised I could scrub in on the next surgery. I want to be a part of the process from initial consult to seeing that dog walk again. Or fitting her for a wheelchair if therapy and surgery don't work."

Todd hadn't budged an inch from behind her, and when Hazel inhaled, her shoulder brushed against his chest. Squashing down an instant imprint of *eeuw* at the contact, Hazel stepped to the side, so she had room to turn and face him. She hadn't batted an eye when, as Ashley had pointed out, Burke had bumped into her. But even this accidental contact with the younger man felt somehow inappropriate. Maybe it was the stress of the long day. Or that awkward conversation with Ashley. Or maybe it was something else entirely that made her anxious to get on with her work. "We'll discuss it later. The priority is the patient's care right now—and that includes the owner as well as the pet."

"The more experience I get, the better. One of these days soon, I'll be finishing my classwork and interning..." Todd rested his hand on the counter beside her, his arm nearly circling around her as he winked. "Then you and I can be full partners."

The message in that letter burned through her pocket and seared her skin. *That* was what bothered her about Todd's tendency to be overly familiar with her. She gently pushed Todd back a step. "Personal space, Todd. We've had this discussion, remember?"

Maybe not such a great catch for her daughter, after all. Todd might be good with animals, but his people skills could use a little work.

He stepped back even farther, putting his hands up in mock surrender. "I don't mean anything by it, Dr. Coop. You know I'm harmless. You're jumpy today for some reason."

No. He was behaving in a way that she didn't appreciate. Not as a boss with her employee. Not as a woman with a man young enough to be her son. Not as someone who'd been receiving anonymous letters that spoke to a disturbing desire for a relationship. She pointed to the door, reminding him that she was the boss here. She didn't have to explain anything to a vet tech who worked for her. "Exam room three."

"Yes, ma'am. Whatever you need." While Todd headed across the lobby to the exam room on the opposite side, Hazel pushed through the swinging door leading into the restricted area where she performed surgery, stored meds and housed specialized equipment. She went straight to the X-ray room to see how poor little Maggie had fared after her fall down a flight of steps.

What she needed was time alone in the darkened room to clear her head. She pulled her glasses from her pocket to study the film. But the moment they touched the bridge of her nose, she thought of the letter and tugged them right back off.

She didn't need to pull out the letter to read it again. She knew every word by heart.

I've been watching you, Hazel.

Your bright green eyes are so intelligent, so pretty. Even when you wear your reading glasses, they shine and entice me. No man deserves you.

I want to be a part of your life. I want us to share everything.

I want you.

I want you.

I want you.

Hazel might not recognize flirting anymore—or maybe she subconsciously chose to ignore it. Her relationship skills might be rusty since her divorce and bankruptcy and the threats and humiliation that had filled her life during her husband Aaron's trial and for several years afterward.

But she'd been a different person then. Now she knew when something wasn't right. A man who wrote *I want you* a dozen times on a letter, and then refused to sign it or even include a return address, did not have her best interests at heart.

This letter, and eight more she had like it at home, told her she'd become someone's obsession.

The feeling of being watched, of being stalked, of feeling terrorized in the places she was supposed to feel safe felt a lot like...

She gasped at the knock outside the open door. "Todd, I said..."

"Whoa." Jedediah Burke filled her doorway again. His hands raised in apology did nothing to lessen the impact of his size dwarfing the tiny room. "Sorry about that. You were really concentrating. Everything okay?"

When Hazel realized she was clutching her hand

over her racing heart, she immediately reached for her glasses again and put them on. With his eyes narrowed on her, she doubted she was fooling him. He'd startled her, and he knew it. Avoiding Burke's probing gaze, she studied the troubling results of the X-ray. "You can't seem to leave."

After a moment he nodded. "I forgot to tell you what time lunch was tomorrow. I know I could have texted, but I was already here." He stepped into the room, stopping beside her chair to glance at the X-ray. Unlike when Todd had invaded her personal space, she knew the strongest urge to turn and lean into him—especially when his hand settled gently on her shoulder. "Did something happen? Lose a patient?"

Damn it. The man smelled good, too. An enticing combination of spicy soap and the subtle musk of the early-October afternoon clinging to his skin that only intensified in the small confines of the X-ray room.

Hazel considered brushing off his concern and sending him on his way. Then her peripheral gaze landed on the brass KCPD badge clipped onto his belt. Burke represented help and safety in more ways than one. She'd known him for five years now. She could trust him with this. She tucked her glasses back into her jacket pocket and tilted her gaze up to his. "Could I ask you something? As a police officer?"

"Of course." He pulled away, the moment of compassion masked by his wary alertness.

She pulled the note from her pocket and spared a few moments to smooth it open against the tabletop before handing it to him. "Would you read this?" He'd probably think she was being paranoid. Or maybe he'd be angry that she hadn't reported the letters sooner. His chiseled expression grew grimmer with every line he skimmed.

"Is that normal?" she asked.

"Who's it from?"

She hesitated a beat before answering. "I don't know."

"Then no, it's not." He leaned against the door frame, facing her again. "Got a jilted boyfriend I need to worry about?"

The friend she knew might be teasing her to help her feel a little less worried, but the cop was waiting for an answer.

She'd asked for his opinion. She owed it to him to give him a clearer understanding as to why an innocuous note could rattle her this much. "At first, I thought my ex-husband, Aaron, was writing me again. You probably remember him from the news a few years back." Burke nodded but waited for her to continue. "He used to send me flowery garbage like that when we were dating. I told him I wasn't impressed, and he stopped. He always said he liked my directness—until he went to trial. Then he wasn't real keen on me telling the truth. The letters he used to write from prison were straight-out blame for testifying against him. Those were angry tirades. I stopped opening his mail and then had a judge stop them altogether. I asked him not to have any contact with me or the girls. There were too many threats back when the trial…back when Aaron was arrested. He ruined a lot of lives when he raided those retirement funds. I didn't need his vile messages on top of the threats we were getting from other victims."

"*Other* victims?" Oh, hell. He'd picked up on that rare slip of the tongue. "Were you a victim, too?"

She shook her head instead of answering the question. "I just meant I thought the obsessive language meant they were from my ex."

"You said *they*?" Burke repeated, holding up the letter. "You thought *they* were from your ex."

Damn. He didn't miss a trick. No sense avoiding the full truth with this veteran cop. "That's the ninth one I've gotten since the first one came on my birthday, August 5."

"Nine letters in nine weeks?"

"The first ones were pretty innocuous. But…he seems to get angrier or more frustrated with each letter."

Burke turned the paper over, inspecting it for identifying clues she knew he wouldn't find. "Did the envelope have a post office stamp?"

"Kansas City. But no return address."

"Is Aaron still in prison?"

Hazel shook her head. "He got out on parole the end of last year. The restraining order should prevent him from having contact with me or the girls. But then these started arriving. They're not exactly a threat, but they're…unsettling."

"Do you know where he is now?"

She stood when he handed back the letter. "Our lives have been a lot more peaceful without him. I didn't want to jinx anything by reaching out to him. Even through a third party."

"I'll look into it." Burke reached for her hand. But it wasn't a reassuring squeeze he offered so much as a warning. "But I'm guessing he's here in Kansas City."

Chapter Two

"Uh…huh…" Hazel drew out her response as she looked through her scope into Gunny's ear. "Everything's looking pink and perfect. No signs of the infection."

Burke mirrored her, scooting around to the other side of the examination table while she moved to inspect Gunny's other ear. Although he trusted that Gunny would maintain his stay command until he released him, Burke had volunteered to hold the big dog while Hazel gave the Czech shepherd a final all clear on his ear treatments. With all the exam rooms full and clients waiting in the lobby, it was clear that Friday afternoon at the clinic was a busy time for boarding drop-offs and medical appointments. Letting Burke stay here to help not only freed up a member of her staff to work with another patient but also gave him a few minutes of privacy he needed to update Hazel on what he'd found out about her ex-husband and the letters.

There was one particularly disturbing item he'd discovered in Aaron Cooper's arrest record. While the cop in him wanted to dig into the details, the man in him wasn't sure how he'd handle what he might find. Besides, Hazel was a private person, and if she had chosen not to mention the incident in the five years they'd known each other, then he wasn't going to bring it up. Not yet, anyway. He understood about divorce and betrayal, and that the injured party did whatever she or he had to in order to move on with their lives.

But if push came to shove and there really was a credible threat here, or he had any inclination that history was going to repeat itself, then privacy be damned. He'd demand the whole truth from Hazel in order to mount the comprehensive security detail she might require. And if she still wouldn't share, he knew other ways to get the specifics he needed. But he wouldn't like going behind her back, and neither would she.

Burke scrubbed a hand over Gunny's brown-and-black head, more to keep the dog from falling asleep than to prevent him from acting up while he lay on the table and let Hazel check him out. His nostrils flared with a calming breath as he edited any emotion from his tone. She'd asked him to do this favor as a professional, not as the man who was finding it harder every day to respect the boundaries she put up between them. "I talked to Aaron's parole officer and notified Officer Kranitz about the letters. He'll ask your ex about them. If Kranitz thinks Aaron is responsible for sending them, he'll remind him about the restraining order. After that, another letter arrives and he's back in jail."

Hazel peered into the scope and nodded. "That can't prevent him from giving the letters to someone else to mail for him. Even at the worst of the lawsuits and legal proceedings, he always managed to have a couple of pals who seemed willing to do his bidding. Still don't know if he paid them to be his allies or relied on his rather convincing charm. One thing Aaron always excelled at was making deals."

Damn. Not one blink to reveal just what her ex-husband had been capable of, and what she must have gone through at his hand. Instead, she straightened and smiled up at him. "This ear is looking great, too. I'd say your partner is fit for duty."

No details today. Burke wasn't going to push, because he had a feeling Hazel would retreat to that unspoken distance between them that he'd worked patiently to overcome. He didn't want any of the closeness they'd settled into in this relationship, which was something more than friendship, yet something less than what he truly wanted, to erode.

"Good." He moved his hand along Gunny's fur to pet his flank as Hazel took over scratching around the dog's ears. He grinned at the way Gunny turned his head into her palm, savoring her touch. He ignored the sucker punch of jealousy he felt and ordered the dog up to a sit. "You're gettin' soft, big guy. I need to get you back to more than just training sessions."

Hazel set the scope on the counter behind her and came back to rub her hands around Gunny's jowls. "Don't you listen to the mean ol' sergeant," she teased. "You're as tough as any cop on the force."

"Don't encourage him," Burke teased right back. "He's already got a big ego I have to keep in check."

Now the examination was done, and they were standing around spoiling his working K-9 instead of all three of them getting back to work. If Hazel hadn't shown him those creepy letters she'd been receiving and asked him to help her reclaim some peace of mind by finding out where they were coming from, he'd have no reason to be here at all.

While he couldn't say for certain who was sending her the anonymous notes, he had done everything he could to give her that peace of mind. "Your building downtown seems secure with the parking gate and coded entry system. While I don't like that wall of windows at the front of your condo where anybody and his brother could look in on you if they're in a high enough location, at least you're not on the ground floor. Plus, they've done a good job installing locks on the front door and fire escape windows."

"A refurbished historic building has structural limitations. I saved long and hard to buy that place. Plus, it's only a few blocks' drive from the clinic. At least it's in a good neighborhood near the library, hotels and convention center."

Burke nodded. No place was truly safe if someone was determined to get to her. And the fact that the perp had said he was watching her made him think he knew exactly where she lived. Or worked. Or both. "I also talked to hospital police regarding Polly and the potential threats. They'll do what they can to keep an eye on things there. Polly and Ashley's apartment has good security, too." His fingers stilled in Gunny's fur beside the KCPD vest the dog wore. "I've also got Aaron's current address. If the harassment doesn't stop and you want Gunny and me to pay him a personal visit, I will."

Her hands stilled as well, and her cheeks went pale. "I hope it doesn't come to that. You've been very thorough."

"How else would I do my job?"

Hazel reached across the dog to squeeze his forearm. Every nerve ending in his body zeroed in on the skin-on-skin caress. "Thank you."

"You're welcome."

He was tall enough that he could lean across the table and kiss her if he wanted. And damn, he wanted to. He wanted to ask her out, too, as evidenced by that half-assed attempt to invite her to lunch last week. There was something about Hazel Cooper that made him stupid like a teenager again. Probably because he hadn't wanted a woman the way he wanted her for a long time. She made him laugh. She got his dry humor. She was a smart woman and damn good at her job, and, despite trying to camouflage them in those scrubs and jeans, she had just about the sweetest curves he'd ever seen. And though he suspected that tomboyish pixie cut of hair was all about convenience, the silvery blond bangs drew his attention to her pretty green eyes, and the short length highlighted the elegant column of her neck—a whole stretch of creamy skin he'd like to nuzzle his lips against and taste with his tongue.

But he respected her unspoken wish to keep a friendly professional relationship between them. Besides, his ex-wife, Shannon, had burned him badly enough that he'd choose a woman whose friendship and loyalty he could trust without question over satisfying any itch he had to find out what Hazel's skin tasted like. Pity he couldn't find a friendship like this and a lover in the same woman. He might not be such a crusty, out-of-practice horndog around Dr. Coop if that was the case.

It took a slurp of Gunny's tongue across Hazel's jaw to break the standing-and-staring spell that had possessed him for a few seconds. Burke wisely shrugged off her touch and pulled away as she laughed. "Sorry about that. I guess he's done. Gunny, down. Good boy."

He petted Gunny's flanks, buying himself a few seconds to set his game face back in place. He should *not* be jealous that his dog had kissed Hazel before he had.

Hazel scratched Gunny near his tail before turning away to the counter to open a cookie jar filled with green chews. "Want a treat?" Gunny's tail thumped against Burke's leg in anticipation of his reward. "Who's the best patient ever? That's right, Gunny. It's you." Hazel held up her hand, giving the dog a command. "Sit. Good boy. Here you go." He liked that she respected the dog's training and didn't simply spoil him with treats and petting, although his K-9 partner had no problem being a hand-fed couch potato when his vest was off and he was off duty. Hazel rubbed Gunny around the ears one last time before opening the door onto the hallway that led to the lobby. Burke was pleased, too, that the dog's ears were no longer sensitive to the touch and itching like crazy. Dr. Coop did good work. She smiled. "Come on, you two. I'll walk you out."

Gunny automatically heeled, noticing the people, pets and displays of food and treats and other supplies around them, without showing much interest or taking his focus off Burke as they followed Hazel to the front counter. The big dog paused once to touch noses and match tail wags with Cleo, the three-legged, one-eyed miniature schnauzer who trotted around the counter to greet him. Hazel brought the smaller senior dog to work with her every day, where she lounged in her own bed beside the reception staff or worked as something of a goodwill ambassador around the veterinary clinic. Cleo had earned the strands of white showing in her gray muzzle, and she made it her business to greet favorite customers and new patients. Gunny was definitely on Cleo's favorites list. If Burke was given to fanciful imaginings, he'd think Gunny and Cleo had a bit of a crush on each other, judging by the way they rubbed against each other and made quick work of the whole tail-sniffing scenario.

Hazel Cooper, however, *was* prone to fanciful imaginings with the animals she worked with. As Cleo danced between her legs and batted at Gunny, encouraging him to play, Hazel reached down to pet the schnauzer's flank. "That's right, your boyfriend's here."

"Cleo does know she's fixed, doesn't she?" Burke teased. "Her flirting's not going to do her any good. Nothing's going to happen between these two."

"A girl can still look, can't she?"

When Hazel straightened, her gaze traveled up his stomach, chest and jaw to meet his. A flare of heat passed between them, and Burke's mouth went dry. Well, hell. What kind of mixed signal was that? The good doctor had checked him out. So it was okay for her to look, too? But she still wanted him to keep things professional and friendly between them? Maybe the rules of dating had changed too much since he'd last taken the plunge and he had no business even considering acting upon the connection the two of them shared.

Whatever spark she'd felt, she either dutifully ignored it or else it fizzled out. Hazel leaned over the counter to speak to the receptionist at her computer. "Go ahead and send today's bill to the police department," she instructed, before tilting her gaze up to his again. Burke liked that about her, too—that she made direct eye contact with him and didn't mince words. At six feet two, he figured he was about eight inches taller than she was, but the veterinarian never let that deter her from meeting his gaze, no matter how close they stood. "I don't need to see Gunny again until his next checkup or shots are due. Just be sure to keep his ears clean. And if he starts shaking his head or scratching again, you can use more of that medicated ointment I gave you. Call me, of course, if that doesn't take care of it."

"Will do." He was out of excuses for hanging around

the vet clinic and Dr. Coop. Gunny had a clean bill of health. He'd stretched out on the floor and Cleo had propped her two front paws on his back, as though standing tall on her big buddy's shoulders made her a big dog, too. But even though Gunny was enjoying the pseudo-massage of the other dog walking on him, Burke was on the clock. And he had nothing left to report on the background investigation he'd done on Hazel's ex-husband. He pulled his KCPD ball cap from his back pocket and adjusted it over his closely cropped hair. "Better get back to work. I'll keep you posted if I find out anything more about—" he glanced around at all the people in the front waiting area "—that matter we discussed."

"Thank you," she mouthed, no doubt appreciating his discretion about keeping her private affairs private. "See you next time." Burke nodded. She pursed her lips together and made a noisy kissing sound to get her dog's attention. "Cleo, come."

After a tumble onto her back leg, Cleo quickly righted herself and trotted over to her mistress to be petted. Then Hazel picked up the stack of mail the receptionist set on the counter for her and started sorting through the letters, a couple of magazines and a padded mailer. Burke had turned to the door and pulled Gunny into a heeling position when he heard the soft gasp behind him.

"Dr. Coop?" He turned to see the lighter envelopes floating to the floor alongside the small package Hazel had dropped. "Hazel?" Her panicked gaze darted up to his when he used her first name. What the hell? He glanced down at the mess around her feet, searching for one that looked like a threat. "Did you get another letter?"

With a curt nod to him and a forced smile for everyone else in the room, she shook off her momentary panic and squatted down to gather up the envelopes and magazines. "Maybe. I don't know. There's no return address on that package, and the label is typed. Like the others. But there haven't been any packages before." Like Cleo, Gunny was curious why his favorite doctor was down at his level. The dogs sniffed at Hazel, sniffed the scattered mail…and then Gunny sat. "The others have gone to my home address. This is the first one to come here." Burke's concern that some anonymous turd had upset Hazel again morphed into something far graver when Gunny tipped his long brown snout up to him. Ah, hell. "Maybe it's nothing. Not everybody puts a return address—"

"Don't touch another thing." He grasped Hazel by the arm and lifted her to her feet, placing her behind him as he backed away from the counter. He scooped Cleo up with one hand and put her in Hazel's arms when the smaller dog tried to sniff the package, too.

"What are you doing?"

Burke pulled out his badge and held it up to identify himself to the entire room in a clear, concise voice. "I need everyone's attention. I'm Sergeant Jedediah Burke, KCPD." He swiveled his gaze to include everyone in the lobby. "I need everyone to stay exactly where you are. Does everybody have control of their animals? Don't. Move."

Hazel hugged Cleo to her chest. "Burke?"

"That includes you. Stay put. Don't let the dog down." He nudged her back another step before clipping his badge back onto his belt and leading Gunny out the double glass doors.

When he came back in with the dog, he was aware of fearful stares, questioning looks and a nervous laugh from behind the counter. But nobody spoke, nobody questioned his orders as he let Gunny nose his way around the shelves of dog food, a cat meowing in its carrier, then along the edge of the front counter and back to the pile of mail on the floor.

Gunny alerted again when he reached the padded envelope, sitting back on his haunches and tilting his nose up to Burke.

Burke swore. He slipped Gunny's chew toy reward between his teeth and pulled him away from the envelope, praising him for doing his job.

Gunny's nose was as reliable as clockwork.

Hazel's love letters had just taken a very sinister, very deadly turn.

He pulled his radio off his belt and summoned Dispatch before looking down into Hazel's worried expression. He couldn't spare more than a glance to reassure her he hadn't completely gone off his gourd because he needed to act.

"I need everybody—people, animals—to evacuate the building ASAP." He swiveled his gaze to include every staff member and client in the lobby. "I want you all at least twenty yards away, in the front parking lot. Turn off your phones. Do not send a text. Do not call anyone." He looked to Hazel again because he knew he could rely on her to keep her head and get the job done, even if she was frightened. "I'll need a head count to make sure everyone is where they should be."

"Of course." She waved the three receptionists out of their seats while Burke positioned himself to blockade the padded envelope, so that no one would accidentally step on it as they hurried to do their boss's bidding. "Linda. Get on the headset, get the staff out of the back rooms. Tell everyone I want them in the parking lot. Get the animals we're boarding on leashes and put them in the kennel runs out back. Todd." She pointed to the swinging door as the young man came out of an examination room. "Get the two dogs we neutered this morning out of Recovery. Ashley—"

"I'll take care of the customers out here, Mom." Hazel's daughter didn't hesitate to do her mother's bidding, but fear was clearly stamped on her face when she stopped in front of Burke and asked, "What's going on?"

"It's just a precaution," Burke answered, nodding toward the exit and urging her to keep moving. "Call it a fire drill."

"There's a fire?" she whispered. "The alarm didn't go off."

Hazel pressed Cleo into Ashley's arms and turned her to the front door. "It's okay, sweetie. Just do as Burke says. I'll go through the exam rooms."

Ashley nodded, then held out her arm to escort one of their elderly clients to the parking lot, where customers, patients and staff were gathering. Hazel opened the doors to each examination room and led the pets and people into the lobby.

"Twenty yards out," Burke reminded Todd as the young man hurried by with the dogs from the recovery room.

Todd spared a worried glance for Hazel as she stepped back from the double doors at the front vestibule. "Dr. Coop, you coming?"

"I'll be right there." Hazel peered through the glass, counting her staff members and assuring their safety before she turned around and came back to find Burke relaying details to the dispatcher. Normally he would have used his cell phone, but he couldn't risk using a wireless signal until he knew more.

"What's going on?" she demanded the moment he signed off. She needed an explanation to fit his evacuation order and calm the panic caused by the sudden mass exodus. "I know there's no fire. I heard the dispatcher say she was sending a unit. Who's coming?"

"The bomb squad."

Her eyes widened before dropping her gaze to the unmarked package. "A bomb? I thought it was just another... I hadn't gotten a letter this week. I'd hoped Aaron would stop once his parole officer spoke with him. Did that just piss him off?" He could tell she was hoping he'd say this was a false alarm when she tilted her face back to his. "You think he sent a bomb to my clinic? With all these people? These innocent animals?"

Burke reached down to rub Gunny's head. "Gunny alerted there was an explosive. That nose of his is never wrong." Taking Hazel by the elbow, he escorted her to the vestibule. He wished he could tell her there was nothing to worry about, that it was okay to smile and erase the fear he read in her eyes. "I need you outside, too. Gunny and I have to clear the building."

"But..." She planted her feet and refused to leave. "That's what the bomb squad is for, right? Shouldn't you have backup?" She splayed her hand at the middle of his chest. His heart leaped against her urgent touch. "Or body armor?"

"Go. It's what we do." He cupped her cheek and jaw in his hand. "But I need you to be safe before I can go to work. I need you to be in charge out there."

She nodded. Then, with those green eyes tilted up to his, she covered his hand with hers. "I'll see you outside," she vowed, as if her will could guarantee that they'd be reunited.

Bombs didn't come with any kind of guarantee. He'd seen far too many of them when his Army unit had been deployed to the Middle East. He'd seen more than he'd ever imagined stateside now that he wore this uniform. The volatility of the explosives Gunny had been trained to detect meant, by their very nature, there were no guarantees he could give.

He traded a curt nod before opening the door and sending her out.

Burke watched her join Ashley and that ponytailed vet tech before he felt the eager tension radiating up Gunny's lead into his hand. The dog thought bomb detections and building searches were a sport that would end with a tug-of-war game with his favorite toy if he successfully found his target. But Burke knew just how serious this job could be.

Backup was en route. But KCFD and the bomb squad couldn't do a damn thing to help unless he could tell them that there were no other explosives, no other potential casualties on-site, no perp lying in wait to take out a first responder. Their job was to make sure it was safe to enter the building to deal with whatever was in the package that some pervert had sent Hazel.

"Gunny, *voran*!" Burke tugged on Gunny's leash and gave him the search command in German. "Come on, boy. Let's go to work."

Chapter Three

"Lookin' good, Shadow." Hazel checked the incision
on the black Lab she'd neutered that morning, adjusted
the E-collar around her neck and petted her chest before closing the door to her kennel.

The big dog yawned and laid her head down on the
cushion inside the kennel, relaxing as though she'd
come for a day at the spa instead of a desexing operation and a bomb threat. Hazel wished she could slough
off the stress of the day so easily. With the fire department and police cars that had blocked traffic around the
clinic gone, and no one left from the bomb squad here
except for Burke's friend Justin Grant, she should be
breathing a sigh of relief. All but one of her clients had
rescheduled appointments and left once the police had
deemed it safe to move their vehicles out of the parking lot. The animals she was responsible for were all
safe. The members of her staff, although understand-
ably shaken by the threat, had gone back to their duties,
like the professionals they were, to finish out the work-
day as soon as the first responders had informed them
it was safe to come back inside the building.

But *safe* was a relative term.

Hazel couldn't help thinking that the vial of C-4 pel-
lets and a trigger mechanism wrapped in a bunch of col-

orful unconnected wires were meant to do more than scare her. Why would a man who'd write love letters— no matter how unnervingly obsessive they were—send her a package of bomb parts? Did he think being afraid would make her turn to him for comfort? Was he angry because she hadn't responded the way he wanted to his professions of love and desire? Not that she could respond one way or another to a man who refused to identify himself. And if the package had come from Aaron, was he still so angry with her that he'd send what could only be construed as a death threat?

Sixteen years ago he hadn't been so courteous to give her that kind of warning.

For a few nightmarish seconds, Hazel's breath locked up in her chest as she relived flashes of memory from that horrific night when Aaron had done what he thought was necessary to stop her from testifying against him.

Even though there were no words, there was a message for her in that package.

If only she knew what it meant, and who had sent it, she could devise coping and security strategies—she could turn his name over to KCPD and move on with the useful, contented life she'd created for herself and her daughters. She'd dealt with death threats against her and her daughters before, years ago when Aaron's crimes had been discovered, and the people who'd trusted him had lost everything. Hell, she'd dealt with Aaron, who'd been even more frightening. But how did she equate *I want you* with the promise of violence and death?

What had she ever done that was so horribly wrong that someone wanted to do this to her? Again.

Hazel pushed to her feet. She hugged her arms around her waist and leaned against the frame of the kennel wall, closing her eyes for a few moments to take in the familiar sounds and smells of her clinic. From Shadow's nasal breathing to the rustle and vocalizations of the other animals settling into their kennels for the evening, from the stringent tang of antiseptic cleanser used on her equipment to the more earthy scents of the animals themselves—this was her world, her safe zone, the place where she felt most at home. She was the authority here, in charge of her own schedule, her own destiny. She was surrounded by her daughter and friends and work she loved. Being here helped to center her and call up the strength that would get her through this nightmare of being the focus of someone's dangerously obsessive attention.

She inhaled deeply, intending to release a calming breath, when the air around her changed its scent. She opened her eyes a split second before Todd Mizner reached for her and pulled her lightly against his chest.

The younger man's supportive hug startled more than it comforted. "You okay, Dr. Coop? That was a big scare, wasn't it?"

If she hadn't felt the trembling through his arms, she might have chastised him for the unwelcome contact. But Todd was probably as rattled by the idea of a bomb threat as she'd been. Like some men, maybe he wouldn't admit his fear, but he took comfort by helping someone else deal with hers. Instead of pushing him away, she settled her hands at his waist and let him hang on to her for a few seconds before stepping back. "I'm fine, Todd. Thanks for checking. Fortunately, no one was hurt. We've reopened for business. I think we'll be fine."

He adjusted his glasses on his nose before frowning at her response. "We've all got your back here. You know that, right?"

"I know that, Todd. Thank you." She squeezed his arm and patted it just like she had the dog and moved on to the next kennel to check her patient there. "Are the staff doing okay?" she asked. "How are you holding up?"

"I'm not the one that package was addressed to." He reached in beside her to adjust the dog's E-collar while she inspected the sutures, brushing his shoulder against hers. Although she often made accidental contact with the vet techs when they were working together with an animal, Todd's next words made her think she needed to have a conversation with him about the difference between *friendly* and *too friendly* when it came to his interactions with the female staff here at the clinic. "You know, if you want to go get a glass of wine or something to unwind and let the tension go after work, I'd be happy to take you someplace."

"Todd—"

When she started to refuse, he put his hands up in surrender, retreating a step to give her the space he must have just realized he'd invaded again. "A bunch of us could go. Celebrate life and all that after our close call this afternoon."

Hazel shut the kennel door before answering. "No, thank you. If you and some of the others want to celebrate, that's great. I love hearing that you all are supporting each other. But I think I'll be heading straight home once this day is over. I'm exhausted."

"You sure?" His disappointment in her refusal to join him, or them, was evident for a few seconds before he rallied with a smile. "Maybe another time."

She made a point of checking her watch instead of

replying to the open-ended invitation. "You'd better get those dogs we're boarding out for their last run before we close up shop."

"Anything you say, boss lady."

After Todd left to do her bidding, Hazel went through her office and the workrooms in the back to grab her purse, turn off lights and close the doors that connected to each exam room. Maybe there hadn't been anything all that unusual about Todd's concern for her. By the time she reached the reception area, her staff had all the computers shut down, and the appointment schedule and prescription orders ready for the next morning. One by one they gave her a hug and wished her goodnight, repeating Todd's invitation to join them for a celebration-slash-commiseration drink. Hazel thanked them all, commended them for keeping their heads in a crisis and ordered them to have some fun.

The sky was gray with twilight and the air smelled of ozone ahead of the promised storm by the time she hooked Cleo to her leash, locked the front doors and headed down the ramp to her truck. Two other trucks remained in the parking lot, both with the distinctive black-and-white markings that identified them as KCPD vehicles. Her gaze instantly went to the broad-shouldered man leaning back against the K-9 truck with his arms crossed over his wide chest in an easy, deceptively relaxed stance. Burke was in the middle of a conversation with the senior officer from the bomb squad she'd met earlier, Justin Grant. Clearly, the two men were friends, judging by the laughter they shared. Justin was younger—blond, slightly taller than Burke, and built like a lanky distance runner. Of course, most men seemed slighter standing next to Burke's muscular build.

Hazel's eyes widened as the surprising observation popped into her head, and she hurried Cleo over to a grassy patch in the landscaping around the parking lot for the dog to take care of business before the drive home. What was she doing? Comparing other men against Burke's standard? Officer Grant was a handsome man, but she had barely noticed him once she'd caught sight of Burke. She wasn't naive enough to deny that she was attracted to Burke on some subconscious level—any healthy woman would be. But when had her conscious thoughts become so attuned to the rugged police sergeant?

Once Burke caught sight of her and Cleo, he straightened away from the truck and smiled. Maybe that was what the distraction was—Burke's attention always seemed to shift to her whenever they were in the same space together. That could explain her hyperawareness of him. Why wouldn't she be equally aware of a man whose focus was concentrated on her?

That was all this was—alert cop, polite man, a few errant hormones appreciating the attention after so many years on her own—and the last years before that with Aaron, when she'd been reduced to invisibility one day, verbal whipping dog the next and, ultimately, the target of his desperation. She and Burke had shared a special friendship from the time when she'd first started working with him and the other K-9 officers at KCPD. He respected her. He was a calm presence. Sometimes he even made her laugh. Her self-preserving guard was a little off after those love letters and the events of today, making her thoughts a little scattered, her instincts a little sharper. There was no need to worry that she might be developing different, deeper feelings for him. Tomorrow she'd wake up with her strength and survival instincts intact, and she could push those feelings into the background, where she needed them to stay.

"Cleo, come." With the dog down to fumes now after staking out several spots, Hazel calmed her off-kilter thoughts and walked past her truck to join the two men. Cleo darted ahead of her, eager to investigate them, or perhaps catching Gunny's scent as the big dog lounged in his air-conditioned kennel in the back seat of Burke's truck. Cleo sniffed Officer Grant's shoes before propping her two front paws against Burke's knee, wobbling on her back leg and wagging her stump of a tail. "Easy, girl," she said.

"Dr. Coop." Justin Grant chuckled as he nodded a greeting, amused by the dog's favoritism. "Who's this little diva?"

"Cleo. She was hit by a car and left by the side of the road. She was with us in recovery for a long time, and since no one claimed her, my staff adopted her and made her the clinic mascot. I get the honor of chauffeuring her home for the evenings. And she has a crazy crush on this big galoot."

"You got everything locked up?" Burke asked. He knelt to scratch Cleo around the ears, easing the schnauzer's manic energy with his deep voice and large hands. "She probably smells Gunny on me. Makes me a hit with all the furry ladies." He talked to the dog, working his trainer magic. "Chill, little one. Gunny worked hard all afternoon and needs his rest. Maybe you can play with him tomorrow. That's a good girl."

By the time he was done talking, the three-legged dog had rolled onto her side and was panting while Burke rubbed her tummy. Some of the tension inside Hazel eased, too, hearing that soothing, low-pitched voice. She'd probably be panting, too, if he whispered little praises to her and stroked her skin like that.

Hazel quickly turned away as a different sort of tension seized her. Where were these sexual thoughts coming from? Why was she allowing herself to react to Burke in a way she never had before? Once Ashley had put those thoughts about flirting and feelings into her head, she hadn't been able to compartmentalize her emotions the way she usually did. She really needed to find out who was behind these threats and get the normalcy of her familiar, predictable life back.

Studiously ignoring the man kneeling beside her and indulging her spoiled dog, Hazel tilted her chin to Justin. "You're certain it's safe to resume business as usual tomorrow morning?"

"Yes, ma'am." The younger officer seemed unaware of the embarrassment heating her cheeks, or else he was too polite to mention it. "Our search teams found nothing you need to worry about except for that envelope."

"An envelope filled with bomb-making parts," she clarified, still in a bit of shock that something so dangerous had traveled through the mail and ended up in her place of work, where she, her daughter and so many of her friends were.

"In this case, parts are just parts," Justin assured her. "Nothing was rigged to detonate. C-4 requires an electric charge through a triggering device like a blasting cap or detonator cord. The small explosion triggers the larger one. As unsettling as receiving a gift like that might be, nothing was going to happen. Even if you struck a match to it, it would burn, not explode. All the same, we've got the C-4 secured, and the envelope is on its way to the evidence locker."

"Nobody sends explosives through the mail for no

reason." Burke pushed to his feet beside her, his shoulders filling up her peripheral vision, making a mockery of her efforts to ignore her awareness of him. "This perp has broken the law just by putting that package in a mail slot and lying about its contents. That's a big risk to take."

Justin nodded his agreement. "The sender may be an expert in explosives who knew the device wouldn't work, and this was either a gag or a warning of some kind. Probably the latter, given those letters you mentioned."

Hazel shivered, feeling the electricity in the air dotting her skin with goose bumps. She was swallowed up by the cold front being pushed ahead of the pending storm, and she hugged her arms around her waist, wishing she had more than her scrubs on to keep her warm. "Someone thinks this is funny?"

She shouldn't have been surprised to feel Burke's arm slide around her shoulders or his hand rubbing up and down her arm. "From the perp's perspective, not yours. Maybe he wants you to know how serious his feelings are for you. Or he's hoping you'll be scared enough to turn to him for comfort."

She was equally surprised at how easy it was to lean against Burke's warmth and strength as the unsettling chill consumed her. "The man doesn't even have the guts to tell me who he is. Does he really believe that threatening me is going to make me ignore the ick factor of those letters and fall in love with him?"

"Another possibility is that he's a novice who has no clue what he's messing with and didn't realize that the contents couldn't go off." Justin shook his head, as though he liked that possibility even less. "I hate to think that he'll keep trying until he gets it right."

"Don't worry, Doc." Burke squeezed her shoulders a little tighter. "Gunny and I are at your service whenever you need us."

She squeezed his hand where it rested on her shoulder. "Cleo and I appreciate it. Thanks." At the mention of her name, the little dog got to her feet and danced around her legs. She wished she could share the old girl's enthusiasm for this conversation. "So you think he'll try again?" Hazel asked the younger man.

"If he's already escalated from letter writing to threats like that, then yeah, as long as he has access to the right equipment, I doubt this is a onetime thing."

Hazel lifted her chin at the grim pronouncement. Sixteen years ago, at the height of her ex-husband's trial, she'd been bombarded with hate mail, anonymous phone calls and threats against her and her daughters—as if she was guilty by association for the way Aaron had destroyed so many lives. If only they'd known how thoroughly he'd destroyed hers, they might have felt sympathy rather than hate. But other than being jostled and spit on by a courthouse crowd, and her daughters being bullied at school—the last straw that had sealed her decision to testify against Aaron and finalize their divorce—none of those threats had ended in violence like this. Not the kind where people died. "He's trying to get my attention. He's probably too much of a coward to actually hurt me."

The two men exchanged a look as though her optimistic assertion was naive. But she wasn't about to explain to a man she'd just met why she had so little naivete left about the world—just a foolish hope that she'd already lived through the worst the world had to offer, and a belief that the future had to be better.

"I hope that's the case," Justin said. "In the meantime, I'll keep working the investigation from my end. See if I can find out where that C-4 came from. The guy has to have connections to construction jobs or the military—or the black market—in order to get his hands on that grade of explosive." He reached out to shake hands with Burke. "I'll keep you posted on what I find out."

Burke nodded his thanks. "Say hi to Emilia and the kids. When is number three due?"

"This summer."

"You know scientists found out what causes that, don't you?"

Justin grinned at the teasing. "Don't lecture me about making babies, old man. You know you love being JJ's godfather."

"I do. Tell him I'll bring Gunny by again sometime for the two of them to play."

"Will do." Justin looked to Hazel and extended his hand. "Dr. Coop. I'm sorry this happened."

"Thank you, Officer Grant."

"Justin." As they shook hands, he nodded toward Burke. "If you're hanging out with this guy, I imagine we'll be crossing paths again."

Although she didn't think that dealing with bomb threats and disturbing letters or even canine ear infections qualified as "hanging out," Hazel realized she had spent more time with Burke in the past week than she had over the past two months. Did Justin think there was something more going on between her and Burke, too? First, Ashley had claimed Burke was flirting with her. And now Justin had practically labeled them a couple. She'd better be careful. Leaning on Jedediah Burke could become a habit she wouldn't want to break. Did she imagine his hand tightening around her shoulder briefly before she decided it might be wiser to break contact and step away from him?

And why was that subtle pressure all it took to keep her snugged to his side?

Justin backed toward his truck. "You need anything else from me, give me a call."

"Roger that." Burke's arm was still around her shoulders as Justin drove out of the parking lot.

The breeze was picking up as Cleo tugged on the leash, apparently ready to do some more exploring if Hazel didn't offer her a comfortable place to nap and Burke wasn't going to be petting her anymore. The wind held an unexpected bite as she moved away from Burke's warmth to let the dog reach the grass. Was the chill she felt physical or mental or both? She rubbed her free hand up and down her arm and turned her face to the sky to see the layers of clouds darting by. The wind whipped her bangs across her eyes and lifted the short waves on top of her head. "Looks like we're going to get a storm."

Burke's sigh was a deep rumble through the air behind her. "Are we reduced to that now? Talking about the weather like a couple of acquaintances who barely know each other?" He stepped up beside her, his callused fingers a soothing caress as he brushed the hair out of her eyes. He repeated the same gentle stroke across her forehead and along her temple before cupping the side of her jaw and letting his fingers curve around the back of her neck. "Promise me one thing. You'll never be afraid to speak what's on your mind to me."

She nodded. "Same here. You've always been a straight shooter with me, and I don't want that to change."

His fingertips pulled against the tension at the nape

of her neck. "Then, in the spirit of honesty…you look worn-out. You doin' okay?"

"Nothing that a good night's sleep and feeling safe again won't cure."

"Anything I can do to help?"

Hazel had closed her eyes against the heavenly massage, until she realized she was just as shamelessly addicted to his touch as Cleo had been. She blinked her eyes open to find Burke studying her expression, waiting for her answer. "I thought I'd have some answers by now—that this obsession would end, not escalate." She reached up to wrap her fingers around his wrist, stilling his kneading long enough to share an embarrassing truth. "What if I can't handle this? I'm not as young as I was when I had to deal with this kind of emotional chaos before. And it nearly broke me back then."

"You're not alone this time." He tugged against her neck, pulling her into his chest and winding his arms around her. "I assume you're referring to that mess with your ex?"

She nodded.

He might not know the details, but he knew enough to understand that she'd been put through hell and had survived. "Maybe you've traded some of those youthful energy reserves for life experience. You'll be smarter about dealing with this mess than you were the last one. And if you are intimating in any way, shape or form that you are over the hill, and not strong or vibrant or able to deal with what life's throwing at you right now, I'm going to have to pick a fight with you."

She huffed a laugh at the compliment. "Have I ever told you how good you are for my ego, Sergeant Burke?"

"Just being a straight shooter, ma'am."

The inner voice that reminded her to maintain a professional distance from the veteran cop grew weaker with every breath she took. She settled against him, soothed by the strong beat of his heart beneath her ear. Her arms snuck around his waist as he nestled his chin against the crown of her hair and surrounded her in his abundant heat. She flattened her hands against his strong back and admitted to the tingling she felt in the tips of her breasts as they responded to the friction of her body pressed against his. God, he felt good. Solid, masculine. He smelled even better. If she wasn't gun-shy about starting a relationship with him, she could see herself falling for Burke far too easily. If he could work such magic with his hands, she could only imagine how sexy and addictive his kisses would be. Would he be gentle? Authoritative? Some heady mix in between?

As for sex... Her experience with Aaron had been all about the bells and whistles after the initial bloom of young love had faded. Just like her trust, their physical relationship had deteriorated to mechanics and trying too hard and finally to disappointment and neglect. Other than her husband, she hadn't had any partners. She had a feeling that, like the man himself, getting physical with Burke would be straightforward. *I want you. I'll make it good. Let's do this.*

Her breasts weren't the only part of her stinging with wakening desire now. Fantasizing about Jedediah Burke, imagining something more between them, reminded Hazel that she was a sexual being who'd denied her needs for far too long. Her marriage had crumbled, and she'd gone into survivor mode. She'd concentrated on being a mother and father to her girls, as well as a successful business owner who could support them and their dreams. She'd found solace in her work and a purposeful way to atone for the damage Aaron had done to the world by helping the animals in her care. But somewhere along the way she'd forgotten what it felt like to be held by a man, to be desired by one, to want something that was just for her.

She parted her lips as the heat building inside her demanded an outlet. As restlessness replaced her fatigue, she shifted her cheek against Burke's shoulder. Even his beard stubble catching a few strands of her hair and tugging gently against her scalp felt like a caress, but she couldn't seem to make herself pull away from his embrace. She opened her eyes to focus on the KCPD logo on the side of his truck, reminding herself why she'd turned to Burke in the first place. "Haven't you already done enough today? If you hadn't been here, I might have opened that package."

But then he pressed a kiss to her temple. His arms tightened imperceptibly around her. "Just doin' my job, Doc."

Hazel shivered at the deep, husky tone, but not because she was chilled by the cooling weather. Her body was responding to the call of his. Were Ashley's observations right? Could this strong, kind man want something more between them, too?

"Haze…"

She leaned back against his arms and tipped her face up to his descending mouth. "Burke, I…"

A beep from her purse interrupted whatever mistake she'd been about to make. A text. She was equal parts relieved and disappointed as she pressed her palms against his shoulders and backed out of his arms. She needed a good friend more than she needed another failed relationship right now. And she didn't imagine the kiss that had almost happened would have resulted in anything else but a complication neither of them needed.

"Sorry." She reached into her purse to pull out her cell phone. "Just in case it's a patient emergency."

Burke turned away, scrubbing his palm over his jaw as she unlocked the screen. She wasn't sure if that was frustration or relief that left him rolling the tension from his neck and shoulders. Instead of worrying about his reaction to that almost kiss when she wasn't sure of what she herself was feeling, she pulled up the text.

She didn't recognize the number or name of any patient, but, needing the distraction, she opened it, anyway. It was an animated meme with a caption. She recognized the familiar shape of her younger daughter's red car and smiled for a moment, thinking Polly had sent her a funny message to cheer her up.

But the number wasn't Polly's. Hazel frowned in confusion. Confusion quickly gave way to a fear that hollowed out her stomach.

The words that accompanied the picture were neither her daughter's nor funny.

I'm coming for you and everything you care about.

Don't make the mistake of thinking I'm not a threat, or that I'm not watching your every waking moment.

You're mine.

The picture exploded with cartoonish fireworks that faded away to reveal the burned-out frame of an automobile.

"Burke…" A mama bear's anger blazed behind her eyes, making her dizzy for a moment. She swung around and held up the awful image. "Burke!"

She showed him the text and he cursed.

He double-checked the time stamp and cursed again, swiveling his gaze 360 degrees around the empty parking lot and light traffic on the street beyond. The strip mall across the street had cars near a restaurant and waiting in line at the drive-through bank. The graying sky reflected in all the windows, keeping her from seeing if anyone was spying on her from inside one of the shops. "He just now sent this. He's got eyes on you. Or he knows your schedule, knows your routine."

Hazel looked, too, but she didn't see anyone staring at her, no one sitting in his car and pointing at her, laughing at how easily he could get under her skin and upset her. "Polly owns a Kia just like that. I'm sure she drove it to work this morning. She's at Saint Luke's Hospital, working and taking classes." Hazel watched the message play again, willing for some sort of clue to appear and reveal her tormentor's identity. "Is he threatening my baby…?"

Whether she was ten years old or twenty-one, her younger daughter would always be her baby. And a sick message like this text did more to frighten Hazel than any anonymous love letter or vial of C-4 could.

Burke clamped his hand around her upper arm and pulled her to the passenger door of his truck. "Get in. Call Polly. We're going to the hospital."

"I can drive."

"No." He opened the door.

"No? She's my daughter. I have to—"

His big hands spanned her waist and he picked her up and set her inside. He bent down to pick up Cleo and plopped the dog onto her lap before she could climb back out. Then he blocked the open door, meeting her eye to eye. "You're angry right now. And you're scared for your child. I don't want you driving while you're on your phone and worried about her."

She had to look away from the intensity in those dark

brown eyes. She didn't need to argue for her independence. He was making sense. She thanked him with a nod. "Good point."

He jogged around to get in behind the wheel and started the truck. "Give me the number again."

Hazel rattled off the caller's ID while Burke backed out of the parking space and picked up his radio to call Dispatch. Gunny sat up the moment his handler had climbed into the truck and whined quietly in the back as they pulled into traffic and picked up speed. Cleo was on her feet, wanting to touch noses with the working dog through the grate separating them, but Hazel wrapped her arms around the schnauzer to keep her in her lap.

Burke identified himself and reported the text as a bomb threat before warning Dispatch to alert the bomb squad and KCFD. Then he recited the phone number and asked her to run a trace on it. After he signed off, he glanced at Hazel. "They'll put an investigator on tracking down that cell number, although I'm guessing it'll be a burner phone." He reached out to rub his hand over the top of Cleo's head. "Once we know Polly's okay—and she will be okay—you and I are going downtown and filing a full report on this harassment campaign."

"Thank you."

He slid his hand along Cleo's back until he caught Hazel's hand and squeezed it. "You and your girls will be safe, Doc. I promise." Returning both hands to the wheel, he nodded toward her phone. "Call."

Hazel punched in her younger daughter's number while the truck sped along Front Street toward downtown. A mist was spitting on the windshield now, and Burke turned on the wipers, along with his flashing lights and siren as they ran into rush hour traffic.

"Hey, Mom. What's up?"

It was a relief to hear Polly's voice. "Are you at the hospital?"

"Where else would I be?" Polly asked. Hazel heard voices and laughter in the background, as though her daughter was safely surrounded by friends. "It's my long day. Classes. Work. My evening volunteer seminar starts in half an hour."

The clouds blinked with lightning, and thunder rumbled overhead, the coming storm adding to the urgency of the moment. "Don't leave the building," Hazel warned. "We're on our way to you."

"We?"

"Sergeant Burke is driving me."

"Ooh, yum." She heard Polly excuse herself from whomever she was with, and the background noise quieted. "Sergeant Hottie McHotterson, who loves dogs as much as you do? Whose broad shoulders fill out his uniform like a man half his age? That Sergeant Burke?"

Hazel groaned, glad she didn't have the call on speakerphone, but she couldn't keep her gaze from sliding across the cab of the truck to verify her daughter's observation. She tried to make her next breath a sigh of relief. If Polly could tease her about her dating life, or lack thereof, then she had to be fine. "You've been talking to your sister."

"There might have been some cahootenizing over a couple of glasses of wine last weekend. You do know we both like him, right, Mom? If you ever decide you want to date again, Sergeant Burke would be on our approved list."

She wasn't having this discussion again. She needed to focus on the problem at hand. "Did you drive your car to the hospital this morning?"

"Of course I did."

"Have you been outside since then?"

"No. I had classes. Went on rounds with Professor Owenson in the maternity ward. I saw the rain in the forecast, and it was clouding up, so I just grabbed a bite of dinner in the cafeteria instead of going back to the apartment." Good. Her daughters shared an apartment, and knowing Ashley had headed home after work, she was relieved to hear that her older daughter wouldn't accidentally run into the danger indicated by that text when she pulled into the parking lot behind their complex.

"Where is your car now?"

"In the west lot." Polly hesitated, no doubt picking up on the urgency in her voice. "Mom, is something wrong?"

"Stay inside the hospital. Do not go to your car for any reason."

Burke motioned for her to hold the phone up and put it on speaker. "Polly? Jedediah Burke here."

"Hey, Sarge. What's going on?"

"Do what your mom says, and contact hospital security to cordon off your car. Tell them not to touch anything. We'll be there in ten minutes." The rain was coming down in sheets now. Could he guarantee that? "First responders are on their way."

"Okay, now you're both scaring me," said Polly. Hazel recognized the tightness in her daughter's tone. "Does this have anything to do with the package Mom got in the mail today? Ashley texted me about it this afternoon."

"Possibly. I don't want to scare you, but I believe someone may have tampered with your car. At least with one that looks like yours."

"Tampered? What do you mean? Like someone let the air out of my tires?" Even over the noise of the storm and traffic, Hazel could hear her daughter's quickened breaths. "I'm heading down the Wornall Road hallway to the south windows. I parked aboveground today. I can see my car from... There it is. Right where I left it. I was here early enough to get a surface-level spot."

"Don't go to it," Hazel warned. "Stay inside until we get there."

"It's okay, Mom. I'm just look—" When Polly gasped and went silent, Hazel nearly screamed into the phone.

But like all the women in the Cooper family, she was a medical professional and knew that panicking wasn't going to help anyone. "Polly?"

"Sergeant? Mom? There's a guy in a black hoodie out there. He's walking around my car, looking in the windows." Polly's soft voice told Hazel her daughter was afraid. "I can't see his face. What's he doing out there with all this rain? Nobody else is—"

"Call security," Burke ordered. He raced through an intersection. Gunny whined with more excitement and Cleo barked.

"He's jogging away. He ran down the ramp into the parking garage. I can't see exactly where he went. I hear sirens—they're not ambulances. Maybe he heard them, too."

"Do what Burke says, sweetie. Contact security and stay inside. We'll be right there."

Hazel heard a muffled thump like thunder in the distance. Had the storm reached Saint Luke's, too?

"Oh, my God." She barely heard her daughter's whisper.

"Polly? Please tell me that was thunder."

Burke shook his head.

Hazel knew by the pace of her breathing that her daughter was running. "I'm on my way to the security desk now."

"You need to talk to me right now, young lady."

"I'm okay, Mom. But get here fast. My car just blew up."

Chapter Four

The rain was pouring by the time the Kansas City Fire Department had extinguished the flames of Polly's car, driving everyone but the crime scene technicians back inside the hospital. Cradling Cleo in her lap, Hazel sat in a chair in the carpeted lobby, absently petting Gunny, who dozed at her feet, eavesdropping on Burke, Justin Grant and a stone-faced firefighter named Matt Taylor, whom Hazel had learned was a younger brother to Pike Taylor, the K-9 officer who worked with Burke.

Once the police had finished interviewing her, Polly had insisted on checking in for the last half hour of her volunteer seminar. Hazel understood her need to stay focused on something other than the danger that had come far too close this evening. Plus, Polly had inherited Hazel's own workaholic tendencies and wanted to finish the job she'd promised to do. Her big sister, Ashley, had shown up minutes after Hazel and Burke had arrived, as worried about Polly as Hazel was. The two young women were so close. Polly had probably texted Ashley for moral support the moment she'd gotten off the phone with Hazel.

Although the stress of the day was wearing on her, Hazel felt better knowing her daughters were under the same roof as she was, and she could keep an eye on them both and know they were safe.

She'd relive those last few months with Aaron a hundred times before she'd let anyone hurt one of her daughters.

Cleo stirred in Hazel's lap, alert to every employee, patient or visitor who walked past. Unfazed by her own physical handicaps, it was almost as though the small dog was keeping watch over her mistress. Or maybe the one-eyed schnauzer was keeping watch over her big bruiser buddy, who panted quietly at Hazel's feet. Unless they were registered therapy animals, dogs, as a rule, weren't allowed inside the hospital. But no one seemed to mind the smell of wet dog on the premises tonight. Burke's Czech shepherd had done his job, alerting to the remnants of explosives inside the front wheel well of Polly's car, his sensitive nose picking up the scent even after the firefighters had soaked the vehicle with foam and the storm had set in while the first responders cleared the scene. With the help of three other bomb-sniffing dogs and their partners, Gunny and Burke had cleared every vehicle in the parking garage and the interior of Saint Luke's itself.

Polly's car had been specifically targeted. Matt Taylor said the fire had been contained to Polly's car, the fuel in her gas tank had accounted for most of the flames, and only minor damage had been inflicted on the nearby vehicles. And though the police and search dogs had determined there were no other explosives on the site to worry about, Hazel still worried.

Her *daughter* had been targeted.

Even now, hours after the initial explosion, knowing Polly hadn't been anywhere close to the bomb when it detonated, Hazel felt light-headed with an overwhelming dose of anger and fear.

If Polly hadn't had such a full day and hadn't decided to eat dinner at the hospital, she might have been in that car, stuck in rush hour traffic, when it exploded. Hazel's baby girl might be horribly injured or… Hazel fisted her fingers in Gunny's long, damp coat. She refused to even think the word.

Threatening *her* was one thing.

Going after her children was something else entirely.

The letters had been upsetting, yes—the bomb parts delivered to the clinic were unsettling. But even with seeking out Burke's help, she hadn't taken the whole stalking situation as seriously as she should have until today. Now her friends and employees and daughters had been drawn into this senseless terror campaign. Her protective mama-bear hackles were on high alert. She could no longer separate the threats from the rest of her life, praying they'd go away, hoping she could handle the situation herself. Now she intended to meet the enemy head-on—protect her daughters, protect her staff—identify the culprit and then sic Gunny and Burke and the rest of the KCPD on him.

Matt Taylor had shed his big reflective coat and helmet, and he stood with his hands propped at the waist of his insulated turnout pants. "If the explosive had been placed in the back near the gas tank, we'd be talking a different story. As it is, other than the shrapnel that dinged the neighboring cars, most of the damage came from the fuel burning. The gas tank never exploded."

Justin looked from Matt to Burke. "So again, either this guy doesn't know what he's doing with these explosives, or he's deliberately drawing this out—upping the stakes with each threat instead of going for maximum damage." His green-eyed gaze darted over to Hazel, indicating he knew she was listening in. Yes, the damage had been more than enough, considering they were talking about Polly's car. But she hoped that locking gazes with him indicated she wanted to hear the questions and answers they were discussing, even if the topic might upset her. "How did our perp know which vehicle to target? The DMV's not a public-access database."

"Because he's watching Hazel and her girls." Burke's chest expanded with an angry breath. "He's inserted himself into their lives somehow, even in a periphery way, so he can learn all he can about them—where they work, where they live, their routines, what they drive." He scrubbed his palm over the stubble shading his jaw. "I need to ferret this guy out. Find out why he's doing this to Hazel and put a stop to it."

"Look, what you and the dogs you train do is invaluable. But you're not a detective, old man," Justin cautioned him.

Burke's glare was part reprimand and all irritation at the reminder. But whether it was the job description or the nickname that he didn't find amusing, she couldn't tell. "If Gunny can find a bomb in a campus this size, then I can damn well find the perp who put it there." He shrugged some of the tension off his shoulders and made a concession. "I won't go cowboy on anybody. I'll keep Detectives Bellamy and Cartwright in the loop. As long as they do the same for me."

Cooper Bellamy and Seth Cartwright were the two detectives who'd come to Saint Luke's to take statements from her, Burke and Polly. Now that the CSIs had set up a protective tarp and fog lights around the shell of Polly's car, Bellamy and Cartwright were out in the rain, getting preliminary statements from the criminologists on the scene and meeting with the guards at the security gate in front of the hospital to see if any of them had glimpsed the man in the black hoodie and could provide a more detailed description of the guy or his vehicle.

Right now, with no traceable phone number, no return address on the letters, and no answers yet on where he'd obtained the bomb parts and explosives, Polly's description of an oversized man in a black hoodie and dark pants who disappeared inside the parking garage was the best they had to go on.

"Keep KCFD in the loop, too," Matt said, extending his hand to shake both Burke's and Justin's. "I'll get you the results from our arson investigator as soon as we know anything more concrete."

"Thanks, Matt."

Matt nodded to Hazel as he strode past. "Ma'am."

"Thank you, Mr. Taylor."

She followed him to the front doors with her gaze and saw the young firefighter exchange a look with her older daughter, Ashley. Although she didn't think they knew each other, Ashley gave him a friendly wave before he walked out into the rain and she returned to the animated conversation she was having on her cell phone.

Hazel's eyes narrowed at the observation. Could something as simple as a friendly wave she didn't remember be the cause of all this terror and destruction? Did some creep fancy himself in love with her because she'd smiled at him or been polite?

Hazel had made a point of not dating for years now. Aaron had given her plenty of reason to be wary of men she didn't know. But even if she had considered getting to know a new man in an intimate way, she hadn't. First, because her daughters had needed her and the stability of being home every night during and after Aaron's trial and the dissolution of their disastrous marriage. And more recently because those years of emotional self-preservation had become an ingrained habit. If she wasn't any better a judge of whom to trust and give her heart to than when she fell for Aaron Cooper, then what business did she have risking another relationship?

It was Survival 101. She didn't lead on any man who might be interested in her. She stated her rules, tried to let him down easy if he pushed for her to bend those rules and kept her heart at a safe distance.

Had she slipped somewhere? She had several platonic relationships with men—like Burke, clients, co-workers, friends. Had she missed a sign that one of them had deeper feelings for her? Had she subconsciously encouraged someone into thinking she cared for him with a wave or a smile or a thank-you?

He's inserted himself into their lives...

Burke's assertion clanged like a warning bell inside her head.

Who was Ashley talking to? Judging by her big smile and lively responses, it had to be a boyfriend—or someone she wanted to be her boyfriend. Did Hazel know whom her daughter was interested in now? She'd broken up with her last boyfriend because he'd gotten too serious too fast for her. And bless Ashley's outgoing, adventurous heart, she didn't have settling down to babies and white picket fences on her mind anytime soon. Ashley claimed they'd parted on good terms. But could a man who'd been talking marriage really be content to walk away after a breakup?

Hazel turned in her seat, looking in the opposite

direction down the hallway leading to the employees' locker room. Polly's ponytail was curlier than Ashley's and a couple of shades darker, but just as easy to spot. She strolled down the hallway, sharing a conversation with an older man wearing tattered jeans and an ill-fitting Army jacket. They stopped before reaching the side exit to the employee parking lot and faced each other. His shaggy beard and faded ball cap on top of his longish gray hair led her to think he was one of the homeless patients her daughter worked with in her volunteer seminar. Polly had a big heart and a bone-deep drive to help anyone in need. Hazel had always been proud of Polly's calling to be of service to others.

But she startled Cleo with a silent jerk of protest when the man leaned over and hugged Polly. Hazel absentmindedly stroked the dog's head to apologize but wasn't feeling any calmer herself. She didn't know that man holding on to her younger daughter as though she was a lifeline. Not that she knew every patient, classmate or teacher of Polly's. But would a man like that fancy himself in love simply because Polly had tended his wound or offered him a smile?

Did Hazel have any men like that or Ashley's phone friend in her life?

Was that how a stalker was born?

Identifying the man behind the letters and explosives meant starting with a single question. Hazel intended to spend some time on the computer tonight, reading through her patient files to refresh her memory about her clients and the salespeople and consultants she did business with. She'd urge Polly and Ashley to do the same with their circles of friends, coworkers and acquaintances. But for now, she was going to find out who that man was with Polly. Plus, it would give her an opportunity to check in with her daughter to see how she was holding up after seeing her most expensive possession and means of transportation be destroyed.

A warm hand folded over Hazel's shoulder, and she yelped louder than Cleo had.

"Easy." Burke quickly drew his hand away and retreated a step. "Didn't mean to startle you. You okay?"

"Sorry." She pulled her focus from her speculative thoughts long enough to reorient herself in the moment. She grounded herself in Burke's narrowed brown eyes and leaned to one side to see the rest of the lobby behind him. "Justin left?"

"Yeah. Detective Bellamy said they recovered more of the bomb parts and wanted him to examine them before they bagged everything up for the lab." She nodded, glad to have all these professionals working to help her now but wishing they had more answers for her. "Bellamy said they've put out a BOLO on the guy Polly described."

"An oversized man in a black hoodie and dark pants is pretty generic, isn't it?"

"It is. But it's a place to start." He must have read the doubt in her expression. And he couldn't miss her gaze darting between her daughters and following the homeless man as he left Polly and strolled around the lobby to the front doors. "Are the girls okay? That guy bothering them?"

"Young women. Not girls anymore." Had the homeless man's gaze brushed across Ashley's back as he walked out into the rain? "And no. Not that I could see. He was talking to Polly. Probably a patient. I guess I'm suspicious of everyone now."

"Everyone?" Burke prompted, perhaps wondering if

he and the other cops and firefighters he'd been talking to were on that suspect list.

"I just wish I knew who was responsible…" Hazel pushed to her feet, setting Cleo down on the carpet beside Gunny. She placed both leashes into Burke's hand. "Do you mind? I need to check on Polly. I can find out who that man is and get at least one question answered tonight."

"I'll keep an eye on Cleo." Burke tilted his head toward the effervescent blonde laughing into her phone. "I'll keep an eye her, too."

Burke's matter-of-fact promise kindled a warm ball of light inside her, chasing away the almost desperate feeling of helplessness that had left her on edge from the moment she'd dropped that package at the clinic. Did he have any idea how grateful she was for his steady presence and ability to take charge of a situation and get whatever action was needed done? He'd been strong when her own strength had faltered. Hazel knew she was lucky that he was a part of her life. She reached up and splayed her fingers against his chest, fingering the KCPD logo emblazoned there. Did she imagine the tremor that rippled across the skin and muscle beneath her hand? "I'm not sure how I would have gotten through today without you. Thank you."

He placed his hand over hers, holding it against the strong beat of his heart. "Just doin' my job."

She shook her head. "You've gone above and beyond the call of duty, Jedediah. How long have you been off the clock? And you're still here with me."

His dark brows arched above his eyes when she used his given name, and she realized she'd never called him that before. He'd always been the big boss of the K-9 unit, Burke. Or Sarge. Or Sergeant Burke.

She liked the rhythmic sound of his name on her tongue. "Is it okay if I call you that? Jedediah?"

"Yeah." His answer was a deep-pitched rumble that danced across all kinds of nerve endings and scattered her vows of friendship and keeping him arm's length from her heart. "Jedediah's good. Do I still have to call you Dr. Coop?"

Good gravy. This man could read the phone book or a grocery list in that voice, and her pulse would race a little faster.

"Of course not. Hazel's such an old-fashioned name, though—I almost always had a nickname. I was named after one of my grandmothers. I was always the only Hazel in class, surrounded by Lisas and Karens and Marys." She wiggled her fingers beneath his hand, tracing the *C* on his chest, idly speculating how a man in his fifties kept himself in such good shape. "I bet there weren't a lot of Jedediahs, either."

"You were unique. You still are."

Why did that sound more like a compliment than a commentary? Was he talking about more than her name? Was she?

How had this whole interchange become more than a thank-you? Could Ashley be right? Had she and Burke been flirting with each other? She had rules in place, damn it. Rules to protect her heart, to protect her family, to keep herself from making the same mistakes she'd made with Aaron. She needed structure. She needed boundaries. Was she falling for this man?

Hazel jerked her hand away, putting the brakes on that possibility. "Excuse me. I'm sorry." Though what, exactly, she was apologizing for, she wasn't certain. Was she leading him on? Making him think that a relationship could happen between them? Did Jedediah want that? Did she?

"Haze—"

But she shook her head, turned and hurried down the hallway after Polly. "I'm sorry."

Hazel clutched her shoulder bag to her chest and followed Polly to the employee locker room at the end of the hall. She did not want to be one of those women who used a man when she needed one, then set him aside. How would that be any different from the way Aaron had treated their marriage? She had no intention of stringing Jedediah along, letting him think he had a chance for something more with her when she couldn't guarantee that was what she wanted, too. Hurting him would be worse than never allowing a serious relationship to happen. Jedediah deserved better than that from her. And she needed to set a better example of an honest relationship for her daughters.

Vowing to have a serious conversation with Jedediah about her rules, once her nerves were a little less frayed by bombs and threats, Hazel caught the door to the locker room before it swung shut. She had her game face back on by the time she stepped inside—even if that air of cool, calm, we've-got-nothing-to-worry-about Mom face was only a facade.

Hazel spotted Polly heading down the center aisle alongside the bench that ran between the rows of lockers. "Knock, knock. Is it okay if I come in?"

Polly waved her into the room. "Sure, Mom."

Nodding to two staff members who were chatting at the front end of the bench, Hazel walked past them. Polly was standing at her open locker door when Hazel wound an arm around her and hugged her to her side. "Hey, young lady. How are you holding up?"

Polly's shoulders lifted with a heavy sigh. "Honestly?"

"Always."

Polly's green eyes darted over to meet hers. "I'm exhausted. This was already a long day without your troubles spilling over into my life." She reached around to share the hug, easing the stinging guilt from her words. "Sorry. That didn't come out right. I don't blame you for any of this. I've just been so worried about you that I didn't realize I needed to be worried about me, too." She smiled as she pulled away and went back to changing out of her scrubs into jeans and a T-shirt. "I'm not looking forward to spending my day off tomorrow dealing with insurance."

"I can help you if you need me to."

Polly tapped her chest with her thumb, asserting her independence. "Grown-up, Mom."

Hazel tapped her own chest, reminding her daughter that some things would never change. "Mother, Polly."

She sat on the bench while Polly exchanged her clogs for a pair of running shoes. She picked up her daughter's discarded scrubs and rolled them up. She wasn't sure what prompted her to dip her nose to the wrinkled bundle and sniff. She inhaled the subtle scents of Polly's shower gel, and the disinfectants and unguents she'd come into contact with throughout the day. Hazel frowned, though, when she realized those were the only scents she was picking up. Was it stereotyping of her to think that a man who lived on the streets would have transferred some sort of pungent odor to her daughter's clothes?

"Don't worry." Polly plucked the bundle from Hazel's hands and tucked them into her backpack. "Laundry is on my to-do list tonight."

"It's not that." Hazel asked the question that had been

worrying her. "Now that I'm paranoid about all the men who encounter my family, I was wondering…who was that man who hugged you?"

"Russell?" Polly pulled her ponytail from the back of her T-shirt and studied her reflection in the small mirror inside her locker door. "He's one of the homeless guys my class is volunteering with. They come to the hospital and we practice routine medical care, or we assist the doctors or senior nurses if they have something more serious to deal with. Tonight gave Russell a dry place to go to get out of this rain, too. He's usually at the Yankee Hill Road shelter, but that's several blocks from here." She muttered a euphemistic curse. "I forgot to ask if he had money for the bus."

"At least it's not chilly tonight," Hazel pointed out. "If he gets wet, he won't catch a cold."

"I'm sure you're right." Polly reached onto the top shelf of her locker. "He reminds me of somebody's grandpa. He said he missed working with me tonight. By the time I got to the area where the group meets, the others were gone. But he waited for me. He heard what happened and could tell I was upset." She pulled out a small rectangle of cardboard and handed it to her. "He gave me this card. Isn't that sweet?"

Hazel supposed she didn't need to worry about a grandfatherly patient paying attention to her daughter. She was the one with the unwanted suitor who was proving to be a threat to them all. Besides, a man who had to resort to crayons and cutting off the front of another card to glue to a piece of cardboard probably didn't have the budget to purchase C-4 and pay for the postage her stalker had already spent on her.

Smiling fondly, Polly sat down to tie her shoes. "Even in Russell's circumstances, he was thinking of me."

Hazel turned the card over to read the message scrawled in three different colors of crayon. *Out of all the people in the world, you're the one I'm thinking of today. Sorry about your car. Russell D.*

"Out of all the people in the world, huh? Your father used to say gushy stuff like that to me when he wanted to apologize for whatever event he forgot or promise he had to break." A message that had usually been accompanied by flowers or a gift they couldn't afford. She'd have preferred a considerate heads-up beforehand if he wasn't going to be at one of Ashley's concerts or plays, or one of Polly's games.

Too many grand gestures and not enough substance and reliability had slowly eroded her trust in Aaron until the girls were the only reason she kept fighting for her marriage. In the end, she'd finally admitted there was nothing left to fight for. And after the night of the accident that was no accident… Leaving with Ashley and Polly had been the best way to protect them from the backlash of Aaron's crimes. Erasing Aaron from her life had been the only way to stop the hateful, then pleading letters from prison. By the time he'd accepted his fate and started writing to Ashley and Polly instead, the girls were too afraid or too disinterested to rebuild a relationship with their father.

Polly bumped her shoulder against hers, cajoling her out of those negative memories. "Hey. I know where your head's at. This isn't Dad we're talking about. Russell loses points for creativity, but I believe the sentiment is legit."

Hazel laced her fingers together with Polly's and squeezed her hand. "You're absolutely right. It's the thought that counts."

"I suppose it's hard to form bonds with people when

you're in a situation like Russell's. But I think he looks forward to me checking his blood pressure every week." Polly returned the card to the top shelf of her locker. "That means I'm making a difference in someone's life, right?"

Smiling, Hazel rose to hug her to her side again. "You've been making a difference from the day you were born, sweetie. I don't think there's a puppy, bug or baby bird you didn't want to rescue when you were little."

Polly scrunched her face into a frown. "Funny. I'm not so keen on the bugs now."

"Can anyone join this party?" Ashley beamed a smile as Hazel leaned into her older daughter to include her in the group hug. "It's good to see you laughing again, Mom."

Hazel's mood had lightened considerably from the gloom and suspicion she'd come into the hospital with. "It feels good," she admitted. "Spending time with my two favorite people always makes me feel better. Are you sure you're both okay?"

"The Cooper women have weathered everything else life has thrown at us. We'll get through this, too. Cooper Power."

"Cooper Power," Polly echoed, trading a fist bump with her sister.

Hazel marveled at the bond these two shared. No matter what she accomplished in her life, she knew raising these two fine young women would always be her greatest achievement.

As Polly grabbed her jacket from her locker, Ashley pulled a business card from her purse. "It's not a new car, but I have a present for you, sis."

"A present?" Polly took the business card and flipped it over to read it.

"Sergeant Burke's card with all his numbers." Ashley pulled a second one from her purse to show she'd gotten one, too. "He said to call if we needed anything— whether he's on duty or at home. Even if we just need someone to walk us to our car at night, or we get a flat tire somewhere." She grinned at her sister. "Not that you're going to get a flat tire anytime soon."

"Way to rub it in, dork." Polly stuffed the card into her pocket. "That's awfully nice of the sergeant."

It was. Even without a word or a touch, Jedediah Burke was working his way past Hazel's defenses. His caring offer to her girls warmed her heart and gave her one more reason to toss aside her rules and embrace the possibility of a new relationship.

Ashley slipped her card back into her bag. "He said I could call him Burke. Most of his friends call him that."

"Is that right?" The daughters exchanged a meaningful look before Polly asked, "What do you call him, Mom?"

Apparently, she was going with *Jedediah* now. But somehow, sharing that—even with her daughters—felt like betraying some sort of intimate secret.

"Don't think I don't see what you two are up to. Burke is a good man. We owe him big-time for all the help he's given us. I'm touched that he would extend his protection to you, too."

"He's protecting you? Ooh." Ashley clapped her hands together. "Like a bodyguard? Or a boyfriend?"

Hazel groaned. "I came back here to see if you were all right. Clearly, you are, if you have time to worry about my love life."

"Or lack thereof," Ashley pointed out.

"Stop it." Hazel pointed a stern maternal finger at each of them. "I want you both to come stay with me. There's plenty of room at the condo. Keep us all together until this guy is caught and no one else can get hurt."

"Stay with you?" Ashley frowned before turning her head toward the locker room door as the two women who'd been chatting earlier opened it wide to leave, giving them all a glimpse of the muscular man waiting out in the hallway with two dogs at his side. Burke was leaning against the wall, studying something on his phone, somehow looking both tired and alert as he formed a protective wall between her little family and the outside world that wanted to hurt them. "What if you're entertaining guests?"

Hazel's eyes lingered on his weary expression as the door slowly closed on him. "One, I am not entertaining Burke or any other man. And two, you and Ashley will always come first, even if there was a man in my life."

She was still watching the last glimpse of Burke and wondering what he did to relax after long days like this, or who he leaned on when he needed a boost of support, when Polly squeezed her hand. "When are you going to put yourself first, Mom? Ashley and I are adults now. Don't use us as an excuse to not move on with your life and find happiness."

"Be smart and find it with *him*," Ashley urged. "Burke's a silver fox. You know what that means, don't you?"

"Yes, I know the term. I'm your mother, not dead."

Ashley grinned. "So, you *do* think he's hot."

That was a given.

"I liked it better when I could send you two to your room." Hazel shook her head, forcing herself to remember that the strength she'd imbued in her daughters was there for a reason. "All right. I'll try not to be so much of a mother hen. But don't forget that this guy is no joke. I want you two to look out for each other."

"We will," Polly promised.

"Keep a watchful eye out for anyone paying too much attention to you. Don't go anyplace by yourself. Lock your doors. You know the safety drill. Call me or the police if anything seems wrong to you. Whatever this man wants from me, I am not going to let it hurt my daughters."

Ashley hugged her taller sister to her side. "I'll keep an eye on her, Mom." She tilted her chin up to Polly. "I've got a date tonight with Joe. Maybe we can double. I'm sure he has a friend."

"No, thank you." Polly pulled away to heft her backpack onto her shoulder and close her locker. "I need to study."

"Who's Joe?" Hazel asked. She knew that wasn't the let's-get-married guy Ashley had dumped. The idea of a stranger entering their lives right now worried her. "That's who you were on the phone with?"

"Uh-huh. He's the guy I met a couple of Fridays ago when I went to Fontella's bachelorette party at The Pickle up by City Market."

"The Pickle?" Hazel frowned.

"It's a rooftop bar with pickleball courts. He's a bouncer there. I told you, didn't I?"

She knew about her college friend's wedding, but not the new boyfriend. "No, you didn't."

"He's cool, Mom," Polly volunteered. "I met him when he picked up Ash for the movie last weekend. He's got more tats than any guy I've ever met. But he was funny and super nice. Don't judge a book by its cover and all that."

Bouncer? Tats? Funny and nice? Her daughters really *had* grown up. "Do I get to meet this guy?"

"Do you mind if I invite him to the apartment, then?" Ashley asked Polly, pulling out her phone, ignoring Hazel's question. "We could order a couple of pizzas, and then Joe and I can watch a movie while you're in your room with your books and headphones being all nerdy."

Polly rolled her eyes before shrugging. "That sounds fine. Then none of us will be alone." She nodded toward the exit door, indicating the man waiting patiently on the other side. "Right, Mom?"

Hazel put her hands up in surrender before pulling each daughter in for a hug. "I guess I'm outvoted. Just be safe. And check in with me tomorrow if I don't see you so I know you're all right."

"We will. Love you." Ashley tightened the hug before pulling back and nodding toward the hallway. "Burke's tired. Hungry, too, I imagine." She gave Hazel a little nudge. "Go. Feed him. He needs some attention."

"He's a grown man." Hazel was arguing against the pull of empathy she'd just been feeling. "He can take care of himself."

Polly took a more logical approach to the relentless matchmaking. "He's been with you all day long. It's after nine o'clock and neither one of you have eaten dinner. Wouldn't that be a nice way to say thank you to him for being such a rock for us today?"

"It's what a good friend would do," Ashley added. She touched her lips. "Although, every man likes a little pretty. Some lip gloss wouldn't hurt."

"Enough with the lip gloss." Hazel tried to stare them down but quickly realized the tactic that had worked to silence an argument when they were children wasn't going to work tonight. Besides, they did have a point.

"Fine. I do owe him for his help today." She reluctantly took the lip gloss Ashley offered and dabbed a little color and shine onto her dry lips before pushing it back into her daughter's hand. But she grabbed onto Ashley's fingers and squeezed, still determined they understood her point. "You two know you can't will a relationship to happen between Burke and me just because it amuses you or you think I'm going to wind up alone and living in your spare bedroom. I'm in a good place on my own. I'm happy with my life—except for that idiot who won't leave us alone. I'm more worried about our safety right now than about falling in love again."

"Did she say *falling in love*?" Polly pointed out to her sister.

"That's what I heard. She likes him. She just won't admit it." Ashley was grinning from ear to ear now. "I can see if Joe has a friend he could hook you up with, if that's more of the kind of guy you like."

Another bouncer with tats who was probably half her age? No, thanks.

Polly linked her arm through hers and turned her toward the door. "Mom…there's nothing wrong with being deliriously happy and falling in love again. If you find the right man. And I can't see any way that Sergeant Burke would be the mistake that Dad was."

But what if *she* was the mistake? What if *she* was the one with the rotten judgment who could be tricked into another unhealthy relationship?

Although their hearts were in the right place, her daughters didn't know every detail of the hell Aaron Cooper had put them through. But she did. They thought they were helping by pushing her toward Burke—and they wouldn't let it drop until she gave in and proved them wrong.

Hazel sighed in surrender and traded one more hug before pushing the door open and marching into the hallway. "Call me when you two get home." Burke immediately tucked his phone into his pocket and straightened away from the wall. Barely breaking stride, she grabbed his hand as she passed by and tugged him toward the lobby. "Come with me."

He ordered the dogs into step beside him before subtly changing his grip on hers, linking their fingers together in a more mutual grasp. "Everything okay?"

"If you call two buttinsky daughters who don't know when to mind their own business okay, then yes, everything's fine."

He halted, pulling her to a stop without releasing her hand. "Did I miss something?"

Hazel glanced up. She couldn't help but smile a reassurance to ease the questioning frown that lined his eyes. "Never mind. Unless you have a better offer, I'm taking you to dinner."

Chapter Five

A better offer? Burke had been waiting for an invitation from Hazel Cooper for a long time. And even though there'd been no declaration of affection, or even an admission that this crazy lust he felt was mutual, getting an invitation to the fourth-floor loft in Kansas City's downtown Library District that Hazel called home felt like taking their relationship to the next level.

By mutual agreement, dinner had ended up being takeout from a burger joint they'd passed on their way from the vet clinic, where she'd picked up her truck and he'd followed her home. He'd been lucky enough to find a place to park on the street a couple of blocks from her building after she'd parked in the gated garage on the street level of the renovated tool and die shop and warehouse. The short walk to join her at the caged-in entrance where she let him in gave Gunny time to do his business before they took the elevator up to the fourth floor.

With only two condos on each floor, Hazel's place felt open and roomy, especially with the wall of floor-to-ceiling windows facing the skyline to the west. He was surprised to see how much of the industrial design of the original building had been preserved in the open ductwork and stained brick walls from when the building had been a hub of manufacturing and commerce near the Missouri River. Although a pair of bedrooms and two bathrooms had been closed in with modern walls, the rest of the loft felt big enough for him to relax in.

Hazel kicked off her shoes the moment she stepped through the front door, fed Cleo and Gunny, and found an old blanket for his dog to sleep on beside the sofa where the smaller dog had curled up. Then she invited him to sit on one of the stools at the kitchen island while she pulled a couple of cold beers from the fridge and set out plates and cloth napkins to make the paper-wrapped sandwiches and fries feel like a real sit-down meal. They talked about the decidedly feminine touches of color and cushy furniture that softened the industrial vibe of the place, her older daughter's apparent obsession with lip gloss that seemed to be part of some joke he didn't understand and her concern about her younger daughter shopping for a new car.

Burke insisted she sit while he cleared the dishes and loaded the dishwasher, offering to go car shopping with Polly. They talked about the rain forcing him to change his training schedule with his officers and their dogs, Royals baseball and whether she preferred the scruffy look he was sporting at 11:00 p.m. to being clean-shaven like when he reported for his shift in the morning. They talked about any-and everything except the bombs, the love letters and the threat she was facing from her unknown stalker.

He decided he liked Hazel's lips, whether they were shiny with gloss, pursed in a bow as she sipped her beer, stretched out in a smile or moving with easy precision as she articulated her words. And though he enjoyed the feeling of intimacy that sharing comfortable spaces and late-night conversation with a beautiful woman gave him, he didn't like that she was avoiding the reason why he and Gunny were here in the first place. He'd always admired Hazel's strength—raising her daughters alone, running her business, caring for others and standing by that strict code of right and wrong she believed in.

But surely, she'd let go sometime. Hazel knew she didn't have to entertain him, right? She didn't have to laugh at his lame teasing or make sure he got that third scoop of ice cream in the sundaes she fixed for dessert. He'd given her apartment the once-over, checking the fire escape and window locks, ensuring the lock on her front door was properly installed, closing the sheer curtains across her living room windows to keep prying eyes from seeing in as she turned on the lights. His offer of security was a given. But he was also here to give her a safety net to drop her guard and give in to the fear and fatigue or whatever she must be feeling.

He closed the dishwasher and turned to face her across the island, catching a glimpse of the big yawn she tried to hide behind the caramel sauce she was licking off her spoon as she finished her sundae. He imagined the swipe of that tongue across his own lips and shifted at the instant stab of heat that tightened his groin and made his pulse race. Man, she had a beautiful mouth. It was getting harder and harder for him to ignore this longing, this sense of rightness he felt every time he spent even a moment with Hazel Cooper. He was 99 percent sure she felt it, too, given the darting glances he spied when she thought his back was turned. But damn that strength of hers. Even as he admired what made her so attractive, he cursed her ability to ignore the possibilities between them.

"Sorry," she apologized around the last bite of the homemade sauce. "It's not the company, I swear."

"Leave something for the dishwasher to do." Burke grinned as he reached across the island to pluck the spoon from her fingers and pick up the empty bowl. He rinsed them off and added them to the dishwasher, carefully choosing his words before he faced her again. "You *do* know that I'm here for you if you need help with anything. An ear to listen. A shoulder to lean on. Someone to watch the place while you crash for a few hours." He braced his hands on the granite counter-top and leaned toward her. "You've been through a lot today. Trust me to have your back. Let me take care of you a little bit while you let down your hair and relax or do whatever you need to do to regroup."

She flicked at the silvery blond bangs that played up the mossy green color of her eyes. "What hair?"

Fine. Make a joke out of his caring. He'd better leave before he argued that he admired how practical her super short hair was, and how it gave him a clear glimpse of the delicate shells of her ears that he wanted to touch and taste. Scrubbing his hand across his jaw, he pushed away from the counter and strode to the back of the couch, where he'd left his ball cap and Gunny's lead. "I guess that's my cue. You don't need me anymore, so I'd better get Gunny home." Even before he gave the command, the big dog was on his feet. "Gunny, *hier.*"

He plunked his hat onto his head and hooked Gun-ny's lead to his harness.

"Burke." Hazel's stool scudded across the wood planks of the floor. Her bare feet made no sound, but he inhaled the familiar tropical scent of coconut from her soap and shampoo before he heard her behind him. "Jedediah." His muscles jerked beneath the firm grip of her hand on his arm, asking him to stop. Her face was tipped up to his when he glanced down over the jut of his shoulder. Her eyes were weary and worried and sincere. "I'm sorry. I don't mean to make light of your feelings. I'm just not sure I'm prepared to deal with them. Or mine. Not tonight."

He curled his fingers over hers, holding her hand against his skin as he turned. "You don't have to apologize," he conceded. "There was a lot more conversation going on in my head than what came out. You and I are so close, Haze, I sometimes forget that you don't want the same thing between us that I do."

"That isn't necessarily true."

He narrowed his eyes, studying her as she paused for a moment. What exactly was she saying here? His nostrils flared as he drew in a deep breath, willing himself to be patient and let her speak when everything in him wanted to pounce on that ember of hope she'd just given him. He missed the touch of her hand when she released him to hug her arms around her middle. But her gaze stayed locked on his, and she didn't back away.

"Maybe I've been on my own for so long that I've forgotten how to open up and be in a relationship..." She shrugged, the gesture reminding him that, other than removing her shoes and socks, she still wore the scrubs she'd had on all day. She had to be running on fumes. And yet she was still going to push through her fatigue and finish this conversation. "I know *friendship* doesn't truly explain who we are to each other. But..." She shook her head and smiled without finishing that sentence. "Thank you for looking out for me today. For looking out for Ash and Polly—giving them your cards. It comforted them knowing there was someone they could depend on besides their mother—and that was a comfort to me."

"*Sitz.*" Gunny dropped onto his haunches beside

him, his tongue lolling out between his teeth as he waited patiently for a more interesting command. Burke fished into the pocket on his utility vest and handed Hazel a business card, as well. "Here." He slipped the card into her agile, unadorned hand, hating that he could get turned on by even the subtle movement of her fingers brushing against his. "Same promise I made to them. You call or text me anytime. Day or night. On duty or off. I will be there for you."

"I know. This makes me feel as safe as one of your hugs. And trust me, I love those." She braced her hand against his shoulder and stretched up on tiptoes to kiss his cheek. "Thank you."

As she dropped back to her heels, she drew her fingertips across the scruff of his beard. His pulse beat wildly beneath the lingering caress along his jaw. She had to feel what her touch did to him. "I may change my mind about this scruff. There's just enough silver sprinkled there to remind me of a wolf." Her breath gusted against his neck, as if she was feeling the same rise in temperature he was. "Like the alpha wolf." She gently scraped her short nails against the nap of his stubble again, and the blood pounding through his veins charged straight to his groin. Her eyes narrowed as she processed an unexpected revelation. "You're the alpha of your KCPD pack, aren't you?"

You don't want the same thing between us that I do. That isn't necessarily true.

Yeah. She felt it, too.

How the hell was he supposed to remain some celibate saint of a hero when she touched him like this?

When her surprised gaze darted back to his, Burke lowered his head and pressed his mouth against hers. Although he half expected her to resist, her lips parted to welcome him. She flattened her palm against his cheek and jaw, moaning into his mouth as he gently claimed her. He sampled the shape and softness of her lush bottom lip with a stroke of his tongue before pulling it between his lips. Hazel gave a slight shake of her head. But, just as he hesitated, he realized she wasn't saying no to the kiss. Instead, she was rubbing her mouth against him, seeming to enjoy the texture of his alpha-wolf scruff against her tender skin, or whatever that silly metaphor meant to her. He translated the words into *I think you're irresistibly hot, too*, and let her kiss whatever she wanted, reveling in the same tinder-like friction kindling between them.

He felt her leaning into him, rising onto her toes to take this sensuous investigation to the next level. Burke brought his hands up to frame her face, his fingertips curling beneath those delicate ears to cup the nape of her neck.

She reached up to push his hat off and rubbed her hands against his hair. Burke smiled at her newfound fascination with exploring him and set out on a journey of his own, peppering kisses along her jaw until he found the warm beat of her pulse beneath her ear. Hazel tipped her head back, arching her neck to give him access to sup there. Her bare toes curled atop the instep of his boot and he felt the imprint of proud nipples pressing into his chest as she struggled to get closer. Burke obliged by sliding one hand down over the curve of her hip to cup her sweet, round bottom and lift her onto the desire straining behind his zipper. Her arms settled around his shoulders and she held on, twisting to bring her mouth back to his.

But he'd waited a damn long time for this kiss to happen, and he hadn't satisfied his fantasy of nibbling on her ear and running his teeth against the simple gold stud on her lobe, savoring the contrast between hard and soft that was symbolic of everything about her.

"How long have we been puttin' this off?" he breathed against her ear, loving how she trembled beneath the whisper of air and brush of his lips. Her fingers clutched in the layers of cotton and mesh, digging into the skin and muscle underneath. He wished he'd taken the time to shed his utility vest or her shirt or both before starting this kiss. "I'm tired of pretending we don't want to taste each other—don't want to hold on to each other like—"

"Enough talking." She palmed his jaw in a desperate grasp. "Just—" He captured her mouth in another kiss, spearing his tongue between her lips, tasting sweet caramel and cool cream, and a flavor that was uniquely hers.

Her sigh of surrender told him he'd given her exactly what she wanted.

Burke fell back against the steel door, taking her full weight and loving every curve that flattened against his body, which had been starving for the feel of her. Her feet left the floor entirely as she tightened her arms around his shoulders and pulled herself into the next kiss.

The friction between their bodies created shockwaves that cascaded through him, triggering a snarling groan of need from deep in his chest. "God, how I've wanted you. How I wanted this."

"Do you know how many years have passed since I've been with someone…since I even let myself think about…kissing…" She might be out of practice, but she hadn't forgotten a damn thing about what turned him on. She was eager to touch, raking her fingers across his short hair, down the column of his neck, across his shoulders. They bumped noses and stumbled as he re-positioned her in his arms. She smiled and went right back to dragging her teeth along his jawline. "It's been so long since I... I don't remember how to satisfy this itch that's screaming inside me." She laughed against his mouth. "Much less yours. I might need a refresher course."

"You'll get no complaints from me."

"But—"

"Enough talking," he teased. The tips of his fingers caught in her hair as he framed her face between his hands, guiding her mouth back to his. "It's okay, babe. I want this, too. I can't believe this is finally—"

"Babe?" She broke off the kiss, going still in his arms, repeating the single word as if it was a curse. Hazel braced her hands against his shoulders and blinked him into focus, as if she was coming to after being lost in a dream. Maybe he'd been dreaming, too, thinking that they'd turned a corner in their relationship. Before he could even catch his breath, she released her grip on him and slid her feet back to the floor.

"Guess I got a little carried away." He straightened away from the door, drawing her back into his arms. "Making out like a man half my age isn't usually my style. Guess I've been savin' up." Despite the joke, he silently vowed to dial it back a notch before he went too far and scared her away.

But, apparently, he already had.

Hazel palmed his chest and pushed him back. "What did you call me?"

Any illusion of dream time was done. Burke shook his head, clearing the lingering confusion from his thoughts. "I don't know. *Babe?* I can do *honey* or *sweetheart* if you prefer—"

"No." She was vaguely staring at the middle of his chest where her hand rested, replaying the last couple of minutes in her head, too. "Don't call me that. Don't call me any of that."

At least she had the courtesy to struggle to soothe her erratic breathing, just like he was fighting to inhale a steady, normal breath. She couldn't lie and say that kiss hadn't affected her, too. "Okay. I won't…" He clasped her shoulders to rub his hands up and down her arms until he could think with his brain again. "We can go slow."

"Burke…" She shrugged off his grasp. Her gaze locked firmly onto his. "Jedediah. We have to stop. We aren't a pair of hormone-fueled teenagers. We're old enough to know better than to give in to our urges. We're both exhausted. We're not thinking straight."

"I am. I'm not second-guessin' any of this." He reached for her again, hoping to ease her doubts, but she strong-armed him out of her personal space.

"Stop."

"Because I called you *babe*?" Burke held both hands out in surrender, understanding her right to end any contact she wasn't comfortable with, even if he didn't fully understand why.

The faint lines beside her eyes deepened with an apology. "That's what Aaron called me."

Swearing one choice word, Burke rubbed his hand across his spiky hair. "How was I supposed to know? I'm sorry I upset you." He could feel the short-circuited desire still sparking through his fingertips. But instead of reaching for her, he bent down to retrieve his KCPD ball cap from the floor beside Gunny. "Guess I ruined the moment, huh?"

Despite his fatigue, every muscle in him was tight with desire. That kiss had been pure heaven. And it had only primed the fuel burning inside him. He wanted more with Hazel Cooper. He wanted the right to kiss her every time he walked away from her. Hell. He didn't want to walk away. He wanted to stay the night. Feel those cute, naked toes running up his leg and her body melting into his as she surrendered to his kisses.

"I'm not blaming you. But it's the wake-up call I needed to remind myself that I have rules. I don't do relationships. I don't want to—not with you."

He heard that message like a slap across the face. He pulled his cap onto his head and reached for Gunny's leash. "That's clear enough."

Hazel's fingers fisted in his vest, stopping him from turning to the door. "Not because I'm not tempted to see where you and I might go…but…because I *am* tempted. I've ignored the attraction between us because I don't want to risk what we have. I don't want to lose you from my life."

Why did the possibility of everything she'd just admitted make her look so sad?

He captured her hand against his heart. "Let me get this straight—you're willing to throw away a chance at us becoming more than friends because you're scared it could be really incredible between us?"

"What if it isn't? I'll admit it—I haven't been with a man in years. And I miss that. But what if this is just chemistry that flares out once we give in and get it out of our system? Or we're two lonely people who are so desperate to make an intimate connection that we're jumping on feelings that aren't really there? Think how that could taint what we already have." She tapped his chest with every sentence. "What I know is real. What I know is good and special."

Real. Good. Special. Sounded like a perfect scenario to him. "The best marriages I know are when the man and woman are friends first. That doesn't mean there's no passion. No soul-deep connection that defies logic. All of that goes into a relationship."

"Marriage? That's quite a jump from our first kiss to exchanging rings." Hazel pulled away, finally putting some distance between them. "You've been divorced a long time, Burke. Are you sure you can do a serious committed relationship? That you even want that?"

Back to *Burke*, huh? Boy, when she pushed him away, she pushed hard. "After Shannon, I never found the right woman I could put that much faith in—until I met you. I've wanted you for years, and in all that time, until this past week, until tonight, you've kept me at arm's length. But I'm still here. I think that shows a pretty solid commitment." After a moment she nodded, at least giving him that. "You've been divorced a long time, too. Maybe you're the one who's afraid to commit."

"Guilty as charged. But I have my reasons."

"I know you do. But, Haze, when your heart's involved, there's always a risk. You're sure you're not just afraid of getting hurt?"

"Why? You gonna hurt me?" She tried to make it a joke, but neither of them laughed. "I know you wouldn't mean to. But the last time I followed my heart, I nearly died. I can't afford to be impulsive again."

"What?" Her marriage had dissolved years before the two of them had met. And though her ex-husband's crimes had been big news in Kansas City, he'd been on active duty back then, stationed overseas, and had never heard all the details. Once he'd gotten to know the woman Hazel was now, he hadn't cared who she or her ex had once been. In his recent research into her ex's criminal history, he'd seen the charge of attempted murder along with the fraud and embezzlement charges. But he had no idea who her husband's intended victim had been.

A cold feeling of dread crept down Burke's spine. "What do you mean *died*?"

Chapter Six

"It's a long story, and I'm too tired to get into all of it tonight." The chill Burke felt must be contagious. Hazel crossed to the back of the couch, where she'd shed her scrubs jacket and pulled it on over her T-shirt and jeans. "I stood by Aaron like a good wife when I found out how he'd cheated all those people out of their investments and retirement funds. Gave him the benefit of the doubt. Hoped someone else was responsible and he was the scapegoat who'd been falsely accused."

"I've heard he put you through hell," Burke conceded. "What does that have to do with us?"

She paced over to the curtains and pulled one aside to stare out into the moonless night dotted with the lights of downtown KC. "Even after Aaron was arrested and the DA was hounding me to testify against him, I did everything I could to make our marriage work. Ashley and Polly were six and four. They didn't understand what was going on around them—why friends suddenly stopped calling, why kids were mean to Ashley in school."

Burke swore. "I had no idea it was that bad."

"I did everything I could to try to keep things as normal as possible for them—to keep our family intact. I gave up my life savings, my self-worth, my happiness and any sense of security because I thought it was the right thing to do. I thought love was going to conquer all." Hazel released the curtain and faced him. "It didn't." She hugged herself around her middle, and every cell in his body begged for the right to cross the room and pull her into his arms to share his warmth and strength. "I've worked hard for a long time to regain everything I lost. I don't know if I'm willing to risk that again."

"You haven't regained everything," he pointed out sadly. "You don't trust your own judgment. You don't trust your heart."

Sad green eyes locked on to his, and she nodded her agreement. "I paid a heavy price for loving Aaron."

To keep himself by the door, Burke reached down to pet Gunny's flanks. Like him, the working dog was getting antsy about staying in place instead of taking action. But Hazel needed to talk. "We all make mistakes, Doc. Hell, I've made my share. We're allowed to learn from them and move on. Mistakes don't mean we don't get to be happy."

"I get the learning part. Most people's mistakes aren't as big as the one I made in marrying Aaron."

He vowed then and there to request Aaron Cooper's case file and court transcripts and read them down to the very last detail. He had a sick feeling there was still more to this story, and he wished Hazel trusted him enough to tell him the worst. But she was locking down tight, letting him know he wasn't getting the answers he needed tonight.

"You can't judge every man by your ex's standard. I'm not like him, and you know it. I would never ask you to change who you need to be. And I'd be pissed if you thought you had to." Gunny whined an empathetic protest and Cleo popped up on the back of the couch to see what was upsetting her friend. "I'm a patient man, but you keep making me work too hard, and I might quit trying."

Hazel scooped up the one-eyed schnauzer and hugged the dog to her chest as she joined him at the door again. "That makes it sound like I've been leading you on. I swear, that's not my intention. That's why I never should have kissed you."

"I know you don't want to hurt me. Don't add that guilt on top of everything else you're dealing with. Your honesty is one of those things that make me want to be with you. Still, it's not fair of me to push when you're vulnerable like this." He scrubbed his fingers around Cleo's ears, glad that Hazel would at least accept comfort from her dog if not from him. "If it makes any difference, you don't have the monopoly on being gun-shy about risking everything on a new relationship. Sticking with you is a risk for me, too. I don't relish failing again."

"You didn't fail," she said, and he couldn't miss how her expression changed to one of unflinching support the moment he shared his own weakness. "When we first became friends, you said your wife cheated on you while you were deployed. That's hardly your fault."

For him, for everyone else, Hazel was a warrior. Why couldn't she put that fight into her own happiness? Did she really believe they were destined to fail if they gave in to their deepest feelings?

"I guess our bond wasn't strong enough for Shannon to be without me 24-7. I must not inspire that kind of loyalty. Not with her—and apparently, not with you."

"Of course you do. Look at the men and women you work with, the dogs you train. Look at us. That loyalty—that unquestioning trust—those are the very things I don't want to jeopardize."

"You can have both—friendship *and* love." He gave up on petting the dog and brushed his fingertip along Hazel's jaw. "If you trust me to be your friend, then why can't you trust me to love you?"

"I won't risk my emotional security for a roll in the hay or a chance at temporary bliss when it all might end in heartache and you walking out of my life."

"Who says I'm offering you a roll in the hay?" he teased, despite the evidence that had pushed against the seam of his BDU a few minutes earlier.

"I'm cautious, not blind." Her gaze dropped briefly to his crotch. It was good to see her smile again. "Promise me one thing, no matter what happens between us. Never lie to me."

He smiled back. "Deal."

"And I promise to do my damnedest not to give you false hope. Not to hurt you."

To hell with tiptoeing around his feelings. He slipped his hand around to cup the back of her head. Ignoring the dog squished between them, he kissed her squarely on the mouth, stealing her gasp of surprise. He kissed her hard. Kissed her well. Kissed her until she understood he'd never tire of kissing that beautiful, responsive mouth, and pulled away. "*That's* chemistry. It isn't a bad place to start a relationship." He reached behind him to unlock the door. "I've been through a lot of life, Haze. I'm tough. I'm not going to break—or walk away when you need me—because of a few dings to my ego, or because we're in different places in our relationship. Loving you may not be as simple as a fairy tale, but that doesn't mean I'm going to stop."

"Burke—"

He pressed his fingertip to her lips, silencing any more protest. "Good night, Dr. Coop. Lock up behind me."

Burke skipped the elevator and took Gunny down the stairs, knowing they both needed to work off some of the energy pent up inside them. He opened the steel mesh door at the pedestrian exit to the parking garage and waited for it to close and automatically lock behind him before jogging across the street to the parking lot framed by a narrow grassy area and let the dog relieve himself.

While Gunny sniffed and staked out a couple of trees and shrubs in regular dog mode, Burke took note of the young couple arguing over the roof of their car in the parking lot. He dismissed their petty whining as no threat and glanced back at Hazel's building. He tilted his head to the bright lights behind the fourth-floor windows, wondering how his favorite veterinarian was coping with the aftermath of that intense conversation and make-out session, which he'd let get out of hand the moment she'd kissed him back. He shook his head and tugged on Gunny's leash to get them moving toward his truck. He couldn't tell if he was angry or hurt. Probably both. "You handled that well, Sarge. All those years of biding your time and you blow it all in one night."

After the rain they'd had earlier, he expected the night to be cool. Instead, a fog of humidity hung in the air, closing in around him.

What the hell did she mean when she said her marriage to Aaron Cooper had nearly killed her? Could the tragedy of that marriage have anything to do with the creepy love letters and bomb threats? Her ex had been out of prison for almost a year now. Were the threats punishment for divorcing him? And did she have any idea how badly he wanted to protect her from bombs and stalkers and a painful past that still haunted her?

He didn't suppose there was any way to hide his feelings for Hazel now—no way to step back from laying it all out there. He wasn't worried about salvaging his pride—he was old enough to have learned that there were things in life worth a lot more than a man's ego. But he was also old enough to know that love was a precious thing, and that trust was probably the greatest gift a person could give him…and Hazel had refused to trust his belief that they were meant to be together in every way. He was stumped on how to get her to take that leap of faith with him. And it nagged at him to think that maybe she'd be better off if he didn't even try.

But losing Hazel… The idea of never working side by side with her or trading dumb jokes or kissing her again gutted him.

He exchanged a nod with a trio of young men they passed on the sidewalk before halting at a traffic light. One of the preppie guys in the front waved to someone up the hill behind Burke and rushed on to meet their friend. The one in the hoodie following a few steps behind them ducked his head and hurried after his buddies.

Could Burke be happy with the status quo anymore?

His phone rang in his pocket as the light changed. He led Gunny around the standing water at the curb and pulled his cell from his utility vest. For a split second, his dark mood skyrocketed at the slim hope Hazel had changed her mind. He wisely cooled his jets, though, knowing that at this time of night, even though they were off the clock, it was probably a work call.

"And the night just gets worse," he muttered when he saw the number.

Gunny jerked against his lead, stopping halfway across the street to glance behind them. Burke figured the low-pitched growl was just the dog tracking where the three young men had gone—or maybe he was sensing Burke's response to the name on his cell screen.

His ex-wife, Shannon.

"Gunny, *fuss*." The dog fell into step beside him again. They reached the next curb before he answered the call. "What do you want?"

"Hello to you, too." Her familiar giggle, which he'd once found so charming, grated on his nerves.

If he wasn't a cop, trained to respond to anyone in need—even the woman who'd broken his heart as a younger man—he wouldn't have answered at all. "It's late, Shannon. Is there an emergency? Is Bill all right?"

"You're not at home."

How would she know that? Ah, hell. Instinctively, he glanced around the intersection, wondering if she'd had someone track down his location. Thankfully, there was no sign of her. Had she gone to his house? It was located far enough away on the outskirts of the city that he could have a big fenced-in yard and some mature trees where Gunny could play. A home that was nowhere near the pricey Ward Parkway neighborhood where Shannon and her husband lived. "Are you at my place?"

"I'm parked in your driveway. The lights are out and no one's home." Her breathy sigh, followed by a dramatic sniffle, told him she'd been crying. "I needed to see you."

Burke slowed his pace, feeling a tinge of concern. Maybe there *was* a problem. "Shannon?"

"Why do I have to hear through the grapevine that my husband was nearly killed by a bomb today?"

And poof. Any concern he felt vanished. Now he

was just annoyed that she'd dropped by his house un-
announced. Gunny tugged on his lead again, curious
about something only a dog could see or smell in the
shadows. Burke tugged right back, demanding the dog
sit and stay beside him. Gunny never ignored a command unless he was off leash. Something had caught
the dog's attention, and Burke had been his partner long
enough not to ignore his partner's instincts.

He paused on the corner, turning a slow 360 to see
if he could spot whatever had the dog's attention. A bar
two blocks up had patrons spilling out onto the sidewalk
with their drinks and smokes. The rock music was loud,
but not illegally so. The arguing couple had driven off,
and the trio of young men had disappeared. But they
could have gone into the bar, turned a corner or gotten
into their vehicle and left downtown. A little farther
up the street, a city bus was brightly lit and picking up
passengers near one of the big hotels.

Burke kept searching for anything or anyone that
would put Gunny on alert. "Don't go all drama queen
on me, Shannon. First, it's *ex*-husband, three times
removed. Unless you've divorced Bill Bennett and I
haven't read about it in the paper yet." The irony that
her fourth husband was a divorce attorney wasn't lost
on Burke. "And second, which bomb are you talking
about?"

"Which…? There was more than one? You and that
dog. Why can't you have a regular pet like everybody
else?" He could picture her wiping away tears from her
dark almond-shaped eyes now that she understood he
wasn't swayed by them. "I'm talking about the bomb
threat at the veterinary clinic. I saw the report on TV."

He'd been clearing the hospital when the evening
newscasts had aired. Maybe a reporter had caught him

on camera. "A friend was sent a package at her work. Gunny identified the explosive and we cleared the building. It wasn't really a bomb. Just the parts to make one. I wasn't in any significant danger."

"Significant? But you were in *some* danger. I was right to be worried."

He was a cop. He'd been a soldier before that. The danger surrounding either job was a given. "Go home, Shannon. I'm not yours to worry about."

Although it had been years since he'd come home from a deployment to find her in bed with one of the attorneys she'd worked for as a paralegal, and the anger, heartbreak and blow to his pride had long since mellowed, her betrayal had left a mark that influenced how he approached relationships in the years since. That was probably why it had taken him so long to realize that Hazel was the only woman he wanted to be with, why he'd been content to let things simmer beneath the surface of their relationship...until tonight.

Burke suspected that, in her own way, Shannon truly had loved him, and maybe part of her still did, judging by the infrequent phone calls like this one. But the infatuation shared by high school sweethearts hadn't lasted. She hadn't been cut out to be a military wife. Even with access to support groups, being alone for extended periods of time, managing the day-to-day responsibilities of running a home, working a job and living a life on her own just weren't in her skill set. Even after he'd retired from the Army and Reserves, he doubted she would have done any better with the hours and dangers of him being a cop, even though he was on home soil.

"That's cold, Jed. You know my heart will always belong to you."

"Don't let Bill hear you say that." Since he hadn't

spotted anything unusual to account for Gunny's restlessness, he headed on toward his truck. "I'd hate to be
the cause of his own divorce."

"About that… You know I've matured since we
were married. We were too young. *I* was too young. I
didn't understand about commitment then. And I was
so lonely. But now I—"

Beep.

"Hold on a second, I've got an incoming message."

Thank God. He'd been down this road with Shannon too many times before. She must have gotten into
an argument with her current husband. Every time she
hit a bump in the road with her latest relationship, she
got these sentimental urges to call Burke to reconnect—
expecting him to fix the issue, comfort her or, *ain't
never gonna happen*, even take her back. Hell. Maybe
she called all her exes looking for sympathy when the
going got rough. He had no interest in a woman he
couldn't trust. And knowing Shannon's affairs had led
her from one husband to the next told him she wasn't
going to change.

Burke pulled up the text and frowned. Hazel's name
was at the top of the screen.

I need you. Bring Gunny.

A chill of apprehension trickled down his spine.
Burke glanced up at the windows of the old tool and
die building. Even from this distance, he could see that
all the lights had gone out in Hazel's condo. Every lamp
and overhead bulb had been blazing when he left.

"Fuss!" Burke was already moving, jogging, pulling Gunny into a loping run beside him. "Shannon, I
have to go."

"Let me guess—work?"

"Goodbye."

"It's another woman, isn't it? You said *her* workplace. Are you seeing someone? It's that doggie doctor, isn't it?" Anger edged into her voice. "You told me she was one of the guys, Jed. She means more to you than that, doesn't she?"

Uh-uh. He wasn't going down that road with her. He wasn't the one who cheated, so she had no right to be jealous, and he wasn't about to feel guilty about answering a friend's call for help. "You should be talking to your husband about whatever's going on, not me. Bye."

"Jed, don't hang—"

He ended the call, texted back an On my way and stuffed the phone into his pocket before lengthening his stride to match Gunny's. In a matter of seconds, they were back at Hazel's building. But the cage that closed in the parking garage and pedestrian access stopped him like a brick wall. He didn't have a key card to swipe or pass code to punch into the access panel beside the door. The fact that there were no more texts to give him any idea of what was going on only ratcheted up his concern.

He quickly typed in Hazel's condo number and pressed the intercom button.

His blood pressure rose with every second of silence before he heard a quiet, hesitant voice. "Burke?"

"It's me, Haze. Are you all right? Let me in."

Gunny barked, adding his voice to the urgent request. The dog was probably picking up on the tension running down the lead from his partner's hand, but it was enough of a confirmation of their identity for Hazel to buzz them in. The lights were on inside, so this wasn't something as benign as a power outage. Hazel was hiding in the dark for a reason. After a quick glance around the lobby, looking for any signs of an intruder, they vaulted up the stairs and knocked on Hazel's door.

"Sergeant Burke, KCPD," he announced, warning anyone who might be a threat on the other side of that door. "Open up."

He heard a yip from Cleo and a muted cry a split second before the dead bolt turned and the door flew open.

Hazel walked straight into his chest, wound her arms around his waist and clung to him as though a tornado might blow her away if she didn't hang on tightly enough. Burke didn't mind the contact one bit. But standing out on the landing, exposed to potentially prying eyes, wasn't the place to do it. He hustled Gunny into the apartment, wrapped an arm around Hazel's trembling shoulders and pushed her inside, kicking the door shut behind him.

"Voran!" He ordered the dog to search the apartment while he held Hazel close and peered into the semidarkness over her head. The only light on in the whole place was the flashlight shining from her cell phone, which sat on the coffee table in front of the sofa. "Anyone here besides you and Cleo?"

Her fingers convulsed beneath his utility vest at the back of his shirt as she shook her head beneath his chin. "I'm sorry. First, I chase you away, and now I can't seem to let go."

"I said you could lean on me." But he needed to know what the problem was first. "What's happened? Why are the lights out?" He spied Gunny moving from one room to the next, with Cleo limping along in his shadow. Surely the small dog would have been making noise if there was someone in here besides his mistress. Gunny cleared the back bedroom and trotted down the hallway toward him to be rewarded with a toss of his ball on a rope. As both dogs took off after the toy, Burke leaned back against Hazel's grip to frame her jaw between his hands and tip her face up to his. Her skin was cool, her cheeks pale. He wanted to punch somebody for rattling her like this. "Haze, you gotta talk to me."

She bravely raised her gaze to his. "He called. Right after you left."

No need to explain who *he* was. "What did he say?"

"Come to the window."

"Tell me what he said first. Did he threaten you?"

"No. That's what he said. That's all he said." Nodding that she was all right enough for now, Hazel took his hand and led him to the curtains. *"Come to the window."*

When she started to open the edge of the first curtain, Burke pulled her behind him and peered outside over the street, parking lot and buildings. Even with the sky covered by clouds, with the streetlamps, the neon signs of the nearby bar and traffic lights, it was brighter outside than it was inside the condo. He saw the same variety of faceless people walking the street and going about their business that he'd seen from the sidewalk below. "What am I looking for?"

"Is he gone?" She tugged on his arm to get to the window. "I just saw… I'm not making this up."

"I know you're not."

"It was him." Hazel drifted away from the window. "In the parking lot across the street. I saw him. Everyone else was going somewhere. But he was just standing there. Looking up at me. His face was weird, like he had some sort of deformity."

"Do you know anyone like that?"

"No. I tried to get him to say something else. I

wanted to know who he was, why he was doing this to me. All I could hear was him breathing. I hung up and texted you. Turned the lights out so he couldn't see me. But he already had."

"Can you describe anything else about him?"

"I couldn't judge his height from this angle, but kind of a beefy build. He had on a dark hoodie. Dark pants. Like the man Polly described at the hospital."

Burke swore, closing the curtain. The man following the preppie boys had worn dark blue pants and a hoodie. He hadn't been one of them. He was... "I saw him. Passed him on the street." Burke had been too distracted by frustration and self-recriminations to piece together what he'd observed earlier. "I never saw his face, but Gunny recognized him. Something about his smell must have been familiar. Or he still had trace explosives on him." Burke pulled the curtain shut with more force than was necessary. "I don't see him out there now."

"He looked right at me. Made a stupid little heart symbol over his chest. Like that would mean something to me. And then he gestured like...boom." She placed her hands on either side of her head, then quickly pulled them away, splaying her fingers. *Head blown.* An all-too-familiar gesture indicating an explosion—a threat meant for Hazel.

"Let me see your phone."

He followed her to the coffee table, where she turned off the flashlight app and pulled up the recent call list. He texted the number to Dispatch and requested a trace, although he'd bet money that the call had come from a burner phone. Then he headed to the door.

"How do I make this stop?" Hazel followed him to the door. "He knows where I live. He knows where I work, who my children are. He has my number..." She caught him by the arm and stopped him. "You're going after him?" The panic fled her voice when she realized his intent. "You said he was gone."

"I said I didn't see him." He squeezed her hand in a subtle reassurance as he pried it from his arm. He had a job to do. She seemed to understand that. Her eyes had lost that wild lack of focus and were trained on him as she nodded. He called Gunny to him and unhooked the shepherd's leash. *"Bleibe."*

"Stay?" Gunny sat squarely on his haunches beside Hazel. "Don't you need him?"

"No." He unsnapped his holster and rested his hand on the butt of his Glock. "He stays with you and protects you, in case this guy has already gotten into the building somehow. What's your entry code?" She gave him the number. "This door stays locked until I get back."

"What if he calls again?"

"Switch phones with me. If that bastard calls, he's going to talk to me."

Hazel handed over her cell and clutched his to her chest. She drifted closer to Gunny and buried her fingers in his fur. "Be careful."

"You, too."

The dead bolt slid into place behind him. Burke made a quick sweep through the building, startling one couple who were enjoying a good-night kiss on the top floor. No hoodie. And though the guy could have easily ditched it somewhere, these two weren't hiding their faces from him. And they both wore jeans. Burke's grim expression and curt command chased them into the apartment. The rest of the building and parking garage were clear of anyone who looked suspicious. Once outside, he moved through the parking lot across the street, checking vehicles and the spaces in between. He entered the bar for a quick once-over and gave the bouncer at the door a brief description of the perp. But there were too many possible suspects who fit the general description for him to make any useful identification. He checked down the street in the other direction. A block farther, and he'd be on an overpass crossing the interstate running through the north end of downtown KC. There was simply too much ground here for one man to cover. Whoever had been terrorizing Hazel was gone.

Burke was jogging back to Hazel's building when her phone beeped with a text. He eyed his surroundings and got no sense of anyone watching him before he pulled it up on the screen. It was a fuzzy picture of Hazel peeking out her window into the night.

Do I have your attention now? I don't expect you to answer. But I do expect you to listen. I want you to know that everything you have belongs to me.

FYI, your policeman and your dog can't stop me from taking what's rightfully mine.

"Hell." Burke ran the last block and typed in the code to enter the building.

By the time he was back at Hazel's, he was worn-out and angry and relieved to see her with color in her cheeks again as she locked the door behind him. He briefly considered trashing the text, so her healthy, confident look wouldn't disappear again. But the cop in him knew he needed to save it as evidence. Making a case against a stalker almost always relied on having a stack of circumstantial evidence that showed a pattern of harassment and escalating danger. Besides, he'd promised to always be honest with her.

"It's decaf." She handed him a mug of coffee she'd brewed while he'd been out. "I used your phone to call the girls. They're fine. They haven't seen anything suspicious at their place." The coffee smelled heavenly and reviving, but he set it aside to capture her gaze. "What is it? What did you find?"

"Nothing. He's gone, or he would have seen me reading this." He handed her the phone. "I doubt he would have kept silent about me interfering with his private conversation with you."

She read the text and went pale again. Without comment, she simply picked up his mug and carried it back to the kitchen, where she lingered at the counter with her back to him. She busied her hands by adding half-and-half to the mug and sipping on the hot brew herself.

"What does he want from me? Revenge? My undying devotion? Is he getting off on toying with me like this?" She stood at the refrigerator door as the flare of emotion ebbed and her shoulders sagged. "I can't tell if he thinks he loves me or he wants to hurt me."

"Maybe both. Obsession can change from one to the other pretty quickly."

She drank another sip of creamy coffee and abruptly changed the subject. "Someone named Shannon called while you were out. I saw her name. Isn't she your exwife? She left a voice mail. I hope it wasn't important."

"It wasn't."

Hazel set down her mug with a decisive thunk. "You're going to think I'm an absolute nutcase, but could you—"

"I'm staying."

She turned to find him draping his utility vest over

the back of the couch. He knelt to remove Gunny's harness. He ruffled the dog's fur and sent him off to play with his rope ball. "The couch will do just fine."

Her smile told him he'd made the right decision. Not that he was giving her any choice.

"Good." She padded down the hallway and brought him a pillow and covers. She made up the sofa and fluffed the old blanket for Gunny. "I have the extra bedroom I keep for the girls. You could sleep on a real mattress."

Burke removed his gun, belt and badge, and set them on the coffee table within easy reach. "I want to be between you and anything that comes through that front door."

"Are you afraid he'll come back? That he can actually get into the building to get to me?"

"Aren't you?" He could see she was by the bleak shadows in her eyes. Burke took her gently by the shoulders and turned her toward her bedroom. She didn't protest as he dug into the tension cording her neck and followed right behind her. "It's been a long day for both of us. We have work tomorrow. Try to sleep. In the morning, we'll call Detectives Bellamy and Cartwright and fill them in on this latest incident."

She stopped at the bedroom doorway, and they shared a smile at Cleo pawing herself a nest in the middle of Hazel's blanket. "I seem to be saying it a lot lately, but..." Hazel turned and tilted her eyes to his. "Thank you."

"Go to bed, Doc."

"I haven't been scared like this for a long time."

"I know."

"I hate being scared. I'm used to handling whatever I need to on my own."

"I know that, too."

"I'm sorry about arguing with you earlier. It's not that I don't care—"

He silenced her with a finger over her lips. "That was a discussion, not an argument. An honest exchange of what we're thinking and feeling. People who trust like you and me can have those kinds of conversations. It helped me understand those ground rules of yours. It helps me be patient." When she didn't immediately turn in or protest his touch, Burke brushed her bangs across her forehead and cupped the side of her face. "You'll be okay, Doc. You're the strongest woman I know. Gunny and I are just here to back you up."

She considered his words, then stretched up on tip-toe to kiss the corner of his mouth. "Thank you for saying that. It helps me believe it. Good night, Jedediah."

After she closed the door and turned on a light inside, he checked the locks and windows one last time. Once the light had gone out beneath her door, he untied his boots and settled onto the couch, tucking his gun beneath the pillow.

They were back to *Jedediah*. He breathed a sigh that was part fatigue and part relief. He hadn't ruined everything by putting his feelings out on the table. Sure, he wanted more than a peck on the cheek, more than a closed door and distance between them.

But he knew Hazel was safe, and for now, that was enough.

Chapter Seven

"Hey, babe. I know I'm not supposed to contact you, but we need to talk. It's really important."

Hazel knew the first voice mail from her ex today by heart now. And the second. And the fifth.

Her phone vibrated in the pocket of her jeans, stealing her attention away from her current patient, telling her she'd just ignored call number six. How dare Aaron Cooper keep contacting her?

Having her stalker call her last night to taunt her had left her feeling vulnerable and afraid. Waking up to find Jedediah Burke sitting at her kitchen island, drinking from a fresh pot of coffee and reading the news on his phone like he was a normal part of a normal day had gone a long way toward restoring her equilibrium. Not only was Burke a familiar presence, but his strength and easy authority made her feel like there was nothing the world could throw at him that he couldn't handle. And that air of calm confidence made her feel like she could handle it, too.

But that equilibrium that had quickly been knocked off-kilter for a very different reason when she sat beside him with her own mug of coffee. She smelled freshly showered man, felt the warmth radiating off his body and filling the space between them, and found herself silently mourning the sexy salt-and-pepper scruff that had vanished from his clean-shaven jaw this morning.

Burke was one of her best friends.

He was also solid and hot and one hell of a kisser.

For a few minutes last night, she'd been a woman on fire in his arms, intimately aware of every sexy attribute the mature man possessed. Jedediah had done far more than make her feel safe. He'd made her feel desirable, hungry, eager to be alive. After all these years of denying herself, he made her want to be with a man again. It had been empowering to be the woman he couldn't resist. He said he loved her. But did she have it in her to love someone again?

The phone vibrating in her pocket was stark evidence of how wrong choices could ruin so many lives. She already had five messages on her phone today to remind her of those mistakes. The first message had been friendly, polite, even apologetic. But with each call Aaron sounded more and more irritated, more like the desperate, dangerous man he'd become before the divorce.

"Hazel. It's Aaron. Pick up. I have a right to see my girls. You once said you forgave me for what I did to you. I know you won't believe me, but you still mean something to me. And I love my girls. I'm not the man I was sixteen years ago. Prison changed me. You need to let me be a dad to them."

There was a reason for the restraining order against her ex that had been in place for sixteen years. Once a man endangered her children, betrayed her trust and tried to kill her, she really didn't want to hear from him anymore.

A stalker with an explosive hobby.

Jedediah talking love and second chances.

Aaron harassing her with call after call today.

How had her safe, predictable life gotten turned completely upside down like this?

"Dr. Coop?" Todd Mizner's hand closed over her shoulder and Hazel startled. "Sorry. Everything okay?" he asked before pulling away.

She glanced up at the concern in his blue eyes and gave a brief jerk of her head. Time to focus on the problem right here in front of her.

She looked across the stainless-steel examination table into the unblinking scowl from her client, Wade Hanson. For an out-of-shape man who must be in his sixties or early seventies, wearing grungy workman's clothes that had seen better days, he still managed to look intimidating. He had every right to be upset by her lack of concentration on this long, rainy afternoon. The dog he'd brought in needed some serious attention, not a vet who was too distracted by her own problems to provide the care the alarmingly skinny cattle dog mix needed. Of course, Hanson's combative stance with his beefy arms crossed over his potbelly, and his jaw grinding away on the chaw of tobacco in his cheek, could have more to do with the suspicions she hadn't done a very good job of hiding.

"It's not good." She tilted her chin, catching Mr. Hanson studying her from beneath the brim of his soiled ball cap. He quickly shifted his gaze back to the skinny dog on the table while she moved the stethoscope and checked for gut sounds to confirm her initial diagnosis.

"You can fix her, though, right?" Hanson spoke without moving his jaw. Probably a good thing since she didn't want to see the tobacco juice staining his teeth. But he gave her the sense that he was a powder keg about to blow—an unsettling analogy considering recent events. Hazel wondered exactly where that anger seething beneath the surface was directed.

One last vibration on her phone told her Aaron had left another message. Ignoring both the pestering from her ex and the critical glare from Mr. Hanson, she finished her exam. Besides the dog being clearly overbred, she could see ribs and hip bones through the mutt's thin skin and spotted tan fur. A stray scrounging for food on the streets would have more body mass than this poor waif. She had no fever or obvious masses to indicate a serious illness. And Hazel didn't want to draw any blood to check for internal parasites until she'd gotten some intravenous fluids in her to increase her blood volume and stabilize her. "This is a working breed. Athena should be compact, muscular. She needs to be spayed, too. You should have brought her to me sooner." Maybe dropped a few bites of whatever had put that paunch on Hanson's belly to the floor for his pet. "Neglect like this doesn't happen overnight." Since the animal couldn't tell her what she'd suffered, Hazel had to ask the owner questions. "Has she been keeping food down?" She bristled when he didn't immediately answer. "Have you been feeding her?"

Wade scratched at his scraggly white beard and grumbled. "I didn't do it. Margery took her to piss me off. I just got Athena back from her."

Interesting deflection of her queries. Even a few days was too long for this dog to be suffering without basic care. "Your wife did this?"

"Ex-wife. Athena should have been mine when she left. But my selfish, vindictive—"

"I get the picture." Unfortunately, this wasn't the first time Hazel had seen a patient who'd been the victim of an unfriendly split. It wasn't the first time she'd defended the innocent pet who'd been either forgotten or used as a weapon to punish an ex. It was just as likely that Hanson was lying, and he'd taken the dog to spite his ex. Either way, she would see to it that Athena got the help she needed. Hazel set her stethoscope on the counter behind her and slid her arms beneath the dog's chest and rump to help her stand. "Todd. Priority one is to get some IV fluids in her."

Todd took the lightweight dog and cradled her against his chest. "You want me to try a half cup of food with her? See if she can keep it down?"

Hazel nodded. "No more than that. I'm guessing she'll eat anything we put in front of her. But she won't be able to digest much."

Interesting that Mr. Hanson, who claimed to be so attached to the dog his wife had allegedly taken from him and abused, didn't pet Athena or even try to talk to her as Todd carried her from the room. Nothing suspicious about that. Right.

"How long have you had Athena?" Hazel asked, once the door closed behind Todd.

"I told you. Just a few days. Margery took her."

Hazel pulled her reading glasses from the collar of her T-shirt and picked up her clipboard to make a notation on the dog's chart. "How long did you have her before that? Did you get her as a puppy? Rescue her? Take her in as a stray?"

"She kept showing up at work, lookin' for handouts." Even when he finally uncrossed his arms, Mr. Hanson's stance still looked defensive. "I'm on a road crew. We're paving a gravel road out in east Jackson County. I figured somebody dumped her out in the country."

Sadly, that might be true. Perhaps he thought he'd done a good thing by helping the dog find a home. But not if he didn't know how to, or couldn't, give the dog proper care. "Is she current on her shots? Has Athena had any vaccinations you know of?"

He pulled off his cap and scratched his thinning white hair. "I dunno."

Not the answer she was hoping for. "Don't take this the wrong way, Mr. Hanson, but…can you afford to keep a dog? There are programs through several vet clinics I work with that provide food and basic equipment like leashes and bedding, even medical care, for pets whose owners need a little extra help. Would you like me to put you in contact with them?"

Muttering something under his breath, he plunked the hat back on top of his head and started to pace. "What's with the twenty questions? Can you help her or not?"

Unless they found evidence of an internal parasite or illness, this was an easy diagnosis. And she hated it. "Right now, we'll treat Athena for starvation and dehydration." She removed her glasses and hugged the clipboard to her chest as she met the resentful glance he tossed her across the table. Probably every woman was on his hit list now. She'd proceed cautiously, but this dog wasn't going back to Hanson or his wife, not until animal control had investigated the case and she knew exactly who was responsible for the dog's deplorable condition. "I'd like to keep Athena here for at least forty-eight hours, to keep her under observation and make sure she's getting the care she needs. When she's stronger, we'll get a complete blood count, urinalysis and biochemistry profile to find out if there are any underlying issues causing her malnourishment. I'll call you with my results, of course."

"You're taking my dog, aren't you?" he muttered,

sliding his chaw into the opposite cheek. The subtle movement struck Hazel as a pressure valve the man used to contain his temper. "You're gonna get me in trouble with the law." He circled around the table to trail his dirty fingers across the counter, touching the handle of every drawer and cabinet along the way. "I told you, it was Margery who let her get like that."

Hazel turned to keep him in her sight as he moved behind her. "I don't have the authority to take your dog, Mr. Hanson. But if I can't find any evidence of a medical reason for her weight loss, then I will report your ex-wife for animal cruelty." She'd be putting his name on that report, too, as the registered owner.

"Do that." He stopped at the door to the lobby and squeezed the knob. "She took everything I had left. And that wasn't much. I'm just glad to get Athena back."

"Divorces can be hard. Even under the best of circumstances."

"Under the worst of circumstances, they're..." He faced her again, nodding toward the fingers she'd curled around her clipboard. "I see you ain't got no ring on your hand. You divorced, Dr. Cooper?"

Hazel curled her toes into her clogs, resisting the urge to back away from those icy gray eyes. "I am."

He splayed one hand on the metal table and the other on the countertop. He pressed a button on her computer keyboard, clearing the screen saver, before pushing down on the scale she used to weigh puppies, kittens and other small animals. The cradle bounced up and down as he released it. She respected a hardworking man and understood the grime that came with a construction job like his. But since this was a medical facility, there was a sterility factor she had to protect. When he reached toward the sharps disposal bin on the wall, she grabbed his wrist and stopped him. "Mr. Hanson, that's a potential biohazard. Some of this is expensive equipment, too. I ask you not to touch it."

"Yes, ma'am." She couldn't tell if that glimpse of yellowed teeth was a smile or a snarl. But he pulled away and crossed his arms over his gut again in that challenging stance he'd used earlier. "You have a successful business here, Dr. Cooper. Your ex pay for it?"

Hazel bristled at the question. "Excuse me?"

"Did you use his alimony to start your clinic?"

Alimony? That was a joke. When her marriage to Aaron had ended, there'd been nothing left to ask for. The simple answer was no, she'd started this clinic and paid off her student loans on her own dime. She didn't need anyone's help to be a good veterinarian and smart businesswoman. But Wade Hanson was practically a stranger. This was the first time she'd seen Athena as a patient. The dog was already three or four years old and hadn't been fixed or had her teeth cleaned. Other than this brief time they'd spent together in the exam room, she didn't know this man. He didn't need to know her history. "I'm here to take care of Athena—not tell you my life story." Since he wouldn't take the initiative to leave, she moved past him and opened the door for him. "I'll make sure she's eating and does her business before I send her home. Now, if you'll excuse me, I have another appointment."

"You never answered my question about starting this clinic."

"I don't intend to." Whatever prejudice he had against his ex-wife or divorced women, Hazel wasn't going to let him get away with the veiled insults. "You'll notice that it's *my* name over the door, Mr. Hanson."

He grunted a smug sound that seemed to indicate

he hadn't really expected her to share the details of her divorce, or that he didn't believe she had become a success in her own right. If Wade Hanson wanted sympathy or someone to commiserate with over the bitterness he felt for his ex-wife, he'd have to make an appointment with a therapist.

"I get the message, Dr. Cooper." He stepped through the open door, turning back to her, and said, "But you get this message. I intend to keep my dog. No woman is going to take him away from me again. I'll call or stop by tomorrow to see how she's doing."

The inner door opened behind her, and Hazel didn't think she'd ever been so happy to see Todd walk into a room. The interruption finally got Hanson moving.

"You're welcome to do that," she answered, dredging up a smile she didn't feel before closing the door after Wade Hanson. Her shoulders sagged in a weary sigh before she straightened again to face Todd. "Did you get Athena situated?"

"She's handling the IV just fine," he reported. "And she wolfed down that pâté like it was going out of style." He opened the door a crack and peeked out into the lobby before closing it again. "Did you get a load of that guy? He was more interested in getting the dog away from his wife than in taking care of it himself. You gonna report him to animal control?"

She'd like to report him for animal cruelty, female bashing, failure to bathe and creeping her out for no good reason.

Instead, she simply nodded, putting on her reading glasses again and pulling up Athena's patient file on the computer to transfer her notations from the clipboard. "Whether it was Wade Hanson or his wife who let the dog get into this condition, it doesn't matter. Someone needs to be held responsible."

"Hey. You okay?" If Todd had put a hand on her, she probably would have snapped. But maybe he was finally learning the rules of conduct she expected from him. "You look a little rattled. You worried Hanson is going to retaliate if he loses his dog?"

She was worried about a lot of things lately. But she wasn't about to open up to her vet tech and give him any kind of encouragement to take their working relationship to a more personal level. "It's been a long day. I'm fine. Thanks for asking."

Todd's eyebrows came together atop his glasses in a frown. But when she refused to elaborate, he opened a cabinet door and pulled down a bottle of disinfectant spray and paper towels. "You want me to clean up in here? I'm happy to help."

"No, I'll do it. I need to get these details into the system before I call the authorities." Plus, she needed to listen to the messages on her phone. If they were all from Aaron, she'd report them to his parole officer, Steve Kranitz. She continued typing. "Tell the front desk I'm taking a short break. I'll be right out."

"You got it." He exited into the main lobby, closing the door behind him.

Alone in the quiet for the first time that day, Hazel rolled out the stool from beneath the counter and sank onto it. She puffed out a weary breath that lifted her bangs off her forehead before she saved the information on the screen and pulled her phone from her jeans.

"Damn it." Six missed calls, all from Aaron.

And one more from a number she didn't recognize that had just come through. She tried to feel hopeful that at least it wasn't the number of the man who had called and threatened her last night. But Burke had said it was easy to buy several burner phones to prevent KCPD from tracing the calls.

Maybe it was a wrong number.

And maybe her stalker got off on finding one insidious way after another to contact her. To declare his love or frighten her or threaten her with whatever his sick agenda might be.

After pulling up her voice mail, she set the phone on the countertop. Before playing her messages, she ripped off a handful of paper towels and picked up the disinfectant spray, keeping her hands busy and pretending to divert her thoughts by cleaning as she listened.

The polite request in Aaron's first two messages turned to frustration and blew up into a curse-filled tirade by the last one. *"Don't make me fill up your voice mail with messages. Pick up the damn phone and talk to me. Or tell me where and when we can meet. We have to talk. I heard what happened to Polly's car. What if she'd been in it, Hazel? Clearly, you can't handle what's happening on your own. Screw your independence. You need me. The girls need me. I'm their father and I'm worried."* Several beats of silence passed, and Hazel stopped wiping down the scale cradle, thinking the message had ended. But just when she moved to save it as evidence for Officer Kranitz, Aaron exhaled a noisy breath and spoke in a calmer tone. *"I blamed you for putting me in prison. But this one could be on me. I may have some enemies. Let me help."*

The message ended with another recitation of his cell number and a beep. Hazel saved the message and returned with an almost compulsive need to wipe down every knob and surface Wade Hanson had touched. If only she could wipe away the memories of every man who was unhappy with her lately—every man who might be responsible for this psychological torture of love letters and threats and bombs.

I may have some enemies.

"You think?" Try over three hundred enemies who'd lost their life savings and retirement funds to her greedy ex. Or the man he'd pointed a finger at as an accomplice during his trial in an effort to get his sentence reduced. Hazel's testimony had put them both behind bars. And that list of potential enemies didn't account for anyone Aaron might have butted heads with during his fifteen-year stint in prison.

The last message started to play, cooling Hazel's manic energy. She stopped working and stared at the phone on the counter, as if it was responsible for the sudden chill in the air around her.

She heard breathing that was measured and crackling with a slight wheeze. When her caller spoke, the voice sounded eerily familiar. *"Ten...nine...eight... Do you feel the clock ticking yet?"* Could Aaron have disguised his voice to the point she didn't recognize it? Had he coerced a friend into calling on his behalf? Or was there some other obsessive lunatic in her life she hadn't yet identified? *"My patience with you is running out, my beloved. Give me what I want. Or I'll take it from you."*

"Take what!" She slammed the bottle down on the counter. "What the hell do you want from me?"

A soft knock on the door reminded her that she'd raised her voice. Was there a client in the lobby, or had someone from her staff overheard her?

She punched off her cell and stashed it in her pocket as Ashley nudged her way inside the exam room. Her green eyes were narrowed with concern as she closed the door behind her. "Mom? You okay?"

"Hi, sweetie." Hazel tossed the soiled towels and put away the disinfectant, buying herself a few seconds to regain her composure before she pointed to the clipboard her daughter carried. "That my next patient?"

"Your last appointment for the day. It's a new patient." Ashley hugged the clipboard to the front of her pink scrubs. "Who was that on the phone?"

"I was listening to my messages." Hazel reached for the printout of patient information.

Instead of handing it over, Ashley tucked the clipboard behind her back. "Who left the messages? I can't tell if that's your worried face or your pissed-off face. But neither is good. I was hoping you'd be in a better mood, because I need to ask you a favor."

"What favor?"

Ashley pointed to Hazel's head. "Explain the face first."

She'd go with the lesser of two evils. Or maybe she was a fool to think either caller was less of a threat than the other. "Have you gotten any phone calls from your father?"

"From Dad? Dad called you?" Ashley shook her head. "No. Not since he first got out of prison and he begged to meet with Polly and me behind your back. That's when the judge expanded that restraining order to include us." Moving closer, she leaned her hip against the counter. "I'm not sure I'd even recognize what he sounds like anymore, unless he identified himself. What did he say?"

What was the best way to explain this honestly, without tainting her daughter's perception of her father? "He saw the news story about Polly's car and the bomb threat here. He wants to make sure you're both okay."

"He cares now? He didn't care sixteen years ago

when all those people were so angry with him and our family."

"He's older. He's had a lot of time to think on what he did and what he lost." Hazel shoved her hands into the pockets of her jacket and shrugged. "He claims that prison has changed him."

"Yeah, but how? What if it just made him a smarter criminal who can't be caught now? Or do you think he really cares?"

"I can't answer that. I know he adored you both when you were little." Hazel leaned against the counter, giving Ashley's shoulder a teasing bump with her own. "I always promised that when you and Polly were of age, if you wanted a relationship with your father, I wouldn't stand in your way."

"Yeah, well, he used to love you, too." Ashley shook her head, dismissing any idea of reconciliation. "Mom, we know what he did to you. Even now that I'm old enough to understand his supposed reasons, I can't forgive him for that. He didn't know how to be a good father then, and I doubt that's a skill one learns in prison."

"So you don't want to have contact with him?" Hazel reached over to pull Ashley's ponytail from the collar of her top and smoothed it down her back. "Don't answer right away. Think about it."

"I don't need to think about it. Polly and I have discussed it more than once. We don't really know him. We don't want to. We don't want him to be a part of our lives."

"I'll talk to him, then. Or rather, I'll have my attorney talk to his." With her mood lifted, Hazel pushed away from the counter. "Now, what about this favor?"

Ashley's expression creased with a smile she could

barely contain. "Well, maybe I can help your day end on a more positive note."

The smile was contagious. "I'm all for that."

"Do you need me to stay for this last appointment? Joe's coming here to take me to dinner. I'd like to change before he picks me up."

"Joe's coming here?"

"Yes. I thought you might like to check him out for yourself and see how sweet he is. After everything that happened yesterday, I thought that might ease your mind a little bit."

Hazel nodded, appreciating the thoughtful plan. "I think it might."

"Great." She handed Hazel the clipboard she'd brought in. "Here's the chart for Mr. Jingles. Looks like a standard checkup for a newly adopted pet."

Hazel scanned the printout on her new feline patient. "I think I can handle one cat without help." Ashley was already heading out the door to the lobby when Hazel stopped her. "Wait. What about Polly? Will she be on her own tonight?"

"I already talked to Sergeant Burke. He's picking her up at the hospital and taking her home. Polly's cool with that. She has to study for a test tomorrow, so she won't be going anywhere." Ashley gave her a quick hug, then practically danced out the door. "Thanks. I'll let you know as soon as Joe gets here."

"Wait. Ash?" She followed her daughter into the lobby. "When did you talk to Sergeant—"

"Excuse me? I'm Mr. Jingles's owner." A hand with polished French-tip nails was suddenly thrust toward her, stopping Hazel in her tracks.

She instinctively took the woman's hand. "Hello."

"Thank you for working me into your busy schedule,

Dr. Cooper." The dark-haired woman wore a polished gray suit and held a carrier with a cat that was equally sleek and dark. "I'm Shannon Bennett."

Chapter Eight

Burke checked his watch and swore. He tapped on the accelerator, pushing his speed as much as he could without turning on his siren.

He was the only one with an emergency here. If he didn't feel it like a fist to the gut every time Hazel's eyes darkened with fear or uncertainty, he wouldn't care so much about running late now that he and Gunny were off the clock. But it was nearly 5:30 p.m. And though he knew she would be the last one to leave her clinic after locking up, he'd gotten caught up in a search on the grounds at the KCI Airport that had required a team effort by KCPD and airport security to cover a large search grid after a multiple-bomb threat had been called in and a suspicious bag had been discovered in a culvert off one of the parking lots. Fortunately, the bag had ended up being an extreme case of lost luggage, and the depressed individual who'd called in the threat had been identified sitting in his car in another parking lot. He'd been apprehended and taken to a hospital. But now Burke's clothes and skin were damp with the rain, his boots were muddy and he smelled like wet dog.

But he'd promised Hazel he'd be there to protect her and her family. Knowing her independent streak, she'd walk across the parking lot and drive home alone, just as she had all those years when there'd been no one in her life to look out for her. She was a smart woman, and strong. But a stalker who knew so much about her, and so much about explosives, created dangerous circumstances that required her to be extra careful regarding her security. Hell, had he reminded her of the basic safety precautions of checking under and around her truck before even approaching it? Did she understand situational awareness? Pinpointing the location of every person in her vicinity, taking note of her surroundings and anything that seemed out of place?

Would she call him if something *did* seem out of place?

He peered through the rhythmic sweep of the windshield wipers to race through a yellow light and cross into the industrial area north of downtown where her veterinary clinic and a neighboring dog park were located. Even though he and Gunny had put in a long day, he wanted to have his partner do a sweep of Hazel's truck before she got in, just in case the perp who was terrorizing her made good on last night's threat and had escalated from blowing up her daughter's unoccupied car into a much more personal attack.

Burke eyed his cell phone in the console beside him, wondering if he should try calling her again. But since his first two messages about waiting for him had gone straight to voice mail, he focused on weaving through rush hour traffic and getting to the clinic as quickly as he could. Either she was busy, ignoring him or he was already way too late. And that was what made everything in him tighten with worry.

His blood pressure dropped a fraction when he spotted the familiar sign of her family animal clinic. He flipped on his turn signal and slowed but had to stomp on the brake as he came up behind a gray sedan that was nearly the same color as the rain. The pricey car was parked at the curb just outside the clinic parking lot. Not the safest place to park, so close to the driveway entrance. The dark-haired driver was going to get her fancy bumper clipped if she wasn't careful.

Taking a wide arc around the sedan, Burke entered the nearly empty parking lot. Relieved to see Hazel's truck, he pulled in a parking stall and shrugged into his still-wet KCPD jacket before he heard the squeal of tires against the wet payment. Climbing out, he adjusted the bill of his cap to protect his eyes from the rain and saw the taillights of the gray sedan speeding away. Maybe the police logo on the side of his truck had made the driver think twice about creating a potential traffic hazard. Or else the driver had been parked there for no good reason.

Wait a minute.

"No way." He pulled Gunny from the truck and jogged to the street. But the gray sedan had merged with traffic and disappeared. Dark-haired woman in a fancy car? She'd been wearing sunglasses, despite the gloomy weather. He hadn't seen her face, and he no longer knew what his ex-wife drove, but that couldn't have been Shannon, could it?

How could she have known he was coming here? Had she asked one of the men on his team? He was off the clock, so even Dispatch didn't know his twenty. Was she so desperate to reconnect with him that she'd hoped for a face-to-face meeting?

His hand hovered over the phone in his vest beneath his jacket while the rain drummed against the bill of his cap. No. He wouldn't give his ex the satisfaction of calling her to ask where she was, and he dropped his hand to Gunny's flank.

Maybe it hadn't been Shannon in that car at all. She'd been on his mind as an annoyance he needed to deal with ever since last night's call. He needed to sit down with her and spell out that they were never going to get back together. His heart belonged to someone else now. He'd just projected Shannon's identity onto the random brunette the way a supposed eyewitness would sometimes misidentify a suspect because their concentration had been off-line due to their emotions.

Unless... Burke planed the water off his cheeks and jaw and turned back toward the clinic door. Could Shannon have been spying on Hazel? Checking out her competition? Not that there was any possibility of a reunion, but it might be worth looking up the make of her car and, if it was a match, paying her a visit. There were already enough things standing in the way of the relationship he wanted with Hazel. The threats. Preserving a friendship. Hazel's stubborn self-protection streak. He didn't need a jealous ex thrown into the mix working against the future he envisioned for them, too.

With an urgent *"Voran,"* he guided Gunny over to Hazel's truck and ordered the dog to search.

He was stowing Gunny in the back seat of his truck after a quick towel off and a dog biscuit when the clinic doors opened. Hazel stepped out and put up a blue umbrella against the steady drone of the rain.

She scooped Cleo into her arms and handed the small dog over to the young couple who followed her out and waited beside her while she locked the door. He recognized Ashley's long blond ponytail as the two women hugged. The young dark-haired man with a tattoo snaking up his neck and a bandanna tied around the top of his head was someone new, and Burke shifted inside his boots, forcing himself to stay put, trying not to make a suspect of every man who got close to Hazel. The young man and Ashley were both wearing bulky rain pants and jackets. Burke had already spotted the motorcycle parked across the lot from his truck and suspected that Tattoo Man belonged to the bike.

Hazel shook hands with the younger man, turning as Ashley beamed a smile at Burke and waved. "Hey, Burke!"

Burke touched the brim of his cap at her enthusiastic greeting. "Hey, Ash."

In a swift move known only to escape artists and matchmaking daughters, Ashley handed the dog back to her mother, slipped behind her and nudged Hazel forward, pulling the man with her in the opposite direction. Burke shook his head at the totally unsubtle move. At least he had one Cooper woman who was in favor of him getting together with Hazel. Ashley and the guy who was apparently her date hurried down the steps to the left of the door, where they unpacked their helmets from the storage compartment on his motorcycle.

Hazel walked down the ramp in the opposite direction at a much slower pace, meeting Burke at her truck, depositing Cleo and her purse inside before facing him. She raised her umbrella over Burke's head so that it sheltered both. "Here you are, showing up at my clinic again. Is this going to be a thing now?"

"Me keeping you safe? I think so."

She eyed his sodden, muddy appearance from hat to toe before narrowing her eyes as she frowned. "Is there a problem?"

"Long day. Turned out okay."

"But I saw you and Gunny searching my truck."

"Overdeveloped protective instincts," he joked. "Just your friendly neighborhood cop making sure you and Cleo get safely home." He thumbed over his shoulder at his truck and the weary working dog relaxing inside. "Gunny didn't hit on any explosives. I wouldn't have let you and the one-eyed fuzz ball anywhere near your truck if he had."

Finally, she smiled, a regular ol' friendly smile, as though she was glad to see him, and not overthinking or regretting the changing status of their relationship. "Cleo and I thank you. Are you coming over for dinner?"

"Would I be welcome?"

"Me spending time with you? I think so." She gave his teasing right back, and his pulse kicked up a notch at the idea of kissing that beautiful smile.

Fortunately, he had wet clothes cooling on his skin and work that still needed to be done to temper his instinctive male reaction to sharing the intimate space beneath the umbrella with her while the rain falling around them cocooned them from the rest of the world. "I won't be there right away. After I drive Polly to her apartment, I've got a couple of leads on your case I want to follow up on."

"Leads? Like what?"

Besides checking with Justin Grant and the crime lab on the details surrounding the bomb parts mailed to Hazel, and those used to blow up Polly's car, Burke thought of the dark-haired woman in the car who had sped away. "Who was that woman who just drove off?"

Hazel glanced around the parking lot. "What woman?"

"The brunette in the BMW."

"My last client left half an hour ago. A routine check on her new cat, Mr. Jingles. She was chatty. He was fine." She nodded toward the couple climbing onto the motorcycle. "Ashley and Joe and I are the only ones here."

"Your last client wasn't Shannon Bennett, was it?"

"Yes. How did you…?" She leaned away from him, scanning the parking lot again. "Wait. *Your* Shannon? The last name was different. I've never met her before… I was focused on the cat, and I didn't think… Was she checking me out? Does she think something's going on between us?"

Hell, yeah, there was something going on between them. Exactly what hadn't been determined yet, but he wouldn't deny the connection between them anymore. "It doesn't matter what she thinks. Shannon's no longer a part of my life, and I don't want her to be a part of yours."

"She was waiting here until you came. To see if you were going to show up." Hazel shoved her bangs off her forehead. They were damp enough to stick up in a wild disarray. "Is she one of those leads you're following up on? You think a woman could be responsible for what's happening to me?"

Burke wasn't ruling out anyone who might be a threat to Hazel. But his ex-wife was at the bottom of his list of suspects. "Shannon has zero access to explosives, and she wouldn't know how to put a bomb together."

"She could have hired someone who does." Frustration was evident as she attacked her sticky bangs again. "If she blames me for stealing you from her—"

"I've been making my own decisions about who I want to be with for a long time now. There is no stealing. I choose."

"And you choose me."

"Damn right, I do."

"But if she's jealous, we should…"

Hazel's smile had faded. Burke wanted it back. "Forget about Shannon. Our marriage was over years ago. I'll have a conversation with her. She won't bother you again." He wasn't giving Hazel another excuse to push aside the feelings that had finally surfaced between them. "Drive straight home to the parking garage." He pulled his keys from his pocket and stepped from beneath the umbrella. "I'll meet you at your place when I'm finished. And I'll bring dinner."

"You don't have to do that."

He strode to his truck. "I'll be there in an hour. Hour and a half, tops."

Hazel grabbed his arm to stop him, sliding the umbrella over his head again. "Jedediah—"

"Gunny's worried about Cleo. He'd like to make sure she's safe and fed and locked in for the night."

She arched a silvery-gold eyebrow. "Gunny's worried?"

This silly conversation was safer than pouring his guts out to her again the way he had last night. "If Gunny had a driver's license, he'd come over by himself. But he needs me to be his chauffeur."

"Oh, well, tell him we're in the mood for something light tonight, like a salad. It's the only way Cleo and I can justify the ice-cream sundae we intend to eat for dessert."

"With your homemade caramel sauce?" He thought of her licking that spoon again and wondered why, since a few decades had passed since he'd been a horny teenager, his body reacted so sharply, so instantly, to the thought of her licking things. Like him. *Wow.* He needed to feel the cool rain splashing in his face again. Since he'd given in to that kiss, his body seemed to have a one-track mind where Dr. Hazel Cooper was concerned. "Is there enough to share?"

"I'll make sure there is." She glanced back to her truck. "Cleo is looking forward to seeing Gunny again this evening."

"Gunny's pretty stoked about it, too."

They weren't fooling anybody here, least of all each other. Hazel reached up and brushed away the moisture pooling on his shoulders. Her fingers hooked beneath the front of his jacket to straighten his collar and settled there. All casual touches. Every one adding to the energy that hummed through him when they were close like this.

"All this innuendo is dangerous for my peace of mind," she confessed. It was reassuring to hear that, although she was fighting the chemistry they shared, she wasn't denying it. "It makes me feel like you and I are becoming *us*."

He feathered his fingers into her hair and smoothed her bangs back into place across the smooth, warm skin of her forehead. "We are, Haze. I believe in *us*. One day, you will, too. As long as we're on the journey together, I'll go as slow as you need me to."

Hazel shook her head. "That's hardly fair to you."

He cupped his hand against her cheek and jaw. "You're worth the wait."

She studied him for several silent seconds, gauging his sincerity before turning her lips into the palm of his hand and pressing a kiss there. "I want to know anything you find out."

"Will do."

Her fingers flexed inside the front of his jacket, as though she'd forgotten she was still holding on to him.

He hadn't. "And thank you for taking care of Polly this evening. You score a lot of brownie points with that."

He liked brownie points. He liked the idea of redeeming them with her even better. "You raised two good people. I'm happy to help them where I can."

The motorcycle engine roared to life, diverting their attention to the opposite side of the parking lot. With the tats, the muscles and the Harley, Ashley's date looked tough. But that alone didn't make him a threat. The young man made sure Ashley had her helmet securely fastened, and he'd waited for the two women to lock up the clinic earlier. Ashley didn't seem to have any problem winding her arms around his waist as he turned his bike toward the street.

"Bye, Mom! Burke!" Ashley waved before latching onto him again and leaning into his back as he revved the motor and pulled out of the lot.

"Have fun," Hazel called after her, but they were already racing away down the street.

Burke watched Hazel wrap both hands around the base of her umbrella. Any tighter and the wood might snap. "Is that the boyfriend?"

"'Fraid so. Joe Sciarra. He's a bouncer she met at a bar." Her grip didn't relax until the couple had disappeared into the camouflage of traffic and rain. "He was actually charming and well-spoken," she admitted, "although he looks like he rides with one of those motorcycle gangs."

"Want me to run a background check on him?"

Green eyes swiveled up to his. "Can you do that? Isn't that an abuse of your position on the force?"

"Yes, and yes."

"I don't want to get you into trouble."

"One of the perks of running my own division is that

I've earned enough clout to call in favors if I need to. The department will give me a little leeway if I ask for it." Since he had no idea yet who was targeting Hazel, this was a no-brainer. "There have been enough threats that I can justify getting the background on anyone suspicious in your circle of friends and acquaintances."

She considered his answer for a moment, then nodded. "Then, while you're at it, could you also run a background check on a Wade Hanson?"

"Who's that?"

"A client of mine. He's got a pretty serious grudge against women. Still, I just met him today, so he couldn't have sent all those letters."

A bad feeling twisted inside him. "Did he threaten you?"

"Not directly."

"Damn it, Haze—I told you to call—"

She splayed her fingers against his chest, quieting him with a gentle touch. "You can't stop me from doing my job. Just like I can't stop you from doing yours. I suspect him either of animal abuse or failing to report the abuse. I had to call animal control on him, and I doubt that will make him happy with me."

Burke covered her hand with his, needing the anchor of her calm strength to keep from going into protective-caveman mode and scaring her away from confiding in him. "Wade Hanson. Got it. Anything else you want to tell me?" he teased, trying to lighten his mood. He didn't expect to see the frown tighten her expression. Ah, hell. There *was* something else. "What is it?"

"Later. There are some messages on my phone I want you to listen to." Hazel fisted her fingers into the front of his jacket and stretched onto her toes to press a sweet kiss to the corner of his mouth. He treasured the gift without trying to turn it into anything more. "Go do what you need to do. Find answers for me. And tell Gunny not to be late."

HAZEL SUSPECTED THE low-lying areas of the city would be flooding by now with all this rain. But the intermittent downpours kept her neighbors from asking any questions as she walked Cleo inside the perimeter of the parking garage. The other residents of the building exchanged a friendly greeting or stopped to pet Cleo when they came home from work or errands. While she appreciated the security of knowing concrete and steel grating surrounded the ground level of her building, keeping threats and unwanted visitors out of her life, she didn't want them asking why she wasn't walking her dog across the street in the minipark or up a couple of blocks on the grassy area between her neighborhood and the wall that blocked the highway at the base of the hill.

Because someone keeps threatening to blow me up.

Nope, she didn't want to have to explain that one—or try to come up with a lie that would convince them that they were safe, even though she lived in the building with them.

One advantage to having a three-legged dog was that she didn't have to walk Cleo very far to get her exercise. A couple of laps around the garage was enough for Cleo to do both her businesses and clean up after her.

One *dis*advantage to having a three-legged dog was that she didn't have to walk Cleo very far to get her exercise. Security aside, Hazel felt entombed behind the garage's metal gate. Mist from the rain filtered through the steel mesh walls and made the air feel heavy. It trapped the scents of oil and dog, and the sharp, earthy smells of waterlogged foliage and mud from the landscaping outside. Although she knew it would be foolish to do so, she longed to get out into the evening air and feel the rain cool her skin and see it wash the sidewalks clean. She could feel the wind if she was out in the open, and maybe that would blow away this sense of uneasiness that left her starting at every new sound and counting the minutes until Burke showed up with dinner and that heavenly smell that was all man and uniquely his.

She needed to figure out what she was feeling and decide where she wanted her future with Burke to go. He'd been too good a friend for too long for her to give him false hope. She wouldn't be selfish and string him along just so she wouldn't lose his caring and companionship. She was a mature woman who hadn't known passion for a long time, but every fiber of her body craved his kisses and the firm, needy touches that had awakened her long-dormant desire. And no woman of any age would want to deny herself the tenderness and respect with which he treated her.

Hazel cared about Burke. She enjoyed spending time with him—eating, working, talking. They shared a devotion to animals and justice and protecting the people they cared about. She admitted a healthy lust for his toned body and grizzled jaw and teasing sense of humor.

But did she love him? Could she surrender her whole heart to him?

Because if she changed her life—if she let herself love again—she wasn't doing anything halfway. Jedediah Burke wasn't a halfway kind of man, either. And that meant it wouldn't halfway hurt if she made the wrong choice.

Although the rational part of her brain insisted on arguing the point, Hazel was beginning to think that, deep inside, she'd already made her decision. The fact that she didn't want to go back upstairs to her lonely place by herself, now that Burke and Gunny had filled up her condo with their presence, was very telling. Maybe Ashley and Polly—and Burke—were right. The only person standing in the way of a second chance at happiness was her.

And the nimrod who kept taunting her with the promise of blowing her to smithereens.

"That's one hell of a pep talk, Dr. Coop," she muttered out loud. "Cleo, what do you think I should do?"

The dog tilted her head up at the mention of her name, and Hazel reached down to scratch around the schnauzer's ears. But the need for affection lasted only a few seconds before Cleo put her nose to the ground and followed an intriguing scent around a parked car to the concrete half wall.

"Good advice," Hazel praised. "Keep yourself busy instead of worrying so much."

Hazel decided that instead of checking her watch every few minutes like a schoolgirl waiting for her first date to pick her up, she'd find something to keep herself busy and out of her head. She pulled her phone from the pocket of her jeans and called Polly.

"Hey, Mom," her younger daughter answered, clearly recognizing her number on the screen of her phone. "Checking up on me?" she teased in a breathy voice. "Or checking up on Sergeant Burke? He left here about an hour ago. Said he was stopping by the precinct office to do some research. He asked if you like taco salad. I said yes."

"He's coming over for dinner tonight to check on me."

"I kind of figured."

Based on the rhythmic cadence of Polly's voice, Hazel guessed her daughter was in the middle of a workout. "You're not out running tonight, are you?"

"No, worrywart," Polly chided with affection. "Yoga. I'm playing one of those exercise DVDs. I won't get soaked in the rain and catch a cold, and no bad guys can chase me."

Hazel followed Cleo along the wall as the small schnauzer tracked the path of whatever had piqued her interest. "Will you be all right by yourself? Do you want to come over here until Ashley gets home?"

"And be a third wheel on your date with Burke? No, thanks."

"It's not a date."

"It should be."

Hazel heaved a deep sigh that echoed Polly's tension-clearing breath. "I need to work through some things before I commit to a new relationship."

"Mom." Her daughter dragged the single word out to three syllables on three different pitches. "You've had sixteen years to work through things after Dad. You have the right to be happy. If you don't grab Burke, someone else will."

As they reached the wide mesh gate at the parking garage entrance, Cleo jerked on her leash, pulling Hazel down the ramp toward the sidewalk, insisting on tracking the scent outside. *What in the world?* Had one of the neighborhood cats sauntered past? Hazel gave a short tug on the leash. "Come on, girl. You don't want to be out in the rain, and neither do I."

"Sounds like Cleo needs your attention. I swear, you spoil that dog more than you ever did Ash or me." Hazel could hear the smile in her daughter's voice and remembered when she'd been that full of energy and certain that everything would turn out all right if she worked hard, stayed hopeful and remained loyal to the people she loved. That had been a lifetime ago, before Aaron's arrest and the divorce. Before the night she nearly died. Hazel planted her feet as Cleo jerked against the leash. When had she gotten so old and cynical? How long had surviving her life been more important than living it? Too long. She'd taught her daughters better but had reached fifty and was no longer practicing what she preached. "Mom? You still there?"

"Yes. Sorry, I got distracted." Hazel vowed to change her life. Right now. She wasn't going to be a coward about living anymore. And if grabbing Jedediah Burke was part of that spiritual renaissance, then so be it. "You're an insightful young woman, Polly Cooper."

"Um, thanks?"

"I have to go." Her gaze followed the length of the leash down to Cleo to see what had caught the dog's attention. Hazel spotted the vague outline of something small but oddly shaped leaning against the garage gate. But the lights from inside the garage cast distorting shadows through the steel mesh, and she couldn't quite make it out. Were those little tufts of fur poking through the bottom links of the gate? Had a small animal taken refuge from the rain? "I think I've made a decision."

"Good. Talking on the phone is messing with my concentration." Polly laughed before taking another deep breath. "Call if you need anything. Good luck with Burke. Love you."

"Love you, too. Bye." Cleo was pawing at one of the tufts of fur, pulling it through the gate. Was that… a tail? "Cleo. Stop." Hazel knelt and ran her hand along the dog's back to calm the frantic thrill of discovery. "What have you found, girl?"

Whatever belonged to that striped tail wasn't moving. Shortening Cleo's leash, she tucked it beneath the sole of her boot to keep the dog away from the creature that could be ill or worse. She turned on the flashlight on her phone and shone the light through the gate. She gasped a quick inhale of compassion.

A cat.

"Oh, sweetie, what's happened to you?" The veterinarian in her quickly squelched her sympathy and she pushed to her feet. A stray must have curled up as close to shelter as it could get and breathed its last breath. Or else some coldhearted clown who shouldn't be responsible for an animal had lost a pet and dumped the creature here instead of paying for a cremation or disposing of it legally.

Hazel hurried to the pedestrian door. She would check the cat's condition for herself and make sure there was no contagious illness or even take it back to the clinic to scan for a microchip. She'd already called animal control once today. She wasn't afraid to make the owner accountable if there was one.

But Hazel froze before pushing open the locked door. Besides the cat at the vehicle entrance, there was something leaning against the bottom of the door here, too. This object had clean, straight lines instead of curves. It was covered in brown paper instead of fur.

Her vision spun with trepidation as she squatted down to inspect the oblong package that had been left just outside her secure sanctuary. She didn't need to see her name on the mailing label to know what it was, to know it was for her.

But she read it, anyway. *Hazel Cooper.* With her home address.

She shivered as the damp air penetrated her skin.

She scooped Cleo up into her arms and made herself breathe, so she wouldn't pass out with fear. Or anger.

Not again. Not here.

Hazel snapped a picture of the package with her phone, then texted it to Burke's number.

He's been here. Left a package. Calling 911.

A shadow fell over Hazel, and Cleo twisted in her arms, barking as though they were under attack.

Hazel looked up at the furious noise.

And screamed.

Chapter Nine

The grotesque features of the red-and-black Halloween mask framed by the hood of the man's jacket quickly took shape. But identifying the devil costume made him no less frightening than the monster that had first startled her. His eyes were recessed behind the mask, shadowed by night and impossible to identify.

Tumbling onto her butt in her haste to retreat, Hazel scrambled away, clutching the growling, barking Cleo to her chest. Even though the steel grating and coded locks kept him from reaching her, it didn't stop the man from curling one set of his black-gloved fingers through the steel links.

And breathing.

He didn't say a single word, but she could hear his breath coming in gusts and gasps, as though he was out of shape or had run up on her fast. Had he hoped she'd step outside to check on the cat? Maybe trip the bomb when she opened the door? Grab her as soon as she was on his side of the security gate? Or maybe this sicko was simply excited to see how badly he'd startled her.

She quickly got to her feet, hugging Cleo as tightly as the squirming, snarling dog allowed. "Get away from me!" she warned.

The only thing that moved was his chest, puffing in

and out as he did that damn breathing. The man's dark jeans and hoodie were soaked with rain and dripping onto the sidewalk. He'd probably been standing outside for a while, no doubt watching her, and she hadn't even realized it. He'd been watching, waiting for her to be alone, waiting for her to move exactly where he wanted her before he approached. He was a dark, shapeless bulk without a human face, oozing malice and a power she didn't want him to have over her. The bottom of his mask puckered as he sucked in a deep breath, and for a moment, she thought he was going to speak. Instead, he reached into his pocket and pulled out an envelope. The dark holes of his eyes never wavered from her as he rolled the envelope into a scroll and pushed it through the grate.

Hazel watched the curled paper drop to the damp concrete in front of her.

"I'm not going to read that." It was hard to tear her gaze away from the sightless holes where his eyes should be. "Keep your damn love letters." She glanced one way toward the package, the other toward the feline corpse. "Stop bringing me these sick gifts. You need to leave me and my family alone. You're making me angry. Not afraid."

He stepped closer and she jumped back a step, making a liar of herself. Okay, so she was angry *and* afraid. But she wasn't helpless, not entirely.

It took several seconds to hear her own thoughts through the muffling drumbeat of rain, Cleo's barking and her roiling emotions. *Do something. Put him on the defensive. Fight back.*

Suddenly, she felt the phone still clasped in her hand and raised it to snap a picture of the man. He flinched at the flash and spun away for a moment. "How do you like that? I'm calling the cops. I'm sending them a picture of you."

Hazel forwarded the image to Burke's phone, then snapped another picture. And another. Not bothering to read the answering texts from Burke.

The man came back, perhaps remembering that his disguise wouldn't give him away. That he had the advantages of strength and anonymity—and possibly a bomb—on his side of the metal links that separated them.

Her phone vibrated with another response, and she finally looked down at the flurry of texts from Burke.

On my way, said one text.

The next read, Go upstairs and lock yourself in. I notified Dispatch. Help is on its way.

Get the hell away from him! read the most recent message.

Hazel retreated another step. With no gun, he couldn't shoot her. With the gate between them, he couldn't reach her. And yet...

Her devilish suitor leaned into the grating, pushing it slightly forward with the weight of his body. He curled his gloved fingers through the links, stretching them toward her, making her feel as though he could touch her.

"Stay away from me." Hazel shook hard enough that Cleo halted her barking and nuzzled her mama's cheek. "It's okay, girl."

But it wasn't. If Hazel gave in to her imagination, the man would dematerialize and slide straight through the steel mesh to get to her.

"Give me what I want," he wheezed in a toneless whisper, finally deigning to speak.

Did she recognize that voice? It sounded like an echo of something familiar, but with its harsh rasp, she couldn't place it. Could she recognize him by his build? Smell? Anything? She hugged Cleo closer to her chest. "Who are you? What do you want from me?"

And then she saw the electronic device he held in his right hand, small enough to fit within his palm. He stroked it with his thumb. A tiny cell phone? A remote? Whatever it was, she didn't for one second believe it was anything good.

"What is that?" she demanded.

"On…" He flipped a cap off one end and pressed a button. Hazel swung her gaze over to the package, instinctively retreating. "Off…"

She flinched when he pushed the button again, expecting her world to erupt with flame and blow her into a gazillion pieces. She looked at him.

"There are innocent people in this building. You'd hurt more than you and me." She pleaded with him to remember his humanity. "Or don't you care how many people you hurt?"

His answer was an angry grunt. He charged the fence, sending a ripple of the rattling noise around the chain-link walls of the garage. "You should talk," he wheezed.

"Me? What did I do?" Hazel punched 9. "I've had enough of these games. I'm calling the police." Then 1. "Why don't you stay there and keep talking to me? Give them a chance to meet you, too." Another 1, and she hit the call button, then put the phone to her ear. "My name is Dr. Hazel Cooper. There's a man at my building. Threatening me. He has a package—I think it's a bomb. He already blew up my daughter's car." She rattled off her building address and the names of the detectives she'd been working with. "I've alerted my friend Sergeant Burke. Jedediah Burke. He runs the K-9 unit. He'll need backup." The man in the mask never moved, except to curl his black-gloved fingers into fists around the links. Not even hearing that police officers, the bomb squad and one very big, very bad K-9 cop who'd sworn to protect her were on their way could budge him.

"They'll be here any minute," Hazel warned him, repeating the dispatcher's last words. "KCPD is coming for you."

His response was to pull his fingers from the grate and slowly stroke the metal links as though he was caressing her face or her hair in some creepy pantomime of a gentle touch.

Hazel shivered. "Stop that."

The man caressed the metal one more time before turning the shadowed eye sockets of his mask toward the concrete floor and the envelope he'd delivered to her.

She shook her head, refusing to do as he asked. "What have I done that's worth killing me for? Worth killing yourself? If you set off that bomb now, you'll die, too. That's not much of a victory, is it?"

No answer.

"Did you kill that poor cat?"

He held up the device in his hand, pushed a button. "On," he whispered.

As much as she wanted him to go away, Hazel realized she needed to keep him here until the police arrived, instead of running for cover or tossing accusations that might scare him away. "All right. I'll read your note." She set Cleo down but kept the dog on a short leash—away from the man—as she stooped down to pick up the envelope and open it. There wasn't much to the typewritten letter inside.

*You're going to be mine. Do you know how much
I want from you? How much I need you to give
me? Everything.*

Everything?

Not *I want you*, but he wanted something *from* her.

Hazel raised her gaze to those missing eyes as understanding dawned. These weren't love letters. They were payback. The bombs and threats were about retribution this bastard thought she owed him. For what? Something she had done? Some perceived slight? Could this terror campaign be payback for something Aaron had done in prison? Did this perv mistakenly think that hurting her would hurt her ex-husband?

Or was this Aaron himself? After so many years apart, would she recognize her own husband if he was disguised like this? Was this some twisted version of what Aaron had done to her all those years ago?

"Aaron?" She squinted through the glare of the garage lights and the shadows beyond them, trying to see his eyes behind the mask, searching for something familiar beneath the shapeless hoodie and baggy jeans. "Is that you? Why are you doing this?"

All he did was breathe.

Maybe this wasn't her ex. But then, Aaron hadn't actually done the dirty work the last time he'd terrorized her, either.

"Why?" There was no answer, of course. She lurched toward the grate, smacked it with the flat of her hand. Cleo barked at the sharp rattling noise. When the man jumped back from the figurative assault, it was very telling. *That* was a lot like Aaron, too. "Coward! Show me your face. Talk to me like a real man."

She hated the tears that stung her eyes. They were a

toxic mix of remembered shock and fear, and anger that her life should come back to the nightmare that she'd barely survived sixteen years ago.

"Talk to me," she pleaded in a softer tone. "I don't understand. I'm tired of being afraid."

His chest spasmed with a rippling movement. And then she heard another sound. Laughter.

She'd admitted she was afraid of him, of his relentless torment, and that made him laugh. Hazel backed away from the mocking sound.

Big mistake, Dr. Coop. You just gave him what he wanted.

Part of what he wanted, at least. *Everything* probably involved a whole lot more than this mental anguish—like panic or torture. Or dying.

"Good," he dragged out in a toneless whisper. He pushed the button on the device in his hand and replaced the cover. *Off.* Then, with a single finger, he traced the outline of a metal link. Hazel shivered as she imagined him touching her skin with that same finger. "I'll take that as down payment on what you owe me."

She frowned. Why couldn't she recognize that voice? Or was she only imagining it sounded familiar?

She picked up Cleo, and for a split second she wished her little schnauzer was as well trained as Gunny. She'd order her dog to bite that stupid, creepily suggestive finger. She wished she had Burke's partner with her here right now to take him down and sink his teeth into him and chew that hideous mask right off his face. She wished she had Burke.

The blare of an approaching siren pulled Hazel from the violent turn of her thoughts and stiffened her spine. "You're caught."

He shook his head in a silent no. Then he picked up

the package and the dead cat and backed away from the gate as swirling lights from the first official vehicle bounced off the trees across the street.

"Wait!" Hazel dashed to the pedestrian exit as the man ran down the sidewalk, disappearing into the curtain of rain and night. If KCPD didn't catch him now, he'd be free to come back and taunt her again, to hurt someone else. One of her daughters? Her neighbors? Her coworkers and patients? His threats had already escalated to the point that she was certain he intended a messy death for her. But how many innocent people did his idea of *everything* include?

She shoved open the heavy door and ran outside into the rain. "You won't get away with this!" The sirens were deafening as the first official vehicle reached her block. She halted as rain splashed her face and soaked through her clothes. Cleo huddled against her as she peered through the distorted lights of emergency vehicles and streetlamps that highlighted individual raindrops instead of what lay beyond them. She couldn't even see the corner of the building, much less the man. She took one more step, and then another, following in a hesitant pursuit. "Don't run from me now! You're not so brave without a bomb to keep me in check, are you! I want to talk to—"

A big black-and-white pickup swerved into the parking ramp in front of her, screeching to a halt on the damp pavement. Hazel jumped back from the truck that blocked her path. "No!" She dodged around the truck, trying to get eyes on her tormentor. "He's getting away."

But she ran into a wall made of man and uniform.

"Hazel!" The KCPD truck was still rocking from its abrupt stop when Burke jumped out from behind the wheel. Leaving the engine running, he circled around the hood and locked his arm around her waist, catching her before she could dart past him. "What the hell are you doing out here?"

"Stop him!"

She shuffled in quick backward steps to stay upright as he pulled her up against the brick wall. "The only thing that kept me from going crazy imagining all the ways he could hurt you was knowing there was that cage between him and you."

She clung to a fistful of his jacket, even as she tried to slide around him. "He went that way. Around the corner. I didn't think it was safe to come out while he was still here. We need to catch—"

"It wasn't." Burke pushed his hips against hers, trapping her between him and the wall. Clearly, he wasn't letting her move away.

"Damn it, Burke." She pushed. Nothing happened. "I don't want to lose… I don't…" Her fingers slowly curled into his jacket and the vest, shirt and man underneath it. Had she never fully realized how tall and broad he was? She couldn't see anything beyond the expanse of his shoulders. And he was as immovable as the brick wall at her back. But her ebbing panic still wouldn't let her settle against him. "I don't want him to get away. He has a bomb. He'll hurt someone. He'll come back. We have to go after him."

"That's my job. Your safety is my priority." He framed her jaw between his hands, tilting her face up to study her expression, stopping any chance of her putting herself in danger. "Are you okay?"

She calmed herself in the warmth and clarity of Burke's whiskey-brown eyes before nodding. "Cleo spotted him. I was walking her around the garage. He had a dead cat he put by the gate. Like bait to lure us to him. Then I saw the package, and the dog started barking and suddenly he was..." Her arm tightened around Cleo as she remembered the devilish mask and sightless eyes. Then she felt the stroke of Burke's thumb across her lips and came back to the present. Back to a warm body and fiercely protective expression. Back to the man who felt like her future.

If she could survive the present.

Hazel eased her grip on the front on his uniform, letting her hand settle over his heart. "He was right there. As close as you and I are now, with only that grating between us. Cleo was having a fit. I backed away and tried to keep him talking, to get him to stay after I texted you."

Burke rubbed Cleo's head. "Good girl. You were protecting your mama."

Feeling his praise of her feisty little schnauzer like a comforting caress to her own frayed nerves, she turned her head toward the curled-up paper on the other side of the gate. "There's another letter."

"Did you read it?"

Hazel nodded. "I didn't want to. But I thought it would keep him here until help arrived. It's like the others—creepy and obsessive. Only... I don't think it's about love. Having him here made it feel like this is all about revenge."

"Revenge for what?"

Hazel shrugged and shook her head. "This isn't some unrequited crush like I thought it was at first. He's... angry at me. I don't know why. He wants to punish me."

Burke started to pull her into his arms, but, with a dog between them and a second and third black-and-white pulling up behind his truck, he ended up sliding his palm to the back of her neck and briefly massag-

ing the sensitive skin at her nape instead. As he stepped
back, she noticed the flashing lights of a fourth KCPD
car blocking the intersection at the end of the street. Another vehicle was pulling into place at the opposite end
of the block to stop traffic, while a SWAT van pulled
into the parking lot across the street.

"You rallied the troops."

"We take bomb threats very seriously." He feathered
his fingertips through the fringe of hair at her nape,
sending a trickle of much-needed warmth through her.
"I take protecting *you* very seriously."

She reached up to wind her fingers around the damp
sleeve clinging to his sturdy forearm, thanking him.
"I know. And I know you want to be more than just a
protection detail. Part of me wants that, too. But I need
you to understand the kind of baggage I come with if
we pursue this relationship."

His eyes darkened with interest. "That's a conversation I want to have. But I need to be a cop right now.
Later. Okay?"

"Okay."

"Sergeant Burke?" Two uniformed officers, wearing plastic ponchos and KCPD ball caps, appeared at
his shoulder.

Burke blinked and the heat in his eyes had vanished.
The veteran police sergeant had replaced the man she
loved. He slipped his hand to the more neutral position
of her shoulder and turned to the two young men. "The
perp ran toward Broadway a few minutes ago. Black
hoodie. Dark jeans. Halloween mask. See if you can get
eyes on him but keep your distance. Chances are he's
carrying a bomb."

"Yes, sir." The officers ran down the block, splitting
up to cover both sides of the street.

She recognized the next cop, Justin Grant, who moved in beside Burke. His green eyes swept over her face. "Dr. Coop okay?"

Burke pushed her toward the lanky blond man before releasing his grip on her. "She stays with you. She doesn't leave your sight." He glanced down at her before giving orders to Justin. "Give your statement to Bellamy and Cartwright when they get here. Take her upstairs. I'll radio if I find anything."

Burke hesitated for a moment, tension radiating off his body, seeming uncharacteristically unsure of his next move. His reluctance to leave her to pursue the suspect reminded Hazel of the independent strength that had sustained her for more than sixteen years. She loved him for his concern but understood that the best way for him to catch her stalker and would-be bomber who could harm so many more people was to assure him she could draw on that strength and be okay without him.

She reached around Cleo to splay her hand at the center of his chest. "Go. Do your job. Gunny will have your back." She curled her fingers into the front of his jacket and stretched up to press a quick kiss to his mouth. Then she pulled away and looked up at Burke's friend. "Justin will have mine."

With his dark gaze never leaving hers, he nodded. Then he hunched his shoulders against the rain and jogged to his truck.

She heard Gunny whining with excitement as Burke grabbed the big dog's leash from the front. When he opened the back door, the Czech shepherd was dancing at the edge of his cage.

"You keep an eye on him, Gunny!" she called out.

"Come on, boy." Burke hooked up his partner and the shepherd jumped down beside him. "You got one more job in you today?" Gunny looked up at him, his tail wagging in anticipation, waiting for the command to go to work. "Gunny, *Fuss!*"

They moved off at a quick pace, following the devil man and the other two officers down the street.

Hazel watched the rainy night swallow up man and dog, trotting off to do battle with a bomb and the monster who wanted her dead.

Chapter Ten

Hazel startled when she felt Justin's hand at her elbow. "The old man said to get you inside, and I do what the boss says."

"He'll be all right, won't he?" Hazel punched in the code to unlock the door to the pedestrian entrance to the parking garage. "I want him to be focused on his own safety, not me."

"This neighborhood is swarming with cops right now," Justin promised. "He's not alone in some kind of *High Noon* face-off against this guy."

"But it's so dark out there. The streetlights won't do much good until the rain lets up. I didn't see him until he was practically on top of me." A fist squeezed around her heart at all the worst-case scenarios that suddenly filled her head. "A bomb and…that man… can do a lot of damage."

Justin followed her inside, locking the door behind him. "It sounds odd, but the best eyes out there are Gunny's nose. He'll smell a threat long before Burke or anyone else sees it."

"All those men and women who showed up—they aren't in Burke's chain of command, are they?" Hazel asked. "I know you're not."

Justin's grin took the edge off her concern. "I don't

know anyone on the force who doesn't move when Sergeant Burke says jump. And we've been doing a lot of jumping lately."

"Because of me?"

"It's not like we don't all owe him for one favor or another. He and his dogs have saved more of our hides than we can count." Justin took off his cap and smacked it against his thigh to remove the excess water before slipping it back over his blond hair. "Besides, it's about time he found something to care about besides work and dog training. It put an end to those awkward conversations with my wife, asking me to introduce him to one of her friends because she's worried about him turning into a lonely old man. I keep telling her he's one of that rare breed of man who'd rather be alone than with the wrong woman." He winked. "I'd bet money that you're the right one."

The right one. Burke would rather be alone than with someone besides her. Something warmed deep inside Hazel, even as she shivered at the pressure that pronouncement put on her vow to remain single and protect herself from getting hurt again. Did everyone in Kansas City except for her know how long Burke had had feelings for her?

"I'm not sure I'm the best choice for him."

"He's decided what he needs. He doesn't do dumb or boring, and he doesn't do disloyal." Justin pulled a plastic evidence bag from a pocket in his jacket. "I'm sure you know how hard it is for him to trust after the hell his ex-wife put him through."

Hazel bristled at the mention of his ex. She admitted there was a tad of jealousy behind her tense reaction. Shannon Bennett had once owned Jedediah's heart. She'd been in his bed and had most likely been shielded from the nightmares the world threw at her by Burke's broad shoulders and protective instincts. He'd probably made her laugh and had shared intimate conversations and given her knee-melting kisses—all those things she could no longer deny that she wanted for herself. But mostly, she couldn't fathom how anyone would willingly hurt the good man she cared for so much.

"I know she cheated on him."

Justin snorted through his nose. "Wasn't just once. Every time he deployed, she made a new friend." Hazel's heart squeezed with anger, but Justin continued as though he was discussing the inclement weather. He knelt beside the curled letter and envelope. "A man likes to be needed, but it's also nice to know your woman can handle it if you're not there 24-7. It's probably why he likes his dogs so much. They're loyal down to the bone."

Was that how Burke saw her? As an independent woman who was also a loyal friend? With all the problems she'd had in her marriage, at least infidelity hadn't been an issue she'd gone through with Aaron. And even after everything had crashed and burned, she'd never considered being unfaithful to her vows. Of course, she hadn't been willing to trust any man enough to seek out a new relationship. Not until Jedediah Burke had walked into her vet clinic. She understood that she was the woman Burke wanted. But could she truly be the woman he needed? Did she have it in her to give him the kind of love and mutual trust that he deserved?

Thankfully, Justin switched his focus from her relationship with Burke back to the investigation. When the bomb squad officer pulled out a multiuse tool and opened a tweezers attachment to pick up the letter, Hazel pointed out that the man in the Halloween mask had worn gloves. "You won't get any prints from those."

"We'll let the lab be the judge of that." He slipped the letter and envelope into a bag and sealed it. "I want them to check for explosives residue. That can be as much of a signature in tracking down this guy as any prints." Once he towered over her again, he walked her to the elevator and pushed the call button. "Let's go."

On the way up the elevator, Justin jotted the date and location on the evidence bag. He read the message on the letter and muttered an expletive. "This guy's a piece of work. No wonder Burke has been working overtime to get a lead on him. Can you tell me anything about the package?"

Hazel absentmindedly scratched Cleo between her ears. Exhaustion was quickly claiming her now that the adrenaline spike of her stalker's visit was wearing off. "I never saw inside it. It was shaped like a long shoebox. Wrapped in brown paper. Addressed to me. He took it with him."

When they reached the fourth floor, Hazel set Cleo down and unlocked the door to her condo.

"Hold up." After flipping the dead bolt, Justin asked her to wait beside the door. Just as Burke had for the past two nights, the younger officer moved through each room of her apartment, checking under beds and in closets, securing every window and the fire escape exit before coming back to her at the front door. "Everything looks good. You can relax."

Right. Relax. That was still a work in progress. She was keenly aware of the difference between fatigue and feeling relaxed.

But out loud, she thanked Justin for his presence.

"Thanks." She unhooked Cleo's leash, and the dog trotted into the kitchen to lap up a big drink of water. Hazel kicked off her shoes on the mat beside the door and peeled off her wet jacket before following the dog to the kitchen. She rinsed out the coffeepot and started a fresh brew before she heard Justin pulling out one of the stools behind her.

"Burke said you got pictures of the perp and the package." His tone was friendly enough, but also like Burke, he was all business when it came to the investigation. "Show me."

Hazel pulled her phone from the pocket of her jeans and set it on the island counter for him to look through. "You can't tell anything just by looking at the picture, can you?"

"You'd be surprised. The key to finding an unknown bomber is to identify his signature—the way he builds his device, the components he chooses." Justin scrolled through the pictures. "For example, how did he pick up the package when he left? Did he move slowly? Make a point of keeping it parallel to the ground?"

Hazel hugged her arms around her sticky T-shirt and realized she was soaked to the skin. That didn't help the chill she was feeling. She looked beyond Justin to the bank of windows and wondered how wet Burke and Gunny were. If they were cold. Tired. If they were facing down the devil-faced man. She'd hear an explosion, either accidentally or intentionally detonated, at this distance, even with the storm muffling the city noises outside, wouldn't she?

"He'll be okay. Gunny won't let anybody hurt him," Justin said. She dragged her focus back to him as he set his cap on the counter and continued as if she hadn't just gone to a very dark place in her head. "Now, tell me about the package itself."

"You're trying to distract me, so I don't worry about Jedediah."

He arched a golden eyebrow. "Is it working?"

"No. Still worried." She summoned a half smile to match his. "But I can multitask." The chocolatey, earthy scent of coffee filled the kitchen as she pulled down two mugs and poured them each a cup. "The man grabbed the box by one end and tucked it under his arm like a football." She replayed the memory of the man's blank eyeholes and labored breathing as he disappeared into the rain. "He ran. As fast as his huffing and puffing would let him."

Justin turned down her offer of cream and sugar and took a drink, barely giving the coffee time to cool. "Then it's not motion activated like most pipe bombs are. More likely, he set it to detonate with a cell phone where he can call in and set it off exactly when he wants. Thrill bombers often use that setup—they want to witness the destruction they cause, but from a safe distance."

A shiver crawled across Hazel's skin at the gruesome image that created. "Like an addict? Only his drug of choice is blowing things up?"

"Exactly."

She remembered the stroke of his thumb over the electronic device in her stalker's gloved hand. "Wait a minute." She picked up her phone and scrolled through the pictures before pointing one blurry image out to Justin. "It's not a great picture, but he held a device in his hand. He kept saying he was turning it on and off. I kept thinking he was going to detonate the bomb then and there."

"A kill switch."

Hazel shivered. "That sounds ominous."

"He was arming and disarming the weapon. That tells me a lot." Justin set her cell aside to text some notes into his own phone. "He might have been using a timer. Stopping the countdown to continue the conversation— or forcing you to do what he wanted." He'd wanted her to read the letter. He'd wanted her to know that he was in complete control of whether she lived or died. Hazel sank onto the stool beside Justin as he talked through his thoughts out loud. "Although starting and stopping the countdown like that would be like playing Russian roulette. A faulty disconnect or losing track of the countdown would put him right there if the bomb went off. He might have some kind of suicide scenario going on in his head—like the two of you ending together. He probably wouldn't want an audience of police officers, though, if that was the case. It would depersonalize the event too much for him. Unless it wasn't a bomb at all." He glanced down over his shoulder at her. "But another fake meant to terrorize you."

Thrill bombers? Kill switches? Suicide scenarios? This winking, easygoing man had a disturbing knowledge of explosive devices and all the ways her stalker could kill her. Not to mention the knowledge to disarm the devices himself. "Your wife must be a very brave woman, considering all the risks you take."

He nodded. "The bravest. Did you know that Emilia helped me with an undercover op when we first started dating? Of course, I accidentally forced her into it."

"Accidentally?"

His cheeks turned slightly pink. With regret? Embarrassment? A remembered heat? "My mission had gone sideways. I needed her to bail me out. She was brilliant."

While Justin told her the story of how he and his doctor wife had met in an emergency room, and a kiss to keep her from exposing his cover had led to taking down a serial bomber and eventually to marriage and starting a family, Hazel heated up soup and made sandwiches for Justin, Burke and herself. Then she changed into dry clothes and set out coffee mugs and towels for the officers who were coming up to interview her. She made a quick call to each of her daughters. Polly told her about Garrett Cho, the police officer who'd been assigned to watch their apartment. Ashley was still on her date with Joe Sciarra, who got on the phone himself to assure her that he'd keep an eye on Ash and would take her home ASAP. And though she didn't doubt that the muscular bouncer could defend himself and her older daughter, it was hard for Hazel to let either of her girls out of her sight—even knowing they were both grown, responsible young women.

Almost an hour passed before Hazel heard a knock on her door and sloshed her tepid coffee over the rim of her mug. Unlike the two detectives she'd buzzed in earlier, she'd given Burke the pass code to get into her building, so she knew he could come straight up to her condo. But still, she jumped at the unexpected sound. Justin was on his feet, his hand on the butt of his gun at his waist, crossing to the door, before Burke announced himself. "It's me, Haze. Tell Justin to let me in."

By the time Justin unlocked the door, Hazel had grabbed a clean towel and was crossing the room.

"Heads up on the muddy paw prints," Burke warned. "Gunny, *sitz—*"

"It's okay." Gunny zipped past her, leaving a trail across the hardwood floor and area rug in front of the couch as he greeted Cleo, and the two dogs sniffed and curled up together on the blanket she'd left out for the working dog. Hazel shook the towel loose and patted the moisture from Burke's face and neck. "Let him warm up and relax. Gunny's okay, right?"

"He's fine."

"And you?"

Burke carried his gear bag in one hand and held out a wilted paper sack in the other. His pants were caked with mud up to his knees and the scruff of his beard was dotted with droplets of water. "I'm afraid dinner's cold and wet. So am I."

Hazel didn't care. She tossed the towel across his shoulders and slid her arms around his waist, walking into his chest. While the dampness of his clothes seeped into hers, she aligned her body with his, tucked her head beneath his chin and squeezed him tight, saying nothing until she detected the warmth of his body and felt a deep sigh roll through his chest. She heard the double thunk of him dropping both bags and breathed her own sigh of relief when his strong arms folded around her.

"I'm drippin' on you, Doc." His voice was a husky growl against her ear.

"Just let me hold you for a minute."

"I've got no problem with that. But I'm fine, Haze." He stepped to one side, pulling her with him as Justin locked the door behind him. "Any issues here?" he asked the officer who'd been guarding her.

Justin shook his head. "The detectives took her statement. Dr. Coop let me rattle on about Emilia, the kids and me."

"You're good at talking," Burke teased. "I'm surprised you didn't put her to sleep with the way you go on sometimes."

"Would you be serious?" Hazel swatted his backside

beneath his gun belt before hugging him at his waist again. "Most people run away from a bomb. You and Gunny ran right toward it. Justin was trying to keep me from freaking out."

"Freak out? Cool-in-a-Crisis Cooper?" His arms tightened around her. "Never gonna happen."

The nylon of his jacket was cold against her cheek. But where her forehead rested against the skin of his neck, she felt the strong, warm beat of his pulse. He was joking with his friend. Teasing her. All normal stuff. He was in one piece. He was okay. She was okay, too, now that she could see and feel his strength and steady demeanor for herself. As the tension that had been building inside her eased to a level much more manageable than freak-out mode, the need to be practical and stay busy seeped back in. Hazel stepped back and removed Burke's soggy cap, hanging it on the coat rack beside the door before pulling open the snaps of his jacket and pushing it off his shoulders. "He got away, didn't he?"

He waited for her to hang up his jacket before answering. "He must have had a vehicle waiting and drove off before we set up the blockade. Gunny lost his scent." Burke held himself still and let her tend him, as though he sensed how badly she needed to do something to help stop the man stalking her, even if all she could do was keep the officers working the case warm and dry. She unzipped Burke's vest and discovered the clothes underneath were just as wet. But when she unhooked his belt and lifted its heavy weight, he took it from her hands and set it on his bag beside him. Then he untucked his uniform shirt and T-shirt and took over the drying job. "Did you call the girls? Are they okay?"

Restless with nothing to do but wonder at the truth and worry, Hazel retrieved a stool from the kitchen so that Burke could sit and take off his boots. "Polly's at home. There's an Officer Cho outside her building."

"Cho's a good man." Burke tousled his brown-and-gray hair into short spikes with the towel. "The boyfriend's not there with them, is he?"

Alarm surged anew through her, and she plunked the stool down with a bang. "No. Joe and Ashley aren't home yet. Why? Did you find out something about him? Joe talked like a bodyguard—like you do sometimes. He promised to watch over her and take her home. She'll call as soon as she's there. Do you have a bad vibe about him?"

His brown eyes locked on to hers. "I've got a bad vibe about anybody I haven't personally vetted who comes in contact with the Cooper women."

Dialing her panic back a notch at his stern assertion, she knelt to untie his boots. "So nothing specific. That's good."

"Maybe not," Burke admitted. "The only Joseph Sciarra I found in the system was sixty years old. No way was the guy on that motorcycle with Ashley sixty. I was expanding my name search when you sent me that first text."

"Could Joe be a nickname?" Hazel asked, hating the idea of a man lying to her daughter more than she hated the stiff, muddy laces of Burke's boots soiling her hands.

"It's a possibility. It could also be something as innocent as him using an alias for his bouncer job. That way, unhappy customers can't track him down after hours if he had to toss them out or call the cops on them." Burke hung his vest on the hook beside his jacket. "I plan to have a conversation with him tomorrow."

"Do I need to call Ashley again?"

"And tell her what?" He pried off his boot and set it on the drip mat beside the door. "Joe can't be the man who was here talking to you because he's been with her all evening. Right?"

Of course. That made logical sense. Her stalker couldn't be in two places at the same time—and she *had* talked to Joe on Ashley's phone. Hazel nodded. She pressed her lips into a wry smile. "I'm the mom here. I shouldn't scare her more than I already have. I guess it's hard for me to trust any man right now."

His fingers cupped beneath her chin to tilt her face up to his. "Any man?"

She rolled her eyes toward the living room, where Justin was reporting the information he and Burke had gathered to another member of his team. She squeezed her fingers around Burke's wrist and smiled. "With a few notable exceptions."

"Glad I made the short list." He stroked his thumb across her lips in that ticklish caress that made things inside her curl with anticipation before releasing her. "If we don't hear from Ashley in an hour or so, telling us she's safely home with Polly and Garrett Cho, we'll call her then."

"Deal." She moved on to the next muddy boot. "What about you? The devil man didn't threaten you, did he?"

"The devil man?"

"The Halloween mask he wore. I saw it up close tonight."

"Like he needs a nickname. No. I never got eyes on him. Just that damn picture you sent me." He pulled her to her feet in front of him. His hands settled at her waist, his fingers kneading an unspoken message into the skin beneath the sweatshirt she wore. "Are you sure you're not hurt or in shock? What did he say to spook you like this?"

The man's words hadn't been as cutting as his laughter. She'd rebelled against his threats and cryptic pronouncements. But his laughter had crippled her like the blows she'd suffered the night Aaron's friend had tried to silence her. If she hadn't been a veterinarian… if she hadn't had her bag and the syringe and the tranquilizer with her…

Her attacker that night had laughed, too. Right up until he felt the needle she'd jabbed into his thigh.

The next day, when she left the hospital, she'd gone straight to the DA's office and told him she was ready to testify against her husband. She'd seen her attorney about divorce proceedings by the end of the same day.

"Haze?" Burke's callused fingers brushed the bangs across her forehead before settling beneath her chin and tilting her face up to his. "You're scaring me a little bit. Tell me what happened."

"Nothing new." She glanced over her shoulder at Justin and used his presence as an excuse to keep her humiliating secrets a little while longer. Mustering a weak smile, she slipped from his grasp. "Exhausted beyond belief, but I'm not hurt." His eyes narrowed with a question she felt too raw to answer. Instead, she smoothed his wild hair into some semblance of order and carried the wet towel to the pile beside the laundry closet off the kitchen. "The coffee's hot. Want a cup?" Not waiting for an answer, she poured him a mug. From the kitchen she heard the thud of the second boot hit the mat. "At least he took the bomb with him, right? If that's what it was."

The next thing she heard was the deep rumble of his voice beside her. "The makings of one, anyway. Gunny hit on the spot by the gate." He took the mug from her trembling hands, tested the temperature and took a long swallow of the strong black brew.

Justin strolled into the kitchen, reminding her they weren't alone. "That confirms there were explosives. I've got Dr. Coop's statement, some decent pics and a pretty good idea of the type of bomb this guy builds. I'll file the report. You good here?"

With a nod, Burke set down the coffee and walked his friend to the door. "I got this. Thanks, Justin."

The two men shook hands. "You need anything, call. Cartwright and Bellamy said they'd post a unit outside once they're done canvasing the neighborhood and taking witness statements. They've explained what to look for to the man watching your daughters' apartment, too. Dark hoodie. Halloween mask. Brown paper packages—and not the good kind."

"I owe you one." Burke opened the door.

"You owe me nothing, old man. You and that mutt have kept my team alive more than once. It's about time you let me return the favor." Justin pulled his KCPD cap over his head and tipped the brim to Hazel. "Dr. Coop."

"Thank you for everything."

The younger man winked and strode into the hall-way. Burke set the dead bolt behind him and turned to face Hazel across the main room. "I need a hot shower, and Gunny needs food and rest."

In other words, he needed her to take care of herself for a few minutes. He needed her to be more than his ex-wife had ever been for him.

She summoned the dregs of her depleted strength and went to work. "I'll fix you a plate of food and take care of Gunny while you change. If you leave your clothes in the laundry basket, I can run them through the wash, too."

Instead of nodding or speaking, or any other response she might have expected, Burke strode into the kitchen, clasped her face between his hands and lowered his mouth to hers. With nothing more than his fingers in her hair and his lips moving over hers, he kissed her very, very thoroughly. Desire sparked inside her, leaping to meet his claim. Hazel rose up onto her toes, pushing her mouth into his kiss. Her lips parted, welcoming him. Her tongue darted out to meet his, and she tasted coffee and a frantic need that matched her own. She clutched at the front of his shirt, then crawled her fingers up into the damp spikes of his hair. Her hips hit the countertop as Burke's muscular thighs crowded against hers. His kiss permeated her body with a transfusion of heat. The faint desperation and sure claim of his mouth jolted through her heart. Her frayed emotions healed beneath the sweep of his tongue and the press of his body and the needy grasp of his hands.

This was what she needed. The touch of this good man. This celebration of life. Jedediah Burke erased the loneliness from her life. He shared her burdens and made her pulse race and her heart smile. He made her feel as though the emotional isolation that had protected her for so long was a mistake—that she could live more fully, love more completely in a way she hadn't allowed herself to for too many years.

But almost as resolutely as the kiss had begun, Burke pulled away with a ragged sigh. He rested his lips against her forehead for a moment, and she felt the heat of their kiss dissipating into the cool skin there.

"I needed to do that earlier," he confessed. "I was so damn scared that he was going to hurt you." He leaned back, brushing aside her bangs with his fingertips to study her expression. His chest heaved in a deep breath that showed far more control than the mewling gasps she could currently muster. "You sure you're okay?"

Where had the man learned to kiss like that? And now that she'd tasted the depths of Burke's passion, she was becoming addicted to every touch they shared. She felt weak yet energized, totally confused and absolutely right. "Is it too sappy to say I'm better now?"

He gave a slight laugh. "Then count me on the sappy side, too." But his handsome, weary expression was dead serious. "You've been acting a little weird since I got here. Did Justin say something that upset you? The detectives?"

Hazel fiddled with collar of his damp T-shirt before meeting his gaze. "I'm keeping it together for now, okay? Let's just leave it at that."

"Doc, you know you can tell me anything. About the case, that emotional baggage you mentioned earlier—anything."

"I know. I will," she promised. "But first things first." She turned him and nudged him down the hallway. "Go. Before you catch a cold. Or else I'll be worried about you all over again. And the only meds I have on hand are for canines."

When he hesitated at the bathroom doorway, she gave him another gentle push. But this time he didn't budge. "I'm not laughing, Haze. Are you sure you're okay?"

She shrugged, giving him an honest answer. "I just need a little time to myself to process…everything. My life is changing, and I need to make sure I'm making the right decisions."

"Fair enough," he answered, understanding that *he*

was one of those decisions. He remembered his bag at the front door and retrieved it. "I usually take a quick shower. Do you need me to linger? Give you more time?"

She shook her head. "Take however long you need. I'll step in after I hear the water running to get your dirty clothes."

Five minutes later, with the shower running and Burke humming a sweetly tuneless song, Hazel's decision was made. She hadn't been whole before Burke strode into her life five years ago with his first K-9 partner. There was a reason she'd turned to him when she'd been afraid of those letters. A reason she worried about the dangers he faced on her behalf and to protect Kansas City. A reason she'd never considered giving her heart and her soul and her kisses to another man.

She loved Jedediah Burke, loved him with a fierce intensity that was as frightening as it was exciting.

She'd been surviving for a long, long time. But she hadn't been living. She couldn't preach to her daughters to embrace life and love hard and trust a good man if she wouldn't do the same for herself. Jedediah was her partner in every way that mattered.

Except one.

Chapter Eleven

Hazel tapped softly on the bathroom door and waited for Burke's invitation before pushing it open. A cloud of steamy, fragrant air filtered past as she entered the room to open the clothes hamper. As the steam rushed out of the enclosed space, she spotted Burke's bag in the corner beside the sink, his open Dopp kit sitting on the counter.

But with his damp clothes hugged to her chest, she froze, her gaze transfixed by the blurry outline of Burke's tall, muscular form through the mottled glass of the walk-in shower door. He'd stopped moving, too. He must have been rinsing his hair or easing the tightness of overworked muscles by letting the hot water sluice over his neck and shoulders. His body was arched forward, his strong arms braced against the tile wall, his head bowed into the pelting spray of water. Even though she couldn't make out a clear visual image, her brain was cataloging every detail. The sprinkles of silver in his dark brown hair. The breadth of his arms and shoulders. The graceful arch of his long back and curved buttocks. The spicy scents of soap and man, and the earthier scents of grit and sweat washing down the drain teased her nose. Something purely female clenched with a sensual awareness deep inside her. Something unexpectedly protective and faintly territorial squeezed at her heart, too.

She was a veterinarian doctor, for Pete's sake. She knew all about anatomy, both human and animal. She'd been married once a lifetime ago. But there was nothing clinical to her reaction to Burke showering in her home, nothing naive about this connection flowing like a strong current between them whenever they got close. This was how her life could be, how it should have been all along, if only she'd loved this man first.

The way she loved him now.

Burke shook his head, then shifted position behind the translucent glass, reaching for the washcloth he'd tossed over the top of the door. "Sorry about the mud. I'll clean up in here. You may have to wash those pants by themselves."

Hazel dropped the dirty clothes she held. She needed to do this. Now.

"My ex-husband… Aaron…" She inhaled a steadying breath of the tiny room's humid air to quell the terrifying memories that rose like bile in her throat. "Sixteen years ago, Aaron paid a man to kill me. To stop me from testifying against him."

Burke's curse was pithy and succinct. Movement stopped behind the glass, although the sound of the water beating down on the tiles at his feet never ceased. "I know I promised we'd talk, but you couldn't have eased into that?"

This was already like ripping a bandage from raw skin. She'd started, and now the past was oozing out like the festering wound it was. Besides, it was easier to share the truth without Burke's dark eyes probing into hers, seeing more than anyone else ever had.

She needed to say this. She needed to say all of it.

She needed Burke to know why she was such a hot mess in the relationship department. "He hired a friend of his—a man who worked for him on and off at the investment firm. Aaron used the money I'd stashed away in an account for the girls to pay him. Out in the country—I was on my way to an emergency call. A dog had been hit, left to die on the side of the road." She wanted to laugh at the prophetic analogy but had never been able to. "Maybe the dog was already dead. Maybe it never existed. Aaron took the call that night. The judge hadn't seized our house as an asset yet, so we were still living together. Separate rooms, but his lawyer said it helped Aaron's image for the press and jury to think we were still a couple, that he still had my support. He knew the DA had been talking to me."

"Aaron set you up." Burke's posture changed behind the glass, from weary like a man at the end of a long day to alert like the cop he was. He quickly rinsed off. "I want to hear all of it."

"I never saw the headlights until they were right on me. He rammed his car into mine. Rolled me into the ditch."

Burke shut off the water and reached for the towel outside the shower door.

"Because of my seat belt and air bags, I didn't die in the accident. But I was pretty shaken up, a little disoriented when I climbed out through the broken window. I knew Aaron's friend. I thought he was there to save me. That he'd stopped to help. I was so grateful. I was asking if he'd seen the dog who'd been hit. Then he smashed my head against the side of the car. He used his fists and his feet to try to finish the job."

Biting down on a string of curses, Burke stepped out of the shower, knotting the towel at his hips. "Hazel…"

When he reached for her, she took a step back, hugging her arms around her waist. He retreated to the bath mat, perhaps sensing how brittle she felt, how she'd shatter into a thousand pieces if anyone touched her right now. It was probably killing him to refrain from taking action, not to be able to fix this for her.

Instead, he raked his fingers through his wet hair. "I know there's more." His voice was tight, deep. "You're here now. Tell me how you survived."

She zeroed in on the oval pucker of his belly button, linked by a line of dark hair down to the knot on his towel. His stomach was flat, his skin beaded with moisture and flushed with a heat that radiated across the room; his muscles were taut beneath that skin. But what turned her on the most was that stellar control, that endless patience that made her feel she could share everything with him. He respected her need to fight her way through her past, to approach this relationship at the speed she needed to go. Caked with mud, dog hair and layers of protective uniform, or practically naked as the day he was born, Burke wasn't just the man she wanted—he was the man she needed.

She lifted her gaze to his whiskey-brown eyes and found them studying her just as intently as she'd expected. "Aaron's friend laughed at me. He sounded crazy. Drunk? High? I don't know. He joked about refunding the money. Said the job was too easy. He was putting me back in the car, buckling me in, telling me how he was going to set it on fire and blame my death on the accident. Once I was inside, I could reach my bag. I had a syringe with a tranquilizer already loaded. In case the dog didn't cooperate. I stabbed him with it. He passed out before I did. I called the police. I don't remember anything more until I woke up in the ambulance."

"That's the Hazel Cooper I know. You used your head and you fought back." He relaxed the fists that had clenched at his sides. "Is that when you decided to testify against your ex?"

"Murder for hire and attempted murder got Aaron a lot longer sentence than the fraud and embezzlement alone would have."

He took a step forward and she didn't bolt. "And the hit man he hired?"

"The tranquilizer I gave him must have reacted with whatever was already in his system. The paramedics couldn't revive him."

Burke's fingers tiptoed across the top of the vanity and brushed against her elbow. Hazel didn't flinch. If anything, she shifted slightly to the left, moving her elbow into the cup of his hand. She'd just admitted that she'd killed a man—but she saw no recrimination in his eyes, felt no pity in his touch. "You weren't charged, were you?"

She shook her head. "Evidence at the scene and Aaron's money trail made it a clear case of self-defense. My testimony gave the DA the victory he wanted. It ultimately doubled Aaron's sentence."

Burke drifted a half step closer, feathering his fingertips into her bangs, brushing them off her forehead. "I've never met your ex, have I?"

Despite the gentleness of his caress, tension coiled beneath each syllable.

"I doubt it. I filed every restraining order in the book to keep him away from Ashley, Polly and me." She shrugged. "He calls me sometimes." The soothing caresses stopped. Hazel reached up to capture Burke's hand against her cheek. "I don't answer. The girls barely remember him. Polly probably wouldn't even recognize him. She was so young when he went away."

He simply nodded as if some sort of truce had been reached. "Do you think your ex is behind this terror campaign?"

"I don't know. It could be Aaron, wanting to punish me for my *betrayal*. It could be someone else he hired."

"I'll follow up on his whereabouts since his release from prison." He stroked his thumb across her lips before pulling away. "What do you need from me right now?"

There was nowhere to retreat in the small room. And Hazel didn't want him to. "I just needed you to listen. I need you to understand why I've put you off for so many years and insisted that friendship was enough."

Lines deepened beside his eyes as he paused. "You want us to go back to being just friends?"

"No." She touched her fingertips to the worry grooves on his rugged face and willed them to relax. "I think you and I are destined to be something more. But I want you to understand that because of everything I went through, I've had a really hard time trusting men over the years. I gave my heart to a man who thought killing me was a better choice than admitting his guilt and giving us a chance to repair our fractured marriage. I trusted that we could at least have an amicable divorce and still both have a hand in raising our girls. How smart does that make me about relationships?"

She was the one drifting closer now, wanting to reassure him. She ran her fingers over the ticklish scruff of his beard, then drew them down his neck and across the jut of his shoulder.

"I know you're nothing like Aaron. But the doubts about myself have always been there. I never dealt with them because, frankly, I had a life I had to live. Children to raise, a practice to build. It's always been easier to bury my emotions than to deal with them. But you make me think about what I feel, what I want and need. I'm afraid of losing everything again. I want to be braver than I am. For you. For us. But—"

He caught her hand and raised it to his lips, pressing a warm kiss against her knuckles. "You are the bravest woman I know. You defended yourself against a man who wanted you dead. You kept your head in the face of danger. You lived your life in the way you needed to, so that you wouldn't be hurt again. And look at all the animals, all the people you've helped along the way. You have the right the live the way you need to, to choose who you want to have be a part of your life, to live—"

"I choose *you*." She took Burke's hands and placed them on either side of her waist. His fingers kneaded her skin beneath her sweatshirt but stayed resolutely where she'd put them. His nostrils flared with a ragged breath. Hazel felt the same warring need to skip the necessary words and get on with the physical connection they both craved as she braced her hands against his chest. "I want you to be a part of my life. But I'm scared I won't be any good at *us*, and I never want to hurt you."

Her thumb might have hooked around the turgid male nipple she discovered beneath the crisp curls of chest hair. His pectoral muscle might have jerked in a helpless response. But he fought for restraint until she'd said everything she wanted him to hear.

"Haze—"

"What if I can't make you happy? I know I try your patience. Why on earth would you want to be with a woman who runs hot and cold and smells like dog poop and antiseptic? Well, not all the time."

A low, guttural sound rumbled in his throat. "You make me laugh. And I didn't do enough of that until I met you. I have more in common with you than anyone I've ever known. Except maybe Gunny."

It was her turn to laugh. "I didn't do enough of that until I met you, either."

"You have sexy hair and the sweetest mouth." His fingers dipped inside the waistband of her jeans. "And a sexy, round—"

"I've given birth to two babies." She wasn't out of shape for a woman her age, but she *was* a woman of a certain age. "I eat too many sweets, and I haven't been with a man in years. *Years*, Jedediah."

"And I'm on the stud-of-the-month calendar?"

"You should be." She framed his strong jaw between her hands and admired the contours of every well-earned line beside his eyes, the firm shape of his mouth and the angle of his nose. He wasn't perfectly handsome, but she couldn't describe him as anything other than perfectly masculine. "You'd get my vote."

He squeezed his eyes shut for several seconds before his dark lashes fluttered open and his eyes looked their fill of her face, as she'd just studied his. "Do you know how badly I want to be with you?"

Hazel nodded. Years and doubts slipped away beneath the heat in his eyes. "I *want* to be with you. Help me heal. Please."

He lost the battle a split second before she did. His hands clamped around her bottom, snapping her to him, but Hazel was already sliding her arms around his neck. She palmed the back of his prickly wet hair and tilted his mouth down to hers. Their lips clashed like waves against a rocky shore. Tongues danced together, retreated like the ebbing tide, rushed in again.

Hazel poured her heart into every tug, every taste. She clutched at his scalp, dug her fingers into the supple muscles of his back.

Just like that wild ocean current, the pain rushed out as desire swept in. Her nipples tightened and her breasts grew heavy with the friction of Burke's chest moving against hers. His hands slipped beneath her shirt, each sure stroke across her skin stirring the storm building inside her. He broke the kiss only long enough to whisk the shirt off over her head. And then his lips were back, grazing the tender skin along her neck, arousing eager nerve endings with the ticklish scratch of his beard, soothing them with the warm rasp of his tongue.

Her jeans felt rough between her legs as the pressure built inside her. She was keenly aware of the front of his towel tenting between them. *Too many clothes. Not enough skin.* Had she ever felt this hot? This demanding of a lover? This powerful? As Burke's mouth blazed a trail over the swell of her breast, she skimmed her hands down the length of his spine to reach the barrier of the damp towel at his hips. She inhaled the spicy scent of his warm skin before she nipped at the column of his neck, eliciting a growl from his throat. "Please tell me I haven't scared you off."

"Nope." His mouth closed, hot and wet, over the proud tip of her breast, pulling it into his mouth through the lace of her bra. Hazel gasped at the arrow of heat that shot straight to the needy heart of her. "All I heard was that you choose me. You want me. Do you have any idea how long I've been waiting to hear that?"

"About as long as I've wanted to say it?"

"I feel closer to you now than I ever have." He moved his attentions to the other breast, and she twisted against him, wanting even more. "Trust is a precious gift. And yours is hard to earn. Knowing I have it—for this—for everything—makes me want you even more."

"Jedediah…"

"Yes?"

Her hand fisted in the towel. "Too many clothes." She tugged.

He sought her mouth with his own and they laughed together as the towel landed at his feet, baring that fine, tight rump to the squeeze of her hands.

As smoothly as she'd rid him of a simple towel, he unsnapped her jeans and pushed them and her panties down over her hips. The bra went next and then he caught her behind the knee to pull her to him, rocking against her core, driving all kinds of delicious pressure into the most sensitive of places inside her. The hard length of him pressing against her told her he was just as ready as she.

"Protection?" he growled against her skin.

Hazel gasped out a curse. "I haven't been on the pill in years. Of course, I haven't needed to be. I don't know if the girls left—"

He silenced the moment of panic with a hard kiss. "Not a problem. Pants?"

"By the hamper. I haven't had a chance—"

He turned her and swatted her bottom. "I'll meet you in the bedroom."

He retrieved a condom from his wallet and joined her before she could finish pulling back the covers. Once he had sheathed himself, he lifted her onto the bed and followed her down, sliding his hips between her thighs and pushing inside her. Her body forgot how out of practice she was. She was tight for a few moments, but he held himself still until she relaxed and stretched to accommodate him. Then she was the one who reached between them and urged him to complete her. She felt more female, more alive than she had in years. She wanted this. She wanted him. Beneath Burke's hands, she felt beautiful, sexy. He coaxed her body to a peak and she crashed over, holding him in her arms and deep inside her as he crested the same wave and found his release. His guttural moan of satisfaction was as heady as any sweet nothing he could have whispered in her ear.

Sometime later, after Burke had brought her a damp washcloth and closed the door to keep the dogs from joining them, Hazel sank back onto her pillow and exhaled a deeply contented sigh. They were lying on their backs, side by side, their naked bodies still cooling from the intense lovemaking they'd shared.

Burke reached for her hand between them. "You okay?"

She laced her fingers together with his. "I'd like to say it's like riding a bicycle. But…it was never like that before. I can't feel my bones. I feel glorious." She turned her head to see him on the pillow beside hers and felt a tug of something precious and fragile in her heart. "You?"

He rolled onto his side, facing her. "You were worth the wait."

Could there be any more doubt that she loved this man? That she needed him? He was good for her ego. Good for her body. Good for her, period.

But what exactly was he getting out of this relationship besides some seriously hot benefits and…vet care for his K-9 team?

"Jedediah…"

"Dr. Cooper." When he leaned in to kiss her again, his stomach growled, saving her from asking the question she needed to. Maybe those seriously hot benefits were enough for him right now.

Laughing against his kiss, she patted his stomach. His muscles jumped beneath the simple touch, and she quickly pulled her hand away from the temptation to repeat what they'd just shared. "We'd better take care of a few other priorities."

Seizing the opportunity to end the encounter on a positive note instead of dragging the mood down with her worries again, she scrambled off the bed and opened the closet door to pull out the T-shirt and pajama pants hanging on a hook there. "We forgot dinner. We should eat before we fall asleep from exhaustion."

Avoiding the questioning look on his face, Hazel quickly dressed, adding a pair of socks and a hoodie. Burke followed more slowly, swinging his legs off his side of the bed and watching her for several seconds before striding across the hall to the bathroom. "I'll take the dogs out one more time while you heat up some food."

Nearly two hours later, Hazel was lying on the bed, curled into a ball, trying to stay warm. Even her socks and hoodie and an afghan snugged around her couldn't chase away the thoughts that chilled her whole body. She heard Burke in the doorway behind her, identifying him by the soft rustle of his jeans and that spicy clean scent that was his alone.

She wasn't sure how long he hovered there, maybe just checking on her, or maybe trying to decide if he'd be welcome to rejoin her. She'd willingly taken their relationship far beyond the friendship level this evening—it wouldn't be fair to backtrack from that closeness. Not to Burke. Not to either of them.

"I'm not asleep." Rolling over, she found him leaning against the door frame, cradling a mug of the decaf coffee she'd brewed earlier. "You don't have to watch over me 24-7."

He shook his head and came into the room. "Doesn't seem to be a habit I can break." The mattress shifted as he sat on the edge of the bed beside her. "You okay?" He set the mug on the bedside table and straightened the afghan around her. "After baring your soul—and a few other things—to me, you should be exhausted. You barely touched your dinner. And no ice cream, so I know something's wrong."

Ignoring his efforts to tuck her in, Hazel sat up to face him, hugging her knees to her chest. "Besides a stalker I can't identify who wants to blow me up?"

He didn't grin at her teasing. "Yeah. Besides that. You don't regret what happened between us, do you?"

"Other than feeling like I took advantage of your kindness?"

"Kindness?" Now he snickered a single laugh. He rested one hand on top of her knee. "I've been dreaming about making love to you for a couple of years now."

"But you kept your distance because I wanted you to."

"And then you didn't want me to. I don't think I could ever get my fill of you, Doc. But I do wonder about the timing. You've been under a lot of stress. And everything you told me—that was a major catharsis for you."

She couldn't argue that. "I needed to feel like me again for a little while. Like life is normal and people can want each other in a healthy way."

"I gather that's the healing part you wanted. But now you've had time to think." He smoothed her bangs across her forehead. "What's going on inside that head of yours? Help me understand."

Hazel captured his hand and clasped it between both of hers. It was strong and a little rough around the edges, but infinitely tender, just like the man himself. "To-night…the devil man… He laughed at me, Jedediah. I was trying to keep him on the defensive, goad him into staying until KCPD got here. But I let it slip how scared I was, and that made him laugh. He said he'd take it as down payment on what I owe him."

His fingers flinched within her grasp, the only outward sign of his protective temper. "Like the jerk your ex hired. You said he laughed. Joked about the money. I'll need his name, too, by the way. In case he has a surviving relative or friend who might be interested in payback."

She nodded. "He's enjoying this. He's getting off on toying with me."

"He wants to get under your skin."

"He's succeeding." Hazel pulled her hands away to hug her knees again. "I've been completely honest with you—told you some things even my daughters have never heard. I know you need me to be strong. And I'd like to think that I am. But this relentless campaign—all the memories it has dredged up—it's wearing me down. It makes me question everything I say or think or do. The last time I was afraid for my life…"

Burke gathered her in his arms, afghan and all, and pulled her onto his lap. "The last time, you didn't have me. I've got your back."

For once, she was glad his patience had run out, and Hazel snuggled in, tucking her head beneath his chin. "Like Gunny will always have yours."

He nodded. "Trust your strength, Haze. Trust mine."

She did. But if there truly was going to be a future for them, she needed to know if she could hold up her end of the bargain, and be what he needed, too. "Can you trust me just as much? I know your ex-wife… You couldn't trust her."

"No. I couldn't," he said, falling back across the bed and pulling her on top of him, keeping her close. "You're a different class of lady. She never would have been so honest with me as you've been tonight. She never trusted that I could be there for her. If she wanted comfort, entertainment, a sounding board to dump on, she'd go find it. She still does. Hell. She'll call me if her current husband can't make things right for her."

"Not everyone is cut out to be the spouse of a man or woman in uniform."

"True. Shannon was sweet and perfect and everything I wanted in a high school sweetheart. But I became a soldier. And a cop. I saw the world—the good, the bad, the weird and the stuff I wish I could forget. I grew up. I don't know that she ever will." He shifted on the bed, angling them toward the pillows. "You're an adult, Haze. An equal. You've faced more adversity than she ever had to. And you dealt with it without compromising your integrity. You found your own strength. You asked for my help, but you didn't expect to be rescued."

Hazel changed topics, suspecting he'd rather talk about something a little less personal, even though she sensed there was more to Burke's past, just as there had been more to hers. "What did Justin mean when he said you and Gunny had saved him and his team?"

He probably recognized the diversion for what it was, judging by the squeeze of her hand between them. "Usually, a K-9 unit is deployed along with the bomb squad when there's a call. We clear the building, make sure there are no secondary explosives planted in the area."

"Have you ever found secondary explosives?"

"Yes."

His simple answer probably downplayed a good deal of the danger he and Gunny had faced helping their brothers in blue and protecting the city.

"You take care of a lot of people, don't you?" she observed. "I don't want to be another burden to—"

"Do not finish that sentence." A warm, callused finger pressed against her lips. "I'm here by choice, not because it's my job. Not because of the crazy good sex we had."

"Will you stay with me?" she asked.

"I thought that was the plan." He pointed to the doorway. "I'll be right out there. Gunny's already sacked out."

"No. Will you stay *here*?" She patted the bed beside her. "To sleep. Is that asking too much of you and your patience?"

He rolled onto his side, pulling her into his chest. "Me holding you? I think I can manage."

"You smell good," she murmured on a drowsy sigh against his soft cotton T-shirt. "Justin has no business calling you *old man*. You're a man, period. Warm. Solid. One hell of a kisser…among other talents. I love touching you. You feel good."

"Do I feel safe?"

She nodded.

He pressed a kiss to her forehead. "Then close your eyes, Doc."

She did. Minutes later, physically and emotionally spent but snug in the shelter of Burke's embrace, she fell into an exhausted sleep.

Chapter Twelve

With his gun on the nightstand beside him, and Gunny dozing by the door, Burke finally dropped his guard long enough to fall into a deep, contented sleep. The dogs would alert him long before any threat reached him. He could use a solid seven or eight hours to re-build his stamina after burning the candle at both ends to keep an eye on Hazel, track down leads on her stalker and work his own shift duties at the training center.

And then there were the physical demands of that frantic, powerful lovemaking session with Hazel. A blissful sense of peace spilled over from his conscious thoughts and filled his dreams.

He was the only man Hazel wanted. He was certain of it. More certain than he'd ever been with his own wife all those years ago. He reveled in the knowledge that Hazel wanted him enough to demand a mutual seduction, needed him enough to trust him with her secrets. She trusted him with her body, her life. And even though he wondered if she recognized it herself, she trusted him with her heart.

An annoying buzz tried to pull him from his sweet dreams, and he shifted in his sleep. Like a man half his age, he ached to be with her again already, to feel her grasping at him, squeezing around him, calling out his name. Although the images were vague, the sensations were as real as the heat cocooning his body, opening every pore, firing up the blood coursing through his veins. He'd dreamed of Hazel before, but not as vividly as this. Laugh by laugh, conversation by conversation, he'd fallen a little more in love with Hazel Cooper every day. Now he wanted to hold on to the closeness he and the curvy vet had finally shared. He had someone in his life again after all this time. He'd waited for it to be right—he'd waited for her. Now he had more than a friend, more than a fantasy dutifully hidden away in his deepest dreams. He had a partner. He'd be safe with her. He could be who he needed to be, do what he needed to do, and never worry that she couldn't understand the call to duty that drove him. She possessed that same sense of duty—to her children, her patients. She wouldn't leave him for something easier, someone immediately available, and he wouldn't leave her. This had been his vision for so long. He knew where he wanted this relationship to go, what he wanted to ask her.

He'd take her to dinner. No, take her to the dog park. He could tie the ring to Gunny's harness and…

The incessant buzzing ruined the future he was planning with her. He opened his eyes to the darkness. As awareness rapidly pinged through his brain, Burke remembered he was in Hazel's bedroom. He was half-aroused from a soft thigh wedged between his legs, and he was suffused with heat. He didn't remember burrowing beneath the covers, and he realized now that he hadn't. Not only was Hazel snuggled in like a blanket with her omnipresent afghan, the dogs had joined them on the bed.

And a phone was ringing.

"Damn." He wasn't on duty for another thirty-two

hours. Something major must be playing out somewhere in the city for an alert to reach out to off-duty personnel. He patted the back pocket of his jeans. "Where's my phone?"

Hazel was awake, too. She crawled to the nightstand on her side. "It's mine," she murmured, lifting Cleo out of the way.

Burke pushed Gunny off his feet and ordered him to the floor. "What time is it?"

"Too early for a phone call." She fumbled for her phone long enough that he reached up to turn on the lamp beside him. "Make that too late. I'm not the emergency vet on call tonight, so it must be one of my own patients... Oh, hell." She hit the answer button and sat bolt upright. "Ashley?"

"Mom!"

He heard the faint cry of panic over the phone and sat up with Hazel, instantly on alert. He braced his arm behind her back and leaned in. "Put it on speaker."

"Sweetheart, what's wrong?" Tension radiated through Hazel's body.

Ashley was panting or sobbing or both. "I need you to come get me. My car is still at the clinic. I'd call Polly, but I don't think it's safe for her to come here."

The distinct sound of glass breaking made Hazel jump. "What was that? Where are you? Are you all right?"

Men swearing and cheering in the background was not a good sign.

Burke clasped a hand over Hazel's shoulder and spoke into the phone. "Ashley, where are you? What's happening?"

"Sergeant Burke?"

No time to explain why he was on her mother's phone at one in the morning. "Answers, Ash."

Like most people, she responded to his calm, succinct tone. "Joe brought me to this biker bar—Sin City. I could tell this place was a dive even before I saw the drunk passed out at one of the tables. He said these are his friends. Only, somebody did something to someone's bike—I'm not sure what happened. This guy joked that I could pay for the damage." She squealed a split second before he heard chairs knocking over. All sure signs that a fight had broken out. "He wasn't talking about money."

Hazel shivered. "Oh, my God."

"That's when Joe punched him. Oh!" She must have dodged a falling man or flying debris. "Can you come?"

"I know the place." Burke was already out of bed, tucking in his T-shirt and reaching for his belt with his badge and gun. He wasn't taking the time to change into his uniform. "Can you get to the women's restroom and lock yourself in? Or get behind the bar and duck down? It's solid."

"The fight's in here." Ashley was breathing fast, either from physical exertion or fear. "Aren't I safer outside?"

"Not in that part of town."

Hazel had scrambled off the bed, too, circling around to keep the phone close to him while he dressed. "Where's Joe now?" she asked.

"In the parking lot maybe? That's where the argument started. It's like gangs taking sides. I came inside to report it. The bartender called the police."

"Good. They'll be there any minute. It's not far from HQ. Tell them you're a friend of mine. I'm on my way." Burke headed across the hall to the bathroom, where he'd left his bag, to retrieve socks and a pullover. Hazel was right by his side. "Can you get someplace safe?"

Ashley considered her options, then started moving. "This place is long and skinny—I don't think I can get all the way to the bathroom in the back. I'm heading behind the bar now."

A deeper, quieter voice sounded closer than the chaos at the bar. *"Come with me, miss."*

"Who's that?" Burke asked.

"I don't know…" Something crashed. There was a grunt of pain. "Oh! Stop that! Are you okay?"

"Sweetie, who are you talking to?" Hazel demanded, handing Burke his second boot to tie on.

"A man. I don't know," Ashley answered. "An old guy who was sitting at the bar. Another guy just clocked him with his elbow taking a swing at someone else."

"Come with me." There was a scuffling sound and a choice insult for some *old man* before the noises of the fight faded.

Ashley spoke again. *"Are you okay? I have some medical training. Here. Put a towel on it. I'll get some ice."*

Then the deep, breathy voice came back within hearing range. *"I can take you somewhere. Home? A friend's house? Coffee shop? Anywhere but here, right?"* His laughter faded into a wheezing cough.

"Do not leave with anybody," Burke ordered, striding toward the front door to retrieve Gunny's harness. Hazel hurried along beside him. "I'm on my way to get you."

"We're on our way. Be safe, sweetie." Hazel disconnected the call.

Burke glanced down at her pajamas and stockinged feet. "I'm leaving in two minutes. As soon as I get Gunny geared up."

She stepped into her discarded shoes beside the door and grabbed her jacket. "No need to wait."

NO WAY WAS Hazel sitting locked inside Burke's truck while he waded through this mess of drunks with leather and attitude to find her daughter. But a stern warning about not needing the distraction of keeping an eye on her when he needed to watch his own back and rescue Ashley made enough sense that she had agreed to wait just outside his truck, where she could watch everything from across the street and pace away her fears. How had her daughter gotten stuck in the middle of all this mess?

Hazel had helped with natural disaster recovery scenes that didn't have this many police cars and uniformed officers on-site. Sin City certainly lived up to its name as a bar where no one with any good sense belonged. Apparently, Joe Sciarra's argument had triggered the rivalry between two motorcycle clubs. And Ashley had been caught in the middle of it all while her soon-to-be-*ex* boyfriend, Hazel hoped, had sided with his bros instead of getting her out of the melee.

The endless days of rain had finally stopped, but the wet pavement reflected the swirling patterns of red and blue lights and piercing fog lamps from the silent police cruisers, distorting the darting figures of innocent patrons hurrying to escape the police presence and bloodied combatants trying to get in one last lick before they were lined up against the wall or ordered to the ground and handcuffed. Like wraiths sliding in and out of the darkness, officers, brawlers and bystanders alike were being shuffled to various locations—to one of the ambulances that were here to treat a variety of minor injuries, to the parking lot to drive or ride away, or to one of the waiting black-and-white police vehicles.

She huffed out a sigh of relief when Burke appeared in the doorway, with his arm around Ashley's shoulders, her daughter clutched protectively by his side. "Ashley!"

Even as she danced inside her shoes, eager to run to her daughter but mindful of Burke's warning to keep a safe distance, Hazel felt her chin angling up with pride at the sight of the crowd parting for Burke, Ashley and Gunny. The man could sure clear a path. He oozed the sort of authority that made his coworkers respect him and the perps shy out of his way. He should have had children, she thought, sadly—he'd make a fabulous father. Protector. Father figure. Friend. Lover. And he was hers. All hers. If she was brave enough to claim him.

When she couldn't wait another second to know that her daughter was safe, and the man she loved was responsible for that gift, Hazel darted across the street. "Ashley!"

"Mom!" Her older daughter pulled away from Burke and fell into Hazel's tight hug.

"I'm so glad you're okay. *Are* you okay?" She pulled back to frame Ashley's face in her hands. Flushed cheeks, a little pale, but no sign of injury or tears.

"I'm fine, Mom." Ashley's smile confirmed that fact. "I had the daylights scared out of me. But I never was so happy to see Burke walking into that bar."

"I know the feeling." Hazel lifted her gaze to the man waiting patiently beside them. She palmed his grizzled cheek, stretched up on tiptoe and planted a firm kiss square on his mouth. "Thank you," she whispered, then kissed him again, lingering as his lips clung to hers. "Thank you."

When she sank back to her heels, heat was simmering in Burke's dark eyes and her daughter was grinning from ear to ear. "Um, what's happening here?" Ashley pointed back and forth between her and Burke. "And are you wearing your pajamas under your coat?"

"Oh, sweetie," Hazel began. "So much has happened—"

"Hold that thought." Ashley's smile vanished and heat flooded her cheeks as her gaze focused on a point beyond Burke. "I need to have a conversation."

"Whoa." When Burke reached out to stop her from charging back into the chaos, Hazel grabbed his arm and silently asked him to stay put.

She'd seen a black-haired man with too many tattoos being handcuffed and led to the back seat of a police cruiser, too. "Let her go."

"Not by herself." Burke clasped Hazel's hand and pulled her into step beside him. With a nod to the officer who initially warned Ashley to stay back, Burke stopped a few feet away, allowing the meeting with Joe Sciarra to happen, but not interfering.

Joe's left eye was bruised and puffy, and a raspberry had been scraped across his cheek. But Ashley wasn't interested in him being hurt. Hazel's girl was fired up. "They said you started the fight. You brought me here, looking to trade punches with Bigfoot over there?"

"Hey!" The overbuilt man's protest was cut short by the petite uniformed officer palming his head and guiding him into the back of her police cruiser.

Ashley waited for an answer from the man she'd been seeing. "It's nothing personal. I owed a favor and Digger needed the cash. You were fun enough to make the deal worthwhile."

"What deal? With who?" Ashley demanded.

"It was a win-win situation, baby." He winked. "You know you liked hangin' with a bad boy."

"What are you talking about? What's going on?"

Joe scanned the street and parking lot before nodding toward the guy in a baggy, long jacket and jeans sneaking down the sidewalk. "Ask *him*."

The notion of something familiar, something off, jolted through Hazel as she watched the man with the graying blond ponytail and shaggy beard walking away. She released Burke's hand and took a step toward the man. Then another. And another. Fury blazed white-hot, clearing her thoughts, and she started running.

"Haze!" A strong hand clamped over her arm, stopping her. "What is it with you Cooper women?" Burke challenged. "I'm trying to get you away from the danger. Where are you going?"

"That man. I know him." She patted Burke's chest, willing him to see the urgency in catching up with the man before he disappeared. "At Saint Luke's Hospital. He's one of the homeless men Polly works with."

Ashley appeared beside her, studying the man as he glanced behind him and quickened his pace. "He tried to break up the fight. Help me get away. But he got hurt. He took a pretty good punch. Cut his lip and bloodied his nose. They were too out of control in there for him to do much good. But I should thank him for trying."

The man turned around and Hazel cursed. Even from a distance, through the night's distorted lights, she knew him. The man looked straight at her, then spun away, quickly disappearing into an alley. "Put Ashley in your truck."

Burke's hold tightened. "You're not following some guy down a dark alley in the middle of the night."

"Then come with me." She tugged on Burke's grip. "Aaron!"

He released her. "As in Aaron Cooper?"

"Dad?" Ashley echoed.

Burke waved an officer over to his truck and told the young man to keep an eye on Ashley. He and Gunny quickly caught up with Hazel in the alley. She halted beside a pile of trash cans and garbage bags that smelled like a used litter box. The setting was fitting for this reunion.

The man turned beneath the light from the side entrance to a neighboring building. The face was a little more weathered from sun and age, but she knew those blue eyes. Once upon a time she'd loved them. Later, they'd haunted her nightmares.

"What the hell are you doing here, Aaron?"

His shaggy appearance was a far cry from the tailored suit-and-tie up-and-comer she'd once loved. "Hazel. How's it goin', babe?"

"Don't *babe* me. This is no coincidence. What are you doing at Sin City on this particular night?"

"I was trying to save my little girl."

She rolled her eyes to the starry sky and curbed her tongue before she spoke again. "You were at the hospital with Polly, too, weren't you? Are you really homeless?"

He shrugged. "I got a place." His gaze drifted over her shoulder to the man standing behind her. "Nothing fancy like the home where we used to live."

"It was a fairy-tale facade you created, not a home. Not at the end." She might have known the truth, but she had refused to accept her marriage was a sham and her husband couldn't be trusted until the night Aaron's friend had tried to kill her. Her love and loyalty had meant nothing to him. His attempt to reminisce and claim there was a bond they still shared meant nothing to her now. "You've insinuated yourself into Polly's life, haven't you?"

"She and I are friends."

"Friends?"

"She's a kindhearted girl." He smiled. "Like you used to be."

"Does she know who you are?"

"She knows me as Russell, an Army vet who's having a hard time adjusting to life outside." She hadn't expected him to admit his deception. The old Aaron would have stuck with the lie to the very end—unless a different lie could save him. "That's not so far from the truth. I'm struggling to adjust to life away from Jeff City. Making the right friends. Finding a decent job. Not being judged."

"Why would someone judge you? A convicted felon." Sarcasm rolled out with a sharp bite that should have embarrassed her.

"Hell, Hazel, she didn't even recognize me. She doesn't remember me at all."

"You were in prison, not the military. You were there because of the choices you made. You could have done the right thing and admitted your guilt and paid back what you stole. You'd have been out a decade sooner and had a lot of years knowing your daughters."

He could justify any action that benefited himself. "If I can't be their father, then I want to know them however I can."

"By stalking them? Do you know how frightening that is? How did you know Ashley was on a date here tonight? How did you know a fight would…" She shook her head, no longer regretting the sarcasm. "What con are you running this time?"

"I'm not hurting them. I just want to be a part of their lives."

The moment he took a step toward her, she felt a strong hand settle at the small of her back. Burke believed that she could handle this confrontation with her ex, but he was letting both her and Aaron know that he was there if she needed him. Sizing up the big man with the big dog, Aaron retreated half a step.

"Polly was easy. My parole officer put me onto Saint Luke's program to help the homeless and those who can't afford health care. I knew it was her the moment I saw her. She looks just like you when we met." He frowned. "Except for the hair. What'd you do to yours?"

Irrelevant. "And Ashley?"

He pulled back the front of his jacket and thrust his hands into his pockets. For a split second she felt tension stiffen Burke's fingers at her back. Had he expected to see a weapon? Wires attached to a bomb trigger? The tension gradually eased as Aaron continued. "I know Joe Sciarra from inside. Gave him some financial advice so he had a nest egg waiting for him when he got out."

"I'm not even going to ask if that advice was legal or not. You got a guy who owed you a favor to charm your daughter and set her up in a situation where she could have been hurt?"

"He wasn't supposed to hurt Ash. Just scare her. Then I could come in and save the day. Make her grateful to me. I guess it got out of hand."

She wanted to walk over and slap his face for manipulating their children like that. But that would involve touching him, and that thought was about as abhorrent as the idea that no one she loved was safe from his machinations. "How dare you put our daughter in danger for your selfish whims. I guess some habits you'll never break."

"I'm sorry, babe, but your damn restraining orders force me to be resourceful."

Hazel shook her head at the utter waste of a lifetime. "I think of all the good things you could have done with that brain of yours. How much you could have accomplished. If you'd used your people skills to help someone besides yourself—"

"Could've, would've, should've, huh?"

She almost felt sorry for the regret that momentarily aged his expression. *Momentarily.*

"Look, I need to talk to you about something," he continued. "I've been worried about you."

"I'm not your concern."

"Right. That's what New Boyfriend is for." He spared a condescending glance up at Burke, then focused on her again. "Then let's say I'm worried about the girls. That's why I wanted to get close to them. I think someone is after me. You know? Fifteen years behind bars isn't enough satisfaction for a lot of people—"

"I can't do this tonight, Aaron. I need to take care of Ashley." She turned to walk away. She'd wanted to confirm that Aaron had insinuated his way into their lives again and to put him on notice that she wouldn't tolerate his games anymore. She wasn't hanging around to make nice or assuage his conscience.

"Gunny, *fuss*," Burke ordered, falling in behind her.

But Aaron had never liked her asserting herself. "This guy has shown up every place I've been. At Saint Luke's. Your clinic—"

Hazel whirled around. "You've been to my clinic?"

"I watch from the strip mall across the street sometimes. Getting a look at what I've lost. You built a nice place for yourself." He grinned smugly at Burke. "Don't worry, I keep my hundred yards away from her. You can't arrest me for parking my car in a public lot."

Aaron had been close by this whole time? "I knew someone was watching me, but I thought… You need to stop."

"I think he's following me. Or he's following the girls…" He swallowed a curse. Was he losing his temper with her? "While you're shacking up with your new boyfriend here, I've been keeping an eye on Ash and Polly. I tried to tell you something was hinky, but you won't take my calls."

"Why would I believe anything you tell me?"

His anger exploded. "I have the right to protect my own children! If you're putting them in danger—"

"That's rich, coming from you."

"Time out." Burke silenced them both. "Priorities, Haze." He moved up beside her, then edged himself closer to Aaron. "Tell me about the man you've seen following Hazel and the girls."

"I don't have to tell New Boyfriend anything. Even if he does wear a badge. Hell, especially if he wears a badge."

"If you really want to man up and protect your children," Burke taunted, "talk to me." Hazel heard the threat in his voice. "The guy you've seen has been playing with bombs."

"Bombs?" Aaron frowned, looking honestly taken aback by the grim statement. "Polly's car? He did that?"

Burke gave a sharp nod. "He's been to the clinic and Hazel's building—with explosives and bomb parts both times. He probably knows where your daughters live, too. I need to find him before he pushes the button that could take out your entire family and a bunch of innocent bystanders."

"Bombs?" Aaron's thoughts wandered away.

"Do you know this guy?" Burke prodded.

"Not really." Aaron shrugged. "But I used to get anonymous letters in prison from some guy who said he was going to be waiting on the outside for me—to blow me up the way I blew up his life."

A chill skittered down Hazel's spine. "Oh, my God."

"Do you still have a client list of the people you cheated?" Burke asked.

When his only response was a resentful glare, Hazel answered. "It's probably in the archives at the DA's office. They were all listed as victims in the lawsuit."

Burke nodded, pulling his phone from his jeans. "It's a long shot, but let me make a few calls. I'll wake somebody up to see if the prison has any record of who sent those letters, and cross-match it with names from the DA's office. Maybe one of your clients has a job with access to explosives. At the very least, we can determine if the letters came from the same person. Here." He handed Gunny's lead to Hazel. "You know most of the commands. Use him if you need to." He gave Aaron a pointed look before he walked off a few steps to use his phone.

The moment they were superficially alone, Aaron grew defensive. "If this guy was one of my clients, he can't blame me for losing his money. There's always a risk with investments. Things happen."

Things happen. Like the man you entrusted your money to might devise a scheme to funnel all your profits into his own offshore bank account, all while selling a bill of goods that would make you want to keep paying him more money.

"You still don't understand that your actions have repercussions that affect your entire family. We're still paying the price for your greed. You may not be directly involved in what's happening to us now, but if this guy was one of your investors, you're responsible."

"The years have been good to you, babe." His wistful tone had no effect on her. "But I miss your long hair."

"It was too much work. *You* were too much work."

"I was a rich man, Hazel. The four of us would be sitting pretty right now if you'd have just kept your mouth shut." When he reached out to touch her hair, Hazel recoiled.

"Gunny?" The big dog growled beside her. Aaron wisely stepped back with hands up in surrender. *"Sitz."* The big shepherd plopped down into a sit position beside her.

"You've changed."

"You haven't." Neither had the threat surrounding her. "Please. Tell me anything you can about the man you saw. The only times I've gotten close enough to identify him, it was dark, and he was wearing a mask."

Finally, either for his daughters or for her or to avoid dealing with Gunny, Aaron nodded. "The guy I saw is about my height. More of a paunch—I did a lot of working out in prison. The loose clothes are part of my disguise." Unimpressed with his sales pitch, she rubbed the top of Gunny's head and waited for him to continue. "He's a white guy. Does manual labor, I'm guessing. Like a mechanic, maybe. He wears a uniform under that hoodie. His hands were dirty. White hair. I never got a good look at his face."

Never missing an important clue, Burke rejoined

the conversation. "Anything else? Did you see what he drives?"

Aaron shook his head. "He was always on foot when I saw him." He snapped his fingers as an idea hit. "Tobacco. I've seen him spit a chaw more than once."

A chaw of tobacco. Why did that seem familiar? Did she know anyone who chewed? Was there something behind the devil man's mask she could identify?

While the wheels turned inside her head, looking for answers, Burke's hand settled at her back again. "You can walk away this time, Cooper. But if you violate your restraining order and come near any of these women again, I'll be there."

Aaron's glare was less pronounced this time. Without thanking Burke for giving him a break, Aaron turned to Hazel. "Would you talk to the girls and see if they'd be interested in getting to know me? Unless you've poisoned them against me."

"I'll ask them. No guarantees. It will be their choice. And frankly, with the lies you've been telling, you're not off to a great start. You'll have to live with whatever they decide. I won't let you hurt them again."

"Thanks." He turned and headed head down the alley toward the next cross street.

"And, Aaron?" He turned to hear her out. "If you really want a relationship with them—no games, no lies. Be patient. Be real." Like this man beside her. She clasped Burke's hand and headed out of the alley. "I want to see my daughter now."

BURKE ADJUSTED HIS wraparound sunglasses on the bridge of his nose as he drove back into the city after spending several hours at the K-9 training center. It felt prophetic to feel the sun warming his skin through the windshield again. After so many days of one rainstorm after another, the October sun felt more like the beginning of a new page in his life instead of the last hurrah of summer.

It had been a long night with little sleep, but he felt energized by anticipation rather than fatigued. His life was changing, and he was ready for it. His patience with Hazel had paid off. They were a thing now—in a relationship. And once he figured out who was behind all the threats and put the crud behind bars, he intended to make that relationship permanent. He ignored his goofy grin reflected in the mirror. There were some things even his patience couldn't wait for.

After leaving the Sin City bar in KCPD's capable hands, they'd driven straight to Ashley and Polly's apartment, where the three Cooper women shared a laughing, tearful "yell me everything that happened" reunion that included several warm hugs for him and thank-you bites of cheese for Gunny. At his insistence, to streamline their security and for their mother's peace of mind, Ashley and Polly packed up their bags, and he loaded them into his truck. Although he was a little amazed at the toiletries-to-clothing ratio each young woman stuffed into her small suitcase, like their mother, they'd been quick and efficient. Then he'd dismissed Officer Cho and driven them all back to Hazel's condo, where she served the girls hot chocolate, encouraged them to talk as late as they wanted to and succinctly announced that he would be sleeping in her room. With her. If the girls had any objections to those arrangements, they could talk about it in the morning.

He didn't know whether to laugh or be nervous when breakfast that morning had been eerily quiet.

Garrett Cho had stopped by to pick up Polly and

drive her to class at Saint Luke's, and Burke struggled with an unfamiliar urge to take the younger man aside and find out more about his background and his interest in Polly. Then he'd driven Hazel and Ashley to work, and gone to his office at the K-9 training center to follow up on last night's phone calls regarding the leads they'd gotten from Hazel's ex. Some of the leads were paying off as Detectives Bellamy and Cartwright ran down the short list of potential suspects from the list of Aaron Cooper's swindle victims. If any of those names connected to explosives, and crossed paths with Hazel's world, then chances were they had their man. Besides, the Cooper women were babying Gunny enough that he wanted to run the dog through his paces to make sure he remembered he was a trained police officer and not a spoiled house pet.

His time with Hazel and her daughters was crazy, chaotic and full of love. It was the life he wanted. He glanced at the dog panting behind him in the rearview mirror. "You okay with that, partner? You know you're still my number one guy, right?"

Gunny whined in response to being talked to. Burke decided to interpret the dog's excitement as an agreement. But his own smile quickly faded as his phone on the dash lit up with a call from his ex, Shannon. Better deal with this issue, too, if he wanted that life with Hazel.

He punched the answer button and immediately put it on speaker. "Sergeant Burke here."

"You know it's me, Jed." Her sultry voice held a little of that poor-me, damsel-in-distress tone. "Is this a good time to talk?"

With her? Never. But there were some things they needed to settle, once and for all. "I know you went to see Dr. Cooper. Were you checking out the competition?" He flicked his signal to shift into the passing lane. "FYI? There is no competition."

"So you two are serious about each other?"

"Yes."

Judging by that huff of breath, it wasn't the answer she wanted to hear. "Do you love her?"

"I do."

"You and I can never…?"

"No." His answer was gentle but as firm as he could make it. "Go home, Shannon. Talk to Bill and work things out. He loves you."

Discussion done, as far as he was concerned. He disconnected the call and breathed a sigh of relief. He was one step closer to the future he wanted.

He was cruising to a stop when his radio flared to life. "Delta K-9 one, please respond." The dispatcher relayed a call to bomb squad personnel summoning him to a Bravo Tango at a Front Street address.

Bravo Tango.

Bomb threat.

Burke swore. He turned on the siren and lights and stomped on the accelerator. He barely heard the dispatcher's apology about calling him in on his day off, or her explanation about the other bomb detection dog being out on another call. He punched in Hazel's number on the phone. It went straight to voice mail.

He picked up his radio. "Delta K-9 one—10-4." He answered that he was responding to the call and raced through the red light.

He knew that address.

Hazel's clinic.

Chapter Thirteen

"What the hell are you still doing in here?"

Six feet plus of angry Jedediah Burke coming through the swinging door of her operating room, armed and dressed in full protective gear, was a scary thing to behold.

Hazel already knew the clock was ticking; she didn't need him startling her like that. "I'm working as fast as I can. I was in the middle of surgery. I had to at least close her up before I could move her." She tied off another suture in the abdomen of the skinny cattle dog mix. "I told everyone to leave and put Todd in charge of evacuating all the animals."

"Nobody's here but you and that dog. Part of our sweep means getting all personnel off the premises before we even search for explosives." He and Gunny circled to the opposite side of the table. "What can I do to help?"

"Get out of my light, for one." She waved him back a step and concentrated on finishing up as quickly, if not as thoroughly, as she normally did. He glanced around the small surgery room, then put Gunny to work searching, making sure this room, at least, hadn't been rigged to explode. "Is it as bad as those sirens out there make it sound?"

"This area's clear," Burke replied, though it didn't help her feel relieved. "How much longer?"

"Todd and I were in the middle of this operation when Ashley told me a client found a brown paper package in the men's room." The picture Ashley had shown her had looked frighteningly familiar. "It's just like the one the devil man had."

"There's another one at the front door. Gunny hit on it."

Her hand shook and she nearly dropped her needle. "There's more than one?"

He moved in beside her, resting his hand on her shoulder. "Easy, Doc. You got this. But work a little faster."

Gunny suddenly jumped to his feet, his sharp ears pricked toward the door. When Burke pushed the door open slightly to check out the canine alarm, she heard the snuffling and whining, too. "Do I hear a dog in the back? Where's Todd?"

"KCPD's set up a perimeter. Nobody is allowed back in the building."

"We have to get him." He gave her a pointed look. One. More. Stitch. "I can't leave my patients…" When she saw that he was about to argue, she shook her head. "You wouldn't leave Gunny behind."

He gave her a curt nod. "I'll get whoever is in the kennel. Finish up."

Moments later, he was back with Shadow, the big Lab, in his arms. "We're all clear. Let's go."

Hazel frowned, remembering something important about the dog on the operating table. Athena had perked up with a little food and fluids, and was fit enough to be spayed.

"What is it?"

"Tobacco."

"What?"

Hazel shook off the unfinished thought. This wasn't the time to be solving mysteries. "Nothing. Go. I just have to give her an injection to wake her up. I'll be right behind you."

"Make sure you are."

He pushed through the swinging steel door. Seconds later, she heard the back door opening and closing. She gave the injection, made sure she had a heartbeat and breath sounds, then disconnected the dog from the oxygen mask and IV. The back door closed again. Burke wouldn't let her be at risk for very long. She wrapped a blanket around the groggy canine and lifted her in her arms. "We're coming."

It took a split second for the odd sound to register. The door hadn't opened and closed a second time.

Someone had locked it.

But she was already pushing through the swinging metal door out of the surgery room. "Burke?"

She pulled up short.

The devil man.

"Ticktock, Dr. Coop." He held up a triggering device, like the one he'd showed her that night outside her building, and laughed. His thumb rested on the button. "Is it on or off? How long do we have?"

She shrank back against the metal door. "How did you get in here?"

"There are lots of places to hide away in all these little rooms. I just had to be patient." The man in the grotesque mask breathed heavily with excitement as he reached inside a different pocket and pulled out another trigger. He pressed that one. "On."

There was no countdown this time. The floor rocked

beneath Hazel's feet and she stumbled as a deafening boom exploded at the front of the building. Some light debris from the ceiling floated down like snow, but more alarming were the pings and instant dents of a dozen tiny missiles hitting the other side of the metal door. That door had probably just saved her life. If she'd still been in the surgery room…

She pushed away from the wall where she'd fallen. "Are you crazy?"

Perhaps not the right thing to say. The devil man took a menacing step toward her and pulled out a third trigger to replace the one he'd just used to blow up the front of her building. He fisted it in front of her face and jammed the button with his thumb. "On! Now I'm finally getting what I want."

A heavy fist pounded on the exit door behind him. "Hazel!"

"Burke!"

"I'm not interested in company, Dr. Coop." The devil man opened the storage cabinet beside the back door and tossed piles of blankets and towels onto the floor so that she could see the bomb behind them.

"Get away from the building!" she warned, afraid that explosive was the one ticking now. "He's put a bomb by the back door!"

She heard cursing and running. The smells of sulfur and ash drifting through from the front of the clinic stung her nostrils.

She smelled something else, too.

Tobacco.

I've seen him spit a chaw more than once.

The disjointed pieces from so many sources finally fell into place. Hazel hugged the dog sleeping in her arms a little tighter and squared off against the man who'd made her life hell for too many long months. "Take off the mask, Wade."

He grunted, as if surprised to be recognized.

"Are you afraid to do this face-to-face? Afraid to show me the truth?"

He tapped one of the triggers. "Off." Then he pushed back his hood and tugged the plastic mask over his head. He grinned at her with his stained teeth. "Doesn't matter if you figured it out. I will destroy you. Just like your husband destroyed me."

"Can I at least get this dog to safety?"

"It's a stupid dog." He picked up the trigger again and frowned, as if he couldn't remember the sequence of the countdown.

Hazel did. But she wasn't going to tell him he'd turned the countdown off. The trigger in the other hand meant another device was already ticking toward detonation. "How can you care so little about life?" she asked, hoping to distract him from turning on the device again.

"Because I don't have one." The distraction didn't last for long. He pressed the button. "On. Aaron Cooper stole all my money. My life savings. My future. I lost my house, my truck. My friends called me an idiot for falling for his lies. I drank too much and finally lost a good job. I've been working on a road crew. I'm a trained engineer, and I've been working on a stinking road crew. That's where I found that dog you're holding."

"But your wife—"

"She left me. Earlier this year." Probably about the time the letters had started arriving. "She said she finally had enough of me being a loser."

"So you picked up the stray and blamed her, so the authorities would investigate her."

"Yeah. Sweet little bonus—causing her grief. If she'd been loyal to me, I might not have had to go to such drastic measures. But mostly I just needed a way to get to you. So I grabbed Athena and brought her in."

Because he couldn't get to Aaron. Maybe because no amount of punishment or atonement could make up for a ruined life.

"And the explosives? You picked them up on your job, too?"

"Where's your husband, Dr. Coop? Why isn't he rotting in prison? Why isn't he dead? Where's my justice?"

"Aaron is not my husband. You're hurting the wrong person."

Her words didn't seem to be reaching him. She couldn't hear Burke outside anymore. She could barely hear her own thoughts over the fear pounding through her pulse. Wade had blocked her path to escape. He'd probably rigged this entire building to blow.

She *did* have a life. She had a career she loved. Two beautiful daughters. She hadn't told Jedediah that she loved him. "How many bombs are there?"

"I've left a present for you every time I came to your clinic, whenever I visited that scrawny dog. I'm gonna bring this place to the ground." He leaned in, running his tongue along his yellowed teeth. His eyes were rheumy with a serious lack of sleep—or madness. "You wanna see 'em?"

She backed away, glancing all around her, wondering if there was any safe place inside the clinic where she could barricade herself from the next explosion. "I believe you."

"Off." He laughed again, enjoying her distress. "Isn't

it fun not knowing how many seconds you have left to live? It's kind of like not knowing how long you have until the next part of your life implodes." He took a step toward her, backing her down the hallway. "And the police have kindly cordoned off the area so it's just you and me and a countdown." Another step. Was he pushing her toward something? Trapping her? "Your husband destroyed my life. Now I get to do the same to him. I want to destroy *everything*." He raised the trigger and clicked it. "On."

She heard the shattering noise of breaking glass from somewhere in the damaged part of the building. Hazel spun around.

"Gunny! *Fuss!*"

A streak of black and brown rushed past her. She nearly cried out with relief because she knew Burke wouldn't be far behind.

With a vicious snarl, Gunny leaped, chomping down on Wade Hanson's upstretched arm and swinging his legs around to pull the man down to the floor. Gunny twisted, his powerful jaws never losing their grip on the man's arm.

Wade was screaming as Burke stormed in.

"Gunny! *Aus!*" Burke gave the command for the dog to stop biting and ordered him back to his side. He pushed Hazel and Athena behind him and leveled his gun between both hands at the man on the floor. "Stay down!" While Hanson writhed on the floor, cradling his arm and complaining about stupid dogs and sharp teeth, Burke cuffed him and explained his miraculous appearance. "He locked the back door. I couldn't get in. When the front of the building blew, I thought the worst."

Hazel appreciated his fear, but there was no time to

talk. "There are more bombs. He had two triggers in his hands. I don't know what they're attached to, but he said they're counting down."

"Then we're getting out of here." He hauled Wade to his feet and shouldered open the back door, shouting to the cops outside. "K-9 officer coming out! Gunny! *Fuss!*"

Running ahead, Gunny led the way to the fenced yard behind the building. Hazel hurried out next, carrying Athena.

Hanson laughed, even as Burke dragged him to safety. "Time's up."

Hazel spun around. "Burke!"

A wall of black protective gear snapped around her body and pushed her to the ground. Her clinic erupted with three thunderous booms. A storm of fire shot high into the air, while debris rained down on the mud and grass all around them.

It was nighttime again by the time Justin Grant, his bomb disposal team and the KCFD let Hazel back onto the premises again.

So much destruction. So much anger.

She and Burke had been treated for minor injuries and released while Wade Hanson was handcuffed to his hospital bed, being read his rights and the long list of charges leveled against him. She herself had cleaned and put a couple of stitches in a cut Gunny had suffered from flying shrapnel, while Todd had seen to Athena's recovery. All their patients had either been sent home or were being boarded at another animal hospital.

With the girls safely ensconced back at the condo, and Burke at precinct headquarters helping Justin fill out paperwork on the case, Hazel had returned to the clinic. Or what was left of it. Between the explosions, fire and all the water from KCFD's fire hoses, there was little left but the concrete slab and the frame of the kennel's back wall.

Sorting through the rubble for anything salvageable, Hazel was surprised that she didn't feel sad. She spotted a metal stool and waded through a puddle of standing water to set it upright. After drying the top with the sleeve of her jacket, she sat, scanning the place she had built all those years ago despite Aaron's wishes to the contrary.

She was happy—no, intensely relieved—that no one had gotten seriously hurt, not even one of her precious patients. This clinic represented her old life. And it had been razed to the ground. She would rebuild. With a more open floor plan with fewer places for crazed bombers with a vendetta to hide. She could upgrade the technology of the facility. She'd come back, stronger than ever.

When Gunny trotted up to her, she petted the dog and smiled. "Free health care for the rest of your life, young man. All the treats and toys you want, too."

"You're making my dog fat."

Hazel stood and smiled at the deep voice that sounded so tired, so sexy. "Did you finish up at work?"

Burke nodded. Somewhere along the way, he'd showered and changed into a clean uniform. "We found all the bombs. Justin and his team neutralized them."

"You mean Gunny found them all," she teased.

"I mean this is finally over." Burke pushed aside a mangled examination table and joined her beside the stool. "Hanson has been arrested. Your ex is on notice and shouldn't cause you or the girls any more trouble."

"I wonder if Aaron will be called as a material witness by the DA's office. That would be an ironic twist. We'll see if anyone rams a car into him to keep him from testifying."

Burke chuckled. "You've got a wicked sense of humor, woman."

She rested a hand against his chest and smiled up at him. "What I've got is hope."

"Yeah?"

"You are the bravest man I know. The most loyal. The most caring. You put your heart on the line with me. Even when you didn't know how I felt yet."

His hands settled at her waist. "I knew how you felt, Doc. You just had to realize it."

She lost the smile, wanting him to understand how serious she was. "I love you, Jedediah Burke. I don't want to waste another day of my life believing that being safe is the same as being happy. I can have both. I deserve both. I'm safe with you. I always have been. I needed to break some old habits and finally believe it. And, God knows, you make me happy."

"You gonna marry me, then?" he asked. "I've been patient for a long time."

Nodding, she wound her arms around his neck and pulled him to her for a kiss. "You were worth the wait."

* * * * *

COLTON 911: SUSPECT UNDER SIEGE

JANE GODMAN

As always, this book is for my lovely husband,
Stewart, who is gone but never forgotten.
We don't say "goodbye."

Chapter One

Griffin Colton's job had its highs, lows and harrowing moments. Although his business premises were based in downtown Grand Rapids, his reputation as one of Michigan's best adoption attorneys meant he was in demand across the state. As a result, he spent too many days like the one that had just ended, during which he had been traveling from one courtroom to another.

He loved what he did and wouldn't trade the feeling that came from knowing he'd helped a child find a place with the right family. Even so, by the time he returned to his office for a late-afternoon meeting, his already-low energy levels had drained even further. The leader of the local adoption fundraising organization was passionate in her commitment to securing financial help for families. Griffin agreed to provide leaflets to his clients and direct them to further support if necessary. Although the exchange was productive, it was late when his visitor left, and all Griffin wanted to do was drive the short distance to his Heritage Hill home, order takeout and eat it while watching an old movie.

He was closing down his laptop when his receptionist, Martha Dunne, appeared in the doorway.

"Dr. Abigail Matthews is here to see you." Her expression was apologetic. "I explained that I could make an appointment for another time, but she said it was urgent."

Instinct told Griffin it wasn't a good idea to talk to Abigail. She was the daughter of the man his family were investigating. Colton Investigations was the private firm run by his elder brother, Riley. Griffin and their four sisters—two sets of fraternal twins— took cases only involving a search for justice. The more they investigated banker Wes Matthews and his pyramid scheme involving selling RevitaYou pills the more criminal activity they uncovered. Could Abigail be on a fact-finding mission to discover how much they knew about her dad?

But on the one occasion Griffin had met Abigail Matthews, he'd been touched by her obvious devotion to her nine-month-old foster daughter. Children had always been his weakness, particularly those who were fostered or adopted. Having been in the foster system himself, he could never resist stepping in when there was a child involved.

If Abigail had come to see him because of her baby, it didn't matter who her father was, or what he had done. He would help her.

Without revealing any CI secrets...

"Show her in." He glanced at the clock. "Then go home, Martha. I can lock up here."

When the receptionist returned, she was accompanied by accompanied by Abigail, whose tall, slender frame was dressed in jeans, sneakers and a cotton shirt. Martha indicated for Abigail to step inside, then left. Although his visitor's expression was distracted, Griffin was struck again by her beauty. Her brown hair was streaked blond and hung in waves past her shoulders. With her huge brown eyes, bronze skin, high cheekbones and full lips, she was breathtaking.

Baby Maya was in the stroller and a heavy bag was slung over one of Abigail's shoulders. The look in Abigail's eyes as she focused on Griffin was painful in its intensity.

"Thank you for seeing me…" As she started to hold out her hand, the bag slipped from her shoulder. Diapers, baby wipes, bottles of formula and bags of snacks spilled out across the office floor.

"Oh." Abigail kicked on the stroller's brake and knelt on the rug. Her cheeks flamed as she picked up items and stuffed them back into her bag. "I'm so sorry."

"Hey, it's not a problem," Griffin assured her.

As he squatted close to the stroller to retrieve a bottle of hand sanitizer, Maya leaned forward to get a closer look at him. With her chubby cheeks, brown eyes, and mass of dark curls, the baby was adorable. She gave Griffin a grin followed by a friendly kick to the shoulder. When he pretended to stagger back in pain, she giggled and did it again.

"You might find yourself doing that all day," Abigail said. "Once she finds a game she likes, she wants to play it over and over."

Despite her underlying distress, there was a warm look in her eyes when she looked at Maya that intrigued Griffin. Abigail proclaimed she had no knowledge of her father's crimes. She had even come to Colton Investigations just a few days ago and told him and his siblings about a horrifying discovery that she'd made. Her research had uncovered that there was a compound of ricin in RevitaYou that could be deadly, depending on the person taking it. She believed it was only a matter of time before there were deaths as a result of her father's con.

Yet Griffin's doubts about her lingered. Was it possible that Wes could have funded the development of RevitaYou without the knowledge of his research scientist daughter? Surely she was the first person he would have gone to for advice and support? He couldn't help wondering if this innocent act was an attempt to distance herself from consequences, now that the criminal activity was being uncovered.

Between being kicked by the baby and gathering up stray items that had fallen from the bag, he didn't have any time to pursue that thought. A final glance showed him that most of Abigail's belongings had been restored to her. A flash of pink under his desk caught his eye and he crawled in that direction. As he reached for the knitted teddy bear, his fingers closed over Abigail's and they lightly bumped foreheads.

She clutched the soft toy to her chest. "It's her favorite."

And there it was. That look in the depths of her eyes was what drew him to this job. That need to help his clients and their kids… But it felt like something more this time. It was a little sharper. A touch deeper. He was drawn to Abigail in spite of his reservations about her family.

Griffin got to his feet and held out a hand to help her up. As he did, he was conscious of a damp, sticky feeling in the region of his right knee. He glanced down.

"Mashed banana?"

Abigail bit her lip as she looked at the stain on his suit pants. "You must have knelt on the bag. I'm—"

He grinned. "Sorry? You don't need to keep saying that. Most days my clothes tell the story of my appointments. Paint, ice cream, milkshake…" He pointed to different points on his shirt as he spoke. "My dry cleaning bill would bring tears to your eyes."

For the first time, she managed a slight smile. "I guess it must be one of the hazards of your job."

"And *I* guess that leads us neatly to the question of why you're here?" Griffin went to sit at his desk and indicated one of the chairs on the opposite side.

Before she sat down, Abigail handed the teddy bear to Maya. When she looked back at him, her smile had gone, and her features were tight with tension. "Maya has been in my care since she was born. Her mom died when she was three months old and it was always my intention to adopt her. This morning, I got a call from my foster care caseworker telling me that my paperwork is being stalled due to an investigation into my fitness to be a parent."

ABIGAIL WAS STRUGGLING to keep her emotions under control. It had taken every ounce of courage she possessed to walk into Griffin Colton's office. She was going to fight for Maya, and to do that she needed help from the best in the business. His professional reputation was well-known. But the reason she had chosen him went deeper.

Abigail had never been under any illusions about her father. Wes Matthews had the looks and charm of a Hollywood idol combined with the heart and soul of a grifter. But his latest fraud had gone too far. When details started to emerge of the RevitaYou pyramid scheme, she had been genuinely surprised that he had kept it secret from her. She was his daughter, and she was a respected clinical pharmaceutical scientist with a reputation as one of the leading independent researchers in the business. Her role involved the discovery and development of new drugs, alongside the improved use of existing medicines. Who better to help Wes keep this new venture on the right side of the law?

Her old insecurities had kicked in. All her life, she'd known she was a disappointment to her dad, who'd made no secret of the fact that he'd wanted a son. For as long as Abigail could remember, she'd been striving to impress him. Her childhood had been a scoreboard on which she'd never gotten enough points. Academically she'd been gifted, getting straight As in every subject. She had never forgotten the time Wes barely glanced at her report card before asking why she wasn't playing more sports. The following year she'd won an athlete-of-the-year award in high school. He turned up late to the presentation, then told her all about his friend's son who was a gifted musician. Now she played piano to concert performance level.

Naturally, she'd believed he hadn't come to her with his plans for RevitaYou because he'd found someone better to provide the clinical support. The old childhood longing for acceptance, never far from the surface, had bubbled up once more. Underneath the hurt, she'd felt a sense of curiosity. What made this wonder drug so special that she wasn't good enough to be part of it? Determined to find out, she'd ordered a thirty-day daily supply of capsules for herself. Although it was not FDA approved, RevitaYou was widely available online.

The pretty green bottle containing the daily vitamin supplement promised to make the lucky user look ten years younger within one week. Instead of swallowing the product, Abigail had taken it into her laboratory and broken it down into its component parts. That was when she'd discovered the awful truth...

"Did your caseworker explain why the process has

been stalled?" Griffin's question drew her attention back to the present. Back to the most important part of this whole horrible mess.

Maya. She glanced at her little girl, grounding herself.

I can't lose her.

One thing Wes had taught her about parenting was that she knew what sort of mom she wanted to be. She'd seen all the mistakes and was determined not to make them with her own little girl. Her love for Maya burned fierce and strong, and she clung to it.

The thought gave her the strength she needed to talk about what she'd discovered. And she reminded herself that Griffin already knew all about her father. There would be no surprises for him in the Matthews family background.

"It has to be about my dad." Even though they had to be spoken, the words burned her throat. For an instant, she thought she saw a flare of sympathy in the green depths of Griffin's eyes. But it disappeared within seconds, if it had ever been there at all, and his professional demeanor returned. "About RevitaYou."

"When you came to the CI office a few days ago, you told us that you were not involved in your father's con." Although his voice was nonjudgmental, his gaze probed her face. "You were very determined to make sure that we knew that."

She gave a bitter little laugh. "Are you giving me a chance to retract my statement?"

"Do you need one?"

She shook her head. Hard. "I was not involved in RevitaYou. Not at any stage. The first time I heard about it was when your team started blasting out warnings on social media and I saw the links to my dad. I only knew about it after it was declared potentially toxic." He didn't respond, and she sighed. "I don't know how to convince you that I'm telling the truth."

Griffin was silent for a moment or two, then his gaze dropped to Maya. The baby was rubbing her teddy bear against one cheek, her eyelids drooping sleepily.

"If I represent you, we would be in a unique situation. One that calls for total honesty." He looked back at Abigail. "And the truth is that you can't convince me that you didn't know about your dad's scamming people out of their investments in a toxic supplement." She winced, and he gave her an apologetic smile. "I'm sure you'd rather I told you that up front and moved on to what's important."

She sucked in a breath. "Which is?"

He nodded at Maya. "Your little girl."

For the first time, tears filled her eyes. "Can you help me?"

"I can try." He drew a legal pad and a pen toward him, then pushed a box of tissues toward her. "I need the name of your caseworker and any other details you can give me."

It hadn't occurred to her until now, but Griffin Colton was a very good-looking man. He had the sort of tall, muscular build that fit his expensive designer suit to perfection. And his dark blond hair, sculpted cheekbones and chiseled features were more rock idol than lawyer. But it was those eyes that captured her attention. They were dark green, with the shifting colors and moods of an evening forest. As he smiled, they looked like sunlight on new leaves.

"This may sound like a silly question, but do you mind if I order pizza?" he asked. "If you join me, we can eat while we talk."

"GOODNESS." AN HOUR LATER, Abigail looked down at the empty pizza box in surprise. "I didn't even know I was hungry."

Griffin smiled and pointed toward the stroller. "And that little lady has slept through everything."

He liked the way Abigail's face changed when she looked at Maya. It was as if a switch had been flicked and she lit up from within. Had anyone ever looked at him that way? He'd entered the foster system at the age of seven when his mother died. He knew his mom had loved him, and his foster parents, Graham and Kathleen Colton, had cared deeply for him. But *that* look? He wasn't sure he'd ever seen it until now.

"Ah. She likes her sleep." Abigail smoothed down the blanket she'd used to cover the baby's legs. "But she'll wake up hungry."

"It's not relevant to the case, but why did you foster her?"

She was quiet for so long he wasn't sure she was going to answer. When she finally turned away from

Maya to look at him, the sadness in her eyes hit him like a punch to his gut. "Maya is my best friend's daughter."

"I'm sorry. This is clearly painful for you—"

She shook her head. "I live with her loss all the time. Talking about it doesn't make it harder. Veronica Pérez and I met in high school. We had a lot in common." A slight smile twisted her lips. "Her parents were from Cuba, and my mother was Cuban, too. Her father worked away a lot. My mom had left my dad by that time and, although I lived with him... Well, I didn't see a lot of him. Veronica and I became each other's family. Our friendship stayed just as strong throughout our adult lives."

As she was talking, her hands twisted in her lap and her eyes focused on a point outside the window. "Sixteen months ago, Veronica came to see me and gave me some devastating news. She had been diagnosed with terminal lung cancer." Abigail turned to look at Maya. "But there was another bombshell. She was also pregnant."

"Her partner...?"

"She didn't have one. Maya was conceived during a drunken one-night stand. When Veronica contacted the father to tell him about the pregnancy, he offered to pay half the cost of an abortion but flatly refused to have anything else to do with the baby. She told him about the cancer, and he said his position hadn't changed."

"Even if he could have been made to accept his parental responsibilities, he doesn't sound like the right person to care for a child." Griffin's expression was grim.

"That's what I said." Abigail nodded her agreement. "And Veronica was an only child with no other family. Her parents had died in a car crash years before. There was no one else."

"Didn't her doctors advise a termination?"

"She wouldn't consider it," Abigail said. "The only treatment available to her was palliative, and she was determined to refuse anything that would affect her baby's chances of survival."

"Even so, you made a life-changing decision when you took her child." The words couldn't adequately express how much his opinion of her had changed. She was Wes Matthews's daughter. As far as the RevitaYou investigation went, that meant he should regard her as the enemy. But Griffin knew how it felt to be ripped out of a home as a child. He knew the damage it had caused to his developing identity. Even though he'd found a loving home with the Coltons, his ability to form bonds had been damaged beyond repair.

That was why Abigail's generous heart touched him so much. She had given Maya everything. A home, a mom, the love every baby so desperately needed. She had given the little girl an identity.

"I didn't have to think about it. Veronica would have done the same for me." She gave a soft laugh. "But you're right. For someone who hadn't given children a thought before this, suddenly becoming a mom *has* been life changing." She pointed to the bulging bag that had been the cause of her earlier embarrassment. "Just getting out of the door is like mounting a polar expedition."

"What happened to Veronica?" He wasn't sure how tactful it was to ask for details about the brave woman who had carried her baby knowing she wouldn't live to see her grow up.

"She died when Maya was three months old." Abigail hitched in a breath. "Although she was very ill during that time, the three of us got to spend some quality time together. After her death, Maya went through the foster system."

Griffin tapped his pen on the desk. "Presumably, if the adoption has been proceeding, the father has given his permission?"

"Yes. That was agreed while Veronica was still alive." She frowned. "There haven't been any problems. Until now."

"Okay." He was surprised by how much he wanted to make this right. The families were important, of course, but usually his motivation was the child's well-being. This time, his focus was equally divided between Abigail and Maya. He checked the time on his cell phone. "It's late and I may not get an answer but let me see if I can contact your caseworker."

Griffin knew most of the caseworkers in the city and he had a vague recollection of John Jones as a young, earnest man who worked hard for the children in his care.

Although he didn't say it to Abigail, because it sounded boastful, he also knew that his own reputation went before him. If the name Griffin Colton came up on a cell phone display—there wasn't a caseworker alive who would ignore it.

Sure enough, John Jones answered almost immediately. Griffin put him on speakerphone so Abigail could hear the conversation. "Mr. Colton? Hi, what can I do for you, sir?"

"I'm representing Dr. Abigail Matthews. She tells me that the adoption proceedings for her foster daughter, Maya, have been put on hold. I'd like some more details about that decision, please."

He was aware of Abigail's dark gaze fixed on his face as he waited for a reply. In the stroller, Maya murmured quietly in her sleep and waved a chubby hand, as though signifying her own impatience to learn more.

"Um. This is maybe something we should discuss face-to-face." Jones sounded uneasy.

"If the issue is the situation with Dr. Matthews's father, we can talk openly about it."

"No, the RevitaYou situation is not the problem," Jones said. "The reason her paperwork has been put on hold is that I've received information that Dr. Matthews is being investigated as part of her clinical trials to halt the effects of memory loss."

From the way she half rose from her chair, it was clear that this information was news to Abigail. Griffin raised a hand, signaling that he would deal with it. To his relief, although she looked pale and tense, she remained silent.

"Do you have any details about the investigation? And who made the allegation?" he asked.

"I don't have any information about who made the allegations. All I know is that the suggestion is that the doctor has been using an illegal enhancement compound—" There was the sound of Jones turning pages as though he was consulting notes. "A designer, non-FDA-approved drug called Anthrosyne. It appears that, instead of merely halting memory loss, Dr. Matthews has been attempting to boost some of her participants memories in order to gain recognition for her work."

"Can you expand on that?"

"Well, uh… the allegation is that, if Dr. Matthews successfully boosted the memories of her subjects, she would gain considerable attention among her peers. But, of course, she would have been playing with people's lives for her own gain."

Abigail gasped and shook her head but when she tried to speak no sound emerged. Worried for her wellbeing, Griffin quickly ended his call with the caseworker and went to crouch in front of her.

"Are you okay?"

"It isn't true." She clutched his hand. "There must be some mistake. I'm working on a research project called Mem10, which aims to halt memory loss in Alzheimer's subjects. I've never even heard of Anthrosyne until just now."

"We'll find out what's going on." If this was an act, it was the best he'd ever seen. "But right now, you have something more important that needs your attention."

As he finished speaking, Maya, who had been starting to stir, sat up straight. Hurling her teddy bear to the floor, she gave them an accusing glare and, opening her mouth wide, let out a wail.

Blowing her nose on one of the tissues she still had clutched in her hand, Abigail nodded. "You're right. She comes first. She always will."

Chapter Two

When she had made the decision to foster Maya, Abigail had taken her usual methodical approach to finding the right daycare. She'd created a spreadsheet setting out criteria such as distance from her home and place of work, qualifications of the staff, and reviews. When she'd looked at the website for each place, she'd given each one a score.

By that time, Veronica's illness had been so far advanced that it hurt Abigail to see how frail she was. When Veronica had reached for her hand, and her fingers were so thin, they felt like the delicate claws of a bird.

"How will you score the way they *feel*?" her friend had asked.

Abigail had been slightly bewildered by the question. "Well, I'll go and look at them, of course. I mean, if any of them didn't seem like a comfortable place for a baby…"

Veronica had laughed. "Go take a look at them. Then tell me what you think."

It was only when she'd walked through the doors of the Rainbow Daycare Center that Abigail had understood what her friend had meant. It wasn't the closest to her home or work, but the small center had a warm, welcoming approach that was exactly what she wanted for her daughter. More importantly, Maya loved it as well. And Abigail had ripped up the spreadsheet, a circumstance that had made Veronica smile.

The morning after she'd met with Griffin Colton, Abigail dropped Maya at the center at her usual time. At least she knew that the baby would be well cared for while she tried to untangle what was going on. After a sleepless night, she was eager to get into work and see what she could find out.

For the past five years, she'd worked as a research scientist at the small, private Danvers University. Her most recent project involved leading a clinical trial on participants to test the efficacy of a new memory-boosting, over-the-counter supplement called Mem10. After a long, difficult fight with Alzheimer's, Abigail's paternal grandmother had died from complications of the disease. The personal aspect meant that this was a field that was dear to her heart.

As she drove from the daycare center to the university, she tried, yet again, to make some sense of what John Jones had told Griffin. But there wasn't anything rational about what the caseworker had said. Abigail was in charge of the Mem10 trial. She knew exactly what had gone on at each stage of the process. If it wasn't for the fact that it was impacting the adoption process, she would have dismissed the idea that an illegal compound could have been introduced into the trial as absurd. She found the idea that she would attempt to enhance her reputation in such an underhand way deeply offensive.

Although she couldn't understand why anyone would breach the security of her laboratory or lie about it being breached, she was keen to get in there and double-check her systems and paperwork. As she pulled into her usual place in the parking lot, she was conscious of a few severe glances sent her way, and she squared her shoulders. Working at the university had always been enjoyable, but that had changed when the RevitaYou scandal broke.

These days, Abigail had grown used to getting the evil eye from people who believed she knew all about her father's fraud. She'd had several of her participants' adult children refuse to work with her. A colleague who she'd considered a friend had even confronted her publicly, humiliating her before vowing to never speak to her again.

As far as she knew, none of these people had actually invested in RevitaYou. They simply refused to believe that she wasn't involved.

Determined not to let her father's actions affect her work, she'd overcome her natural reticence and held a meeting to assure her colleagues and participants she knew nothing of her father's pyramid scheme and that she had no idea where he was.

It had been one of the hardest things she'd ever

done. Staring at a sea of politely disbelieving faces, she had plowed through her explanation. Although everyone had listened to what she had to say, she knew that she hadn't changed their minds. The realization had hit home. Her name would forever be linked to the RevitaYou scandal.

She had felt it again when she'd met with Griffin. It was obvious that his reaction to her plight had been driven solely by his desire to help Maya. The difference had been Abigail's reaction. She'd wanted to do whatever it took to persuade him of her innocence. . It was only her pride that had made her hold back.

He'd agreed to take her case. She'd secured the best attorney to help her keep Maya. He didn't have to like her or believe in her. So why, when she had so many other things on her mind, did his opinion of her matter so much? The question still occupied her thoughts as she left her vehicle.

"You've got some nerve." someone said from behind her as she walked to her office. The man's voice was soft, but there was no mistaking the menace in his tone.

Abigail swung around sharply. She recognized him immediately. Ryan Thorne was the son of one of her former participants. When the RevitaYou scandal broke, he had withdrawn his father from the Mem10 trial. Although Abigail had tried to persuade him that his dad, Billy, was showing signs of improvement, Ryan had been adamant. He wasn't going to let his dad be experimented upon by a doctor who he thought had been involved in a pyramid scheme.

"Mr. Thorne." She glanced around. The parking lot was quiet and they were all alone. "How's your dad?"

"Not good, thanks to you." He took a step closer.

"I'm sorry to hear that. But you know his place in the program is still open."

He gave a harsh laugh. "You think I'd let you near him again after what I know now?"

"Please believe me, Mr. Thorne. I am not involved in the RevitaYou scheme." As she spoke, another car pulled up close by and she recognized one of her administrative team.

"That line might work with other people. Not me." Thorne threw her a look of disgust. "I've been talking to the others who've withdrawn their parents from your program. You'll get what's coming to you. Just wait and see."

Shoving his hands into his pockets, he stomped away. Shaken, Abigail entered the building and crossed the lobby toward the elevators.

"Dr. Matthews?" Abigail turned to see her boss, Dr. Evan Hardin, standing by the reception desk. His presence in the building a full hour before his usual arrival time was enough to set alarm bells ringing, but the way he used her title instead of her first name worried her most. "Would you come into my office, please?"

Her legs had started to shake so violently that she had to take a moment to get them under control before she could follow him. Under the interested gaze of several of her colleagues, she went along the main corridor in his wake. Following on from her encounter with Ryan Thorne, she wasn't sure she was strong enough to deal with a confrontation with her boss.

"I'm sorry." Dr. Hardin closed the door behind him. "There's no easy way to say this. I'm suspending you pending an investigation into allegations that you've been using an illegal enhancement compound as part of the Mem10 trial."

"Evan—" Abigail could barely hear her own voice for the roaring sound in her ears. "Who made this allegation?"

"I'm not at liberty to divulge that information."

Abigail shook her head from side to side. She had to know who was responsible for these malicious rumors. If no one would tell her, she'd have to track down the source on her own. "You can't believe I would do this."

"It doesn't matter what I think." His face was sympathetic but determined. "I have a duty to the Mem10 program and the participants. Until my investigation is complete, I can't let you continue to take part in the trial."

The tremors had taken over her whole body and Abigail sank into one of the chairs opposite his desk. Her boss was a kind man, and they'd worked well together over the years. She could tell from his manner that he didn't want to take this action, but he was right. He couldn't allow his personal feelings to jeopardize the research—or their subjects. Even so, Mem10 was her project. She overseen its every step. There was so much more than her reputation at stake here.

As Evan handed her a glass of water, she forced herself to focus on the practicalities. "We're at a crucial point. If you halt the program now, it could have a detrimental impact on the outcome."

He lowered his gaze. "I won't halt the program."

Abigail took a sip of water. "What do you mean? You don't have time in your schedule to take over."

"I will appoint a replacement to oversee Mem10 in your absence."

"Oh." Her professional pride shattered into a thousand tiny pieces. At the same time, she thought of the individuals involved the trial, each of whom she had come to know so well. Their lives would be impacted by any change, however minor. "Please choose wisely. There are several competent researchers on my team, but few are qualified to do the role justice."

He lifted his glasses, rubbing his nose wearily. "Thank you for your concern. In addition to this investigation into the illegal use of Anthrosyne, I have another, equally urgent, staffing matter to attend to. If you'll excuse me, Dr. Matthews…"

And that was it. He was no longer using her first name, even in private. It was a polite way of reminding her that she was off the program. And that she should go.

She walked to the door, the shaking in her legs replaced by an unnatural stiffness. Once she was outside and in the corridor, the oddest thought flitted through her head. She really needed to speak to Griffin about this. But why? He was an adoption attorney. He couldn't help her with an employment issue, but most of his siblings were in law enforcement and this was a false allegation. Maybe the CI team could help... She reached into her pocket and drew out her cell, swiping through her address book for his number. As she did, approaching footsteps made her look up.

"Hi, Abigail." The woman approaching gave her a sweet smile. Until recently, Dr. Jenna Avery had been Abigail's closest friend at Danvers University. They'd eaten lunch together each day, gone out for dinner now and then after working late in the lab, even met up at the gym a few times. Then Jenna had confronted Abigail one morning in front of the whole team, hurling abuse at her over RevitaYou. It turned out Jenna was one of the people who'd bought a bottle of the tablets and got sick.

Thanks, Dad: Destroy my reputation. Kill my friendships. Oh, and use your RevitaYou vitamins to poison people for money.

This was the first time Jenna had spoken to Abigail since she'd publicly humiliated her.

"Dr. Hardin has sent for me. I guess he wants me to look after the Mem10 program while you're away." Without waiting for Abigail to reply, Jenna stepped inside Dr. Hardin's office.

It couldn't be true. Jenna Avery was barely competent in her job. Her work was often shoddy, and Abigail had been forced to challenge her in the past when she'd falsified results. At the time, Abigail had been horrified that Evan had kept Jenna on and had privately wondered if he might be sleeping with her colleague. Those doubts surfaced again now. Jenna wasn't qualified to lead a complex trial like Mem10. Evan must know that...

Choking back a sob, Abigail stuffed her cell back into her pocket and ran from the building. It was only when she reached her car that she realized she hadn't told Evan about Ryan Thorne and his veiled threats.

GRIFFIN HAD SPENT the morning in court dealing with four back-to-back cases. By the time the last one was over, he was running late for a meeting with his siblings and he left the court building at a run without pausing to check his messages. Luckily, his office wasn't far from where the Colton Investigations headquarters was located. Once the family home, the mansion on Grand Avenue now belonged to his brother. Although Riley Colton, a former FBI agent, ran CI, Griffin and his sisters contributed their own expertise while working at their full-time jobs.

Since the RevitaYou scandal had hit, and new developments had been breaking almost constantly, the team met more regularly than usual to share information. As he drove the short distance, Griffin reviewed the details of how the story had come to light.

Brody Higgins had been a smart, kicked-around eighteen-year-old foster kid with a small string of misdemeanors when Griffin's dad, Graham, had gotten involved in his case. Brody had been arrested for murder, but Graham had believed the boy was in the wrong place at the wrong time and declined to prosecute. The decision, and subsequent capture of the real killer, had solidified the name of Graham Colton as a hero in Michigan. It also helped turn Brody's life around. Since then, the Coltons had looked out for Brody and treated him like family.

Now aged twenty-seven and a law school graduate, Brody had only wanted a high-paying corporate job and the good life. So it had come as a surprise to Riley when he turned up at his office the previous month looking nervously over his shoulder. The explanation for his behavior was that a big-time loan shark was after him. He'd borrowed five thousand dollars to get in on a can't-fail product called RevitaYou. The vitamin supplements claimed to turn back the clock ten years and the drug was so new that the FDA hadn't even seen it yet.

Although Riley had been incredulous that anyone could have fallen for this illegal pyramid scheme, Brody explained that he happened to pass by a promo for a seminar about making six figures overnight by becoming a member of the exclusive RevitaYou "team" that invested in the product, recruited new members and sold the vitamins. He'd gone along to the seminar where he met real people, including a scientist, four other investors and people who took the vitamins for just two weeks. They produced amazing before and after photos, and gave testimonials raving about the product.

Brody had wanted to pay back his huge law school loans and impress his older girlfriend. He'd felt so sure about RevitaYou that he borrowed the money to invest from an anonymous group called Capital X. Riley in particular had heard about the dangerous operation from the FBI but had never been able to bust them. Capital X used a unique incentive to get their clients to pay up on time. If any payment, including the very high interest, was late, Capital X goons would break two bones at a time until the outstanding amount was paid.

Riley's blood had run cold when Brody showed him his left hand. The ring finger and pinky had been bandaged together. To make things worse, Brody had given his girlfriend a bottle of RevitaYou as a gift, hoping to recruit her to sell the product because he'd get extra bonuses. Instead of being impressed, she'd dumped him. Not only had RevitaYou left her looking ten years *older* but she'd been sick for two days after taking it. Apparently, she was still having issues that seemed to be related to the vitamins. In the light of Abigail's later discovery about ricin, it seemed that Brody had handed his girlfriend a bottle of poison.

Brody had immediately called Wes Matthews, the guy who'd taken his money in cash transfers, to demand his investment back and report the problems with the product. Wes had emailed back that he never received the money and that Brody must be mistaken.

After that, Wes, and the whole RevitaYou operation, including the fancy website, had disappeared.

The timing of Brody's recklessness couldn't have been worse. The CI team didn't have five minutes to spare; all his siblings were all busy. But this was Brody, so Riley had called an emergency meeting of his siblings to discuss next steps. Brody, who had agreed to go into a safe house, hadn't shown up for the meeting and sent a message to let the Coltons know he had gone into hiding. While he was concerned for Brody's safety, Griffin felt it was typical of the younger man to run away from his problems.

Traffic up ahead was at a standstill and Griffin leaned back in his seat.

"Feels like stepping back in time." The murmured words were a reference to his feelings about Brody and the way it felt like everyone sprang to attention whenever *he* needed help. On one level, Griffin knew he was too hard on Brody, on another, he felt like someone had to be. And, to be fair, Brody never resented that slight distance between them.

He sighed. But it wasn't like stepping back in time. Brody could be in real trouble this time. And, no matter, how much Griffin resented the easy attention Brody received within the family group, he didn't want to see him get hurt.

Griffin had been reluctant to get involved this time around. He'd insisted Brody should have known better than to get involved in a pyramid scheme and with a loan shark. Sometimes, the support his family had given to Brody had grated with him, even though there was no reason why it should. His feelings of isolation were his own issue rather than anything to do with the way he was treated within his family. Ever since his birth mother had been killed, he'd felt alone.

He was honest enough to admit that, but it didn't change anything. He still thought Brody got preferential treatment. Griffin knew he'd been cared for and loved as much as any member of the family. But Brody's personality meant he liked an easy ride and these problems he was having now were part of that. If the Coltons had been tougher with Brody when he was younger, maybe things would have turned out differently.

The vehicles in front were moving and he straightened, glad of a break from his thoughts.

In the end, the search for justice—always uppermost with the Coltons—had prevailed. The siblings all wanted con artist Wes Matthews caught before he could steal from more people. Despite his reservations about stepping in to save Brody from his own foolishness, Griffin had said he was in, and they'd taken on the case to honor their dad's memory.

As he pulled into the drive of the house that had been his home since he was eight, Griffin reflected that they couldn't have known at that point how quickly things would escalate. The last they'd heard from Brody was a text from a burner phone, telling them that the Capital X henchmen were on his tail.

Right now, they had no idea whether he was dead or alive.

As if Brody's troubles and the subsequent RevitaYou commotion wasn't enough to occupy his mind, Griffin's thoughts had been turning toward Abigail Matthews throughout the day. It was an inconvenience he could do without. Still not convinced of her innocence in the RevitaYou con, he couldn't allow himself to be drawn in by her plight. Particularly as he wasn't even sure it was her difficulties that were the reason he wanted to get involved. For the first time in as long as he could remember, he had felt a powerful attraction to a woman. And *that* wasn't happening.

Just as he was reminding himself of that, his cell rang. Bringing his vehicle to a halt, he reached into his jacket pocket and drew out his phone. He checked the name on the display. *Abigail Matthews.* A glance around the drive told him his sisters were already there. He didn't have time to take the call. He should let it go to voice mail, but there was no way he was keeping Abigail waiting.

"Griffin Colton."

"I got suspended from my job today." He could tell she was crying.

Griffin studied the facade of the beautiful old house as he took a moment to consider the issues. Bringing Wes Matthews to justice had started out as a campaign for justice but it had spiraled into something bigger. As the scale of the con became clear, it had turned into a crusade on behalf of each individual who had lost their cash, their health or both.

Abigail's role in RevitaYou was still unclear. Had she been involved and was now trying to paint herself as an innocent dupe? It was always possible that she had genuinely been unaware of her father's exploits and was trying to help him now, but could he afford to be open-minded about that? If she was attempting to infiltrate CI to find out what they knew he couldn't let her get too close. His brother and sisters certainly wouldn't allow it.

And the story about being framed for using an illegal drug? Was that just another layer in the con? Could he believe anything she told him?

But the pain in her voice was real. And it was not something he could ignore. She might be a complication. He might not want her in his life but he felt responsible for her. She had come to him for help, and he wasn't going to let her, or Maya, down.

"I'm at the CI headquarters. Meet me here."

It wouldn't be the first time he'd been out of step with his siblings.

It was only when she thought about going to the CI headquarters that Abigail stopped to consider what she was doing. And more importantly about what *Griffin* was doing. She didn't think for a minute that his invitation was an indication that he, or his siblings, believed in her innocence. It might even be a way of drawing her in so they could find out more out about her dad and his whereabouts. If they only knew the truth. His daughter was the last person in whom Wes would confide.

She had never felt so scared or alone. Her mom had died when she was thirteen, but she hadn't seen her for many years before that, and her dad had hardly been a nurturing figure. Seeing her best friend die only months before had been hard enough, but now, she also faced the prospect of losing her career and maybe even Maya, all through no fault of her own. Her name had already been tarnished through association with her father's misdeeds. Now, she was being accused of skewing the results of her trial to boost her own reputation. Who would believe she was innocent?

When she had arrived home that morning, after collecting Maya from daycare, she had sent a quick email to Dr. Hardin.

It may be nothing, but I was confronted today by Ryan Thorne, the son of a former Mem10 participant. He is very angry about my perceived involvement in RevitaYou and said he had been in contact with the families of other former participants. He said I would "get what's coming." His anger seems to be directed against me personally but I thought you should be aware.

Although she had copied the email to the university HR department, she had no real idea where the allegations against her had come from and who was making them. Until she found more information, she couldn't begin to build a defense. Frustrated, hurt and disbelieving, she had called Griffin in the hope that he had heard something more from John Jones. When he suggested meeting him at the CI headquarters, she'd been so relieved at the thought of seeing someone who was on her side, she'd have agreed to anything. It was only when she ended the call that she questioned her decision.

Because... *On her side?* Were those really the right words to describe Griffin?

She had gone to him because of his professional reputation. In her situation, she couldn't take any chances. Losing Maya wasn't an option. But these latest developments were making her question her decision to choose a Colton. If the CI team believed she was guilty of assisting in the RevitaYou con, her suspension from her job would give them additional ammunition against her.

Griffin had been sympathetic toward her, and she believed he had been genuine when he said he wanted to help her keep Maya. But he wouldn't break with his siblings. Of that she was sure.

So, right now, stepping inside would be a little like walking into enemy territory. For the second time.

The first time, she'd dashed headlong into the beautiful old house, determined to let the Colton siblings know what she'd discovered about RevitaYou. Even though it reflected badly on her dad, they had to know that there was a deadly compound in the vitamins.

Acting on a hunch, she had ordered a bottle of Re-vitaYou and, instead of swallowing the pills, taken them into her laboratory and analyzed their component parts. That was when she had discovered the truth. So many people were ingesting a poison. It was only a matter of time before deaths would result.

Abigail wanted to tell the world she didn't believe her father would be behind such an awful scheme. But that would be a lie. The truth was, if he thought it would make him money, he was capable of anything. His personal life had always been a reflection of his business dealings. She remembered her mom, Sofia Barroso, as a sweet, beautiful woman. When she realized what a cold-hearted, conniving man Wes really was, Sofia had left him. Although she had tried to get custody of Abigail, who had been ten at the time, Wes had determinedly fought her and kept her away from her daughter. Sofia had died three years later in a car accident. Wes never remarried and, although he'd dated, his relationships never lasted. Abigail realized later that his self-absorption meant he was unable to feign an interest in another person for long.

Abigail couldn't share the outrage most people evidently felt when Wes had gone into hiding instead of facing his accusers. It was exactly the behavior she'd expect of him. If he didn't look good, he'd walk away. And he certainly wouldn't stick around to face prosecution. Life behind bars? That wouldn't suit Wes Matthews.

None of this soul-searching was helping in her decision about whether she should go ahead and meet with Griffin. Would she be better finding another attorney? Someone who had no preconceptions about her and her father? Someone whose last name wasn't Colton?

She had almost made up her mind to call Griffin and tell him she wouldn't be meeting him, when Maya woke up from her nap. Abigail had tucked her into the crib in the living room, noticing, as she did, how much the baby had grown. Soon, she'd be too big for the cradle next to Abigail's desk…

The thought brought a panicky lump to her throat. If Abigail couldn't adopt her, who would be there to oversee the milestones in Maya's life? She had to be the one. At first, she'd loved the little girl because she was a link to Veronica. She had made a promise to her friend and had been determined to see it through. Over time, that had changed, and she had fallen in love with Maya for her own sake. Now she was Maya's mom. She couldn't imagine the world without her little girl in it.

As if reacting to Abigail's fears, the little girl reached up her plump arms and gave a beaming smile. Even though Veronica had lived for a few months after giving birth, she'd made sure Maya always viewed Abigail as her mom. The extensive palliative treatment she was undergoing, together with the fact that she knew she wouldn't be around to care for her daughter, meant she wanted to make sure Maya identified right from the start with the parent who'd be there.

Although it had broken Abigail's heart, she'd known her friend had been right.

Now, as she lifted Maya from the crib and held her warm, sweetly scented weight against her shoulder, love surged through her, reigniting her strength and resolve. Her life had spun wildly off course recently. She didn't know why, and events had been out of her control. But starting now, she was going to fight back. Maya, her job and her reputation were all too important for her to give up on.

There was only one person she trusted right now. She didn't know why, since his role in the RevitaYou investigation automatically made him suspicious of her. But Griffin Colton appeared to have an aura of integrity, and he'd said he would do his best to help her.

"I guess that's as good a place to start as any," she told Maya, as she gathered up the baby's bag, together with her cell phone and car keys.

Chapter Three

Griffin entered the house through the door at the rear, which took him straight into the family kitchen. He could hear voices coming from the formal dining room and guessed the rest of the team had already gathered around the table in preparation for the meeting. As he approached the room, Pal, Riley's German shepherd, scurried up and thrust a wet nose into his hand.

"Good girl." Griffin patted her head and the dog immediately flopped over onto her back, inviting him to tickle her belly. "Sorry. I don't have time." He lowered his voice. "I'm already about to make myself unpopular."

"Griffin?" His sister Sadie gave him a smirk as he entered the room. "We thought you weren't coming."

"That's not fair. Or funny." Her fraternal twin, Vikki, gave her a reproachful look. "We've all been late now and then."

"Except Riley," Pippa pointed out.

"That's not surprising," Kiely, Pippa's twin, laughed. "He lives here."

Riley looked up from the electronic tablet he'd been studying. "Plus, I'm the responsible one, remember?"

Although there was a twinkle in his eye, Griffin knew there was a world of meaning behind the words. As the oldest of six children, Riley had grown up with a sense of responsibility. His father's career had been time-consuming and required a lot from both his parents, which meant many of the daily parenting duties had fallen to Riley. He had often been expected to babysit, to mentor them, support them with homework and help out with sports and other hobbies. He had the same opportunities as the others, but he'd also done his share of caring.

The former FBI agent was forty-three and Griffin had figured he'd been determined to remain single. In the last few weeks, however, events had taken an unexpected turn. Riley had protected social worker Charlize Kent, with whom he'd had a one-night fling, when she was in danger. Now Riley and Charlize were engaged and expecting a baby and Charlize had moved in with Riley. Griffin was delighted for his brother, but the change in Riley's circumstances once again highlighted his own isolation.

Although he dated, Griffin had never had a close relationship with a woman. In the same way that he was welcomed into the family group, but slightly apart from it, he figured it was to do with his reluctance to show his feelings.

Griffin took a seat at the table and was grateful for the cup of black coffee Sadie pushed in his direction.

"Strong enough that it could have come out of a volcano. Just the way you like it." She gave him a sympathetic smile. "Rough morning?"

"Is there any other kind?"

Sadie, a crime scene investigator with an equally heavy workload, nodded her agreement. Since Riley seemed about ready to start the meeting, they turned their attention his way.

"Let's start with the most important thing… Has anyone heard from Brody?" Riley didn't appear hopeful as he looked at each of his siblings in turn. There was a collective shaking of heads in response. "Pippa, you're the one he was always closest to. He may contact you first."

"I've tried texting him a few times," Pippa said. "But he doesn't reply."

"Clearly, he's still lying low and is terrified about what the Capital X goons will do if they catch up with him." Riley tapped a finger on the table. "All we can do is keep trying to get in touch with him and also attempt to find out more about Capital X."

"Do we have any new information about other aspects of the investigation since our last meeting?" Griffin asked.

Riley consulted the notes on his screen. "We know that Detective Emmanuel Iglesias of the GRPD has opened a RevitaYou case file. I've been sharing information with him. Before Brody came to see me, sixteen people had come forward to say they believed they'd been conned into investing in Wes Matthews's pyramid scheme. Brody was number seventeen and Charlize's aunt, Blythe, was the eighteenth." He looked up. "What about Capital X? Griffin, you'd been looking into them."

Griffin shook his head. Although the CI team was committed to breaking open the underground loan operation, Capital X had proved good at covering its tracks. "I only have what I've already shared. They seem to have unlimited capital because of their brutal tactics and interest rates. They operate underground and on the dark web. No one knows who runs the operation. Everything is anonymous and everyone uses burner phones."

"There must be a way to get in there." Kiely frowned impatiently. She was a freelance private investigator, and Griffin could almost see her formulating plans to get information about the shadowy organization.

"We'll keep trying to find a way," Riley said.

"This stuff is poison." Pippa wrinkled her nose, the expression a reflection of how the family felt about the dangerous vitamins. "And that fits with what Wes Matthews's own daughter told us. There is a ricin compound in the tablets and it's only a matter of time before someone dies."

"What about Abigail Matthews?" JAG attorney Vikki cast a quick glance around the table. "Has anyone checked her out? I find it hard to believe she didn't know what was going on, or that she doesn't know where her dad is now."

Griffin glanced at his watch. Even allowing for time to get Maya ready, Abigail would be there soon. It was time to speak up…

"Dr. Matthews is on her way over."

The five pairs of eyes that turned to look his way pinned him in place the same way the family cat used to fix its prey before it pounced. Griffin had never felt like a real Colton, but he'd never wished he wasn't part of the family unit. Right now, he wasn't quite so sure if he still felt that way.

"You mean you've asked her here because she has more information for us, is that right?" Although Riley was offering him a way to help out the team, his brother didn't sound hopeful.

"I didn't ask her for that reason. She was suspended from her job today and I don't think she has anywhere else to go for help right now." Under their skeptical gazes, he quickly outlined the details of his meeting with Abigail, the investigation into her alleged use of Anthrosyne in the Mem10 program and its impact on her adoption of Maya.

"You realize that none of this makes her appear more trustworthy?" Sadie asked. "If anything, it reinforces the idea that she's likely to be as unprincipled as her father. If she wouldn't hesitate to use an illegal substance in one drug she's trialing, why would she think twice when it came to RevitaYou?"

"Whoa." Griffin held up a hand. "Firstly, the allegation against her is just that. Nothing has been proved and the Anthrosyne investigation hasn't even started.

Secondly, Abigail is the person who came to us with the information that there is a ricin compound in RevitaYou. Why would she do that if she was responsible for putting it there? Why wouldn't she have gone into hiding with her dad?"

Even though his questions were greeted with silence, he could tell he wasn't convincing anyone. Why would his family buy into her innocence when he wasn't sure about Abigail himself? It was a strange situation but, even though he had his doubts, he wasn't prepared to let anyone else make a judgment before they had all the facts. To be fair, his brother and sisters, having been raised with such a strong belief in justice, were equally unlikely to jump to unfair conclusions.

Despite that, Kiely couldn't resist voicing a concern. "What if telling us about the ricin was a ruse to make us think she wasn't involved in RevitaYou? If we believe her, she escapes prosecution and keeps her career and reputation. It also raises the possibility that she can get information from us to find out what's happening with our investigation." She gave Griffin an apologetic look. "If Abigail gains the confidence of someone on the inside, she could relay confidential information back to her father."

There was murmur of protest around the table. "None of us would share details of a case unless we were sure it was okay to do so," Riley said.

"I'm sorry." Kiely reached across to place her

hand over Griffin's. "I didn't mean to suggest that you would."

"I know you didn't." As he returned the grip of her fingers, Griffin reflected that this was all part of his dilemma. By supporting Abigail, he was risking more than an attraction that pulled him out of his comfort zone. The reality was that he shouldn't take her case. No matter how sorry he felt for her, or how much he wanted to help Maya find a permanent home, this situation was too complicated. Even if Abigail had had no knowledge of what her father had done, they were on opposite sides here. And he couldn't foresee a good outcome from that.

The tense atmosphere was interrupted when Pal started barking, signaling that someone was on the premises. Clients and other visitors had to park on the street and walk up the long driveway. Griffin got up from his seat and was heading out into the hall when there was a knock on the front door.

With his emotions in turmoil, he went to open it. After the conversation he'd just had, did he even want to see Abigail again? If there was even the slightest chance that she could come between him and his family, the answer had to be no. At the same time, his heart was racing at the thought of being able to do something to help her.

When he opened the door and saw her face, his doubts vanished. She was pale, with dark circles under her eyes, her hair was untidy, and there was a stain on her lapel that looked like dried oatmeal. She was still the most beautiful woman he'd ever seen. And there was no way he could believe that her behavior was an act to dupe him into revealing information about the RevitaYou investigation.

Maya, who appeared to be full of life, greeted him with a wide grin, then held out her arms as though he was a long-lost friend.

"Can I hold her?" Griffin asked.

"Oh, please do." Abigail handed the baby over. "She's getting heavy now, and today's been…" Her lip wobbled. "I'm sorry."

"Hey." Shifting Maya into the crook of his right elbow, he slid his left arm around Abigail. She leaned gratefully against him as he drew her into the house. "I can only imagine how tough it's been." He paused. "My family are all here. Is that going to be too difficult for you to handle right now?"

She remained still for a moment or two with her head resting on his shoulder, then she straightened. When she looked up, her expression was determined. "I'm ready to see them. Why wouldn't I be? I have nothing to hide."

ALTHOUGH SHE'D SAID she was ready to face Griffin's family, Abigail experienced a moment of near panic as she followed him into the large dining room where the Colton siblings were assembled. It was the same room in which she'd met with them when she'd rushed to tell them her findings about the ricin compound she'd discovered in RevitaYou. She had no regrets about sharing that information, but she knew the CI team had questioned her motives.

Everyone questions my motives.

And she didn't really blame people. It was unfair, and it hurt, but she could understand how she must look to anyone who didn't know her. And, now that Veronica was dead, there was no one with whom she was really close. Loneliness and grief squeezed her heart until she wanted to cry out for the pain to stop. Instead, she held her head a little higher and faced Griffin's brother and sisters.

"Dr. Matthews." Riley Colton got to his feet and indicated an empty chair. "Griffin has been telling us about the problems you've been experiencing."

Abigail sat down and Griffin took the chair next to hers with Maya in his lap. The baby, clearly deciding that all of these people had assembled just to see her, clapped her hands and waved. The gesture broke the ice a little as everyone laughed and Griffin's sisters returned the waves. Overwhelmed by this response, Maya buried her face in Griffin's shirt front and played with the end of his tie.

"I don't know if anyone will believe me, but I did not use an illegal compound to enhance my subjects' memories." There. Saying the words out loud made her feel stronger and strengthened her determination to clear her name. "And I don't know who is trying to frame me."

She wasn't sure if her conviction swayed anyone in the room, but no one looked away or was openly hostile. Pippa Colton, who was an attorney, leaned forward. "But we can assume that this non-FDA-approved substance *has* been used as part of your program?"

"What are you getting at?" Griffin frowned at his sister.

"It's a simple enough question," Pippa said. "If the Anthrosyne drug has definitely been used, but Abigail wasn't responsible for it, the investigators need to take a broad approach to their inquiry."

"Of course." Griffin turned to Abigail. "The Anthrosyne investigation should consider the possibility that someone else could have introduced this substance into the program."

"But I'm in charge of the Mem10 trial." Abigail was confused by the suggestion that anyone else could have intervened. "I don't understand what another person would have to gain from using an illegal compound in this way. It's my name that would be on the research papers."

"If someone else was involved, maybe the motive would become clear when that person's identity was uncovered?" Griffin suggested.

"It's possible, I suppose." Abigail remained skeptical. She had a small team of part-time research scientists who had assisted her with the Mem10 trial since its inception two years earlier. Most of them were dedicated to the university and to the projects in which they were involved. She couldn't imagine a situation in which any of them would risk damaging a piece of work in this way. More importantly, she could see no reason for them to do it.

"I know this isn't a good time to ask you this—" Riley cleared his throat.

Abigail knew what was coming. "You want to know if I've heard from my father?" She shook her head. "It's hard to explain but…" She felt there was a chance she might be able to make this group of people understand her relationship with her father. They seemed prepared to listen to her and, for some reason, she sensed they were trying hard not to judge her. "My dad and I aren't close. I'm probably the last person he'd get in touch with."

"Even so, without consciously knowing where he is, you could have some clues about where he may have gone," Griffin said. "You may have overheard him talking about places he's been to, contacts he has, even other countries he wanted to visit. There's no reason why he would stay in America. In fact, it would make sense for him to get as far away as possible."

"I've been going over and over those things in my mind, but I can't think of anything." As she spoke, Abigail's breathing became more rapid and shallow. Her chest tightened as though a hurricane was building inside her. Was this what a panic attack felt like? Because all she wanted to do right now was snatch up Maya and flee.

"It's okay." Griffin placed a hand over hers and his warm, strong touch restored some of her calm. "No one is asking you to come up with answers here and now. But something may come to you. If it does, you know where to find us."

She bent her head, feeling some of the anxiety recede. He was right. The sense of urgency she felt was being driven by everything that was going on in her life, but it had no basis in fact. Although it would be helpful to the CI team and the Grand Rapids police to find her father quickly and get the answers to their questions, it didn't have to happen right this minute. This feeling that she couldn't breathe until things were resolved was caused by stress, not reality.

When she looked up and met Griffin's gaze, she saw a measure of understanding in the green depths of his eyes. She couldn't tell whether he knew the direction of her thoughts or simply guessed that she was hurting and wanted to help. Either way, she was glad of his comforting presence.

The conversation continued around her and she was grateful to the Colton siblings for speaking freely about the RevitaYou investigation. Their frustration and distaste was obvious. They clearly could not comprehend a mindset such as her father's. Wes Matthews had always placed his love of money and material things above all other considerations. Even, it had now become clear, the law.

The meeting ended with Riley and his siblings discussing his meeting with two elderly couples who had invested in RevitaYou. Ellis and Reva Layne and John and Cassie Winslow had no idea where Wes could have gone and had gained no clues from anything the man said to them.

"At least I took their story to the local news station," Riley said. "I gave a reporter details of the RevitaYou scam, the sickness caused by the tablets and the disappearance of banker Wes Matthews. The anchor interviewed Detective Emmanuel Iglesias on camera, and he was able to give a warning not to take the product."

"It still doesn't get us any further along," Sadie sighed. "It feels like we've stalled when it comes to finding Matthews and cracking open Capital X."

"I could do some more searching and see if I can find more about who else has worked with my dad on the RevitaYou formula," Abigail offered. "He's not a chemist. Someone had to come up with the formula for the pills."

"That would be helpful," Griffin said.

Maya had been happily tugging on his tie and peeping through her fingers at his siblings. Now, she was getting restless and started to wriggle to be put down.

"It's getting close to her dinnertime." Abigail held out her arms, and Maya launched herself toward her. "I should take her home."

"I'll see you out." Griffin got to his feet and helped her up from her chair.

"I hope you'll feel able to join us at our next meeting, Dr. Matthews—" Riley broke off with a slight smile. "And perhaps we should use first names from now on?"

She managed a smile. "Yes. Call me Abigail. And I hope I'll have more information for you next time we meet."

Griffin escorted her out into the hall and opened the front door. "I hope that wasn't too difficult?"

"In a strange way, it was useful." She frowned as she tried to find the words to express what she meant. "I can see how hard you and your family are working to make this right and I want to help. I still find it hard to believe that my dad is the person responsible for all of this." She looked out at the driveway. "I just…"

He waited for a few moments before prompting her. "You just…?"

"On top of everything else, I was threatened by the son of one of my participants today."

"You need to go to the police." His expression was concerned. "Threats can turn nasty."

She shook her head. "It wasn't an explicit threat. Hopefully once the group who object to me because of RevitaYou know I'm off the Mem10 trial, they'll forget their objections and get back on board. I just don't want to be alone with my thoughts tonight. Once Maya is asleep, I know I'll keep going over and over this allegation."

"How about I finish up here and then come by your place with takeout?"

She looked at him in surprise. "You don't have to do that."

"I know I don't have to. I want to." He patted Maya's cheek. "You get this little one home and I'll see you in a few hours."

Unable to speak because of the lump in her throat, Abigail nodded. His kindness had caught her unawares once again and, as she headed toward her car, all she could think was how nice it would have been to have discovered this sweet side of his nature in different circumstances.

Chapter Four

Griffin had a mountain of reading to get through for a court case. He also had an early start the following day and he needed a good night's sleep. So why was he bringing dinner over to Abigail's house, wondering what sort of food she liked and agonizing over whether he should take wine or beer? He knew nothing about this woman. Actually, that wasn't true. He knew plenty about her—just not about her tastes.

Yet his instinct persisted. He wanted to help and protect her. Damn it. He didn't even know if she drank alcohol. He added soda to the order on the delivery app he used, then returned his cell phone to his pocket and, having saved his files, closed down his laptop.

He didn't understand what was going on. His natural caution had deserted him and, in its place there was a fizzing excitement that he'd never experienced before. Even when he should be thinking about other things, Abigail intruded into his thoughts. He'd never had a crush, not one that had lasted more than a day or two, but he imagined it felt a lot like this. Out of all the women he could have been attracted to, he had to choose the most unsuitable one. At thirty-two years of age, he was seeing the emotions over which he'd always exercised such tight control rebel in spectacular style.

He'd sometimes wondered if the timing of his adoption was the key to his feelings of isolation. Although he was still young when he'd been brought into the Colton family, he'd been old enough to already have an identity, a sense of who he was. The sense of difference came from within, not from anything imposed by his adoptive family.

Surely this change was a good enough reason *not* to go over to Abigail's place. After spending his whole life feeling like he didn't fit in, Griffin was always afraid that in his personal relationships he would either be too distant, or that his craving for love would overpower a partner. As a result, he dated, but never allowed himself get close to a woman. This attraction he felt toward Abigail was stronger than anything he'd ever known. Could he rely on his usual self-restraint?

At the same time, the urge to see her again was overwhelming. And, just for once, he wanted to stop being cautious. Just for once, he wanted to act on impulse and see where it led him. Snatching up his car keys, he headed out of his apartment door before discretion took over again.

His apartment was close to the CI headquarters but Abigail lived in a small house near the Danvers University campus where she worked. The drive took about twenty minutes, during which time Griffin grew impatient. Having made up his mind that he wanted to see her, he was in a hurry to get over to her place. She had impressed him earlier with her resilience, but there was no doubt about the tough time she was having. Other than helping with the adoption case, he wasn't sure what else he could do. But he knew for sure that he wanted to try. If he could lift some of the burden from those slender shoulders and take the haunted look from her eyes, he would.

He knew what his siblings would say. Griffin had always identified with the underdog. Possibly it was why he resented Brody, who had an air of expectation about him. Probably because of his own difficult start in life, Griffin wanted to support those who were struggling to help themselves. Abigail wasn't weak, but the odds were stacked against her in every part of her life right now. Was that the root of this attraction? Was he drawn to her because of her vulnerability?

When she answered her front door, he almost laughed out loud at the question. In that instant, his feelings for her had nothing to do with her fragility, or her need for protection. They had a lot to do with the fact that Abigail Matthews was *gorgeous*. Then she smiled, and he got the first clue that this might be something more than a physical attraction. Putting his heart out there wasn't going to be part of the deal.

"Maya finally fell asleep about half an hour ago," she said, as he stepped inside a small hall. "She was tired, but she wouldn't settle."

"She can probably sense your mood." Griffin followed her into a small, cozy kitchen and dining room.

Abigail nodded. "She's had such a difficult start in life. I always try so hard to keep things light, but babies are very intuitive." Her lip wobbled slightly, and she sucked in a breath. "I'm all she has, so she's bound to pick up on how I'm feeling."

"Hey." He placed a hand on her arm. "Maya is a very lucky little girl. She's loved. Sadly, I see many instances of kids who are not."

"Oh, goodness." Her eyes were troubled as she scanned his face. "That must be so difficult for you to deal with."

It was almost a shock to realize that she got it. For the first time ever, someone understood, without being told, that Griffin didn't do a bland nine-to-five desk job. His siblings had an idea about the heartbreak he saw on a daily basis. Otherwise, no one appreciated that he spent most of his time trying to undo tragedy.

For an instant, his throat tightened, and he didn't trust himself to respond. Instead, he turned the conversation to a safer direction. "I ordered the takeout to be delivered here. I hope you like Chinese food?"

"Love it." She smiled. "And, in spite of everything that's been happening, I'm hungry."

He checked his cell phone. "It should be here in a few minutes."

"Just enough time to get ready."

She moved quickly around the kitchen. Reaching into cupboards and drawers, she handed Griffin plates, glasses and forks, which he placed on the small table. Just as Abigail was filling a jug with water, there was a knock on the door.

"Perfect timing." They shared a smile before she headed to answer it. When she returned, she pretended to stagger under the weight of the brown paper bags she was carrying. "How many people are you expecting?"

Griffin laughed. "My family will tell you that I always overcater."

"That's okay. I love leftovers for breakfast." She hesitated, apparently aware that her words could have held a double meaning. "That is… I don't know if… What I meant was…"

Griffin came to her rescue. "Don't count on there being any leftovers. I haven't eaten all day, and that smells good."

She gave him a grateful smile. "It sure does."

They sat at the table and spent the next few minutes opening the various cartons and piling food onto their plates.

"I didn't know what you'd want to drink." Griffin indicated the selection of beer, wine and soda.

"I don't usually drink on a work night—" She gave a little gasp as she realized what she'd said, then shrugged. "But I guess that won't be a problem, so I'll take a beer."

Her attempt at lightheartedness didn't quite work. As he reached for one of the chilled bottles, Griffin caught a glimpse of the hurt in her eyes. It seemed impossible to believe that if she had been responsible for using the illegal substance in her research, she would be so shocked and hurt at the treatment she was getting.

His head might be telling him to be wary around Abigail, but his heart was giving him a different message. He had been brought up in a family that had a strong emphasis on care and support. It had been one of the biggest motivators in his life. He had come late to being a Colton, but he didn't walk away from people who needed his help.

"Have you heard any more from your boss?" he asked. "They should move quickly on this Anthrosyne investigation. Keeping you waiting would be unfair."

"I had an email confirming the decision to suspend me and outlining the reasons. It didn't tell me anything that I don't already know." Although her expression was gloomy, he was glad to see her scoop up a forkful of rice and start eating.

"And do you have legal representation? I can help you with the adoption case, but I have no experience with employment law."

"I guess that's the next step," she sighed. "I know nothing about this sort of thing. I wouldn't know where to start looking for a decent attorney."

"Leave it to me." He pushed a carton of chop suey in her direction. "My sisters will know someone, particularly Pippa, who is an attorney."

She bent her head over her plate. "Will this affect my chances of keeping Maya?"

"The fact that you are under investigation for a serious misdemeanor, one that could potentially lead to a criminal charge, is already impacting the adoption process. That's why we need your employer to get the Anthrosyne investigation completed quickly." He didn't want to give her any false hope, but he felt confident in his next statement. "You shouldn't worry that anything will happen immediately. That fact that you are under investigation will not be enough for Maya to be removed from your care."

"What—" She fiddled with the label on her beer bottle before taking a slug. "What about RevitaYou? Most people think I was involved in that, too."

"But you weren't." As he said it, he knew he believed it. "Which means there's no real evidence against you. This is Maya's home. She won't be taken away from you over some unfounded allegations."

When she finally met his gaze, he saw a sheen of tears in her eyes. "Thank you."

They ate in silence for a few minutes, then Abigail returned to the subject of Griffin's job. "I would imagine it can be rewarding as well as emotionally draining."

"It can. There's nothing quite like that feeling of knowing you've helped a child find the right family."

"What made you choose that career?" she asked.

He didn't usually talk about his early life. These days, no one ever questioned his status as a Colton. When he was younger, if the subject ever arose, his adoptive parents, Graham and Kathleen, would always reassure him about how loved and wanted he was. And he'd always wanted to believe them…

"I was taken into foster care at the age of seven after my mom was killed by her abusive partner." He wasn't sure he'd *ever* said those words out loud.

"Oh, my goodness." Abigail reached out and took his hand. "How terrible for you."

"I listen to people now who speculate about how much a child of that age can remember, and I want to tell them to rip up their books and studies and start over again. Because I remember everything about my mom," Griffin said. "I know how she looked, how she smelled, and the clothes she wore. I can hear her voice, her laughter. I remember the stories she told me, the songs we sang together. I can still taste her awful cooking." He laughed. "Do I really remember those things? Maybe not. But I think I do."

Abigail returned his smile. "She sounds like a wonderful person."

"She was. But she was also very vulnerable. I never knew my dad. He left when I was a few months old. After that, my mom dipped in and out of relationships with several deeply unsuitable men. I know that now because there were always social workers in our lives. Some of the 'uncles' she brought home weren't nice people."

"But she wouldn't have put you in danger, surely?" Her grip on his fingers tightened.

"Not intentionally. I'm certain of that. But she was very sweet and gullible. I imagine the guys she dated promised her the earth." His lips twisted into a sad smile. "It's a pattern I see a lot. Then, one night, she left me with a neighbor while she went out to a bar with a new man. She never came home."

"What happened?"

"There were plenty of witnesses, who all told the same story. They both got drunk. Another guy asked her to dance. She said 'yes' but the boyfriend objected. They started arguing and he swung a punch. My mom fell and hit her head on the corner of a table. The bar staff acted quickly but she was dead before the ambulance arrived."

She shifted in her seat so she was facing him. "What an awful thing for you to face as a child. Did you have any other biological family?"

"No. It had always been just the two of us. My mom had spent her own childhood in a series of foster homes—" He shrugged. "The irony is that she'd been determined to make sure I wouldn't go the same way."

"She couldn't have predicted what would happen." Abigail sounded almost fierce. "No one could. What about your father? Didn't he come forward when he knew your mom was dead?"

"My dad was forty-two when he met my mom. She was twenty. He was diagnosed with bipolar disorder, receiving a pension from the army following a breakdown during basic training twenty-six years earlier. When I was born, he had been addicted to alcohol and over-the-counter painkillers for most of his life," Griffin said. "He couldn't care for himself, let alone a child. When officials from the Michigan Department of Health and Human Services tracked him down, he told them he wanted nothing to do with me. Years later, I read my file. The caseworker in charge commented that, in the circumstances, no contact would be best for both of us."

Although he was able to look back now and feel empathy for the broken man who had fathered him, his memories of that time, in contrast to those from before his mother's death, were shrouded in murky terror. The nightmares, the tears, the need to see his mom again, and the ever-present "who will care for me now?" questions were as real to him today as they had been back then. Over time the feelings of abandonment and rejection had subsided, but they'd never gone away. He'd learned to understand that no one had been at fault. His mom had been struggling to do her best against the background of her own problems. Through no fault of his own, his dad had been unable to offer even the basic requirements of fatherhood. Even his mother's killer hadn't meant to cause her death.

There was no blame. Only fragments of broken lives. Through the years, Griffin had examined them, tried to understand, but never fully pieced them together to make sense of his life story. By the time he became a Colton, he was already his own person, destined to be forever in the middle of two lives.

"You must have needed so much help. Please tell

me you were given the right kind of support," Abigail said.

"There were certainly people who wanted me to talk to them. But I'm not sure they understood what I needed." Griffin frowned as he tried to explain what he meant. "I was seven years old. I didn't want to talk about my feelings. I just wanted my mom."

"That's so sad." She reached for one of the paper napkins that had come with the takeout order and blew her nose. "It must have been the most awful time in your life."

He was amazed that, with everything that was going on in her own life, she could be moved by his story. Having been brought up from the age of seven in an empathetic family, he was used to people tuning into his feelings. This felt different. It was as if Abigail was so in tune with his emotions, she was absorbing some of the hurt he always carried with him. The thought was comforting and scary at the same time.

"What happened next?" Abigail asked.

"Graham Colton defended the guy who killed my mom." Griffin scooped up a forkful of noodles and ate them before continuing. "He was charged with murder, but Graham got the sentence reduced to assault."

"Oh." She blinked in surprise. "How did you feel about that?"

"At the time, I knew nothing about it. I was protected from what was happening. Now? I guess it was the right outcome. He was a jerk, but he didn't intend to kill her."

"I don't know if I could be as forgiving." The corners of her mouth turned down. "But you found a home with the Coltons?"

"Yes. Graham told Kathleen about the case, and she was moved by my story. They adopted me soon after."

Griffin had never encountered anyone with a gaze as a perceptive as Abigail's. It was as if those hazel eyes were probing his thoughts. "It must have been very hard to adjust to a new family so soon after losing your mom."

"It was." Although she was easy to talk to, he now found himself hitting the emotional equivalent of a brick wall. If he got started on what he'd lost and gained when he became part of a new family... Well, he just wasn't ready to go there. Instead, he held up one of the cartons. "Care to split the last spring roll?"

AS THEY FINISHED the meal, Griffin steered the conversation toward less personal topics, including a local news item about a spate of thefts from a bakery. Security footage had shown that the perpetrator was the owner's dog. Although she laughed at the story, Abigail remained shocked by what Griffin had told her about his early life.

Now, it appeared he had retreated behind a barrier as though he was afraid he'd revealed too much. She didn't want him to regret having confided in her, and she wanted to let him know how much she valued his trust in her.

Would it help if he knew they had something in common? She figured it was worth a try.

"The circumstances were different, but I lost my own mom when I was very young," she said.

"I know you said she left your dad."

"When I was ten. I never saw her again after that and she died in a car crash when I was thirteen."

"I'm sorry. I didn't know."

"Why would you?" Abigail managed a slight smile. "I'm guessing your research into my family has covered my father's business activities rather than our personal lives."

"You're right." His expression was somber. "But telling you about my own mom could have been triggering for you. I didn't consider that."

She shook her head. "That's not why I'm telling you this. You shared your story with me. I wanted to do the same."

"Why didn't you see your mother after she left? That's a very unusual situation."

"Looking back, I'm amazed she stayed with him as long as she did. I found out later that she tried to leave and take me with her on several occasions, but my dad stopped her each time. In the end, it all became too much. She sneaked out one night to a place where he couldn't find her. With the help of some friends, she started a fight for custody." She bent her head, studying the wood grain of the tabletop. "He used every cheap shot he could come up with to make sure she couldn't win and that we never got to see each other."

"If you never saw her again, how do you know all of this?" Griffin asked. "Did your dad tell you he used unfair tactics?"

"No, although he wouldn't see it as a bad thing. He takes pride in being good at fighting dirty. My mom wrote me a letter just before she died. Actually, it was one of many, but it was the only one I received. I don't know what happened to the others, but I guess my dad intercepted them. Somehow, this one got through."

Whenever she remembered that time, the confusion and grief she'd experienced resurfaced. Her dad had told her that her mom had gone because she no longer cared about them, and the absence of any contact had seemed to reinforce that. For a long time, Abigail had questioned her own role in the breakup. Had it been her fault? Had she somehow caused her mother to fall out of love with her dad? With her? Feeling unloved and rejected, she had withdrawn into herself.

"Do you want to talk about what it said?" Griffin asked.

She reached for another napkin and dabbed at the corners of her eyes before blowing her nose again. Such a good look. Was this what he'd expected when he offered to come over? But he was such a good listener, and they'd established an almost instant bond through their similar backgrounds. For the first time since Veronica's death, she didn't feel embarrassed about showing her feelings in front of another person.

"Mom wrote how much she loved me and how hard it had been to leave. In the end, my dad had made her life such hell that she'd had no choice. His wild business schemes, debts and dubious acquaintances were taking over his life and, at the same time, his controlling behavior toward her was increasing. He wouldn't allow her to leave the house without him and wouldn't give her any money of her own. In that letter, she told me how hard she'd tried to get custody and to have contact with me." She managed a laugh. "The thing is, my dad never really cared for me that much. Keeping us apart would have been driven more by the desire to hurt my mom than any love he felt for me."

"I'm sure he cared for you in his own way." His voice was gentle.

"Are you?" she asked. "Think about what you know of the RevitaYou scam. Do you think the man behind that sounds like he would be a loving parent? And yet, his own mom was loving and kind. I grew up close to her, even though my dad wasn't a family man. She died of Alzheimer's and that prompted my interest in the disease."

"Yet, even despite your mom's letter, you didn't get to see her before she died?"

"The letter made things worse. I tried confronting my dad but he refused to listen when I asked to see my mom. When we got the news that she was dead—" She tilted her head back and looked up at the ceiling for a moment or two. "The first thing he said was that at least I would finally stop annoying him about contacting her."

Although Griffin didn't comment, his fist clenched

on the tabletop. After a few moments, he pointed at her empty beer bottle. "Another?"

"Thank you, but two is my limit. Maya will wake me up at about six tomorrow morning, so I need a clear head."

"Did you go to your mom's funeral?" he asked.

"Yes, even though my dad told me I couldn't. Veronica and I sneaked out of school that day and went to the service. I'm glad I got a chance to say goodbye."

"You should have been able to do so much more." His voice was gruff. "Too many people are inclined to view divorce as just another episode in a child's life. It's not. It's a major trauma that changes the whole trajectory of a person's future. In your case, you had so much else to deal with in addition to your parents splitting up."

She smiled at him. "You are the most amazing advocate for children."

"I do my best."

When he smiled, she realized that she'd been mistaken. He wasn't cold. He was shy.

"When Riley checked on your dad's background, he discovered that Wes was an investment banker." Griffin changed the subject.

"That's one of the jobs he had," Abigail said. "He used to be good with money, but then his age became an issue for the firm he was at. He started complaining about younger people being given all the opportunities. He was always a scammer and what he meant was that he was missing out on the chance to make more cash. He said he was leaving to start a new venture. He was a grifter and I guess RevitaYou and the pyramid scheme was his latest plan. I feel so bad for all the people who got taken in and lost money."

"It's not just about money. The reason we started to investigate this con is because of a man called Brody Higgins. My dad got involved in Brody's case when he was wrongly accused of murder. Since then, we've all looked out for Brody—he's like part of the family. Brody borrowed five thousand dollars from a loan shark company called Capital X to get in on RevitaYou. When he didn't meet the first payment, they broke two of his fingers. Now he's on the run trying to avoid the next attack."

"That must be so worrying for you and your family," Abigail said.

"More for them than for me. Brody might have been another late addition to the family but he was a very important one."

There was something about Griffin's expression as he spoke that drew her attention. She sensed there was a tension in him about how the Coltons treated Brody. Clearly, his past was complicated and still affected him today. Yet he had turned all that hurt into a powerful force for good. She knew about the amazing work he did for children, not just in his job, but for nonprofit organizations in the Grand Rapids area. It told her so much about the sort of man he was that he could empathize so strongly with children in the foster and adoption system and he would devote his life to helping them.

"I should go." He indicated the clock over the stove. "Goodness, how did it get to be after midnight?"

He laughed. "I'd love to stay and talk some more but I have an early start. And you did say you'll be woken at six."

She walked with him to the front door. He paused and faced her in the confined space of the hall. As he raised his arms, she thought he was going to pull her in close for a kiss. Her heart started to beat a little faster and she held her breath. He hesitated for a second, then rested his hands lightly on her shoulders.

"I enjoyed tonight, even though the circumstances weren't ideal."

She nodded. "And some of the topics we talked about weren't exactly uplifting."

"But it was good to be able to share those difficult parts of our lives." He moved his hands down to her upper arms, warming her flesh through the thin material of her shirt. "Let me know if you hear any more about the Anthrosyne investigation. I'll keep you informed if I get any information from your caseworker."

When he'd gone, Abigail locked the door and slid her hands down her arms, touching the place where his fingers had just rested. Surely it was wrong to feel happy when her life was falling apart so spectacularly?

Wrong or not, being with Griffin made her feel good and she was glad of his protective presence in her life. And the fact that she found him so attractive? Well that was a complication she would have to deal with. *How* she would deal with it, though—that was something she hadn't quite figured out yet.

Chapter Five

That night, Abigail surprised herself by actually sleeping for a few hours. In addition, Maya slept past her usual time the following morning. As a result, the baby woke with a raging appetite and immediately demanded food. For someone who couldn't yet talk, she sure knew how to voice her requirements. After strapping her into the high chair, Abigail was preparing oatmeal and pouring milk into a sippy cup, when the doorbell rang.

Frowning, she went to answer it. It was still before eight. She had called the daycare to let them know they were running late but she had no idea who could be calling at that time, particularly as she would usually be heading out about now.

When she opened the door, the tall man standing on the doorstep had an air of authority that was reinforced when he held up his police badge. "Dr. Matthews?"

"Yes." The sinking feeling in the pit of her stomach was intensifying with each passing second.

"I'm Detective Emmanuel Iglesias of the Grand Rapids PD. May I come in?"

A wail from the direction of the kitchen signaled that Maya was growing impatient. Although Abigail would have liked to find out more about why there was a police officer at her door *before* she asked him in, she wasn't prepared to keep her daughter waiting any longer.

"I need to feed my baby while we talk." She stood to one side to allow the detective to step inside.

As she led him through to the kitchen, her imagination was going wild. Had they found her dad? Had he somehow implicated her in the RevitaYou con? Had he committed another crime? Or had the Anthrosyne investigation become a criminal inquiry? There were so many things going on in her life and she just couldn't imagine any good reason why a detective would be knocking on her door at eight in the morning.

The blood in her veins seemed to have been replaced with ice water and, when she went to take the oatmeal out of the microwave, her hand shook.

"It's okay, honey." She forced herself to sound normal for Maya's sake. "Breakfast is coming right up." She turned to Detective Iglesias. "Can I get you anything? Coffee, maybe?"

He shook his head. "I can see you're busy, so I'll get straight to the point. I'm investigating the murder of Dr. Evan Hardin."

Abigail had been about to stir the oatmeal but, at

those words, the spoon slipped from her fingers and clattered to the floor. "What?"

She must have misheard. Things like murder inquiries belonged on TV and in the movies. They didn't happen in real life.

"Dr. Hardin was found dead in his office this morning. The time of death is still to be confirmed but we believe it was sometime yesterday evening."

Mechanically, Abigail picked up the spoon from the floor and placed it in the sink. After getting a clean one from the drawer, she went to sit beside the high chair. Maya babbled happily and opened her mouth like a baby bird. A rush of nausea washed over Abigail and she bowed her head until it passed.

"You said he was murdered?" Images flitted through her mind of the kind, serious man who had been her supervisor and friend throughout her time at Danvers University. Why would anyone kill Evan Hardin? He was an academic. The sweetest, most inoffensive man she'd ever met.

"He was hit over the head from behind with a blunt object. A blood-stained glass bowl, from his awards shelf, was lying next to the body. I'm in the initial stages of my inquiry but it appears that it was the murder weapon. Nothing appears to have been taken." He took a small notepad and pen out of his shirt pocket. "I believe Dr. Hardin was your boss?"

"Wait." Abigail looked away from Maya's oatmeal covered face. "Am I a suspect?"

"All I'm doing right now is making some preliminary inquiries." He was close enough for her to see that he had written the date and time next to her name at the top of a blank page. "But I've been given information that you and Dr. Hardin had an argument yesterday. Something to do with your suspension from your job because of your use of illegal substances?"

Her situation was bad enough, but what he'd just said made it sound so much worse. And, if Evan's body had been found only that morning, who had given the police false information about her? Was it the same person who had provided details of the use of Anthrosyne in the Mem10 trial? Either way, Abigail felt under pressure. She had no way of defending herself against an invisible threat and yet it felt like the evidence was stacking up against her. The *nonexistent* evidence.

"I want to speak to my attorney before I answer any questions." If that made her sound guilty, she didn't care. Because of RevitaYou, the rest of the world already viewed her that way. From now on, she was putting herself, and Maya, first.

"You have that right, of course."

There was just one problem. Abigail didn't have a lawyer. At least, not one who specialized in criminal law. What she had was an adoption attorney. But she trusted Griffin. Because of the connection that had sprung up between them, she knew he would support her better than anyone.

She spooned the last of the oatmeal into Maya's mouth. "I need some privacy while I make a call."

He rubbed a hand over his chin and gave her a weary look. "I could come back later."

"Thank you." She wasn't going to let him make her feel guilty about taking control. Even after a reasonable night's sleep, she was tired and stressed. Her future with Maya was too important to risk on a wrong word to a detective. "I'll have my attorney call you to arrange a convenient time."

When he'd gone, Abigail leaned against the wall for a moment or two. Her knees were trembling, and she wanted to cry. But she didn't have time to be upset.

Please let Griffin answer...

With fingers that shook slightly, she found his number in her cell phone and swiped to make the call. It went straight to voice mail.

Choking back the sob that rose in her throat, she forced herself to speak calmly. "Please call me back as soon as you get this message. It's important."

For now, that was all she could do. Maya needed normality, and that was what Abigail would give her. Pinning on a smile, she returned to the kitchen.

"Hey there. How would you like to go for a walk in the park?"

Maya showed her appreciation of the idea by hammering her spoon on the tray of her high chair before throwing her sippy cup on the floor.

Her stress levels were off the scale, but she was a mom and Maya's care was at the top of her list of priorities. As she focused on packing a bag with the baby's essentials, she found her breathing slowly returning to normal.

Staying in control. For now, it was all she could do. And for Maya's sake, she would do it the best way she knew how.

"I'M NOT SURE I can help you." Griffin hated saying those words, but the couple sitting opposite him had brought him a case that was outside of his experience. "I think you need to take this to the police."

"That's what I said." Liam Desmond placed an arm around his wife's shoulders.

"But—" Shelby Desmond pressed a tissue against her lips before continuing. "We don't want to press charges. We just want our baby. Isn't that what you do? You bring families together?"

The Desmonds had come to Griffin in desperation when the private adoption they'd arranged had gone wrong. A woman on social media who said she knew about their fertility problems had approached them. After striking up a conversation via social media, the woman, who called herself Dr. Anne Jay, had explained that she ran MorningStar Families, an online adoption agency.

Liam and Shelby were desperate for a child of their own, but the waiting list was a long one and they had agreed to adopt the baby of a young woman called Kitty. They had sent regular payments to Dr. Jay who, in return, had obligingly sent them photographic evidence of Kitty's pregnancy and medical records. On the day the baby was due, they had transferred ten thousand dollars to MorningStar Families' bank account. Immediately afterward, Dr. Jay had stopped communicating with them on social media. They had no other way of contacting her. Griffin had spent some time looking into the online agency, but had been unable to find any contact details.

"To be honest, I would be surprised if there ever was a baby." Although Griffin spoke gently, he wanted them to know the truth right from the start.

Shelby covered her face with her hands and began to weep quietly. Her husband regarded Griffin with a mixture of annoyance and helplessness. "You think this woman could have done this before?"

"It's possible. Like I said, you need to talk to the police."

He didn't add that the arrangement the Desmonds had made with MorningStar Families was a questionable one and the chances of them getting their money back weren't high. The police should still be informed about the online adoption scam so that they could try to prevent it from happening again.

"Since you work with families all the time, maybe you could help to warn other people against this sort of thing?" Liam asked.

"I'll certainly try," Griffin said.

"If we send you some details, would you share them publicly?"

"Send them and I'll see what I can do." He would check with Pippa before making any promises, but he couldn't see what harm there would be in adding a paragraph to his monthly newsletter warning his followers to be aware that this sort of con existed.

When the Desmonds had gone, he checked the time. He had half an hour before his next meeting. Luckily that was routine and required no preparation. A regular lunchtime get-together with some of his fellow family law attorneys, at which they discussed their workload and difficult cases.

He just had time to check his messages. As soon as he picked up his cell phone, he frowned. Abigail had called him almost four hours earlier. As he listened to her message, he grew even more concerned.

When he called her back, she answered immediately. "Oh, thank goodness."

"Is something wrong?"

"My boss has been murdered." Her voice wobbled. "And I think I'm a suspect."

"Have the police said that?" He was reaching for his jacket and car keys as he spoke.

"No, but the detective who came around here made a comment about how Evan and I had a bad relationship. I told him I wasn't prepared to speak to him until I'd consulted my attorney." He heard her indrawn breath. "All I could think of was that I needed to call you."

"That was the right thing to do. I'm on my way over."

Before he left the building, Griffin arranged for his receptionist, Martha, to call his colleagues at the forthcoming meeting and offer his apologies. As he headed out to his car, he called Riley.

"Dr. Evan Hardin of Danvers University has been murdered."

"What? Isn't he Abigail Matthews's boss?" Riley sounded as shocked as Griffin felt. "What the hell is going on?"

"That's where I hope you can help me out. I don't have any information. Can you check the news channels, websites and social media to see what you can find out, then get back to me?"

"Leave it with me."

Griffin ended the call as he reached his vehicle. Riley's question was a perfect summary of his own thoughts. What the hell *was* going on? Could Abigail have killed her boss? His brain refused to process that possibility. As an attorney, he should be able to keep an open mind. As a man…? No, unless he was presented with undeniable proof, he wasn't going there.

When he arrived at Abigail's house, he was pleased to see her looking pale but calm. They went through to the den, where Maya was playing on the rug with a stack of colored wooden blocks. When she saw Griffin, she waved an aimless hand, but returned to her game.

"Don't be fooled into thinking she'll stay there," Abigail said. "She doesn't crawl, but she wriggles on her stomach. If I look away, she can be across the room in seconds."

"She's gorgeous." They watched the little girl together for a few seconds. "You are very lucky to have each other."

She nodded. "And I intend to keep it that way."

Although he was glad to see her fighting spirit was intact, Griffin noticed the tightness in her jaw muscles. He wanted to take that tension away.

"Tell me what happened."

"A detective from the GRPD came to see me just before eight o'clock this morning. He told me that Evan—Dr. Hardin—had been murdered. He was found in his office early this morning but they think he was killed yesterday evening. The police officer, a Detective Iglesias, said he'd been given information that Evan and I had a bad argument. That was when I told him that I wanted to speak to my attorney before I answered any questions."

"I know Emmanuel Iglesias," Griffin said. "He can be trusted to conduct a fair inquiry."

"But someone has already influenced his judgment of me," Abigail pointed out. "The way he spoke made it sound like he'd been told I was guilty of personally using a banned substance."

"Then we need to make sure he is given the facts instead of hearsay. Although—" Griffin frowned as a thought occurred to him. "If Evan's body was only found this morning, and Detective Iglesias was here by eight o'clock, the person who talked to him about you must have done it very quickly."

"What do you mean exactly?" Abigail asked.

"Think about it. I'm not sure how early your building is opened, but presumably the body was found by a cleaner or maintenance worker. That person would have called the police. A crime scene investigation team would then have arrived at Evan's office and Emmanuel Iglesias must have joined them as soon as he could. It gives a very short time frame for someone to contact him with information about you. How did anyone even know that Evan was dead?"

"You're right. Unless it was someone in the building," Abigail suggested. "Scientific research isn't a nine-to-five job, so people are around early in the morning. If anyone saw the activity in Evan's office and found out what was going on, they could have approached Detective Iglesias with information."

"But why were they in such a hurry? The police will question everyone in time." Griffin stooped to pick up some of Maya's blocks that were beyond her reach. As soon as he handed them to her, the baby threw them away again. "No, someone was very keen to get your name out there from the start. They wanted the police to see you as a suspect even before the investigation started."

She appeared lost in thought for a few seconds. "Do you think that person was trying to frame me?"

"I do. And we have to consider that it could be the same person who introduced the illegal compound into your research program in order to sabotage your career."

"But surely—" She lifted a hand to her throat. "How far would a person go to make me look bad?"

"Were you going to say that no one would have killed Evan Hardin in order to place the blame on you?" She nodded. "I'm not so sure."

Abigail sat down abruptly on one of the two small sofas. "This can't be happening." The color had drained from her cheeks and she raised scared eyes to his face. "How could anyone hate me *that* much?"

Griffin went to sit next to her. Placing an arm around her shoulders, he drew her close and she immediately nestled against his side.

"You have to remember that this is not about anything you've done wrong. The reason behind what's going on here could be something you are completely unaware of. Until we know the identity of the person behind this, we won't know why they're focusing on you. Can you think of anyone who would do this?"

"I don't think I'm going to win any popularity contests right now. There are plenty of people out there who wouldn't rush to help me up if I fell in the street. But this?" She shook her head. "Tampering with a drug trial is bad enough. Killing my boss to make me look bad? I can't even begin to comprehend that."

"You said you'd been threatened by a former participant?"

She lifted her head, appearing momentarily confused. "Ryan Thorne? He's the son of a former Mem10 trial participant. Ryan withdrew his dad from the program when news about RevitaYou broke. He confronted me in the university parking lot yesterday before I met with Evan."

"What did he say exactly?" Griffin asked.

"He repeated the usual allegations about my involvement in RevitaYou. He's said in the past that there's no way I'm not part of it and how I'm the worst doctor in the world for creating such a terrible drug. Then he said he'd spoken with some other families who had withdrawn participants from the program. He said I'd get what was coming."

"Those were his exact words?"

She nodded. "I thought he meant I'd lose my job, or maybe be prosecuted."

"How many people withdrew from the Mem10 trial when they heard about RevitaYou?"

"Five." She bit her lip. "We started with fifteen people involved in the trial. But after your family started putting out social media blasts about the dangers of RevitaYou, a third left the program."

"I'm sorry. We didn't foresee the impact it would have on the work you were doing at Danvers University."

"How could you? And you needed a way to get the word out fast so that people stopped taking those dangerous vitamins," Abigail said. "I'm glad you acted quickly. I hope I'm wrong, but RevitaYou could prove even deadlier than anyone expected. Do you really believe that Ryan Thorne's threats could be connected to Evan's murder?"

"Believe me, having grown up in the Colton household, and doing what I do, my eyes have been opened to the best and worst of what people are capable of.

And sometimes the most unlikely things can trigger a disproportionate and unpredictable response." Privately, Griffin could picture several situations in which an irate relative of a participant might turn his, or her, anger against Abigail's boss. Possibly Dr. Hardin had refused to discuss the Anthrosyne investigation, or listen to a complaint against Abigail, and the situation had gotten out of hand. He didn't want to distress her further by speculating. "I want to find out who was so eager to talk to the police immediately after the murder. If it was Ryan Thorne, or someone else whose relative is involved, they have some explaining to do."

ABIGAIL WAS STILL nervous when Detective Iglesias returned. But with Griffin at her side she felt stronger and more prepared to face him.

"Griffin." The police officer nodded as he took a seat in the kitchen. Since Maya was sleeping in the den, Abigail had switched the baby monitor on. Now and then, faint sounds of snoring reached them. "Riley has already been in touch, but I told him I don't have much information about this case."

"Who else have you interviewed?" Griffin asked, as the three of them sat at the table.

"Dr. Matthews is the first person I've spoken to in connection with this murder." There was a definite change in the detective's manner. With Griffin he seemed slightly defensive, as though conscious that he would be required to explain his actions.

"And what are your reasons for questioning her first? We know she wasn't the last person to see Dr. Hardin alive," Griffin pointed out. "Dr. Jenna Avery entered his office immediately after Abigail. And, since that was early yesterday morning, it seems unlikely that he didn't speak to anyone else during the course of the day."

Emmanuel rubbed his nose thoughtfully. "Look, I'm not making any judgments here. But I was told that Dr. Matthews and Dr. Hardin didn't have a good relationship after a recent incident. I wouldn't be doing my job if I didn't check that out."

"Ah, yes." As Griffin spoke, Abigail was seeing a different side to his character. She could picture him in a courtroom, tearing holes in the opposing side's argument. "The information you received straight after the doctor was killed. Who told you about that?"

Emmanuel looked surprised. "It was a message that was left for me at the university reception desk. I don't know who it was from."

"And you're happy to act on an anonymous note?" Griffin shot back angrily. "Is that how the GRPD operates these days?"

"Hey." Emmanuel was clearly riled. "I told you I wasn't reaching any conclusions here. This is a starting point. That's all."

"It's okay." Before Griffin could continue, Abigail placed a hand on his arm. "I'll explain the situation to Detective Iglesias. I have plenty of emails from Evan to back up my story. They show that our relationship was a good one."

"Okay." Griffin's expression lightened slightly, but, as he looked at Emmanuel, she could tell he still wasn't happy. "But I want you to do everything you can to find out who sent that note."

The detective held up his hands. "I'll try but it won't be easy."

"Then I want it on the record that my client is freely helping the police despite being questioned on the strength of one very dubious piece of evidence."

"Your client?" Emmanuel raised an eyebrow. "You're practicing criminal law now?" Griffin gave him a frosty look. "Okay. I get the message. Attempts at humor will not be appreciated."

"Dr. Hardin and I did not have a difficult relationship," Abigail said. "On the contrary, we had worked well together for a number of years. I am in charge of one of Evan's research programs. It's a series of clinical trials to test efficacy of a new memory boosting over-the-counter supplement called Mem10. My paternal grandmother died from complications from Alzheimer's and this field has always been dear to my heart."

She bowed her head. This was the hard part and she still couldn't believe she was having to explain this to anyone, let alone a police officer.

"I recently learned that my bid to adopt my foster daughter has been stalled. That was when I discovered I was being investigated over an allegation that

I'd used an illegal enhancement compound, a designer, non-FDA-approved drug called Anthrosyne, to boost some of my participants' memories and to gain recognition for my work. The allegation was false, someone is trying to frame me. I have no idea who would do that, or why, but yesterday morning, Evan suspended me from my job pending an internal investigation."

"How did you feel about that?" Emmanuel asked.

"How do you think she felt?" Griffin snapped. "How would you feel if you were suspended from the job you loved over something you didn't do?"

"I have to ask," Emmanuel said. "You know that."

Although he continued to scowl, Griffin held up his hands in a reluctant gesture of surrender.

"I was devastated but I understood Evan's position," Abigail said. "Neither of us would ever do anything to jeopardize the success of the program."

Emmanuel made a few notes before looking up. "What will happen to the Anthrosyne investigation now that Dr. Hardin is dead?"

"I don't understand." Abigail regarded him in confusion. "I expect another of the Danvers University leadership team members will take over. Why?"

"Just wondering." He tapped his pen on the table. "So the investigation doesn't go away because the guy leading it is dead?"

"Of course not."

"I think what Emmanuel is getting at is that, in terms of the Anthrosyne investigation, you had nothing to gain from killing your boss." For the first time, Griffin looked at the police officer with approval.

"I had nothing to gain in *any* terms." She wanted the words to be forceful, but her voice shook. "I am not a killer."

"Dr. Matthews, I am not suggesting that you are—"

Griffin cut across the detective's explanation. "Do you have a precise time of death?"

"The coroner has estimated that Dr. Hardin was killed between four and six yesterday evening. Until he completes his examination, we won't have anything more accurate," Emmanuel said. "He lived alone, so no one reported him missing. Unfortunately, his killer was in the building when he was working there. Why do you ask?"

"Just that Abigail was at Colton Investigations yesterday afternoon and I was here with her until after midnight last night. If her boss had been murdered around either of those times, I'd have been able to provide an alibi." As Griffin spoke, the doorbell rang. "Are you expecting anyone?" he asked Abigail.

"No." She shook her head.

Emmanuel checked his cell phone. "It's one of my colleagues. Some new evidence has come to light."

"Good," Griffin said. "The sooner you clear Abigail's name the better."

When Abigail went to the door, the second police officer introduced himself as Detective Daniel Lopez. He accompanied her into the kitchen and nodded briefly to Griffin before turning to Emmanuel.

"We found something under Dr. Hardin's desk. It was missed in the initial search, but the CSI team recovered it when they conducted a more detailed examination of the murder scene."

He held up a plastic evidence bag containing a gold charm bracelet with the initials *A* and *M.*

"Is this yours, Dr. Matthews?" Emmanuel asked.

Abigail turned to look at Griffin, her eyes widening as the implications of what she was seeing hit her. "Yes. I lost it at work about a week ago."

Chapter Six

When the two detectives left, Griffin accompanied them to the door. "I don't want to tell you how to do your job—"

"Whenever anyone says those words, they always follow them up by telling us how to do our job." Emmanuel exchanged a weary look with his colleague.

"Don't you think it was odd that the bracelet was missed on the first search?"

Daniel Lopez bristled. "Are you implying that our CSI team didn't do their job properly?"

"No. I'm going one step further than that and suggesting that someone is trying to frame Abigail Matthews." Griffin fought to keep his anger under control. "She hasn't told you this, but she was threatened by the son of a former trial subject yesterday. He told her she'd get what was coming. His name is Ryan Thorne."

"We'll check him out," Emmanuel said. "But, right now, Dr. Matthews still looks like our chief suspect."

"You don't have enough to charge her." Griffin was certain of that. An anonymous note and an item of jewelry that placed Abigail in Dr. Hardin's office at some point? Any decent defense lawyer would get the case thrown out within minutes.

"Not yet. When we do, we'll be back." It sounded a lot like a threat.

"Check the security footage in and around Dr. Hardin's office yesterday evening and this morning, if you haven't already." To hell with not telling them how to do their jobs. "Was Abigail Matthews in the Danvers University building? And find out if anyone went into his office after the first search and before the second one."

Neither detective replied but he could see them processing those instructions.

"Also, Abigail was at the CI headquarters with my family yesterday. My brother and sisters can vouch for that. She left in the middle of the time period during which you're suggesting Dr. Hardin was killed. If she crossed town to kill him, she'd have hit the rush hour traffic. When you have an exact time of death, you might want to check out the times to see if she could have done it within the time available. And, as I've said, I was with her and Maya at her house until after midnight."

Griffin watched the two men walk across the small patch of lawn to their vehicles before he returned to the house. When he reached the kitchen, Abigail had her head in her hands and her slender shoulders were shaking.

Moving swiftly to her side, he drew her to her feet

and held her tight against him. His intention had been to convey his belief in her and reassure her that he would be there for her during this fight. But, as he cradled her head to his chest with one hand and placed the other in the small of her back, a different feeling took hold.

With the warm softness of her breasts against his ribcage and his thighs pressed to her hips, the moment was magical and intimate. Ever since his mother's death, Griffin had believed that physical closeness was overrated. He loved his adopted family, but there had been a distance between them that he'd been unable to overcome. Holding Abigail was about more than wrapping his arms around her. He was enfolding her with his whole body, healing himself as well as her.

"I didn't do it." Her words were muffled by his shirt.

"You don't have to say that to me."

She looked up, her face streaked with tears and her eyelids red and swollen. "Thank you. You don't know what it means to have someone who believes in my innocence."

Her lips were close. So temptingly close that her breath brushed his lips when she spoke. Without thinking, he leaned in to kiss her. Gently, his mouth met hers. Taking all the time in the world, he softly explored the delicate curve of her lips. As she tilted her head to one side, he caressed the seam of her mouth with his tongue.

Winding her arms around his neck, she lightly

nudged his tongue with her own. And passion ignited in an instant…but he knew he had to nip that in the bud. So… Griffin leaned back, examining Abigail's face. "Was that bad timing?"

"Possibly." She gave him a watered-down version of her usual smile. "But it was still very nice."

The doorbell rang and he felt a tremor run through her whole body. "You don't think it's the police again?"

"I'd be surprised if they came back so soon. Why don't I check it out while you make coffee?"

Although her expression didn't lighten, she headed toward the coffee machine on the counter while Griffin went to answer the door. The man who stood on the doorstep looked to be in his late twenties. His expression was serious, even slightly harassed, and he double-checked the front cover of the file he was holding when he saw Griffin.

"I'm looking for Dr. Abigail Matthews."

"Who are you?" The way the day had gone so far, Griffin was in no mood to waste time on politeness.

"My name is John Jones. I think we spoke on the phone recently, Mr. Colton?" Of course. This was the caseworker who oversaw Abigail's guardianship of Maya.

"I don't think Dr. Matthews is expecting you?"

"No. But I need to speak to her. It's urgent."

Griffin didn't like the sound of that, but he could hardly keep the guy standing there. Holding the door wide, he stepped to one side to allow Jones to enter.

When they reached the kitchen, Abigail swung around to face them.

"John? Is everything okay?" It was clear from the strained look on her face that she didn't think it was.

"I'm sorry, Dr. Matthews. I've received information that you are a suspect in a murder case. In the circumstances, I have no choice. I have to remove Maya from your care."

I HAVE RECEIVED INFORMATION…

Those words were suddenly dominating Abigail's life and she had no idea who was behind them. All she knew in that instant was that she couldn't let this man take Maya away from her.

"Please—" Sobs tightened her throat and she couldn't continue.

She couldn't see any way past the pain in her chest. The grief was too much. Then, from somewhere deep inside her came the will to fight. And that was what she needed. For Maya's sake, she would get past the hurt and keep going. "Abigail is not a suspect." Griffin's voice was calm. "As far as I'm aware, the police have no suspects."

The caseworker gave them both an apologetic look. "I've spoken to Detective Iglesias. He tells me that Dr. Matthews is under scrutiny for a number of reasons. Firstly, there is her father's connection to the RevitaYou pyramid scheme. Then, of course, there is the Anthrosyne investigation and Dr. Matthews's suspension. Finally, we have the possibility that she may be implicated in Dr. Hardin's murder. And I believe there have also been threats issued against her as a result of some of these issues. Believe me, I wouldn't do this unless the situation was serious."

"But you can't think I would harm Maya," Abigail said. "And surely that's the only reason to take her from me?"

"You've been threatened, and that means that Maya could also be harmed..."

"Abigail has been Maya's only caregiver since her birth," Griffin interrupted. "And you must know that the baby is in no danger from her own foster mother."

"That's true. There is no question that Maya is in any danger from Dr. Matthews," John admitted. "But we have to consider Maya's overall welfare. The threats that have been made against you are too vague and could pose a danger to the baby. There are just too many negative elements for me to consider this a safe place for her."

"When will you be taking Maya?" Griffin asked.

"Right now."

"Oh, no." Jolted out of the shock that had kept her passive while they talked as though they were in a court of law and she wasn't there, Abigail made a move as if to block the door. Her thoughts broke free like a dam breaking. No one was taking her little girl. Not while she had breath in her body. "No." She choked back a sob, terror gripping her. "This is her home. I'm her mom. You can't take her from me."

"I'm sorry." John looked uncomfortable.

"We both know Children's Protective Services is stretched to the limits and that includes the foster system," Griffin said. "Where will you take Maya?"

"I'll be honest with you, I don't know right now. We're so backlogged with cases that I don't have a clear plan. All I know is that Maya will have to be placed elsewhere until Dr. Matthews is fully cleared."

Abigail sank into one of the chairs, feeling the blood draining from her face. Clearly alarmed for her well-being, Griffin squatted at her side. "Breathe deeply. In through your nose and out through your mouth."

She gazed at him blankly. As she followed his instructions, the faintness that had threatened to overwhelm her gave way to a shard of pain in her gut. "My baby..."

She couldn't continue. All she could think was that she couldn't let this happen, but at the same time, her body was going into shock. Cold fear was spreading along her limbs and all she could do was stare at Griffin, as though searching for an answer in his eyes.

"*I'll* take Maya." He turned his head to look at the caseworker.

"Pardon?" John stared at him as though he'd just grown another head.

"I have been certified as a foster parent for five years. I keep my registration up-to-date and I'm known to your agency." He gripped Abigail's hands tightly. "What objection could there be?"

John gave him a doubtful look. "This is an unusual situation. I need to call my boss before I give you an answer." He gestured toward the hall. "Can I step outside?"

Abigail nodded. "Of course."

When the caseworker had left the room and closed the door, she picked up the still sleeping Maya and held her close, burying her face briefly in the little girl's hair, before studying Griffin's face. "I am not going to turn down this offer but what made you decide to become a foster parent?"

"Firstly, let me make it clear that, although I have certification, I have never actually fostered a child. I know very little about being a parent." He paused for a moment as if gathering his thoughts. "Being adopted shaped who I am, and not always in a good way. Don't get me wrong. I love my Colton family. I appreciate them and I am thankful every day that they are a part of my life. But I grew up feeling different from them. We don't share the same genes. I never had those bonding moments when you look at someone across the room and realize that you resemble them."

He shook his head as though wondering where this outpouring was coming from. She thought again about her first impressions of him as a stiff, unyielding figure and how wrong she'd been.

"In spite of that, what Graham and Kathleen did when they offered me a place in their family has always resonated with me. I am in awe of people like them." He lifted her hand to his lips briefly. "And like you. People who offer a loving home to a child who is not theirs by birth. If the time came when I was faced with a situation that needed me to step up, I wanted to be able to do it. But the paperwork to register as a foster parent can be time consuming."

She rolled her eyes. "Tell me about it."

"The agency screens the home and life of prospective foster parents, including family background, employment history, determination of any past abuse, criminal background checks, finances and medical history. They conduct a physical examination of the home, which includes cleanliness and condition, sanitation, fire safety and nature of the neighborhood in which the home is located. There is also a consideration of the desire and motivation to foster." Griffin ticked each item off on his fingers. "That sort of detail doesn't happen in a hurry. I decided that, if I was serious about being ready to step up at any time, I needed to have my certification in place and keep it up-to-date."

"And this is your time to step up?" Her voice was husky.

"I figure it's better than letting Maya go to a stranger or into a childcare facility."

She choked back a sob. "I don't know how to thank you."

"Hey." He used his thumb to wipe away a tear that trickled down her cheek. "You don't have to thank me. And there are some logistics we'll need to talk about—"

Before he could continue, John Jones came back

into the room. "My boss has given his approval for you to foster Maya."

Griffin got to his feet. "I have a condition."

The caseworker and Abigail both regarded him warily. "I'm assuming that Maya will need to come and live in my home as part of the foster care plan?"

"That's right," John said.

"She's a nine-month-old baby who has only ever known the care of one person. Dr. Matthews is her mother. This is a very delicate stage in Maya's development. I am not prepared to do anything to unsettle her." He drew himself up to his full height, ensuring he had their full attention before making his next statement. "Which is why Dr. Matthews must move into my house with us until this matter is resolved."

Gratitude flooded through Abigail, leaving her speechless. This man, who she barely knew, was prepared to do this for her and Maya. He was going to turn his life upside down to make sure they could stay together. She already knew he was a good man. She was only just realizing that he was truly remarkable. Any woman would be lucky to have him as her partner and the father of her children.

"I'm not sure—" John tugged at his lower lip.

"What objection can there be?" Griffin asked. "I will be Maya's foster parent. I'll take full responsibility for her welfare and safety. And you've already admitted that she is in no danger from Dr. Matthews. The perceived danger is from those who might wish to harm Dr. Matthews."

"But you work full-time," John said.

"I'll take a leave of absence. My junior colleagues can pick up my cases and I'll supervise them from home."

"In that case, I guess it will be okay," John conceded. "There will be some paperwork to go through."

"You can bring it around to my place." He turned to Abigail. "Does this arrangement suit you?" She nodded at him over Maya's head. "Right now, Abigail and I need to get started on packing Maya's stuff."

ALMOST IMMEDIATELY AFTER John left, Maya woke up and started to wail.

"Since the child welfare authorities will do regular assessments going forward, I need to do some actual parenting." Griffin followed Abigail into the den and watched as she lifted the baby from the crib. "But I told you, I know nothing about this. I'm at a loss. Is she in pain?"

"No. She always wakes up hungry." The baby calmed down a little when she was cradled against Abigail's chest. "She has been eating solid food since she was six months old, but she still has formula several times a day. Although I keep it chilled, and there's no reason why she couldn't drink it at that temperature, she prefers it a little warmer."

As she spoke, she went back into the kitchen. Expertly holding Maya on one arm, she heated water on the stove, took a bottle of formula from the fridge, then poured the water into a jug and placed the formula into it.

"It only takes a minute or two." She smiled down at Maya as she spoke. "But this little lady doesn't do patience, so we have to sing songs while we wait."

Griffin regarded her in alarm. "I can't sing."

"Maya won't be judging your singing ability. It's the sound of your voice she's interested in." He thought he glimpsed a gleam of mischief in her eyes. "She likes rock ballads."

"You have got to be joking—"

"Quick. Or she'll start crying again."

He gave her a reproachful look and, from the depths of his memory, dredged up a song that his dad, Graham, used to play when he was driving. Fumbling his way through the first verse, he reached the chorus and was just starting to feel more confident when Maya, who had been regarding him with a horrified expression, threw back her head and started to scream.

"I told you I was no good at this," he told Abigail.

She made a suspicious choking sound. "I don't think she likes that particular band."

"In the future, make sure you give me her playlist in advance."

"Luckily, her formula is now ready." She retrieved the bottle from the jug of water and dried it with a muslin cloth. "You can redeem yourself by feeding her."

Maya had stopped crying, but she was still watching him with distrust. "Will she be okay with that?"

"As long as you have the magic bottle, she'll be fine." Abigail pointed to a chair. "Sit down and I'll hand her over."

Once Griffin was seated, Abigail placed Maya on his lap. Gripping her under her arms, he studied her with concern. She appeared to be quite robust. But how was he supposed to maneuver her so that he could get the bottle to her mouth?

"She's a baby, not a ticking bomb." There was a hint of sympathy in Abigail's smile.

Taking one of his hands, she drew it around Maya's body and eased the little girl back into the crook of his arms before holding out the bottle. The baby instantly grabbed it and pulled it to her mouth with a contented sigh. As she drank, her intent gaze fixed on his face and Griffin felt a new warmth bloom deep in his chest. This little person was somehow reaching out to him with that look, trying to figure out who he was, and establish a connection with him.

"Do you talk to her while she drinks?" Suddenly, getting it right was about more than food, and warmth and shelter.

"Yes. She likes that," Abigail said. "Don't worry about what you say. It's the sound of your voice that matters most."

She moved away and started to stack items of baby food together on the counter. After giving the matter some thought, Griffin decided to talk to Maya about a subject close to his heart.

"You may not know this, but there is a hockey team

called the Grand Rapids Griffins. Their logo is a griffin. It's a legendary creature with the body, tail and back legs of a lion, and the head and wings of an eagle. You'd think it would be cool to be named after something like that, wouldn't you? And maybe it would be. For some people." Even though she had her back to him, he sensed Abigail was listening carefully. "Anyway, the Grand Rapids Griffins play at Van Andel Arena. We should go there during the season and you can help me cheer them on. You and your mom."

Maya drained the last of her formula and let out a loud belch.

"Not a hockey fan, huh? I guess if we can't enjoy the same sports, we can find out if we have other things in common. What do you like to do in your spare time?"

"She enjoys putting things in her mouth, especially things that shouldn't be there," Abigail said. "Cruising around the furniture is a new favorite, and she never tires of throwing things out of the bath, stroller or high chair."

"I guess I could learn to share her appreciation of those things."

"Right now, it's time for a diaper change." Abigail moved purposefully toward them. "And that's something Maya definitely isn't fond of."

"I'd forgotten about diapers." Griffin rolled his eyes.

"Get ready for your first lesson."

"I may have to ask my brother for some advice. We

have two sets of twins as siblings and he took on much of their care when we were growing up."

"He sounds like a good person to have on speed dial."

She took Maya from him and carried her through to the den. In a corner of the room, there was a changing mat and a plastic box with all the things that were needed for a diaper change. As soon as Abigail knelt and put Maya on her back on the mat, the baby giggled and rolled onto her front.

"You need to be fast." Abigail flipped her gently but deftly over again. Keeping one forearm across the little girl's stomach, she reached into the box and produced a toy that looked like a bunch of keys. When Maya saw it, she waved her chubby hands in the air until Abigail handed it over. She then alternated between shaking the keys wildly and chewing them. "And you need to distract her."

"Should I be taking notes?" He knelt beside Abigail, watching in fascination as she swiftly removed Maya's socks and pink sweatpants.

"Don't worry. I'll be right here at your side."

He wanted to tell her how much he liked the sound of that, although maybe not in the context of dirty diapers, but she was reaching into the box again.

"Talk me through what you're doing."

"I'm getting unscented baby wipes, so I can clean her skin. That's the best way to prevent diaper rash. If a rash does develop, she needs plenty of diaper-free time and some ointment to help her heal." Abigail placed the pack of wipes next to the mat. "We also need a biodegradable bag so we can dispose of the used diaper." She looked at him with a grin. "At least she hasn't pooped this time."

"How do you know?"

"Oh, you'll know when she's pooped." She leaned over to look Maya in the eye. "Go easy on Griffin. He has yet to encounter you at your stinkiest."

Maya chuckled and waved her toy keys in a celebratory gesture. It seemed to take Abigail only a few seconds to remove the old diaper, clean Maya's delicate skin and have her completely changed. Griffin was certain he would not be able to perform the same series of actions on the small, wriggling body so skillfully or quickly.

Once Maya was upright again and seated on the changing mat, she offered Griffin her toy. Touched by the gesture, he reached out to take it, only to have her snatch it away at the last minute. Still holding the keys, Maya clapped her hands and grinned at him.

"That's another thing she likes," Abigail told him, as she cleared away the changing accessories. "Playing teasing games." She sat back on her heels. "How will it work? Us moving into your place?"

"I have plenty of space. I grew up in Heritage Hill and always loved it. When it came to finding a home of my own, I knew there was only one place I wanted to live. Of course, those old houses aren't really suitable for a man on his own but I found a first floor apartment that needed renovation just a few blocks from the house where Riley still lives and from which he runs Colton Investigations."

"Those buildings are amazing." There was a genuine note of envy in Abigail's voice. "I remember walking around that neighborhood with my mom when I was very small. It was like stepping back in time."

"Trying to rebuild my place and stay true to the original style has been hard," Griffin said. "It's almost finished but it's been a labor of love. Anyway, I have three bedrooms, two bathrooms and a garden. There's plenty of room for Maya to play. There is just one thing I think we should talk about."

"What's that?"

"I think it's important to decide how we're going to introduce Maya to Lucy."

Chapter Seven

The fact that Griffin had mentioned introducing Maya to someone called Lucy implied that this person was significant in his life. At that moment, Abigail realized she had made an assumption that he was single, based on the attraction between them. That, and the kiss they had shared. But she barely knew him. It was possible he was in a relationship and he cheated on his partner.

She wasn't comfortable with that image of him. No, it went deeper than that. She had started to develop feelings for him and she felt betrayed. Yet, it was at odds with her instincts and everything she had learned in the time she had known him. Griffin Colton was trustworthy when it came to his work. She *knew* that. But that left some unanswered questions about how he acted in his personal life.

She may as well start with the obvious one. "Is Lucy your roommate?"

He laughed. "That's one way of describing her." He drew out his cell phone and started scrolling. When he found what he was looking for, he held it up. "This is Lucy."

Abigail studied the picture on the screen. At least it wasn't a gorgeous woman. Instead, it was a cute creature with a pink nose, a circular blond stripe around its light brown face and teddy-bear ears. "Is it a kitten? No. A mongoose?"

"Lucy is a ferret. Full name Lucy Fur. As in Lucifer. Because she's a demon."

She cast a worried glance in Maya's direction. "When you say 'demon'—?"

"Oh, Lucy doesn't bite. She just steals things. And hides. And eats things she shouldn't. Like shoes and electrical cables." Griffin rolled his eyes. "There are some states that don't allow ferret ownership. I've told her I'm going to move to one, but Lucy doesn't respond to threats."

Abigail laughed. "What made you choose a ferret as a pet?"

"I didn't. Lucy chose me," Griffin said. "About two years ago, I found her in my garden. She was only a youngster and she was badly injured. I think she may have been in a fight with a cat or a dog. I took her to the vet, and they took care of her, but they had nowhere for her to go. Unlike cats and dogs, there are few animal rescue centers that welcome ferrets. I couldn't bear to see such a sweet, healthy animal euthanized, so Lucy came home with me."

"It sounds like she and Maya will get along just

fine." She chewed her lip nervously. "But don't ferrets carry disease and bite?"

He looked relieved. "Lucy has a cage. It's not like she has the freedom of the house all the time. We can introduce them gradually and make sure they are always supervised."

She stooped to pick up Maya, feeling comforted by the baby's warm weight on her hip. "I don't want to disrupt your life, Griffin."

"Leaving my ferret in her cage for a little longer each day will not have an adverse effect on my well-being." He grinned. "Quite the opposite."

The temptation to return his smile was irresistible but she wanted to let him know she was serious. "You know that's not what I meant."

He placed a hand on her arm. "I want to do this for you, Abigail."

She studied his face, searching for something behind the smile. Growing up with Wes Matthews had made her suspicious of everyone's motives. With her dad there was always another angle, always a reason to turn on the charm. Although she knew there was such a thing as a nice guy, her judgment was skewed by her past experiences. Could Griffin be what he appeared? Strong, kind, dependable and protective? She hoped so, but she had learned to hold part of her trust back. Just in case.

"Why?" The word slipped out, and she winced. Would he think her ungrateful? Questioning his motives wasn't the best way to start this new relationship.

"Because I think you're innocent and you've had a raw deal. Because I want to make sure that Maya doesn't suffer because of what is going on." He took a step closer. "And because I like you."

Oh, goodness. The warmth in his eyes made her heart develop an extra little beat. Feeling like a school-girl with a crush, she gazed up at him. Clearly feeling that the moment had stretched out a little too long without any action, Maya reached out and gave Griffin a punch on the chin. The action broke the mood and, as they started to laugh, Maya clapped her hands.

"We should probably think about getting your things together ready to take to my place."

She sighed. "That's going to be such a big job."

"It doesn't have to be." He always managed to sound so reasonable and soothing. "It's not like you have to do it all at once. Pack enough for a day or two. We can always come back for more." He hesitated. "I don't want to pry, but are you going to be okay financially?"

"Yes. I have savings and a small legacy from my mom." She cleared her throat. "If you need me to pay rent…"

He looked horrified. "That was *not* why I asked. I was wondering if you needed a loan."

She started to laugh. "Are you always so sensible?"

"Do you mean boring?"

She shook her head, eager to reassure him. "That is the last word I would use to describe you."

"Maybe you can do some PR within my family? I

could use some help to lose the reverse-rebel label," Griffin said. "Don't get me wrong. I don't want to be considered wild. But I've been the don't-know-how-to-party animal among my siblings for too long."

"If you're expecting me and Maya to change all that, you definitely don't know much about babies. I guarantee you'll be too exhausted to even think."

He laughed. "You're joking, right? How difficult can it be, taking care of one small child?"

At six o'clock the next morning, Griffin was seated at his own kitchen table. Uncertain whether he was dreaming, he gulped down a mouthful of coffee. It was hot and strong, the way he liked it, but his body was in shock after a sleepless night and he shuddered.

"Okay. I think the fact that my taste buds are working must mean I'm awake."

Abigail, who was slumped in a chair next to him, slowly turned her head in his direction. The movement seemed to require more effort than usual. "You took over pacing the floor with Maya from me. That was at two-thirty. She finally fell asleep at five. So, yes. Unless you've been sleepwalking all this time, you're awake."

Griffin rubbed a hand along his chin, feeling the stubble scratch his palm. "You said looking after a baby was exhausting, but last night was beyond anything I imagined. Is it always like this?"

"No." She sat up straighter. "Most of the time, Maya sleeps through. The only times she has a problem are if she's unwell, or teething. I think she had trouble settling last night because she's in a strange place."

"At least she's sleeping now," Griffin said. "I felt so sorry for her. And so helpless. It's awful seeing her get upset."

"You did a great job of comforting her," Abigail said. "It's distressing because babies don't know they're tired. They just know they feel bad. If Maya could just sleep, it would all be okay. But, of course, she cries and that makes her more exhausted and unhappy."

"I don't want the change of environment to have an adverse effect on her."

"She's resilient," Abigail said. "And, as you said, she has me to keep things normal for her. I'm sure she'll be okay." She smothered a yawn behind her hand. "Although we may be in for a few more sleepless nights before she gets into a routine."

Although she was pale, and her hair was mussed up, she still managed to look beautiful. Her pajama shorts and tank top showed off her long, tanned limbs and, even though he was so tired that lifting his coffee cup felt like a superhuman effort, her nearness was intoxicating. It was one of the things he hadn't thought through when he'd proposed this solution to her problems.

His first thought had been that Maya must not be placed with strangers. By offering to foster Abigail's daughter, he hadn't considered that mother and child would come as a package. Having them under his roof would bring him more challenges than he could have foreseen. And among them would be the attraction he felt for Abigail.

Or was he fooling himself? When he'd issued the invitation for Abigail to stay at his place with Maya, he'd realized that they would be in close proximity. Hadn't he been excited at the prospect and the opportunities it would bring? He was torn. Part of him wanted to take things further and act on the attraction between them. At the same time, he was conscious of her vulnerability.

Abigail was in danger. He was certain of that. Someone was trying to ruin her life and that person was so determined to succeed that he, or she, had already committed murder. Griffin was committed to protecting her and helping uncover the truth. Yet he was also part of the team working to find her father and bring him to justice. It would be stepping outside of his supportive role if he began a relationship with a woman in Abigail's position.

He had always taken such care to safeguard his heart. For the first time, he had an urge to set caution aside and see where his feelings might take him. The irony was that he couldn't act on it. He didn't know what the future held, but he'd have liked the chance to find out if Abigail had a part to play in his.

As Abigail tried to hide another yawn, he decided to focus on how he could provide practical help in the present. "Why don't you take a nap while the baby is asleep?"

"What about you?" Abigail asked. "We're equally tired."

"I need to check my emails and messages. I can always rest this afternoon."

"If you're sure?" She got to her feet. "Come and get me when Maya wakes up."

He placed a hand on his heart, pretending to be hurt. "Do you think I won't be able to cope?"

"I didn't mean—"

He laughed. "Get some sleep. Maya and I will be fine."

When Abigail opened her eyes a few hours later, she was confused by the light streaming through a gap in the drapes and by the strange room. Her first reaction was panic as she wondered why she was sleeping in the day and where Maya could be. As she came fully awake and recalled the events of the past few days, the initial alarm subsided. But the anxiety that had been with her since she had learned about the allegations against her remained.

She was still struggling to come to terms with how dramatically her life had changed. She had stepped outside her comfort zone when she'd agreed to adopt Maya but that had proved to be one of the best decisions of her life. Having lost Veronica, she not only had a permanent reminder of her friend in her life, she also now had a child of her own. The love she felt for Maya was as all-consuming as it had been unexpected at first.

But struggling with the loss of her closest friend, and still getting used to motherhood, she had then been hit with the shocking news about her father's role in the RevitaYou con. As a child, she'd been dazzled by him. His stories were magical. There was the pet monkey that played checkers with him. The time he smuggled diamonds out of South Africa. His heroic military record. As Abigail grew older, she began to see flaws in his anecdotes. Sometimes, the details changed...

She'd had other questions. Why did he have so many cell phones? Why did people call him by different names? Wes always had an explanation. Finally, just before her mom left, he had confessed. He was a spy, working at that time on a top-secret mission to foil a dangerous enemy plot against the government. Fascinated, and eager to see him in action, she'd followed him out of the house one afternoon. He'd gone to a local bar, gotten drunk and thrown up in the gutter on his way home.

And that was when it had hit her. Everything her father had told her about himself was a lie. Twenty-five years later, she wasn't surprised that he was still lying and cheating his way through life. What upset her most about RevitaYou was Wes's complete lack of concern for the consequences while he was taking people's money, often their life savings. Surely he must have foreseen that packaging a product that contained a poison and labeling it as a vitamin would cause harm to at least some of those who used it? The fact that he had gone ahead anyway was an indication that he didn't care.

What hurt almost as much was that so many people still believed that Abigail was part of the scheme. Ever since that day when she had realized that her father was a liar, she had been scared of her own genetics. Whenever she was faced with a tough decision, a little voice inside her head always wondered, "What would Wes do?" The answer was straightforward, of course. Wes would take the easy way, not the right way. So far, Abigail had been hand-on-heart happy with her own choices. She didn't take after her dad. Sadly, the rest of the world didn't know that.

Except for Griffin. She didn't know why he believed in her. She just knew he was genuine, and she was glad of his strength and encouragement when everyone else seemed determined to condemn her. His support had become doubly important since the Anthrosyne investigation and Dr. Hardin's murder. Without Griffin... She sat up abruptly. Fortunately, she had Griffin at her side. Picturing the loneliness and despair of fighting these allegations alone was a waste of time and emotion.

The apartment was very quiet. Too quiet for a place that contained Maya, who must be awake by now. Pushing back the bedclothes, she got to her feet. Still dressed in her shorts and tank, she slipped her feet into sneakers and pulled on a lightweight sweatshirt before leaving the bedroom. Following the central hall, she headed toward the kitchen.

There was a small closet to one side of the back door, and this housed the cage belonging to Lucy, the ferret. Although Griffin had shown his pet to Abigail and Maya on the previous day, Lucy had proved elusive, hiding in her bed with only the tips of her ears showing. Now, as Abigail passed, the little creature darted up to the bars and watched her with bright, beady eyes.

"Maybe we can hang out later," Abigail said. "Right now, I need to find my daughter."

It wasn't difficult to track Griffin and Maya down. All she needed to do was follow the trail of destruction. In the kitchen, there was cereal, milk and flour—*flour?*—on the floor. Going through to the den, she found most of Griffin's books pulled off the lower shelf of his bookcase and thrown onto the floor. Photograph frames were tipped over, cushions thrown from the chairs. Abigail recognized the hand at work. The scene looked like her own home most days.

She heard Maya's laugh and looked out the window. Griffin was sitting on the small lawn and the baby was wriggling on her stomach toward him. She appeared to be holding a plant.

Abigail retraced her steps through the kitchen and went out the back door. The yard was small and neat and the first thing she noticed was that a row of herbs had been pulled out of their pots and scattered across the steps.

"You should stop her when she goes into destructo-baby mode," she said.

Griffin greeted her with a smile. "Yeah. You'll have to show me how you do that. So far, nothing I've tried has had any impact."

When Maya saw Abigail, she dropped the leaves she'd been holding out to Griffin and raised her dirty hands to her mom instead.

"Come here, you." Abigail scooped her up and swung her round, causing Maya to squeal with delight.

She was conscious of Griffin watching them attentively. It was possible he was enjoying the moment or hoping to pick up some tips on how to deal with a nine-month-old whirlwind. But when she looked up and met his gaze, the heat in the depths of his eyes threatened to burn her up. It also ignited an answering flame deep inside her. A wave of emotion washed over her and she lost herself in that instant.

It was incredible that she could feel so attracted to him, in spite of the turmoil in her life. When she was with Griffin, she felt happy and at peace in a way she'd never experienced before. She only wished it was something they had time to explore.

"I saw that Maya trashed the kitchen. Did she happen to also eat breakfast?"

"Yes, she had cereal and a cup of milk. I wasn't sure how much to give her but, when she was finished, she threw the leftovers on the floor." He came closer and tickled Maya under the chin. "I sat her on the counter to clean her up and that's when she tipped a bag of flour over as well. She's fast."

"She is," Abigail agreed. "And stubborn. Once she decides that she wants something, she doesn't give up."

"What about you? Did you sleep okay? Would you like some toast and coffee?" There was that smile again, the one that warmed her and made her shiver at the same time. "Although it's closer to lunch than breakfast now."

"I slept really well." She looked down at her unconventional outfit. "But maybe I should shower and change before I think about food?"

"You look great to me." As he spoke, he appeared to have second thoughts about the message his words might convey. "I mean, your clothes look fine." He paused, clearly thinking some more. "And so do you, of course."

Abigail laughed. "It's okay. Neither my clothes nor I need any further explanation of your meaning."

He rubbed a hand along his jaw. "I'm not used to this."

"Really? I'd never have guessed." They exchanged a teasing look that was lost when Maya rubbed a grubby hand down Abigail's cheek. "Why don't I take this little lady with me? That way we can both shower and change."

"While you do that, I'll make lunch," Griffin said. "And then I thought we could do some research into the scientist who assisted your dad on the RevitaYou scheme."

Abigail sighed. "I like part of that plan. And I guess we have to do the other part if we are going to move forward with the investigation."

Chapter Eight

RevitaYou came in pretty green bottles, each containing a thirty-day supply of capsules. The accompanying glossy brochure was written in flowery language and promised to make the lucky purchaser look ten years younger within one week of directed use.

"Look." Griffin pointed to the very small print on the last page. "There are no contact details, but your dad is listed as the founder of the company. There is no information about who might have collaborated with him on this breakthrough invention."

They were seated side by side at the desk in his small office. Maya was taking a post-lunch nap and Abigail had brought the baby monitor into the room. The occasional mumble or snort reminded them of her presence.

Abigail leaned closer, her hair brushing his cheek as she squinted at the tiny writing. "I still have access to the forums on the university website. It's possible the project was mentioned when it was in its early stages."

Griffin shrugged. "We've done everything we can think of at CI. It has to be worth a try."

For the next half hour, they sat in silence while Abigail followed different threads and tried new searches. Just as she started to lean back in her chair with an expression of gloom, her gaze fixed on the screen.

"Landon Street. Ugh. I know that guy."

Griffin turned his head to look at her, trying to focus on the conversation instead of the fact that their faces were inches apart. "The way you said that makes me suspect that what you know of him isn't good."

"Landon Street has to be the most unethical chemist in the country. He worked at Danvers University a few years ago." The corners of her mouth turned down. "If there was a way to cut a corner, Landon would find it. He constantly skirted close to the edge of illegal practice. His research papers were sloppy, and he let his colleagues down time after time. I can't remember how many violations he had in the short time he worked at the university."

"What happened to him?"

"He took his shoddy methods a step too far. He'd already been moved into a lesser post because he couldn't be trusted. On the occasion in question, he was supposed to assist in a new clinical trial that would help elderly subjects with pressure sores. His supervisor gave him a schedule in which he needed to check each person weekly. Landon decided that was too often and, without consulting his boss, reduced the checks to once a month. The result was that one man developed an infection and almost died."

"That's criminal." Griffin was outraged.

"You're right, of course. The problem was that Landon's conduct reflected badly on Danvers University." She gave a helpless shrug. "It would not have been my way of dealing with the matter, but I believe the university settled out of court with the family and let Landon go but stopped short of suggesting his license should be revoked."

"That's appalling. He could have gone on to kill someone."

She pointed at the screen. "If I'm right, Landon could be responsible for formulating RevitaYou, and that may still happen. In this thread, there is a suggestion that he is working on a new vitamin."

Sensing her distress, he placed a hand on her wrist. "What happened to Landon after he left Danvers University?"

She frowned. "I don't know. Why do you ask?"

"I'm wondering how your father got to know him. Do crooked scientists advertise their credentials anywhere in particular? Maybe they offer their services to con artists through dedicated webpages or on social media?"

She managed a smile. "It's an interesting idea. But I'm not dodgy so I wouldn't know."

"I would never suggest that you were." He gripped her wrist a little tighter before opening his laptop. "Let's see what we can find out about Landon Street."

An internet search took them along a convoluted path. After leaving Danvers University, Landon Street's name cropped up in connection with a number of medical practices. It seemed he would lend his name to any venture, mainstream, alternative, even wacky. More recently, however, he had been involved in a few shady undertakings. There were beauty products, anti-aging drugs and miracle cures with his name attached to them. Quick fixes that had gone out of production within months, or even weeks, of their launch.

Scrolling through his history made depressing reading. If Wes Matthews had gone looking for an unethical scientist to assist him with RevitaYou, these credentials would have put Landon top of the list.

"Wait." Abigail was studying the search results with a puzzled expression. "Can you click on that link?"

It was an entry in article in a Danvers University online academic journal, written several years earlier. The writer had included a photograph of a team of scientists at Danvers University who had received an award for their pioneering work in researching prevention of early miscarriage. As she read it, Abigail leaned closer, the frown line between her eyes deepening.

"Is there a problem?" Griffin asked.

"Yes." Abigail pointed to the text on the screen. "This has been altered. See here, where the participants in the program are listed?" She pointed to a paragraph near the end of the article. "I was part of that research project and I know my name was in-cluded when this piece first went out. You can see from the photograph that I was among those who re-ceived the award. I'm right there, front and center. But all references to me have been removed."

Griffin whistled. "Why would anyone do that?"

"I don't know. To discredit me, maybe? But there's more. Landon Street is listed as one of the team who won the award. He didn't even work at Danvers at the time. He's not in this photograph."

Griffin followed the line of her finger as she pointed to the individuals on the podium holding up their awards. "How can you be so sure that the article has been altered and not that these were mistakes to the original?"

She scrolled down to the end, indicating the name of the author. "Because I wrote it."

AN HOUR LATER, Abigail slumped back in her seat. "I don't believe this. We've checked five articles so far. Each of them included references to work I've done They have all been altered so that my name has been removed and another scientist has been inserted in my place."

"But a different person has been substituted each time," Griffin said. "Only the first one gives credit for your work to Landon Street."

"Even so, it's like someone is trying to obliterate my achievements and ruin my career." She rubbed her eyes with her knuckles. "On top of everything else."

"Since we know he's crooked, let's start with Landon. Could he be the one who is behind the other attempts to discredit you? Even the murder of Dr. Hardin?" Griffin asked.

Abigail took a few moments to think about what he was asking. "Landon is not a nice guy, that much is clear from his actions. But is he capable of premeditated murder? I honestly couldn't answer that question because I don't know him well enough. And that's why I don't think he's the person behind the attempts to ruin me. He doesn't have a motive."

"He doesn't have a reason *that you know of,*" Griffin said. "But if he has ties to your dad, who knows what's been going on behind the scenes? They could have fallen out and getting at you is Landon's way of paying Wes back. Or if Dr. Hardin antagonized him, Landon may have believed you were behind it, even though you weren't."

"Oh." She sprang to her feet, crossing her arms over her chest. "I wish we knew what was going on. This feeling that someone is out to get me without know who is just so frustrating."

He got up and came to her, placing strong hands on her shoulders. "And frightening. I know how scared you must be."

She rested her forehead against his chest. "I've never known anything like this. The idea that I've made someone hate me so much—"

"Hey." He placed a hand beneath her chin, gently

tilting her face until she was looking at him. "This is not about anything *you've* done."

She drew in a breath. "Try telling that to the person who killed my boss."

"Whoever murdered Dr. Hardin did it for reasons that were outside of your control, Abigail. The killer will try to justify it by blaming you, but you must never be drawn into that." He stroked her cheek with his thumb. "Stay strong. We'll get through this together."

Together. She liked the sound of that more than she could say. Rising onto the tips of her toes, she lightly touched her lips to his in a butterfly kiss. The gesture triggered a storm that nearly knocked her off her feet. Griffin's arms tightened around her, enfolding her in his embrace. He took hold of her chin with one hand, tilting her face up to his as he moved his lips over hers. This kiss was strong and warm, filled with passion, letting her know how much he wanted her. Instantly, her body ached for more. Arousal powered along her nerve endings, awakening a need within her, filling her with a passion that was unlike anything she'd ever experienced.

She clung to him, lost in the magic of his mouth caressing hers. He teased her, nibbling at her lower lip, flicking his tongue over the sensitive flesh. Sighing into his mouth, she surrendered to the delicious feelings churning through her. This was what it should feel like to be held by a man. She felt cherished and wanted. As though she had truly come to life at his touch.

Her lips parted, welcoming his tongue inside her mouth. She savored the velvet feel and warm, sweet taste of him. As their tongues danced and explored, he twisted his hands in the length of her hair. Finally, he broke the kiss and gazed down at her. The tenderness in his eyes said more than any words ever could.

"I think we forgot to be serious, dedicated investigators for a moment, there." She flashed a mischievous smile his way.

"Is that what we did?" His answering grin did something sinful to her insides.

Briefly, she rested her head against his shoulder. "Let's not get carried away. Maya will wake up soon."

He squeezed her upper arm. "Okay. Back to Landon Street."

Abigail groaned. "You sure know how to kill the mood."

He laughed. "You were the one who said we shouldn't get carried away."

"So it's my fault we go from delicious kisses to bad guy scientists?"

His eyes gleamed. "Delicious, huh?"

She bumped his shoulder with her own. "Oh, come on. You must have been told that dozens of times."

"Funnily enough, I haven't." His expression became serious. "Prior to getting involved in RevitaYou, Landon seems to have been lying low. Which makes me wonder where he is now. I need to call Riley."

"Do you want me to give you some privacy?"

He shook his head. "You're part of the CI team now."

As he got out his cell phone and found his brother's number, she studied the laptop screen, glad of a distraction. *Part of the CI team.* Apart from her job, she'd never felt part of anything. Even then, she'd always been the geeky girl on the fringes, rather than Miss Popularity. Coming soon after that incredible kiss, Griffin's words had caught her unawares and left her feeling shaken.

It was *him.* Griffin was the reason for her confusion. In the short time she had known him, he had turned her world upside down. His presence was reassuring and disturbing at the same time. And, while she loved the sensations this new attraction brought her way, she feared them as well. Until recently, her only meaningful relationship had been with her career. Now she was a new mom. She had responsibilities that were beyond anything she'd ever known before. Surely it was too soon to consider a romantic relationship as well? And with a Colton?

No. The hugs were wonderful. The kisses were even better. But she had to put them in context. Her life was in turmoil. She was scared, confused and lonely. Griffin had offered her shelter and protection, and he was the only person who appeared to believe in her. Was it any wonder she found herself drawn to him?

Try this attraction out another time. Like when life is back to normal. Whenever that might be...

"Riley? I need you to trace someone for me as part of the RevitaYou investigation." Griffin was talking to his brother. "A Dr. Landon Street. He's the person Wes Matthews used to develop the RevitaYou formula. I'm going to send you some links to his background but I also need to know where he is now. He may be able to help us find Wes."

He ended the call after chatting briefly to Riley about other matters.

"Do you think Landon could still be in touch with my dad?" Abigail asked. "They are in this together, after all."

"It's a possibility. The bad publicity following the social media blasts will have spooked them both. We know Wes is lying low, but there's a chance he and Landon have been in contact with each other. Maybe Landon even knows where Wes is hiding."

"It's like every piece of information we find about RevitaYou paints a worse picture." She shook her head. "And it was my dad who did this. He was the person who thought up this con. For the sake of the people whose lives have been affected, he has to face justice. But, and this sounds horribly selfish, I know that Maya and I will be tainted by what he's done."

"That's not true. When he's found, and the truth comes out, people will see that you had nothing to do with his schemes."

"But I'll always be Wes Matthews's daughter," she

said. "And, even though Maya has never met him, she will always be his granddaughter. Assuming the adoption goes through."

"Maya will always be the daughter of the strong, beautiful woman who chose to raise her." His voice resonated with sincerity. "I wish there was something I could do to make this better for you."

"You do make it better, Griffin." In that moment her doubts faded to nothing. He hadn't come into her life at the wrong time. When she needed him, he was at her side. The future might bring its challenges, but that simple truth was enough for now. "Just by being here, you do."

ABIGAIL WAS AMAZED at the way the Colton family worked so well as a unit. Griffin had told his siblings that they needed more of Abigail and Maya's belongings brought from home and the next thing she knew, there was a whole moving process underway.

The Coltons had packed up her place and delivered boxes and suitcases with clothes, toys and various baby items; unpacked; and put the contents away almost before she could tell it was happening. At the same time, with all the coming and going, Abigail was able to observe Griffin interact with his family.

It soon became clear that, in a group of big personalities, Griffin was the quietest of the siblings. Perhaps because he hadn't been born a Colton, he exhibited different traits and it showed most when the group was all together. While the others competed to talk, he remained reserved, cautious and introspective. His sisters, it seemed, were keen to let Abigail know the best ways to handle their strong, silent brother.

"He needs space," Sadie said, as she staggered through the door carrying a box of Maya's toys. "Give him time to think about things before expecting him to make a decision. He's self-conscious and he likes to consider options and consequences. If you're prepared to wait, he'll appreciate the lack of pressure and become more at ease with you."

"That's really helpful." Abigail helped her to carry the toys through to the den. "But you do know we're not in a relationship, don't you?"

"Oh, that." Sadie waved a hand in an airy gesture. "I just thought it would be useful advice."

"Yes." Kiely joined in the conversation. "I used to think that when Griffin was still and silent he was angry. Turns out, he's just recharging, or people watching."

Even in the midst of the lively family group, Abigail found herself watching Griffin more than any of the others. She wondered how someone so shy could be so successful in a career that required so much persuasive human interaction. And he was also able to switch on a forceful persona, such as when he dealt with her caseworker.

In the end, she was so fascinated by the contrast between his personal and professional personalities that she decided to ask him about it later that night when they were bathing Maya.

"Damn it. Just when I thought I was doing so well at disguising my introversion that you might actually believe I was outgoing."

"I just wondered," she explained. "You do such an amazingly complex job, yet I don't think you enjoy being in a large group of people.

"You're right. Social situations don't come naturally to me. I don't do small talk and I prefer solitude to crowds. But my job requires me to mingle and to appear confident. So, over the years, I've developed a secondary personality. That's the person I become in social or work situations."

"That must be hard," Abigail said.

He shrugged. "It's second nature now."

As he leaned over the edge of the bath to splash water over Maya's upper body, the baby squealed with pleasure, making them both laugh.

Abigail sent him a sidelong glance. "Sadie was very keen to tell me how to handle your shyness."

He started to laugh. "I'll bet she was. My sisters are relentless matchmakers."

"Oh." She glanced his way again. "Have they been trying hard to find you a partner?"

"Why not come right out and say it? I'm thirty-two and still single. A hopeless case."

"What does that make me?" She held out a towel. Griffin handed Maya over and Abigail wrapped the baby up. "I'm thirty-five and not a man in sight."

"All I can say is that there must be something seriously wrong with the men of your acquaintance."

Embarrassed, she bent her head as she tended to Maya. "That doesn't sound like something an introvert would say."

"I don't feel very introverted when I'm with you."

When she looked up again, he'd left the room.

"How CAN YOU be able to climb the furniture before you can walk?" Griffin lifted Maya down from the coffee table for the fifth time that evening. "I don't understand how that works."

While Abigail prepared dinner, he and Maya were spending some time together. Although he had decluttered the living room, he'd underestimated the baby's ability to get into mischief. Wriggling on her belly, she managed to get around the room pushing buttons, pulling wires, emptying bins and throwing, or chewing, anything she could find. As Griffin removed each item from her reach, she moved on to the next. Her own toys lay in a neglected pile on the rug.

At nine months old, she either didn't understand the word *no* or she'd developed selective hearing. Each time Griffin moved her away from a harmful item, she gave him an angelic smile and went straight back again. He knew babies were meant to be lively and inquisitive, but he hadn't been aware that their mission in life was to wear out the adults who cared for them.

He had a sudden flash of inspiration. "I know what you'd like. There is someone in this house who is even faster and nosier than you."

He'd taken Maya to look at Lucy in her cage a few

times and the little girl and the ferret had regarded each other in fascination through the bars. So far, he had released Lucy only when Maya was asleep, taking the ferret for walks in the yard, or to climb in the park. Lucy was very tame and didn't mind wearing a leash and harness. As long as she could snuffle in the grass and under shrubs, or run up trees, she was happy.

Aware that ferrets had a reputation for nipping fingers, he didn't want to take any chances with his pet in close proximity to Maya. Probably because of her sad start in life, Lucy had the sweetest nature of any animal he'd ever known. She had never even scratched him, but a baby and a wild animal were a potentially volatile combination. With that in mind, he checked with Abigail. She was happy to leave the dinner cooking for a few minutes to help supervise the introductions.

"You're sure Lucy will be okay around Maya?" Abigail regarded the bright-eyed little animal with a combination of interest and caution.

"I'll keep Lucy in her harness," he promised, as he gently stroked the ferret's head. "I just thought Maya might like something else to do as a change from destroying electrical items."

"You could read her a book."

"Tried that." He rubbed his head reminiscently. "She hit me with it."

"There are educational games on my tablet." Although Abigail's expression was prim, her eyes danced with laughter.

"When she found out the tablet wasn't edible, she tried using it to hammer out a beat on the table. I think she may have a future as a drummer in a rock band." Maya, who had been looking from one to the other as they spoke, clapped her hands and bounced up and down on Abigail's knee. "See, she likes that idea. And I know a place where they can fix the screen on your tablet."

Abigail rolled her eyes. "Okay. Let's try the wildlife option."

After getting to his feet, Griffin placed Lucy on the floor. The ferret immediately scurried around, nose to the ground, her long body wiggling with pleasure. Holding the end of her leash, he followed her as she checked out every inch of the room. After a few minutes, having satisfied herself that there were no predators or rival ferrets lurking in any of the corners, she shimmied up the drapes.

Turning to look at Maya, Griffin saw that the baby was completely still, her eyes wide and her mouth open.

"All these books and lectures about parenting," he said, as he drew closer to Abigail. "And all that's really needed to keep a baby quiet is a small, furry creature on a leash."

She punched him lightly on the upper arm. "You do know that Maya will want to copy Lucy, don't you? From now on, she'll have a burning ambition to climb everything in the room."

This was what he'd been missing. Lighthearted exchanges and laughing over nothing. Little things that added up to big things. He wanted more of these moments with her.

Abigail's cell phone buzzed, and the moment was lost. She checked the number and frowned. "It's Dr. Wallis Porter. He's a member of the Danvers University administration."

"Do you want me to take Maya out of the room?" he asked.

She shook her head. "I guess it will be about the Anthrosyne investigation and I'm fine with you hearing what they have to say." Her hand shook slightly as she swiped to answer the call, and he'd have given anything to have been able to take that nervousness away. "Dr. Abigail Matthews."

She listened intently for about a minute, her expression becoming more and more disbelieving. When she spoke again, her voice betrayed a combination of hurt and anger. "You must be mistaken. Dr. Jenna Avery is my subordinate. You can't appoint her to lead an internal investigation into my conduct."

It was clear to Griffin that Abigail was not convinced by any explanations she was hearing from the person on the other end of the call. Her cheeks flushed and her jaw tensed. After a moment or two, she cut in sharply. "I don't care how busy you are, Dr. Porter. You and I need to meet to discuss this. Tomorrow morning."

When she ended the call, she stared at Griffin, her eyes wide and scared. "What is going on?"

He used his free hand to grip her knee. "I don't know. Not yet. But we will find out."

Chapter Nine

The next morning, while Abigail and Maya were still asleep, Griffin checked his emails. His colleagues had already dealt with most work-related items but there were a few things that needed his attention.

One of his messages was from Liam Desmond, the man who, with his wife Shelby, had been on the receiving end of the adoption scam. Griffin had been thorough in his research and Liam was thanking him for his work. Griffin scanned the items Liam had sent again. Not only were there copies of all social media interaction between the Desmonds and Dr. Anne Jay of MorningStar Families, he had also included any links he'd found to her and her online adoption agency. These were admittedly few, and vague.

Among the lengthy records that Liam had sent, the only interesting thing Griffin had found was an old profile picture from one of Dr. Jay's dormant social media accounts. She'd been more careful recently to protect her identity, leaving no photographic trail, or other evidence that could be used to identify her. There was no guarantee that the woman in this picture was actually her. And, of course, the name Anne Jay was likely an alias, the title "Doctor" fake as well. Even so, it was a possible link, if the police ever tracked her down. Taken from the side, it wasn't particularly clear, but it showed she was young, possibly early thirties, white, and her hair was cut in a sleek, dark bob.

Griffin replied to Liam's email, reminding him again to contact the police and suggesting that the photograph might be helpful to them. He didn't point out that unless the police had a suspect, it was unlikely that they would be able to track down the perpetrator of the adoption con from a single picture. Ultimately, he believed that the Desmonds would have to accept that they had been the victims of a nasty fraud. Dr. Jay had probably moved on to her next target and a new scam. In all likelihood, she also had a new name.

"Coffee?" Abigail's voice from his office doorway provided a welcome distraction.

"Please." He studied her face. "You look tired."

"I didn't get much sleep," she admitted. "Maya has settled well after her bad first night. In fact she's still asleep now. But this new development in the Anthrosyne investigation is bothering me."

Griffin closed the lid of his laptop. "Let's go get that coffee, then we can talk about the issues in more detail."

They went through to the kitchen and Abigail prepared their drinks. When they sat at the table, she cradled her cup in her hands as though trying to get warm.

"Tell me why you think putting this Dr. Avery in charge of the Anthrosyne investigation is another attempt to undermine you," Griffin said.

"Jenna Avery is one of my team on the Mem10 program and we worked together on the miscarriage project. She is a talented research scientist, but she's lazy. She cuts corners and doesn't complete paperwork to a good-enough standard. Until recently, I would have said she was also one of my friends at Danvers University. We used to eat lunch together, go out for dinner now and then—we'd meet up at the gym occasionally." When she looked up from her coffee cup, he could see the haunted look in her eyes, the one that usually meant she was thinking about her father. "That all changed one day in a team meeting. Without warning, Jenna started shouting abuse at me over RevitaYou. It turned out she'd bought a bottle of the tablets and got sick."

"Then she can't investigate you. Never mind that she's junior to you. She has a conflict of interest."

"I never thought of that." Abigail gave him a grateful look. "I wish you could come with me to this meeting. I'm so nervous I'm sure I'll mess it up."

He considered the matter for a moment. "If you want me there, I'll come. I'm your attorney. I know my specialism is adoption, but my role is to support you."

She started to lift her cup to her lips, but her hand shook so badly that she placed it back on the table. "Would you do that for me?"

"Of course. I'll admit I'm intrigued as to why the

Danvers would appoint Dr. Avery to head the internal investigation. It sounds like she's not up to the job, but leaving that aside, it's not a smart move on their part since it leaves them open to allegations of incompetence or deliberately trying to get rid of you. Either way, I'm happy to help you fight back."

He was taken by surprise as Abigail leaned across the distance between them and wrapped her arms around him in a hug. It wasn't the most comfortable of positions, since she was on one chair and he was on another, but Griffin wasn't about to complain.

"Thank you." Her lips were pressed up against his neck and the sensation was maddeningly good. "There's just one thing we need to think about."

"What's that?" he asked.

She lifted her head, momentarily distracting him with the nearness of her mouth to his. "What will we do with Maya during this meeting? I've told daycare I'm on leave."

"If you're in agreement, we could ask Riley and Charlize to take care of her for an hour or two. It'll be good practice for when their own baby comes along."

"I don't know." She gave him a troubled look. "I've only ever left her at daycare."

He tightened his grip on her waist, enjoying the way she leaned closer. "You'd never introduced her to a ferret until yesterday. Now she has one as a new best friend."

"I'm not sure how your brother and his fiancée will feel about being compared to a small furry animal…and I don't want you to think that I don't trust your family."

"You don't have any reason to trust my family. But I hope you know that our investigation into your father's schemes would never affect our judgment where you or Maya are concerned."

"I'll admit I was worried that you and your siblings could have reached a decision about my guilt without knowing me," she said. "But now that I know you, I can see that you have higher standards than that." He could tell she was still fighting her natural caution where Maya was concerned. "If you're sure Riley and Charlize won't mind?"

"Once they get used to the exhaustion and know they have to hide anything that can be thrown or spilled, I'm sure they'll be delighted."

She started to protest, but he silenced her by pressing a kiss to the corner of her mouth. As he did, the baby monitor crackled into life with a series of demanding cries.

"Oh, that's something else I need to warn Riley and Charlize about." He flashed a grin at Abigail as she got to her feet. "Maya has perfect, or maybe I should call it *imperfect*, timing."

AFTER LEAVING MAYA with Riley and Charlize, Griffin drove them to the Danvers University administrative offices. Having observed her daughter closely with Griffin's brother and his fiancée, Abigail felt reassured that Maya would be fine. Actually, she felt slightly concerned that she would return to find her daughter had taken charge of the household.

"She doesn't have to get her own way all the time," Abigail had told Charlize, as Maya was pointing to a stack of pancakes on the kitchen counter while fluttering her eyelashes and making cooing sounds. "It's fine to say no."

Since Riley had been gazing at the baby with a besotted expression, and Charlize had already been reaching for a bowl and spoon, she had little expectation of being listened to. It had always been at the back of her mind that she and Maya had no family except each other. Wes was their only close relative and he had never shown any interest in his foster granddaughter. He was hardly a conventional grandfather and his recent behavior made his credentials even less appealing. Uncle Riley and Aunt Charlize were just what her daughter needed.

But she was getting a little ahead of herself. They had stepped in to babysit as a one-off. It wasn't like Griffin's family would be there for life. The thought had caused her cheeks to burn. Distractions were not what she needed. Not today.

As Griffin found a space in the parking lot, Abigail gazed at the familiar building. It had been her workplace for the last five years, yet it felt hostile to her now. The decision to appoint Jenna Avery was so bizarre it felt like a declaration of intent. As Griffin had said, it either meant her employers were incompetent, or that they intended to get rid of her. And she didn't believe the university administration was incapable of doing its job. Dr. Wallis Porter had headed up the human resources department for over twenty years and he was as sharp as a tack.

Which left her with a nasty reality. She was no longer welcome at Danvers University. Could she blame those in charge for reaching that decision? She was the daughter of the man behind a particularly nasty con. The publicity surrounding the dodgy vitamins hadn't impacted the university yet but it was only a matter of time and Abigail felt that the clock was ticking. They were on a countdown to the first RevitaYou death...

The fallout had already been felt, though. Ryan Thorne might be the most vocal, but she knew that others had made complaints about her, asking how the university could continue to employ someone with her connections. It didn't matter that, in reality, her record was blemish free. All that counted was the perception.

Wes Matthews's daughter. Tainted by association.

Add the Anthrosyne allegation into the mix, and even before the investigation started, she was doomed.

"Why didn't I see that?" She spoke aloud without thinking.

"Pardon?" Griffin turned his head to look at her.

"I can't survive this, can I?" She bit her lower lip to stop it from trembling. "It doesn't matter who conducts the Anthrosyne investigation, or what the outcome is. My reputation is ruined, both here at Danvers University and as a research scientist."

"Once we clear your name, the damage will be undone," he said. "People have short memories. Before long, they will move on to the next story."

She nodded. "I know you're right. It's just so hard when we're in the middle of this one."

He pressed her hand. "Let's go get 'em."

They exited the car and crossed the parking lot. The sensation that she was being watched from the building made Abigail square her shoulders. She'd done nothing wrong. She'd worked there happily for so long. She wasn't about to enter the place now like a condemned woman.

Once inside, she went to the desk. The receptionist looked up with a smile. "Oh, Dr. Matthews. Hi."

The friendly greeting made the situation seem even more surreal. "Dr. Porter is expecting me."

The receptionist consulted her computer screen. "Yes, he is. Please come with me."

The last time Abigail had been into this part of the building, she had accompanied Evan Hardin to his office. As she and Griffin followed the receptionist, the thought chilled her. Was there something she could have done that day that would have changed the outcome for Evan? Had anything she had said or done contributed to his death? It was impossible to believe that the man she'd known and cared about was dead, that his murder could somehow be linked to her. The thought jogged something in her memory. Something Evan had said...

When they reached Dr. Porter's office, the receptionist knocked before moving aside to let them enter. The administrator rose from his seat behind his desk when they stepped into the room. Although he was nearing retirement, he still had the air of a man who had occupied a position of authority for many years.

"Dr. Matthews." After nodding to Abigail, he turned to Griffin with an inquiring look.

"Mr. Colton is my attorney." A brief look of annoyance flashed across Dr. Porter's features and Abigail was glad. She wasn't here to make things easy for him.

"I'm not sure—"

"You're not sure if Abigail is entitled to representation at a meeting with her employer?" Griffin's tone was pleasant, but his manner reminded Abigail of a hawk about to swoop on its prey. "Why would you be in any doubt about that, Dr. Porter?"

"That's not what I meant." There was a hint of snappiness in the response and Dr. Porter waved them to two seats on the opposite side of his desk as he resumed his own seat. "I was simply unaware that this meeting required such formality."

"Clearly it does," Griffin said. "Since the person you have appointed to replace Dr. Hardin as the Anthrosyne investigation lead is not only junior to Abigail, she is also known to be antagonistic to her."

Dr. Porter frowned. "I'm not aware of any antagonism."

"Jenna Avery was publicly and recently confrontational to me," Abigail said. "She accused me of being involved in the RevitaYou con and blamed me for the fact that she had become ill after taking some of the vitamins. Her allegations were witnessed by at least twelve Danvers University staff."

"This raises a number of issues for you, as the head of Human Resources, at this university," Griffin said. "The first, of course, is the potential damage to Abigail's well-being from being subjected to such a distressing personal attack in her workplace." Griffin leaned forward slightly in his seat, ensuring he had the other man's full attention. "She prefers to hope that these accusations, whether they are from the families of participants, or whether they are anonymous, will die out over time. However, it was particularly upsetting to be confronted in this way by a colleague, someone who should have the intellectual strength and emotional resilience to know better. Abigail has not raised a formal grievance against Dr. Avery. Although she could."

He paused, allowing the impact of his words to sink in. Abigail felt a little of the tightness around her heart loosen. She didn't know if Griffin had managed to change Dr. Porter's mind. But he was on her side. He had thought about this from her perspective. He'd said he would help her fight and that was what he was doing. Win or lose, she would always remember this moment and the look in his eyes.

"I will look into this." Dr. Porter's whole body had stiffened as though concrete had been injected into his veins. "But your other objection, Dr. Matthews, that Jenna Avery is junior to you is not valid. Prior to his death, Dr. Hardin sent an email to myself and the other members of the Danvers University leadership team informing us that he was removing you from the Mem10 project with immediate effect. You were demoted and Jenna Avery was to be your replacement."

For a moment, Abigail felt as though the earth had tilted off its axis. A curious sense of acceptance came over her. So that was it. She had lost her job without even knowing. Jenna had said as much when Abigail had seen her outside Evan's office but she'd hoped it wasn't true. Jenna was incapable of doing justice to the project to which Abigail had dedicated so much of her time and expertise. And now Jenna would oversee the Anthrosyne investigation and do everything she could to implicate Abigail further.

"How long before Dr. Hardin's death did he send that email?" Griffin asked.

"I don't see why the timing is important," Dr. Porter blustered.

"It could be very important. Dr. Hardin was killed on the day he told Abigail she was being investigated. From what I've heard of him, he was a very fair, very ethical man." Dr. Porter inclined his head in agreement. "It seems odd to me that he would make the decision to replace Abigail without having even started an internal investigation into the allegations. It is even more strange that he would have informed you about it without telling her."

Dr. Porter tented his fingers beneath his chin. "What are you suggesting?"

"I think the police would like to take a look at that email, particularly in relation to the time of Dr. Hardin's death and his other activities that day."

Abigail raised a shaking hand to her throat. "Do you think it was written by someone other than Evan?"

"I'm almost certain it was," Griffin said. "And I'd like a copy of that email so I can take it to Detective Emmanuel Iglesias."

WHEN THEY ARRIVED at the Grand Rapids Police Department building, the front desk cop, Michaela Martin, recognized Griffin. Some of his cases brought him into contact with the police and, of course, his CI work meant he liaised closely with local law enforcement.

"I need to speak to Detective Iglesias," he told Michaela.

"Join the queue." She rolled her eyes and pointed to a stack of papers on the reception counter. "Those are his messages."

"It's urgent."

Something in his tone must have resonated with her because she looked from him to Abigail, then nodded. "Let me see if I can contact him." She moved away from the desk.

"Will Detective Iglesias listen to what we have to say to him?" Abigail murmured. "It all sounds so far-fetched."

"He'll listen." Griffin was now certain that whoever killed Evan Hardin was also trying to frame Abigail. That person was determined to ruin her life and he, or she, had to be stopped. The idea of a faceless killer plotting to harm her made his blood run cold. If anything happened to her or Maya… "I'll make him."

A few minutes later, Emmanuel approached the desk. He looked tired and distracted.

"Griffin. Dr. Matthews." He nodded at them in turn. "I haven't been in touch because I don't have anything new to tell you—"

"We have some information for you," Griffin said.

"In that case, you'd better follow me."

He led them along a corridor to a small office. If the amount of paperwork on his desk was any indication, Emmanuel was either very busy, or very disorganized. He cleared stacks of files from two chairs so that Griffin and Abigail could sit down. After moving to the swivel chair behind his desk, he took out a pad and pen.

"I take it this new information relates to Dr. Hardin's murder?"

"Indirectly," Griffin said. "I told you I believed someone was trying to frame Abigail."

"That's right. You asked us to look at the son of one of her former patients." Emmanuel flipped through his notepad. "A Ryan Thorne."

Griffin drummed his fingers on the desk. "He's one of several people you need to consider. But there is new evidence of attempts to ruin Abigail's reputation. If you can find out who is behind those, it might bring you closer to discovering who would make it look like she killed her boss."

Quickly, but succinctly, he outlined how he and Abigail had found out that her name had been removed from articles on the Danvers University website. "We haven't checked every report that credits Abigail. Of the few we have, we've found evidence of tampering."

"Who has administrator rights to the university website?" Emmanuel asked Abigail.

"When I've written articles for inclusion on the website, I've submitted them to Dr. Porter's personal assistant. They are then approved and uploaded to the website," she said. "I'm not sure who else has access to the website."

"I guess it could have been hacked?" Griffin suggested.

"That's something I'll need to check out." Emmanuel scribbled a note on his pad. "I agree that this appears to be a campaign against Abigail but I'm not sure it's strong enough to link it to the murder of Dr. Hardin."

"There's more." Griffin outlined the conversation they'd had less than an hour ago with Dr. Porter. "On the day of his death, Dr. Hardin allegedly sent an email to Dr. Porter and other senior colleagues. In it, he told them that he was going to demote Abigail and replace her with a junior colleague, someone who was not qualified to lead the Mem10 program."

"I can see how much this troubles you." Emmanuel looked from Griffin to Abigail. "But I don't work in your world, so I need you to explain why."

She cleared her throat. "Evan Hardin and I had worked together for five years. He was one of the fairest men I knew, and he always upheld the high standards of the university. He had been appointed to lead an investigation into the allegation that I had used Anthrosyne in my research. He would not have taken his responsibility to me, or the university, lightly. There is no way he would have made the decision to demote and replace me before he'd even started that investigation or proven the allegations' veracity."

Emmanuel tapped his pen on his pad. "I see what you mean. If he'd done so, it would have looked like he'd already made a judgment that you were guilty."

She nodded, and Griffin could see the relief in her eyes. This police officer understood. "Exactly. And, even if he had concluded his investigation and decided that I could no longer be part of the Mem10 trial, Jenna Avery was not qualified to be my replacement. Danvers University has a small faculty, but there are half a dozen others who could have stepped in to take over my role."

She turned to look at Griffin. "I haven't told you this, but I remembered something while we were at the university. When I was in Evan's office on the day before he was murdered, he told me that, in addition to the Anthrosyne investigation, he had another equally urgent staffing matter to deal with."

"Did he give you any details?" Emmanuel asked.

"No. That was all he said."

"Have you done as I asked and checked the security camera footage of the area around Dr. Hardin's office before and after his death?" Griffin asked the detective. "We need to know if anyone entered after the first crime scene search and before the second. That would tell us who could have planted Abigail's bracelet."

"The security cameras were disabled," Emmanuel said.

"Well, isn't that convenient? Looks like someone didn't want to be seen." Griffin shifted impatiently in his seat."

"Thank you. It had occurred to me." Emmanuel turned to a clean page in his notebook. "Tell me about Dr. Avery."

"Oh, goodness. I wasn't implying—"

"I have to look at everyone involved in a case," Emmanuel said. "I'm already aware that Dr. Avery was one of the last people to talk to Dr. Hardin. Now it seems that she may have more information that can help with my inquiry."

Abigail cast a doubtful look in Griffin's direction. "No one is suggesting that you are trying to cast blame on Dr. Avery," he assured her.

The corners of her mouth turned down. "I'm not sure she would see it that way. She already hates me."

"Dr. Avery bought some RevitaYou vitamins and

got sick. She blames Abigail and has been publicly confrontational with her about it," Griffin told Emmanuel.

"It certainly sounds like she has a reason to hold a grudge against you." Emmanuel made a quick note as he spoke.

"If you're using RevitaYou as your baseline, there are a lot of people who have a reason to hold a grudge against me," Abigail said. "Does the fact that one of them happened to work with me make her more likely to be behind these attacks?"

"Maybe not. But it certainly gives her better access to the Danvers University website. And to Dr. Hardin," Emmanuel said.

"Doesn't it also mean she had a better chance of stirring things up among the families of the Mem10 participants?" Griffin asked.

Abigail frowned. "There's been no suggestion that anyone did that."

"So far," he said. "But the group who took their family members off the Mem10 program when the RevitaYou scandal broke seems to have been quite organized and vocal. I think it's worth considering whether they were being fed information from behind the scenes."

"It's something I'll look into when I speak to Ryan Thorne and the others who withdrew their family members from Mem10." Emmanuel spent a few moments reading through his notes. "I have a fairly detailed picture of Dr. Hardin's movements during his last day. Do you have a copy of the email he sent to Dr. Porter and his other colleagues? The one in which he told them he was replacing Abigail with Jenna Avery. It will be useful to place it in the time frame of what else he was doing."

Griffin took out his cell and found the email. "Dr. Porter was a little reluctant to share it with me but we told him we were coming straight here after we left his office, so he knew it would only be a matter of time before you subpoenaed his records."

He handed the phone over to Emmanuel. After reading for a minute or two, the detective looked up. "Okay. Here are my initial thoughts. We have Dr. Hardin's work laptop and his cell phone in our possession and I've already seen the messages he sent during the few days prior to his death. Although this message was sent from his Danvers University email address, it was not sent from either of those devices. Forward it to me and I'll get our technicians straight onto finding out where it *was* sent from."

"Do you agree with Griffin that there's a chance Dr. Hardin didn't send it?" Abigail asked. Without looking in Griffin's direction, she reached for his hand. When he clasped her fingers, they were cold as ice, despite the summer temperatures.

"I know he didn't send it. And the device is not my reason for saying that." Emmanuel paused, clearly weighing his words. "This is confidential, but at the time this email was sent, Dr. Hardin was undergoing emergency dental treatment. Clearly, he could not have sent the email."

"Which means that someone else did," Griffin said. "And, when you find out who it was, you'll know who is trying to frame Abigail."

Chapter Ten

They drove to Heritage Hill in silence, both wrapped in their own thoughts. Abigail was relieved that Emmanuel seemed to be taking her claim that someone was trying to frame her more seriously. At the same time, it made the looming threat of a shadowy figure who wanted to harm her even more real. More than ever, she was glad of Griffin's reassuring presence.

"I don't want to launch into a full-on conspiracy theory," he said, as they approached CI headquarters. "But we have to consider the possibility that there is a group of people behind the effort to discredit you as a response to your father's criminal activity. They could have someone—not necessarily Jenna Avery—working inside the university feeding them information about you."

Abigail shivered. "That's a horrible thought."

"I'm not trying to alarm you. But the RevitaYou con has made a lot of people angry. And it's receiving attention on social media. Who knows what people are saying about your father, or how they're planning to get back at him? I'm just suggesting that we should look at all the angles." He turned his head briefly to look her way. "And we need to be prepared for them. Let's not take any chances with your safety, or Maya's."

"I could consider the possibility that people might have gotten together and plotted revenge if it wasn't for the fact that Evan has been killed," Abigail said. "That's too extreme. No matter how angry people are at what my father has done, I can't picture a situation in which a group would see that as suitable revenge."

Griffin pulled into the drive of the house where he had lived as a child and pulled up in the small parking lot at the rear. "You're right, of course. It would only take one reasonable person within the group to hear of such a plan. They would immediately report it to the police."

"So we're back to a lone person with a grudge against me?" Abigail said, as they exited the vehicle.

"I guess that was always the most likely scenario. But let's keep an open mind."

Although Riley lived in their childhood home, which also served as the CI headquarters, Griffin had already explained that the other Colton siblings still came and went as they pleased. They entered through the rear door, which led them straight into the kitchen.

"It looks remarkably tidy," Griffin said. "Maya can't have been in here."

Abigail dug him in the ribs with her elbow. "Just because *you* let a nine-month-old walk all over you…"

The sounds of laughter drew them along the hall and into the den. Riley and Charlize were both sitting on the rug with Maya. Their dog, Pal, was lying nearby, with her nose close to the baby's feet. Griffin and Abigail paused in the doorway to watch the game that was in progress. Riley passed a ball to Charlize, who then passed it to Maya. The baby took it from her but, instead of passing it to Riley, she attempted to give it to Pal.

Looking up, Charlize beckoned them into the room. "She's done this every time. It was love at first sight between Maya and Pal."

Riley grinned. "I think you might have trouble when you try to leave. Pal is convinced Maya is her puppy."

At that instant, Maya saw them. Giving a welcoming screech, she waved her hands.

"Hi, honey." Abigail scooped her up into her arms. "It looks like you've been having fun." The darkness of the day receded as her little girl snuggled close and tucked her head into Abigail's neck. When Griffin approached, Maya reached out a hand as though inviting him to share the embrace.

"Hey." As he leaned in close and stroked Maya's cheek, Abigail could see how moved he was. "It's good to see you, too."

"She's gorgeous," Charlize said. "The sweetest little girl ever."

The two women shared a smile over Maya's head. Abigail didn't have many friends, but admiration of her baby was a surefire way to win a place among that select group. When Charlize went to make coffee, Abigail and Maya accompanied her, leaving the Colton brothers to discuss CI business.

Pal followed them and Maya, who, despite her inability to speak, was good at making her wishes known, demanded to be put down. As soon as Abigail placed her on the floor, she wiggled her way over to the dog.

"Do they all do that before they crawl?" Charlize asked.

"The wriggling like a worm? I don't think so. All babies seem to find different ways of getting around. I'm not sure if Maya will ever crawl. She gets around so fast on her belly she may stick with that until she starts walking." They watched as Maya grabbed a handful of Pal's fur in each hand and hauled herself upright. "That's one patient dog."

"Pal has to be the most good-natured canine in the world," Charlize agreed. "I only hope my baby is as good-natured as Maya." She placed a hand on her belly. "I'm blissfully happy, but this whole thing has been quite an adjustment—moving in with Riley, the pregnancy, getting engaged…"

As they watched it was as if some unspoken communication passed between the baby and the dog. Slowly, Pal took a tiny step and, still clinging to the canine's coat, Maya moved with her. Pal glanced over her shoulder as though checking the little girl was okay before repeating the action. Gradually, they made their way across the small kitchen.

"I would not have believed that if I hadn't seen it for myself," Charlize said.

"Pal sure is a special dog." Abigail shook her head. "You and Riley won't need to buy a fancy baby walker for your own little one."

They were still laughing when they returned to the den. Charlize carried a tray with the coffee cups while Abigail hoisted Maya onto her hip. Pal followed close behind, nudging Abigail on the leg every now and them as though checking that the baby was okay.

"I've been bringing Riley up to date with the latest developments in the Anthrosyne investigation and the attempts to frame you for Dr. Hardin's murder," Griffin said.

"I know these incidents don't officially form part of a CI case but, given the seriousness of the situation and the overlap with our inquiries into RevitaYou, I think we should call a team meeting." Riley's expression was somber. "Particularly since the information you have about Landon Street could prove useful to the other CI members." He turned to Abigail. "Are you happy to share all of this information with our sisters?"

"Of course." She nodded. "The circumstances might not be ideal, but Griffin tells me that I'm part of the CI team now and that's a comforting thought."

A brief look flashed between Riley and Charlize. Although it was over in seconds, it was a lot like an

I-told-you-so glance. But *what* had they been saying to each other about her? She didn't know and she certainly didn't feel comfortable asking.

"There's a lot to talk about. How about we do it over dinner tonight?" Riley asked.

"Sounds like a plan," Griffin said. He pointed to Pal, who had her head on Abigail's knee as she gazed lovingly at Maya. "And a reunion."

WHEN THEY REACHED Griffin's apartment, he carried a sleepy Maya inside and turned to face Abigail. "I have something important to say to you."

"Goodness." She regarded him nervously. "From the look on your face it must be serious."

"It *is* a very serious subject. I think it's time."

She swallowed hard, a faint blush staining her cheeks. "For what?"

"For me to do a solo diaper change." He beckoned her closer. "And it's a stinky one."

Abigail wafted a hand under her nose. "Are you sure about this?"

"As sure as I'll ever be. You stay here while I get suited up in rubber gloves, put a clothespin on my nose, get the goggles and find a scrub top."

She giggled. "If you can laugh, you are halfway to winning the diaper battle."

"I am serious." His solemn look turned into a grin. "Just stay close by in case I need help."

She started to laugh. "From the smell, you may

need reinforcements. Luckily, this little one is ready for her nap, so she may not put up a fight."

Although she was tired, Maya appeared to view those words as a challenge. Griffin carried her through to the bedroom that she shared with Abigail. As soon as he placed her on the changing table that they'd brought from Abigail's apartment, she tried to roll away from him.

Distract her, then pin her down. He remembered Abigail's tactics and handed Maya a toy. She threw it on the floor and started thrashing wildly from side to side.

"She's cranky and trying to get out of being changed," Abigail said. "Just power through and, even if she screams, remember it's for her own good."

Determinedly, Griffin got on with the task in hand. Sure enough, Maya, outraged that he refused to stop, even when she threw herself wildly around, began to cry loudly.

"This is no fun for me, you know," Griffin told her. "In fact, if we're being honest, I'm the one who should be shedding tears."

When he finally got her cleaned up and into a fresh diaper, Maya lay back on her mat and studied him with a resentful expression.

"Do you think she'll ever forgive me?" Griffin asked Abigail.

"You go and wash up while I sing her favorite rock ballad. She'll be asleep in no time, and when she wakes up she'll have forgotten that you're the nasty man who changed her when she wanted to stay dirty."

After he'd disposed of the dirty diaper and washed his hands, he returned to the bedroom. Abigail was placing the sleeping baby in her crib. When Griffin moved to stand at her side, she placed a finger on her lips. Side by side, they watched over Maya as she slumbered.

The little girl looked so tiny with one hand tucked under her cheek and her dark curls fluffed up around her head. Griffin was blown away by the strength of the emotions that Abigail and Maya aroused in him. But it was more than that. There was a feeling of rightness to having them in his life that warmed him and scared him at the same time. Because what would happen when this was all over and they left? How would he cope with a normality that no longer contained them?

Abigail turned her head to look at him and he saw some of his own thoughts reflected in her eyes. She placed her hand over his where it rested on the wooden rail of the crib.

"I'm not good at this." Why did he always have to spoil things by explaining?

"At what?" Her voice was husky.

"Everything." He resisted the temptation to groan. "Life. Relationships…"

"Is that what this is?" She moved a fraction closer. "A relationship? I wouldn't know, you see. I've never been in one."

"Nor have I. Not really. I don't know how to relate to other people on a personal level—"

She placed a finger on his lips. "Can we stop talking now?"

"I think we should."

He caught hold of her around the waist, moving her backward away from the crib.

"Wait." Abigail stopped him before they reached the door.

He released her immediately. "Is this not okay?"

"It's more than okay." She smiled up at him. "It's wonderful. But spontaneity and babies don't mix."

"Ah." He returned the smile. "Bring the baby monitor to my room."

She rose on the tips of her toes to kiss him. "Any man who can say that at a time like this definitely knows how to relate to people on a personal level."

THE FEW MINUTES between Griffin entering his bedroom and Abigail following him in felt like a lifetime. They also gave him just enough time for the doubts to set in. He closed the drapes and started pacing. This had to be a bad idea. Even if they discounted everything that was happening, neither of them was relationship material.

Who said this is leading to a relationship?

He couldn't argue his way out of things that easily. This wasn't about sex. He almost laughed out loud at the thought. *Not about sex? So why are we sneaking into my room in the middle of the day while the baby is asleep?* That wasn't the point. The physical attraction between them was undeniable but there was so much more to it.

Even if they weren't falling for each other deeper and deeper with each passing day, they were living under the same roof and sharing the care of Maya. They couldn't rush into anything…

"I'm sorry," Abigail whispered, as she closed the door behind her. "Maya stirred and I thought she was waking up."

Then she was walking toward him and every thought went out of his head except the need to take her into his arms. Heat flared between them as soon as they kissed. When they broke apart, Abigail reached for his hand, leading him toward the bed.

"Wait." She stopped, her expression questioning. "Are you sure about this?"

"Totally." Her gaze scanned his face. "Are you?"

"Yes." And he was. The doubts of a few minutes ago were gone. "I've never been more certain of anything in my life."

Her smile was radiant. "What a lovely thing to say."

As he looked down at her, it hit him. There was no need to be afraid. This beautiful woman wanted him as much as he wanted her. And right here, right now, that was all that mattered. The future could wait.

With a soft growl, he lifted her off her feet and carried her to the bed. Before he could place her on it, Abigail put a hand on his chest.

"I want to see you." Even though the light was

dim, he could see the color that stained her cheeks. "All of you."

"Works both ways."

Shyness and patience were forgotten as, within minutes, they removed their clothes and lay facing each other on the bed. Abigail wrapped her arms around Griffin's neck, pressing the length of her body tight to his.

"This feels very, very good."

Pushing her arms above her head, he gently eased her onto her back and knelt between her legs. Pausing for a second, he checked her face, looking for any signs of hesitation. Her figured that her half-closed eyes and the way she slowly ran her tongue over her bottom lip were encouraging.

Then she whispered, "I want you." It was the only signal he needed.

Dropping his forehead onto hers, he pressed a lingering kiss onto her lips. Abigail wrapped her long legs around his hips and pulled her body up to meet his, rubbing against him. Griffin gripped her thighs, caressing them before moving his fingers closer to her core.

A little moan escaped Abigail's lips as she fisted the sheets on either side of her hips. "Oh, please..." Her voice was a hoarse rasp.

"Please what?"

"Please touch me."

"I am touching you." He smiled into her eyes.

"Ah, Griffin. Don't tease me." She looked down the length of her body at him. "Please touch me *there*."

"You mean here?"

Leaning forward, he took one long lick at her center. Abigail cried out, her head falling back on the pillow as her whole body trembled. Holding her steady with his hands on her hips, Griffin swiped his tongue through her folds, over and over. Burying her hands in his hair, she thrashed wildly, grinding her hips up toward his face.

"Oh, oh." Her cries echoed around the room.

Grasping her thighs tightly, he parted her legs wider before taking her clit in his mouth. As he sucked, then flicked his tongue across the surface of the sensitive flesh, Abigail came apart.

"Griffin!"

She was jerking and shaking as he held her down, murmuring in pleasure at her reaction. After a minute or two, she reached up and wrapped her arms around his neck, pulling him down into a kiss. He groaned into her mouth, tilting their heads so that he could kiss her deeper and harder, his own desire burning further out of control.

"I almost forgot." Abigail raised her head to look at him. "Do you have protection?"

"Yes." He leaned across and reached into the top drawer of his nightstand.

She trailed a hand down his body. "Then I think we should use it."

ABIGAIL COULDN'T BELIEVE that the amazing orgasm Griffin had just given her with his mouth had only partly satisfied her. Only minutes later, she wanted to feel him driving into her, their bodies slick with perspiration, their hearts pounding in time. This wild side to her personality was as new as it was unexpected. But she knew she could trust Griffin and maybe that was why she was able to let go of her inhibitions with him.

Moving her hands down Griffin's body, she gripped his taut ass and pulled him tight against her. The moment their hips met, and she shifted beneath him, a groan rumbled deep in his chest. The depth of emotion in his eyes took her breath away.

"I didn't know it was possible to feel this alive." As he tore open the condom packet, she sensed he was having trouble speaking.

Abigail moved one hand down between their bodies and stroked his hard, throbbing shaft. "So big."

He thrust his hips, moving in her grip. "Any more of that kind of talk and I'll be so turned on the condom will be a waste of time."

"Then maybe I should help you with that?"

She rubbed her thumb across his head before taking the latex sheath from him. Using one hand to pinch the top of the condom at the tip with her thumb and forefinger, she rolled the condom down while stroking his length. From the way Griffin drew in a sharp breath, she figured he approved of her technique.

He leaned toward her and kissed her mouth, and

she wrapped her legs around his back, opening herself up to him. She could taste herself on his lips, but she could also taste *him*. And she loved his flavor.

He moved his right hand down, guiding himself to her and she tilted her pelvis. As he slowly pushed into her, then retreated again, she gasped at the sensation of him filling her. It was so intense and pleasurable that her inner muscles spasmed just at that first entry. She gripped his waist, holding on tight as he drove deeper each time.

Her body was on fire, the flames starting at the point where their bodies connected and blazing a path along her nerve endings. Whimpering in frustration, she ground her lower body tighter against his. Lifting his head, he smiled into her eyes before pulling back slightly. Holding him tighter, she jerked upward, trying to force him to go harder and faster.

In response to her action, he kissed her deep. As she sucked on his tongue, he lost some of his control. His hips bucked and he plunged wildly in and out.

"Yes." Throwing her head back, Abigail arched her back.

He surged forward, filling her completely before holding still. She loved the feeling of every inch of him pressed into her sensitive inner walls. But the longer he held himself still deep, the more she needed the motion of him powering into her, rubbing his flesh against hers.

She lifted her hips, pleasuring his length with her body and chasing her own fulfillment at the same time. She was so close. Maddeningly, deliciously close. Griffin moved in time with her upward motion, and her body started to convulse. She cried out, holding on tight to Griffin's forearms. As he let go of all restraints, her body spasmed around him and she welcomed every thrust.

She tightened her inner muscles around him as light and color exploded through her body. After a moment, Griffin jerked and cried out as his own climax hit.

Wanting to keep the connection between them for as long as possible, she wrapped her arms around his waist. He bowed his head into the curve of her neck and they remained still, breathing hard for several minutes. When he finally collapsed on the bed beside her, Abigail turned toward him, tucking her body tight against his. She could hear the pounding of his heart against her ear as he stroked her hair.

She felt curiously conflicted. Her body was at peace, but she wanted to laugh and cry at the same time. It was as if a cork had been popped and her emotions had come pouring out like champagne from a bottle.

Griffin was her rock in a stormy sea. He was the only person she trusted. Now he had become so much more than that. What had happened between them was so much more than sex. She hid a smile against his chest. *Although the sex was pretty amazing.* It had confirmed everything she'd hoped and feared.

She wasn't falling for Griffin Colton. She'd already fallen.

Chapter Eleven

"I think I should try looking after Maya on my own.,
Griffin said the next morning. He looked like a man
who couldn't quite believe he'd said those words out
loud.

Abigail gave him a doubtful glance. "What am I
supposed to do while you two have a little bonding
time?"

"Anything you want to. Take a bath. Read a maga-
zine. Go for a walk."

"A bath would be nice," she said longingly. "I can't
remember the last time I soaked in some scented bubbles."

"That's settled." He placed a hand at the small of
her back and steered her toward the door. "We'll be
fine."

Before she left the room, she looked back over her
shoulder. Griffin was seated on the rug with Maya
and the baby was trying to poke him in the eye. Of
course, they'd be fine.

Griffin's master bathroom had a huge roll-top tub

and Abigail eyed it with pleasure as she turned on the faucet. She'd just removed her clothes and was preparing to step into the steaming water when Griffin yelled for her.

"Abigail! Come quickly."

The panic in his voice had her running naked into the den.

"There's something wrong with Maya." He was on his feet, his face ashen as he pointed to the baby. "I think she's having a seizure."

Maya was lying on her back on the rug. Every few seconds, her body would jerk and her spine would arch upward from the floor. Each time it happened, she let out a squeak. When Abigail knelt beside her, the little girl grinned at her, then rolled away. The jerking and squeaking continued as she moved.

Abigail bit back a smile, determined to reassure Griffin instead of laughing at him. "There is nothing wrong with Maya. She has the hiccups."

"Seriously?" He ran a hand through his hair. "That's all it is?"

She nodded. "It happens a lot."

He started to laugh. "I guess I overreacted a little."

Abigail got to her feet. "Just a little." She raised an eyebrow as his gaze roamed over her body. "What are you doing?"

His eyes twinkled. "Just admiring the view."

She wagged a finger at him. "That's not allowed when you're minding the baby."

He held up his hands. "I was only looking."

"How about you look in that direction?" She pointed at Maya, who was on her way out of the door. "And let me get back to my bath?"

Muttering an apology, he hurried to retrieve the baby while Abigail returned to the bathroom. While she knew that Maya would be fine with Griffin, she spent most of her "me time" listening for the sounds of chaos.

Although there were a few bumps and thuds, she didn't hear anything that caused her any alarm. Finally, she relaxed and lay back in the scented bubbles. Half an hour later, she emerged. After taking time to dry her hair and dress in clean sweatpants and a T-shirt, she wandered downstairs.

"That was wonder—" she broke off. "What happened here?"

Griffin's den looked like a scene from a disaster movie. An earthquake, or possibly a hurricane, Abigail decided as she surveyed the scene. Possibly even the aftermath of a nuclear explosion.

Griffin was seated on the floor, picking up the pieces of a shattered picture frame. He looked like a man who had stared into the abyss and no longer had anything left to fear. For some reason, his hair was wet. Maya was trapped in a corner between the coffee table and a chair, but she seemed happy enough as she bashed one of her dolls over the head with a rattle.

"Her diaper was dirty," Griffin said. "I mean, industrial-level dirty. So I started to change her. I was doing a good job until I realized I didn't have a bag to put the dirty one in." He closed his eyes briefly. "I only moved away for a second. Just long enough to get a bag."

Abigail placed a hand on his shoulder. "Don't tell me. She got the dirty diaper?"

"You've been there?"

"I think most parents have." Her voice was sympathetic.

"There was poop everywhere." He shuddered at the memory. "All over Maya, the rug, the sofa, the TV. And, when I tried to stop her, she grabbed me by the hair."

"Oh, Griffin."

"Abigail..." His eyes were round with horror. "I had baby poop in my *hair.*"

She sat on the floor next to him, picking up a few shards of glass that he'd missed. "What did you do?"

"You mean when I'd stopped retching?" She nodded. "I took her through to my room and we both got into the shower. Then I cleaned up in here. I tried to hold onto Maya with one hand but she still grabbed a few things and tried to trash the place."

"So, um, did you enjoy looking after her on your own?"

He gave her a suspicious look. "Are you laughing at me?"

She tried to keep a straight face, but the laughter bubbled up. "Maybe a little."

Griffin stared at her in disbelief for a moment or two, then a slight smile touched his lips. "It would have been just my luck if John Jones had arrived while this place was Poop City."

"At least if the police had turned up to arrest me, the stink might have put them off." Abigail leaned against him, chuckling.

As they toppled onto the rug, giggling uncontrollably, Maya, who was clearly tired of being left out, threw her rattle at them.

ALTHOUGH CHARLIZE HAD made a chicken casserole, Griffin noticed each of his siblings brought a contribution to the evening meal. As a result, the table was overloaded with food at the family dinner that took place before the CI meeting. Maya, who was refreshed after a long nap, ate even more than usual and enjoyed having an audience.

Maya was seated on Griffin's knee and he stopped her as she leaned over and offered the dog a piece of cornbread. "No, don't give that to Pal." Giving him a radiant smile, she carefully rubbed her buttery fingers over the front of his shirt instead. "Thank you for sharing."

He looked up to find his sisters watching them. All four of them wore the same expression. It reminded him of the way they'd looked when they were kids and the family cat had given birth to a litter of kittens.

"You're so sweet," Sadie said.

Griffin got the feeling she was talking to him as well as Maya. Ordinarily, he'd have been uncomfortable at being the center of attention but, all of a sudden, he got it. This was what it was all about. This was family. His sisters were watching him interact with his little girl.

His little girl? Where had that come from? He was fostering Maya on a temporary basis to help Abigail through a difficult period in her life. There had never been any suggestion that it would become anything more. He knew, from his foster parent training, that it would be easy to form bonds with a child in his care. He also knew that, when the time came, he would have to let go. But this felt different.

He knew why. It was because of Abigail. He looked across the table at where she was talking to Charlize and his heart constricted. He'd never known emotion like this existed. And it terrified him. Because he didn't know how to deal with it. All his life, he'd maintained a distance from those around him, scared that his craving for love would be overpowering.

He'd told himself that dating was enough. He didn't want more than a casual relationship now and then. But in Abigail, he'd met a woman who had turned his whole life upside down. A woman who'd made him rethink everything he knew about himself. Because now he knew exactly what he wanted. He wanted her. And Maya. He wanted a family. He wanted *everything*. And with that knowledge, the old doubts resurfaced. Was this about her? Or his longing for love? How would he ever know the difference?

When he held her in his arms, when he kissed her, and drove deep inside her, his fears vanished. In those instants, she was his and there was no need for words. It was when he tried to rationalize his feelings. That was when he was transported back to the night his mom died and he just knew that everyone would be snatched away from him sooner or later. So why bother with love? It was so much easier to do without it.

"Ugh." He was brought back to reality as Maya seized a handful of his hair and tugged hard.

"Hey." Moving swiftly around the table, Abigail came to his rescue. "That is no way to treat Griffin after everything he's done for us. His hair has been traumatized enough for one day."

She leaned against his shoulder as she released him from Maya's eye-wateringly tight grip. Her hair tickled his cheek and her scent invaded his nostrils. As she turned her head to smile at him, he knew his own warnings were a waste of time. He was lost in her, sinking deeper by the minute, and enjoying every second.

AFTER DINNER HAD been cleared away, the family gathered around the table once more for a business meeting. Abigail had brought toys for Maya, and the baby played happily on the rug with her wooden animals.

Griffin started the CI meeting with a summary of what had happened since the team last got together. There were shocked faces around the table as he gave his sisters more details about the murder of Evan Hardin and the various attempts to frame, or discredit Abigail.

"Surely the police can't seriously believe that Abigail killed her boss?" Pippa asked.

Griffin shrugged. "You know what a police inquiry is like. It takes time for them to examine every lead."

"An anonymous note and a bracelet found in Dr. Hardin's office?" Kiely shook her head. "It's not enough evidence for them to consider Abigail as a suspect."

"The police haven't gone that far," Griffin said. "To be fair to Detective Iglesias, he is pursuing every angle."

"Good. Because I'll be asking him to track down a certain research scientist." As he spoke, Riley held up his electronic tablet to show his siblings a photograph. "I've had no luck finding him so far."

The image was of a tall man with a beer belly. His blond-gray hair was tousled, and his blue eyes peered at the camera from behind silver wire-rimmed glasses.

"This is Dr. Landon Street. He is credited by Wes Matthews in his glossy brochure as the person who devised the RevitaYou formula."

Vikki pulled a doubtful face. "I know it's only one picture, but he does not look like someone I'd trust to design a brand-new vitamin that people would take hoping it will change their lives."

"Your instinct would be right," Riley said. "Abigail has first-hand knowledge of Landon Street's dubious methods, but the guy has basically broken every rule there is. It's a miracle that he's avoided jail. He appears to have been saved each time by his employers' reluctance to draw attention to their own shoddy practices. Rather than face justice, he quietly moved on and, as a result, he's continued his dodgy behavior in the next place. Then the next. In the case of RevitaYou, his carelessness has reached the point where someone might die as a result."

"Is this because of the ricin you found in the pills?" Sadie asked Abigail.

"Yes. Ricin is an extremely deadly, naturally occurring poison found in castor beans. It can be created from by-products of the making of castor oil. The compound Landon Street created and added to RevitaYou causes cell death and does wonders for smoothing wrinkles. Not everyone who ingests it will die and they will look younger."

"But they're dicing with death," Sadie said.

"Exactly." Abigail nodded. "We don't know who, and we don't know when, but people will die as a result of the ricin compound in RevitaYou."

"Do we know how Wes Matthews and Landon Street met?" Vikki asked. "Have they been friends for a long time, or did they only make contact recently?"

"As far as I know, they didn't know each other when Landon worked at Danvers University," Abigail said. "Neither of them mentioned knowing the other to me and I think Landon probably would have. He'd find any excuse to chat rather than work."

"Landon offered his services as a freelance researcher." Riley found a web page and again held it up so that everyone could see it. "Is that something you've seen before, Abigail?"

"I'm not familiar with it, but I guess there are independents in every profession. It's a worrying thought, however, because there would be no one to regulate the services offered on a site like that."

"Clearly." Riley nodded. "I compared Landon to some comparable experts. His credentials didn't match up but he was cheap. I'm guessing that would be the appeal for Wes."

"So we figure Wes went shopping for a scientist to make him some vitamins. He came across that site and he found Landon. They agreed on a price and Landon made him the formula for RevitaYou." Griffin shook his head. "It was that easy for them to come up with a product that could kill people?"

"Yes. We know the FDA hasn't seen RevitaYou, so Wes's customers didn't have that protection," Pippa said. "Although it would never have reached the marketplace, of course."

"I don't think Wes and Landon set out to kill anyone." Vikki sent a sympathetic glance in Abigail's direction.

"But they didn't care if they did," she replied. "Don't worry. I know what my father is."

"And now Landon is missing. Just like Wes," Kiely said. "Could they be together?"

"Since we don't know where Wes is either, it wouldn't help us if they were." Riley ran a hand through his hair in frustration.

"I've been trying to think of places my dad might go." Abigail withdrew a folded piece of paper from the pocket of her jeans. "He was born in Michigan and spent most of his life here, but I think he would move on if he felt cornered here. My mom was from Cuba, but they met here in Grand Rapids. They were divorced and I don't think he had anything to do with her family after she died, but I suppose it's always possible that he could have made contact with them." She moved her finger down the list she'd written. "He used to talk about his cousins who lived in Texas, but I don't know where exactly. I know that's not helpful."

"It's very helpful." Griffin covered her hand with his. "It gives us a starting point."

"There was something else. It may be nothing, but he always talked about wanting to go deep sea fishing." She looked around the table. Each of the Colton siblings was watching her with understanding and support. For the first time since her mom had walked out, she felt included. Even wanted. "I just wondered if he might go to a place where he could hide away on a boat. I'm sorry. I know it's a big world out there, with a lot of boats…"

"Any information you can give us is helpful," Riley told her. "We can start looking at whether Wes made travel arrangements in the past, or if he knew anyone who organized boat charters."

"We also have to consider that Wes might do the exact opposite of what is expected and choose a place no one would ever think to look for him," Griffin said.

"On that subject, FBI agent Cooper Winston, who is working the RevitaYou case, has asked me to call him. I'll do that now so that you can all hear the conversation."

The others waited in silence while Riley contacted the Grand Rapids field office. When he got through to Agent Winston, the two men exchanged greetings.

"Cooper, I'm in a CI meeting with my siblings. Wes Matthews's daughter, Abigail, is also here and so is my fiancée, Charlize Kent. Is it okay if I put you on speaker phone?"

Once he'd secured the other man's agreement, Riley continued the call so that everyone in the room could hear. "We've been discussing likely places Matthews might hide."

"Since there's no sign of him, we have to assume that he's living under an alias and in disguise," Cooper said.

"If that's the case, we need to come up with a way to trap him or lure him back to Grand Rapids." Griffin's patience appeared to be wearing thin. It was clear he wanted a resolution and was frustrated that they couldn't find one. Abigail was touched to realize that it was for her sake.

"We'll keep trying to find him." From the weary note in Cooper's voice, the FBI were experiencing the same level of annoyance. "I'll let you know as soon as I have any information for you."

"We'll do the same," Riley said. Before he ended the call, he let Cooper know what they'd learned about

Landon Street and promised to follow the details up in an email.

After Riley ended the call, the mood was despondent. It seemed that the RevitaYou investigation was stalling. No one had heard from Brody, and the siblings were growing increasingly worried about his well-being.

"We should consider two possibilities in regard to contact between Wes and Landon Street," Griffin said. "Either they are still in touch and watching out for each other, or the stress of the investigation and the social media campaign has driven them apart. Either way, if one of them is caught, we should use that against the other."

"What do you mean?" Sadie asked.

"If Landon is arrested first, we should put out a social media blast saying that he's given police details about Wes, even if it's not true. And vice versa."

"Good thinking." Kiely nodded. "Play the bad guys off against each other."

"We have to catch one of them first, remember?" Pippa covered her mouth as she yawned. "Sorry, guys. I had an early start this morning."

It was the cue for the meeting to wind down and, after exchanging a few more details, the siblings started to leave. Abigail gathered up Maya's toys and carried the baby through to the kitchen to thank Charlize. After a few minutes, Griffin joined them.

"Are you ready to go home?"

She had never heard a sweeter question. For a moment her throat constricted. Then she managed a smile. "Home sounds like the best idea ever."

WHEN MAYA WAS ASLEEP, Abigail joined Griffin in his bed. Wrapping her arms around his neck, she twisted her fingers in the hair that grew slightly longer over his nape to draw him closer. His tongue licked hungrily over the seam of her lips, and her mouth parted eagerly for him. He slanted his lips over hers, holding the back of her head and tilting her into a kiss that became hard and deep.

Need surged through her, wild and wanton. She had never felt like this before, and she welcomed it, her need for him escalating, spiraling out of control until she was shaking with the intensity of it.

Griffin jerked his head back and stared at her, his eyes gleaming with a hunger that scared and delighted her.

"I want you more than I have ever wanted anything in my life." His voice was hoarse with need.

She drew his head back down to hers, brushing her lips against his, triggering a series of hungry kisses. She couldn't get enough of him. Couldn't get close enough to him. She needed his tongue in her mouth, the hard muscles of his chest against the softness of her too-sensitive breasts, his hands exploring her body. She needed everything he could give her. Measured and gentle wouldn't do. Self-control wasn't good enough. What Abigail wanted there and then was raw and out of control.

Griffin eased her down so that they were lying side by side and she pressed her hips tight to his until the heavy ridge of his erection pressed firmly against the intimate mound between her thighs. Her hands slid to his chest, her fingers trembling as they slid through the crisp hair. Hunger raged out of control throughout her body. She was intoxicated by the sensual storm gripping her.

Griffin tugged her T-shirt up, and she raised her arms so he could pull it over her head and cast it aside. Her bra followed and his lips were an impatient heat against her nipples as he drew first one delicate tip, then the other, into his mouth. Abigail arched her back and cried out, as a whole new spectrum of sensation swept over her. She was spinning out of control, giving herself up to rapture.

She ran her hand down the front of his body, smoothing over the hard muscles of his chest and down over the ridges of his abdomen. Griffin sucked in a breath as her fingertips lightly brushed his straining erection.

Giving a shaky laugh, he took hold of her hand and guided it so she could wrap her fingers around his shaft. He was raw, pulsing heat beneath her touch. "That feels like heaven but it may test my self-control to the limit."

As she caressed his warm flesh, Griffin's hand moved inside the elastic of her sweat pants, one finger parting her swollen folds. Abigail gave a gasp and he paused. "Is that okay?"

She nodded vigorously. "It's wonderful."

"Then let's get rid of these." She raised her hips so that he could pull her sweatpants and underwear down over her hips and legs.

She let her eyes wander down his body. He was so big and hard, his erection heavy and straining toward her. His silken flesh looked like it was made to be stroked. She knelt on the bed, moving toward him on her knees.

"Let me taste you."

She wrapped her fingers around the base of his shaft and lowered her head, swiping her tongue over the engorged tip. Griffin's whole body jerked, and he hissed in a breath. Abigail gave a little hum of pleasure.

"You like that?"

His groan told her that he did. Repeating the action, she flicked her tongue back and forth over the throbbing crest. His flesh tasted clean and salty, yet darkly erotic. As she became more adventurous and closed her mouth over his head, Griffin moaned, thrusting in small movements against her lips. It seemed natural to suck, and he fisted a hand in her hair in response. Abigail looked up at his face, enjoying his response. His eyes were half-closed, the cords of muscle in his neck standing out.

Gently he eased away from her. "I don't want this to be over before we've even started."

Placing his knee on the bed, he tipped her onto her back. Pressing her onto the bed, he lowered his head between her thighs, and her senses went wild. His tongue rasped over her most tender flesh with the lightest, softest strokes, licking at her, and she writhed in ecstasy, burning to lift herself closer.

"Please..." She needed more but her voice didn't seem to be working.

Luckily, Griffin seemed to know what her wail of need meant. His tongue found the tiny bundle of sensitized nerve endings and flickered over it, sending fire pulsing through her. She dug her hands into his hair in an attempt to draw him even closer. His hands hooked under her knees, pushing them back and wider apart as his tongue stroked her entrance. She felt a pressure, then he was probing just inside her. Color flamed in her cheeks. It was so sweetly, deliciously exciting.

An aching need was building inside her, hunger driving her toward a longed-for release. His lips covered her, his tongue returning to torment that tiny nub, and Abigail's whole body exploded. It propelled her into a cataclysmic ecstasy, tightening her muscles and sending shooting stars of rapture through to every cell in her body. Griffin held her down as she writhed and convulsed, calling out his name deliriously.

She became vaguely aware of him tearing open a condom wrapper before moving in place between her thighs. His lips were gentle on hers as she felt the heavy pressure of him pushing against her still-throbbing entrance.

"Don't go slow." She lifted her hips to accommodate him, gasping as her muscles began to stretch, easing the way for his steel-hard erection. "I want you…all of you."

A powerful thrust of his hips pushed him deeper into her, the tight friction causing her to arch up to him. She twisted mindlessly beneath him, demanding more, and Griffin pulled back before driving into her again, seating himself fully inside her this time. She was as full as she could be. Full of him. It was glorious. Now she needed him to move. To pound in and out of her. Until she screamed.

She wrapped her legs around his hips, urging him on, and heard his groan of surrender. He drew back, then filled her again, impaling her on his thick length. Mindless pleasure washed over her. She gave herself up to sensation. Reality was lost as Griffin drove into her hard and fast, exactly as she had begged.

His erection was a hot length of iron powering into her, rubbing over tender tissue, building the friction, stoking the pleasure, until Abigail thought she might go wild. Her breath was suspended, meaning she couldn't even scream as he increased the tempo, his rapid-fire thrusts driving her ever closer to the edge.

This time, when her release slammed into her, her muscles gripped him, heightening the intensity of each spasm. It felt like liquid velvet had been poured into her veins. Her body was languid, yet every sense was heightened as she pulsed and contracted, each perfect wave ebbing and flowing rapturously over and around her.

She felt his hard flesh stiffen further, his body jerk-

ing to a standstill as the white-hot force of his own release claimed him. Abigail wrapped her arms around
him, wanting to hold him to her, to capture the moment for all eternity.

Eventually she collapsed beneath him, shuddering
in the aftershocks of unimaginable pleasure.

"That was…" When her breath returned, she floun-
dered, searching for the right words.

"Perfect." He sighed the word against her ear as he
drew her into his arms.

"It was."

"I meant you. *You* are perfect."

THE NEXT MORNING, Griffin woke early. His arms were
full of Abigail's warm curves and, for a few minutes,
he just enjoyed how that felt. Waking up with her was
too new, too perfect, to rush. Then he remembered
what he'd been thinking about the previous night and
he eased carefully away from her.

Going into the kitchen, he made himself a cup
of coffee before heading for his study. Once he was
logged in to his laptop, he accessed the Danvers University website. He figured he could have asked Abigail for the information he was looking for but for
some reason he wanted to do the research himself.

The lab's staff members were all listed under their
individual faculties. Although Dr. Hardin's profile remained in place, there was a banner above the research
department with an obituary honoring him and the
work he had done at the university. Griffin scrolled

down, studying the photographs and biographies. He wasn't sure what he was looking for. There was just something at the back of his mind that told him that they were overcomplicating things. The reason for Evan Hardin's death would turn out to be much simpler than they realized.

He skimmed past Abigail's biography, moving on to the junior staff in the department. One of the names caught his eye. Dr. Jenna Avery. What was her role in this? Why had Evan Hardin, or someone acting on his behalf, tried to use this woman to get at Abigail? Her profile was respectable, and he glanced at her photograph. Then he looked again. She was early thirties, pretty, with her dark hair cut in a short bob. And she looked familiar. But surely it couldn't be…

Quickly, he opened another tab and scrolled through his emails, finding the one that he'd sent to Liam Desmond about the online adoption scam. There it was. The old profile picture that Griffin had taken from Dr. Anne Jay's old social media account. The head of MorningStar Families was half-turned away from the camera, and the angle wasn't good, but Griffin was almost certain that Anne Jay and Jenna Avery were the same person.

"Damn it." He ran a hand through his hair. "Even the name is a clue."

Yet… Surely no one would be that arrogant? If Jenna Avery was the person behind this scam, would she really use an alias whose initials were the reverse of her own first name? It seemed too obvious, yet his job and his involvement in CI had taught him that there were no surprises when it came to criminal behavior. People who thought they were above the law often believed they were so clever that they could afford to make jokes at the expense of their victims and the law enforcement agencies who pursued them.

Even so, he was having trouble picturing anyone leading such a bizarre double life. Respectable research scientist and online fraudster? The two didn't fit well together. It was like picturing a librarian who was also a bank robber, or an accountant who mugged old ladies. Stranger things might happen, but it was hard to imagine what they might be.

An internet search didn't give him much more information about Jenna Avery than her Danvers University profile. He glanced at the time on his laptop screen. It was still early. He could wake Abigail, but did he really want to take these suspicions to her and alarm her before he'd even fully thought them through? There was one person who could always be counted on to listen without judging.

"Riley? I need to run the wildest idea by you." It was only when he heard the murmur of voices that Griffin remembered that his brother now lived with Charlize. "Sorry. Did I wake you?"

"Yeah. But it's okay." Riley yawned. "Tell me what this is about."

Quickly, Griffin outlined his thinking about Jenna Avery. "I'm being overimaginative, right? It couldn't possibly be the same woman."

"Send me the picture and the link to the university website. I'll take a look and call you back."

While he waited for his brother to check out the information he'd sent, Griffin reread the email he'd sent to Liam Desmond. As part of his investigation, Griffin had researched MorningStar Families. Despite glowing references on social media, he had been unable to find evidence that the company actually existed, or that it had helped any families to adopt. He had concluded that it existed only as a means of conning people like Liam and Shelby, who were desperate to have a child of their own.

Riley called back five minutes later. "I agree that both pictures could be the same woman, but it's not conclusive. The best thing to do is hand them over to Detective Iglesias. The police have specialist imaging equipment with which they can make a comparison."

Griffin rubbed a hand over his face. "It feels like this whole case is based on hunches and suppositions. Whenever I talk to the police, I sense them rolling their eyes."

"If you're right about this, they'll be glad you persisted," Riley said. "In the meantime, maybe you and I should have a chat with Dr. Jenna Avery."

Chapter Twelve

It was lunchtime and the Danvers University campus was busy as Griffin drove around the parking lot a few times before he finally found a space.

"There are no guarantees that Jenna Avery will see us," he said, as he and Riley exited the car.

"No, but Jenna said that the RevitaYou vitamins she bought made her sick," Riley reminded him. "We'll tell her that we are interviewing all victims of the con, whether they are investors, or those who have been unwell as a result of taking the pills. She felt strongly enough about it to confront Abigail publicly, so hopefully she will be willing to talk to us about her experience."

Once inside the building, they approached the desk and asked for Dr. Avery. The receptionist took their names and Riley's business card, then spoke on the telephone.

"Dr. Avery is on her way," she told them, when she ended her call.

Even without her name badge, the woman who

stepped out of the elevator a few minutes later was instantly recognizable from her profile on the university website. Jenna Avery was petite and attractive, but Griffin sensed she had a watchful air about her. The receptionist handed her Riley's business card and pointed to where the Colton brothers were standing.

Jenna dug her hands into the pockets of her white lab coat as she approached. "I can only spare a few minutes, so it would be helpful if you could tell me straight away what this is about."

"My brother and I are working with the police and the FBI to bring those behind the RevitaYou con to justice," Riley said.

Her expression was hard to read but Griffin saw something shift in the dark depths of her eyes, as though she was weighing up how she could make the most of this situation.

"I can take my lunch early, if you don't mind joining me while I grab a coffee and a sandwich."

There were a few places to eat around the campus and Jenna led them to a small coffee shop. Although the place was busy, they got a table in a quiet corner. Once they'd placed their order, Jenna gave the two men a thoughtful look. "Why have you come to me to talk about RevitaYou?"

"We are talking to everyone who has had a bad experience with the vitamins," Griffin said.

"But how did you know I'd had a problem with the product? I haven't been to the police. I haven't even tried to make a complaint to the manufacturers."

There it was again. That manner of hers was more than watchful. It was suspicious.

Griffin thought for a moment about the best way to answer her question. They already knew she was antagonistic toward Abigail. If he introduced her into the conversation too early, he risked driving Jenna away. "We spoke to someone else at the university who'd had a bad experience with RevitaYou. They mentioned that you'd spoken publicly about your own issues."

"Issues." Her eyes narrowed slightly. "Is that what they called it? Yes, I had issues with RevitaYou."

"Could you tell us what happened?" Riley asked.

"I bought some of the pills, took them and got sick." She shrugged. "Isn't that what happens to most people?"

"Actually, no," Griffin said. "Many RevitaYou users report no side effects."

Their server arrived with Jenna's lunch and their drinks and they waited until he had left before resuming the conversation.

"How soon after you started taking the pills did your symptoms start?" Griffin asked.

"Look." Jenna sat up straighter. "The only reason I agreed to talk to you is because I want that con man, Wes Matthews, and his high-and-mighty daughter to get what's coming to them."

To get what's coming to them. Was it a coincidence that they were the words that Ryan Thorne had used when he threatened Abigail? There was something about Jenna that felt off to Griffin. It was as if everything about her was fake.

"The police have no reason to believe that Abigail Matthews is involved in the RevitaYou fraud." Griffin kept his voice deliberately calm. "Do you have any evidence to suggest otherwise?"

Color flared in her cheeks. "Only what I know of her. That she pretends to be better than the rest of us, yet she wouldn't miss an opportunity to betray a friend—" she broke off. "I think this conversation is over."

Griffin got to his feet. An idea had occurred to him and he just hoped Riley would see what he was doing and go along with it. "Just one more thing."

Jenna gave him a resentful glance. "What is it?"

"What did you do with your unused RevitaYou pills?"

"I threw them in the trash. Why?"

"Oh, no reason. I just hoped we could take them from you for analysis." He half turned away and then looked back. "I suppose the pretty RevitaYou bottles were just too attractive to resist."

Jenna paused in the act of taking a sip of coffee. "What do you mean?"

"I was simply surprised that a scientist would purchase an unlicensed product like RevitaYou. But then the packaging and marketing were very appealing." He smiled. "Especially the pink bottles."

Out of the corner of his eye, he saw Riley frown. His brother knew, of course, that the RevitaYou bottles were green, not pink. He gave Riley a pleading look. *Stick with me on this.*

Jenna shrugged. "We've all fallen for a product that looks good now and then."

"I guess we have. Thank you for your time, Dr. Avery."

They left the building and made their way outside. It was only when they reached the parking lot that Riley placed a hand on Griffin's shoulder.

"Nice work. She has never seen a RevitaYou pill bottle, has she?"

"No." Griffin's lips hardened into a line. "So why does she have a grudge against Abigail?"

ABIGAIL LISTENED IN silence as Griffin recounted the details of his and Riley's meeting with Jenna Avery. As he was speaking, tiny darts of panic prickled her skin. How had her life gone so wildly off course in such a short space of time? Luckily, Maya was napping, and they had a half hour or more of quiet in which they could talk without interruption.

"I don't understand. Are you saying that she didn't know what color the RevitaYou bottles are?" she asked at last. "If she used them, she must have known that they're green."

"Exactly. Your dad did a good job of marketing his product. Those bottles are very distinctive. If Jenna had bought any RevitaYou vitamins, there is no way she would get confused about the color of the bottle." Griffin took her hand. "For some reason, she made up the whole story about getting sick as a result of taking the pills."

Abigail shook her head. "Why would she do that?"

"I can only think of one reason. Jenna must be the person who wants to get at you."

"But why?" Abigail's head was spinning. "We were friends. I wasn't close with her like I was with Veronica, but we got on. I never had any reason to suspect that she disliked me or had a grudge against me."

"I guess we'll find out in time," Griffin said. "But sometimes these things can be quite minor. It may even have been an imagined insult. Maybe she said 'good morning' one day and you didn't respond. Or you forgot her birthday or sat in her favorite chair."

"Even if one of those things *was* the trigger, I can't believe she would be guilty of killing Evan."

"Jenna Avery has proved that she is a liar. Riley and I have told Detective Iglesias about our conversation with her. Now it's up to him to find how far she would go. Is she also a murderer? Only a police investigation can uncover the truth."

Abigail got to her feet. "I'm still struggling to understand how any of this could be happening."

Just then the baby monitor kicked into life. "Does Maya need food?" Griffin asked.

"No. She's eaten lunch," Abigail said. "A drink and some fruit will be enough to keep her going until dinner. Why?"

"Let's go out. Some fresh air will take our minds off what's going on."

Although she appreciated the suggestion, Abigail couldn't help wondering if anything would distract her from her thoughts. She was being pursued by a sinister figure who wanted to destroy her. Until today that person had been faceless. The possibility that it could be Jenna had shaken her to the core of her being. Someone she had known for so long, worked beside every day, talked to and laughed with… It made everything so much worse than if her attacker had been a stranger.

When Griffin brought Maya through from the bedroom, the baby's usual post-nap grumpiness lasted for as long as it took Abigail to change her diaper. Once she'd been placed in her high chair and given a snack of formula and stewed fruit, Maya was all smiles.

"My sisters were like that when we were kids," Griffin said. "The best way to keep them happy was to feed them. Sometimes it still is."

It was rare for him to talk about his family and, as she checked that Maya's bag was stocked with everything they needed, Abigail sent a sidelong glance in his direction. "Growing up in a house with two sets of female twins. Did that make you and Riley closer?"

"No." His expression was closed, and she thought he wasn't going to say any more, then his shoulders relaxed. "You must have guessed by now that I didn't entirely fit in."

Even though she had figured out that he felt out of place within his adoptive family, Abigail sensed that this was an area where she had to tread carefully. All the research she'd done prior to Maya's birth had told

her how necessary a sense of identity was to an adopted person. It was critical that she didn't do or say
anything to undermine Griffin's self-worth.

"I can see that you are very important to your siblings."

He appeared to consider her words carefully as
though the idea hadn't occurred to him until now. "I
think that's true. And, if you asked my brother and
my sisters, I'm sure they would strenuously deny that
I am not one of them."

"But?" Abigail probed gently.

"I can only speak for myself. And I have never *really* felt like a Colton."

"That must be very hard." She covered his hand
with her own.

He shrugged. "There are worse things in life."

She watched his face, unsure how far to push him.
Physically, this man shared so much of himself with
her. When she examined her feelings for him, she
knew that Griffin Colton had changed her life forever.
But she was forced to hold her own emotions back because she knew he was afraid of letting go. So maybe
it was time for her to take his and lead him...

"Like knowing your parent had been killed?" As
soon as she'd spoken, she regretted the words. The
pain that flitted across his face almost took her breath
away and she reached up to touch his cheek. "I'm
sorry. I shouldn't have said that."

"No. You're right. I was very lucky to have been
given a home by Graham and Kathleen. I was loved

and cared for. In many ways my life with them was privileged but I was also given a sense of responsibility and social justice." He caught hold of her hand, pressing it to his lips. "Even so, they didn't shape who I am."

"Your mom did that." Tears stung her eyelids at the thought of the child he'd been and the pain he'd endured.

"Everything I am is because of her."

"She would be so proud of you, Griffin." Abigail reached up and drew his face down to hers so she could kiss him lightly on the lips.

"Thank you for that."

Maya, clearly feeling she had been left out of the conversation for long enough, let out a loud belch. When it got them both to turn around, she clapped her hands.

"Oh, no." Griffin shook his head. "We are not going to start applauding bodily functions."

She gave him one of her cheeky grins and drummed her heels noisily against the high chair.

"Does that mean you want to get out?" Griffin asked.

Maya held up her arms in response. Griffin lifted her from the chair and held her up while Abigail cleaned her face and hands with baby wipes. As she did, two things occurred to her. One was how quickly they'd gotten into a baby care routine. The second was that Griffin's expression had lightened. Even though he hadn't really opened up about his childhood, she sensed that the first barrier had been breached.

As their eyes met over Maya's head, he smiled, and she knew he was letting her know that she was right.

SHERIDAN PARK WAS busy with families and dog walkers. Griffin took Lucy on her harness and leash and, as usual, she attracted a mixture of reactions. Most people admired the cute little ferret, who performed a range of gymnastic tricks. Several were curious and asked questions about her. Only a few were wary and regarded the unusual animal anxiously as though she might be about to break free and go into attack mode at any minute.

Maya, watching from the comfort of her stroller, chuckled at the antics of her ferret buddy. As they strolled around the lake, Griffin was pleased that Abigail appeared relaxed and reasonably content. She'd taken the news about Jenna hard but he admired the way she dealt with everything that came her way. Lately, just when she thought things couldn't get worse, she was rocked by more bad news. Yet she faced each blow with determination and courage. Her inner strength was amazing, and he figured it must have built up when she'd had to cope alone during the difficult years of her childhood. Even though their personalities were different, they had so much in common.

"I used to come here with my mom," she said, as they followed a path around the water's edge. "My dad was very controlling, and he didn't like her to leave the house without him, but she tried to make my life as normal as possible. We'd sneak out and spend time here, feeding the ducks and eating ice cream."

"She sounds like a remarkable woman."

"She was. Most people don't understand that because she left me behind when she finally ran out on my dad. They figure that only a very selfish woman could have done something like that to her child." Her face was half-turned away from him as if she was watching the wildfowl on the water, but he sensed her mind was focused on another time and place. "But you have to know my dad to understand the circumstances. He'd made her life a living hell and she'd reached the point where she had to leave before he broke her. She couldn't have known when she went that he would stop her from seeing me again."

"When someone is driven to take desperate action, they often can't see any alternatives," Griffin said.

"My mom was scared and in hiding. She had no money, no family and no one to help her fight him." Abigail turned to look at him. "She needed someone like you to advise her."

"Let me see if I've got the math right. You were ten when Sofia left Wes left, right? That means I was seven." He bumped her shoulder gently with his own. "I don't think I'd have been much use to your mom."

Laughing, she dug him in the ribs with her elbow. "You know what I meant."

Just as Griffin was enjoying the carefree moment,

his cell phone buzzed. Although he was tempted to ignore it, there were too many claims on his attention. His junior colleagues were all good at their jobs, but there were times when his expertise was needed. And the Colton siblings had an agreed code that they would be there for each other at all times. Then, of course, there was always the possibility that the police had news.

Sure enough, the call was from Emmanuel Iglesias. The detective didn't bother with a greeting. "I just stopped by your place." There was an urgency in his tone that concerned Griffin. "Where are you?"

"In Sheridan Park. What's this all about?"

"Are Abigail Matthews and her daughter with you?"

"Yes. But what—?"

"Go to the coffee shop at the park entrance and wait for me there. I'm on my way." The detective ended the call before Griffin could say any more.

He stared at the screen of his cell for a few seconds, his mind running through a list of possibly reasons for Emmanuel's unusual behavior. If he was coming to arrest Abigail, Griffin wouldn't let that happen. Not without a fight.

Abigail's hand on his arm drew his attention back to her. "What was that about?"

"Emmanuel Iglesias wants us to meet him at the coffee shop."

Her face paled and he could tell she was having the same thoughts as he. Had her anonymous tormentor managed to plant more evidence to convince the police of her guilt? Was Emmanuel on his way to finally slap the cuffs on her?

She swallowed hard. "Why?

"He didn't say." Gently, he placed her hand on the bar of Maya's stroller and covered it with his own. "But there's only one way to find out."

Chapter Thirteen

To Abigail, each step that took them closer to the coffee shop at the park entrance represented the clanging of a closing prison door. Why else would Emmanuel need to see them with such urgency?

Her feet were moving in time with Griffin's, but every nerve ending was crying out for her to swing the stroller around and run in the opposite direction. The person who wanted to frame her had won. The police were coming to get her. But she couldn't be parted from her baby…and Griffin.

When they reached the entrance to the coffee shop, Griffin stopped. "We can't take Lucy inside." He looked around. "Since there's no sign of Emmanuel, we'll wait here."

There were a few people around and Abigail's attention was instantly drawn to a small, slight figure dressed all in black. It was such a warm day, and it seemed odd that anyone would wear a sweatshirt with the hood pulled up. As the person moved toward them, she noticed that he, or she, was also wearing shades.

At the last minute, she saw the outstretched hand and the knife pointed directly at Maya. Her throat tightened with dread. When she tried to cry out and let Griffin know what was happening, no sound came out. With only a split second to act, she threw herself between the lethal weapon and her baby.

Time slowed. Heat seared Abigail's upper left arm as the knife sliced through her flesh. The stroller tilted and she tumbled with it to the ground. Scrambling desperately to protect Maya, she lay over the top of the stroller and anticipated the next slice of the blade.

As if from a distance, Griffin shouted, and Maya started to cry. When Abigail looked up, the hooded attacker was standing over her holding the bloodied blade inches from her face. As she lifted her right hand to shield her face, a tiny, furry figure darted out from beneath the stroller. Lucy sank her sharp teeth into the assailant's left wrist at the top of the gloved hand that held the knife.

Letting out a screech, the hooded figure dropped the weapon and tried to shake Lucy free. With her leash hanging loose, the little ferret hung on tight.

Pain washed over Abigail. Warm blood was pouring down her arm and her vision started to fade. Desperately clinging to consciousness, she tried to look around to see if Maya was okay. Unsure whether the pounding in her ears was her own heartbeat or running footsteps, she was relieved to hear Emmanuel call out a warning.

"GRPD. Stay right where you are."

Ignoring him, the attacker finally knocked Lucy away and spun around. Although Abigail couldn't see what was going on, she heard the detective talking into his radio. "Sheridan Park. Close down the exits. The suspect is on foot and moving fast. She's injured and leaving a trail of blood."

She?

Griffin was kneeling beside her, but his face was an indistinct blur as he removed his T-shirt and used it to apply pressure to her injury. "We need paramedics here. Fast. She's been stabbed."

"Maya?" She clutched his wrist with her right hand.

He slid an arm around her, and she rested her head against his shoulder. "She's unhurt. Detective Lopez has her. We'll take her to the hospital with us."

"What about Lucy?" She managed to gasp out the question. "She saved my life."

"Emmanuel doesn't know it yet but he's about to take a ferret into protective custody."

When he joined them, Emmanuel was carrying Maya and holding Lucy's leash. "The paramedics are on their way." As if to confirm the truth of his statement, they heard the sound of approaching sirens. "Uh. What do you want me to do with the rodent?"

"Get someone to take her to my sister, Sadie. She'll look after her until I can collect her," Griffin said. He took Maya from Emmanuel and, although the baby tucked her head into his neck, Abigail was pleased to see that her tears had subsided. "Then, you need to explain what's going on."

"Yeah." Emmanuel nodded. "After I've coordinated the search and taken care of the wildlife, I'll follow you to the hospital."

Detective Lopez had done a good job of keeping any onlookers back and the ambulance was able to drive right up to the steps of the coffee shop. As it stopped, Emmanuel started to walk away.

"Wait." Abigail's voice was a croak. Shock was setting in. She was shivering wildly, and her teeth chattered as though she was freezing. But she had to know *now*. Later wouldn't do. "You said the person who attacked me was a she. Does that mean you know who it was?"

"Yes." His expression was grim. "It was Jenna Avery."

ONCE THEY WERE in the ambulance and on the way to the hospital, two paramedics examined Abigail. Griffin's anxiety for her was off the scale, but he maintained a calm exterior for Maya's sake. Although the baby had recovered from the shock of having her stroller overturned, she had picked up the tension in the atmosphere and was clingy and whiny.

The paramedics had guided him to a seat that was out of the way of the action and requested that he fasten himself and Maya in so that they were safe during the ride. It meant Maya couldn't see her mom and she kept up a loud protest throughout the journey.

"It's okay. I'm here," Griffin told her. She gave him

a tear-stained look that told him that, right at that moment, he wasn't what she wanted.

It wasn't easy to hear what the paramedics were saying while he was trying to comfort the distressed baby, but he strained to listen to their conversation. "Vital signs are all okay, but the wound is deep and she's lost a lot of blood."

"I'm calling ahead. We need the trauma team prepped and ready for surgery."

Surgery. What did that mean, exactly? Could Abigail lose the use of that arm? Was amputation a possibility? *Tell me she's not going to die...*

When they reached the hospital, there was an emergency team waiting for them. Griffin caught only a brief glimpse of Abigail's face as they rolled the gurney past him and into the building. She wasn't conscious. Her beautiful features were as pale and still as a marble statue. Her T-shirt was stained a deep crimson.

"She's lost so much blood. Will she be okay?" He unfastened himself and Maya and got to his feet.

"If you follow the signs to the family room, sir, someone will be with you as soon as they can." It wasn't an answer.

Tuning into his mood, Maya hooked a hand behind his neck and rested her cheek against his chest. For an instant, he battled to keep control of his emotions. Holding Maya firmly, he walked into the building.

The family room was small and cozy with bright pictures on the walls and a well-stocked toy corner.

There was no one else around and, after sitting Maya on the rug with some play items, Griffin took his cell phone out of his pocket. There were messages from all his siblings. One of Emmanuel's colleagues had taken Lucy to Sadie's place and, while handing over the ferret, had given her a brief account of what had happened to Abigail. The family support system had already swung into action. For the first time in his life, Griffin felt like a Colton.

On our way. Riley's text was brief, to the point. And very welcome.

He knelt on the floor beside Maya, trying to distract himself by playing with her, but his whole body hurt. He couldn't get enough air into his lungs and his heart felt as if it was trying to burst out of his chest. Even as he talked to Maya about the toys, his brain was asking "what if?"

Panic was like an iron fist tightening its grip on his gut. This couldn't be happening. He couldn't have found Abigail only to lose her this way. When he thought back to all those doubts he'd had about her and how hurt she must have been… He clenched a fist on his thigh. That was in the past. They'd moved on. Even so, what if she died without knowing how much he cared?

Although he was alone in the darkness of his thoughts for less than half an hour, it felt like forever. When Riley and Charlize finally dashed into the room, he felt the first burn of tears at the back of his eyelids and blinked hard. He needed to be strong for Maya. And Abigail...

"Oh, my goodness." Charlize fell to her knees beside Griffin, wrapping her arms around him. "How are you holding up?"

He drew in a shaky breath. "I'd be a lot better if I knew what was going on."

"You mean no one has told you anything?" Riley looked around at the empty room.

Griffin got to his feet, leaving Charlize and Maya playing together. "I figure they need to be with Abigail, not out here talking to me."

"Even so, you must be out of your mind with worry. Why don't we stay here with Maya while you see if you can find someone who can tell you what's happening?"

When Griffin tried to thank him, his voice refused to work and the only sound that emerged was a grunt. He saw the understanding in his brother's eyes as Riley placed a hand on his shoulder and steered him toward the door. When he left the room, he noticed a sign directing him to the reception desk. Before he began to follow it, a female doctor approached him.

"Are you here with Dr. Matthews?"

There it was again. That tightness in his throat that made it hard to talk. "Yes."

Suddenly, he wanted to walk away and not hear what this woman had to say. Right now, everything was okay. She could change that with a few words.

"Please follow me." She led him along a corridor

and into a small office. "May I ask what your relationship is to Dr. Matthews?"

It was a tricky question and one to which he didn't know the answer. Since this was not the time or place for soul-searching, he decided to be as honest as he needed to be. "We live together."

She seemed satisfied with that. "Okay. I'm Dr. Reynolds. I led the surgical team who operated on Dr. Matthews. We had to stabilize her condition and reduce the bleeding before we could treat her injury. Because of the severity of the wound, we administered a general anesthetic to determine the extent of the damage. Although there was significant trauma caused by the blade penetration, I'm hopeful that there will be no long-term effects to her arm. The greater concern was dealing with the amount of blood Dr. Matthews lost."

"What treatment has she been given?" Griffin asked.

"After cleansing the wound, we closed it using sutures. We are administering intravenous fluids and antibiotics and she has been given a blood transfusion. It's possible she may need more blood but that's something we'll judge when she comes around from the anesthetic. We'll continue to monitor her vital signs, of course and, longer term, she'll need physiotherapy."

"But she will recover?"

She placed a hand on his arm. "Yes. I have every confidence that she will make a full recovery."

He bowed his head, the relief that flooded through him almost as overwhelming as the fear it replaced.

Abigail was alive and she would be okay. "Can I see her?"

"Yes. She's awake now and has already asked for both you and someone called Maya."

"That's our daughter." He said the words without thinking but as soon as he heard the phrase out loud it made him pause. *Our daughter.* Two little words that contained everything he wanted for the future. "Can I take her to see Abigail?"

"Of course. You can see her together."

WHEN SHE FIRST came around from the anesthetic, Abigail felt like she'd been sleeping for too long and too deeply. Now, she was tired but impatient to see Griffin and Maya. Obediently following the nurse's instructions to rest, she had her eyes closed when she heard Maya let out a cry of delight as they entered the room.

"Yes, it's your mom." Griffin was talking softly. "But we need to be quiet so we don't disturb her."

"I'm awake." Even though she'd been conscious for some time, there was still a slight slurring to her words, as if she was tipsy.

Griffin was at her side instantly. "I'll call the nurse."

"No. I'm fine. She said to use the call button if I need anything." She turned her head slightly so she could look at him and Maya. "This is nice. Just us."

"How do you feel?" He shook his head. "Stupid question."

She lifted her right hand and touched his wrist before stroking Maya's cheek. "Jenna ran away. Did they catch her?"

"No." The voice came from the doorway as, with perfect timing, Emmanuel strode into the room. "I'm sorry I don't have better news for you, but she mingled with the crowds in the park and we lost her. We're still searching, of course."

"I've been waiting for you to tell us exactly what's going on," Griffin said.

"Are you strong enough to have this conversation now?" Emmanuel asked Abigail.

"I need to know why I'm in this hospital bed." She tried to shift position and winced as pain shot through her injured arm. "And whether I have to worry about the future."

"Okay." Emmanuel pulled up a visitor's chair and indicated for Griffin to do the same. When Griffin was seated, Maya settled onto his knee and, by the way her eyelids were drooping, it looked as if she would soon be asleep. "I followed up the information from Griffin and Riley about Jenna's dishonesty over the RevitaYou pills and paid her a visit. When I interviewed her, she came across as very edgy. There wasn't anything specific, but I got the definite impression that she was hiding something. After I left her apartment, I decided to hang around and watch the place. Sure enough, ten minutes later, she came hurrying out carrying a large travel bag. She got into her car and drove off like the hounds of hell were chasing her."

"Did you follow her?" Griffin asked.

"I tried but I lost her after a few blocks. We didn't have enough evidence to get a search warrant for her home address but, after Dr. Hardin's murder, I was able to search Jenna's office at Danvers University. She hadn't been very careful about covering up her obsession with you, Abigail."

"Obsession?" Abigail reached out her right hand and Griffin took hold of it.

"In one drawer of her desk, she had a file containing pictures and cuttings from academic texts. It must have contained everything that was ever printed about you," Emmanuel said.

"But why?" Abigail asked. "We were friends."

"Not according to this." Emmanuel withdrew a book from the inside pocket of his jacket. Although it was contained within an evidence bag, Abigail could see that it looked like a journal of some kind. "This is Jenna's diary. In it, she helpfully documents how she added Anthrosyne to the Mem10 trial and tried to frame you for it. How she wanted to further ruin your reputation by pretending to have taken RevitaYou and gotten ill. She goes into detail about how she killed Evan Hardin because he was about to fire her from her job but how she callously used his death as another chance to get back at you. And, as I already said, she outlined her plans to kill you and Maya, if the police get close to her."

"Get back at me?" Abigail couldn't manage to raise her voice above a whisper. "For what?"

"She has always been jealous of you, both person-ally and professionally. There is a lot of ranting in the diary about your looks and how you rose to your current position at the university. But she seems to have become unhinged recently because she believes you were investigating her role in an online adop-tion scam."

Griffin sat up a little straighter and Maya gave a sleepy grumble. "So she *was* living a double life as Anne Jay?"

"I don't understand." Abigail looked from one man to the other in confusion.

"I didn't have time to talk to you about my suspi-cions," Griffin explained. "But one of my cases in-volved an online adoption scam. The woman at the heart of it looked a lot like Jenna. From what Emman-uel is saying, it appears it *was* her."

"It was," Emmanuel confirmed. "Jenna had been conning childless couples in an online adoption fraud for several years. Basically, she used the miscarriage project you were both involved in to target childless couples. She targeted them through social media, in-troducing herself as the head of MorningStar Families, a private, online adoption agency. After building up a relationship with the vulnerable person, or couple, she would 'introduce' them to the pregnant woman who was supposedly carrying their child and ask for money for expenses. Over the course of the so-called pregnancy, photographs and documents would be ex-changed as well as cash. The pregnant woman didn't exist, of course, and when the nine months were over, Jenna simply ceased all contact with the couple who had been paying her."

"But that's awful." Abigail was horrified.

"Preying on people when they were at their most vulnerable is something that I see too often," Griffin said. "And social media allows people like Jenna to do it anonymously."

"But she knew someone was on to her. Her social media accounts were being tracked and someone was making inquiries about MorningStar Families," Emmanuel said. "You, Abigail, had been talking openly about your research into adoption. Jenna put the two things together and became convinced that you had discovered her guilty secret. She lied about RevitaYou to make you look bad. When Evan called her into his office and told her she was fired, she was certain you had reported your findings to him. The truth was that she'd been falsifying records again. He'd covered up for her in the past because they'd had a brief affair and she was using it to blackmail him but this time she'd gone too far. The details were all on his computer. It looks like she killed him before he had time to explain because she continued to blame you."

"*I* was the person who was on to her." Griffin lightly squeezed Abigail's hand. "When I think what could have happened…"

He looked torn apart with tiredness and worry. She returned his grip. "Hey. I'm still here."

"We need to talk about that," Emmanuel said. "I

hate to do this right now, but Jenna is still on the loose and she's sworn to kill you and Maya."

GRIFFIN'S FEARS WERE BACK, only this time they were stronger than ever. Jenna Avery was unhinged, and she wanted to harm his new family. And no one knew where she was, or when she would strike.

"How are you going to look after them?" he asked Emmanuel.

"While Abigail is in the hospital, we'll put a guard on this room," the police officer said. "Detective Lopez is in the family room with your brother and his fiancée. He can take the first shift."

"But what about Maya?" Abigail's face, already pale, turned ashen as she looked at the baby, who was now sleeping in Griffin's arms. "Jenna's threat was directed at both of us."

"I won't let her out of my sight," Griffin promised.

Tears brimmed in her eyes. "I can't bear this. How can I lie helpless in this bed, knowing that Jenna is out there just waiting to snatch my baby and harm her?"

Griffin knew exactly what she meant. He also knew it wouldn't do her recovery any good to be separated from her daughter at a time like this. Abigail would be distraught with worry every second she and Maya were apart.

"I need to talk to the doctor." Easing Maya into the crook of his arm, he got to his feet. "You'll be here with Abigail the whole time I'm gone, right?" He asked Emmanuel.

The detective nodded. "You can count on it."

Still carrying Maya, Griffin returned to the family room. Riley and Charlize were deep in conversation with Daniel Lopez and he figured that Emmanuel's partner had given them all the details about Jenna and her obsession with Abigail. All three of them looked up when he entered.

"How is Abigail?" Riley asked.

"She's going to be okay." He still felt the weight of everything those words meant about his feelings and his hopes for the future. "I have to go find the doctor and then I have something I need to run by you."

"Anything we can do to help." Riley placed a hand on his shoulder. "You know that."

"Let me take Maya." Charlize was on her feet in an instant, and he carefully handed the sleeping baby over.

"I guess you know about the threats from Jenna Avery?" Griffin spoke directly to Daniel Lopez.

"Don't worry." The detective nodded. "I'll be right here with your baby."

"Thank you."

When he reached the reception desk and asked for Dr. Reynolds, Griffin expected he would have a long wait. She was an emergency surgeon, after all. He was surprised when she joined him after a few minutes.

"My shift is just ending," she explained as they walked into her tiny office. "How can I help you?"

Quickly, he outlined the situation. "While I understand that Abigail may need recovery time in the hospital, I'm concerned about the effects on her well-being if she is separated from her daughter at such a difficult time."

The doctor frowned. "What are you proposing as an alternative?"

"If Abigail can be moved to my brother's home in Heritage Hill, my siblings and I will be able to take full-time responsibility for her care. She would be with Maya, and the police would have them both in one place, so their protection would be simpler. Her caseworker will need to agree to this arrangement as well, of course."

Dr. Reynolds was silent for a few moments. "I had envisaged Dr. Matthews being hospitalized for at least a few days. Since the circumstances are unusual, I'm prepared to consider your suggestion on the condition that we arrange for a nurse to visit her each day. And, if she shows any sign of a temperature, sickness, or the wound appears to be infected, then she must return to hospital immediately."

"Of course. I won't do anything to put her in danger," Griffin assured her. "All I want to do is protect her."

"I can see that." The doctor smiled for the first time. "She's a very lucky lady."

"After everything that's happened to her recently, I'm not sure she'd agree with you."

He returned to the family room and shared the details of his plan with Riley, who immediately started making plans. As Griffin listened to his brother making calls to the other siblings, alerting them to the situation and enlisting their help to get a room ready for Abigail at the CI headquarters, his heart expanded with warmth. This was his family and now they were opening their arms to Abigail and Maya the same way they had accepted him all those years ago.

"How about we take Maya home with us now?" Riley asked when he finished his calls. He turned to Detective Lopez. "Does your vehicle have a car seat?"

"No, but I can get one here within minutes that does." He started talking into his radio.

"What about your vehicle?" Griffin asked.

Riley flapped a hand. "Details. We can sort that out tomorrow."

Griffin briefly gripped his arm in a gesture of gratitude. "Thank you."

"Hey. Maya will have a little cousin soon enough." There it was. That assumption that Maya's place in their lives was permanent. Griffin only hoped Riley was right. "I know you'd do the same for us if the time came."

They spent the next few minutes getting the sleeping baby out to the parking lot and into the patrol car that had pulled up outside the front entrance of the building. Detective Lopez got in the driver's seat with Riley next to him. Charlize sat next to Maya in the rear.

Before the police officer drove away, Griffin leaned into the window to speak to him. "What are the chances that Jenna Avery could be watching the hospital?"

"It's a possibility."

"Could she follow you? Or the ambulance that takes Jenna to the CI headquarters?"

"If she does, we'll be ready for her." The detective's lips thinned into a line. "But don't build her up into something she's not. She's a woman on the run and, thanks to your weird pet, she's also injured."

For now, Griffin figured that was the best he could hope for. He stepped back, watching the vehicle as it drove away. A quick scan of the area outside the hospital showed nothing suspicious and, reassured that the police were protecting Abigail and Maya, he went back inside.

Chapter Fourteen

By the time the ambulance reached the CI headquarters, Abigail was exhausted and aching all over. But she wasn't going to complain. This solution of Griffin's meant she could heal in a safe place among people she knew. And the best part was that she didn't have to be parted from Maya.

When the emergency vehicle pulled up at the rear of the house, two orderlies carefully pushed her wheelchair into the building.

"I can walk," Abigail protested. "My arm is in a sling, but my legs work just fine."

"I don't know." One of them regarded her dubiously. "The doctor told us to use our judgment and you do look pale."

"How about she takes my arm?" Griffin said. "That way she can lean on me?"

The orderlies appeared to feel that was an acceptable compromise. As Griffin helped her from the wheelchair, and her legs trembled, she realized just how weak she was. When she finally stepped into the house, she felt like she'd just run a marathon.

"Where's Maya?" she asked.

"She's having dinner with my sisters." He pointed in the direction of the dining room. "Do you want to go through there and join them, or shall I take you to your bedroom so you can rest?"

She smiled. "I want to see Maya, of course."

He gave an exaggerated sigh. "Sure you do. Even though the doctor told me to make sure you got plenty of rest."

They walked slowly to the room where the entire Colton family were gathered around the table. Exclamations of delight greeted Abigail's arrival, and Griffin escorted her to a chair next to Maya's high chair. The baby cooed with pleasure and offered her mom a mangled piece of toast.

"It's okay, honey. The doctor advised against pre-chewed food at this stage of my recovery."

"It's so good to see you." Kiely reached across the table and pressed her uninjured hand. "What a terrible ordeal."

"The hero ferret can stay at my place as long as she needs to," Sadie said. "I borrowed an old cage from a neighbor whose dog had pups recently, so she's secure and I stopped by Griffin's place to pick up her toys and food."

Abigail was struck again by the genuine niceness of these people. They were investigating her dad, so they knew exactly what he'd done, and there was a

time when they'd believed she was part of his schemes.
Even if that was no longer the case, they could be for-
given for believing that Wes Matthews's daughter was
no good. Raised by a crook, she might have turned
out to be every bit as bad as her father.

But they'd been prepared to believe in her. Although
she knew part of that was for Griffin's sake, it felt good
that they'd been open enough to judge her on who she
was rather than on her notorious relative. And now, as
Sadie pressed her to have a hot drink and Vikki asked
if she was too warm, she felt like she'd been part of this
group forever. This was what a family felt like. How
wonderful that she was able to experience it for herself.

Tiredness settled over her and she let the conversation continue around her without attempting to be part
of it. The siblings were discussing the police protection for her and Maya and whether they also needed
to employ private bodyguards.

"While my instinct is to get an army and surround
the place, we have to consider what Detective Lopez
said." Was it her imagination, or did Griffin seem
more comfortable in his place at the table than he had
on the other occasions she'd seen him there? "We can't
build the threat from Jenna out of proportion. She's
a lone woman on the run and Lucy gave her a hell
of a bite. She has to be hurting badly. Possibly that
wound is even infected. Even if she tries to carry out
her threat, she's up against all of us and the police."

He looked around the table and Abigail could see
him checking whether he had the agreement of the
other members of the family.

"I'm not prepared to put Abigail and Maya at risk, so we have to be extra vigilant. But Riley, Charlize and I will be here full-time. In addition, Emmanuel is putting a police guard on the house 24/7. Plus the rest of you will be checking in regularly. Between us, I think we will be able to keep them safe until the police have Jenna in custody." He turned to Abigail and the smile in his eyes drove her weariness away. "The final decision has to be yours."

"I feel safe with you." After a few seconds, she remembered that they weren't alone. "All of you."

"Then that's settled. But we'll keep reviewing the situation and, if necessary, we can bring in additional security."

There was some general conversation, then Pippa let out a little cry.

"What is it? What's wrong?" Sadie asked.

"It's a text from Brody." Pippa held up her cell phone so they could see the display. "It just came through a second ago."

"I guess it makes sense he would contact you," Riley said. "Out of all of us, you are the one he has always been closest to."

"He's still in hiding." Pippa read the message to them. "He's terrified and desperate to know if Wes Matthews has been caught yet. He knows that's the only way he'll get his money back and be able to pay Capital X so he can come out of hiding and stop living in fear."

There were gloomy faces around the table and Abigail bowed her head.

"I hate to give Brody bad news when things are going so badly for him, but I'll have to reply and tell him that Wes is still on the run," Pippa said. "The only hope I can offer him is that we're working on it round the clock."

"Wait." Griffin stopped her before she could start typing out her response. "Maybe we should just pay back Capital X for Brody so he can come out of hiding?"

There was a stunned silence around the table and Abigail remembered the way Griffin had spoken about Brody when they'd first met. She'd gotten the impression that his feelings toward Brody were complicated. Clearly, she'd been right.

"Would you do that for Brody? And do we even have that kind of liquid cash?" Pippa asked.

"He doesn't deserve what's happening to him," Griffin said. "No one does."

"I'll text him back right away and tell him that we'll pay off his debt to Capital X." Pippa sent the reply and set her cell phone down on the table. There was an expectant hush in the room, but nothing happened. When there was no reply after a few minutes, the tension level wound down a little.

"It looks like Brody's gone silent again," Kiely said.

"Maybe he's had to start running again?" Sadie suggested.

"Or he could be too proud to let us pay his debt," Vikki said.

Griffin moved around the table to sit next to Abigail, checking that she was okay. "Which do you think it is?" She spoke quietly so that only he could hear. "Is he on the run again, or is he too proud?"

"I don't know." He lifted Maya from her high chair and held her on his lap, making sure that the baby could touch Abigail without hurting her. "But if Brody has gone quiet because it would hurt his pride if we paid to help him out of this situation... Well, it would make me think a lot more kindly of him than I've done in the past."

She studied his face. "Was that hard for you to say?"

He shrugged. "Not as hard as it would once have been. Brody found life easy. I found it hard. For a long time, I struggled to accept that it was because we're different people not because my family treated us any differently."

She placed her uninjured hand over his. "You're a good man, Griffin."

He smiled. "You're just saying that because you know you need my help. You can't change a diaper one-handed."

THAT NIGHT, GRIFFIN shared a room with Maya, while Abigail slept in the first-floor room that Charlize had prepared specially for her. Despite the painkillers, she had a restless night. The following morning, Griffin persuaded her to rest for most of the morning while he took care of Maya. When she finally insisted on getting out of bed, she asked him to send Charlize to help her shower.

"I can do that," he said. "Riley and Maya are playing with Pal in the hall."

She gave him a stern look. "Griffin, I will be more than happy to share a shower with you when my arm is mended. But you are not going to be my nurse."

He slid an arm around her waist and drew her close. "I want to take care of you."

"You do." She rubbed her cheek against his chest. "And I—" She stopped and hitched in a breath. "Couldn't manage without you."

"That's not what you were going to say."

"No, it's not." She tilted her head back and smiled up at him. "But there's a time and a place for everything. And this time and place are for me to shower and for you to make me lunch."

She gave him a playful shove toward the door with her right hand. As he followed her instructions and started to prepare lunch, Griffin wondered what she *had* almost said. *And I...what? "And I love you?"* Was that too much to hope for? There were times when he didn't think it was. He knew she cared for him. The closeness they shared didn't need words. But he wasn't sure about what she wanted for the long term. And that terrified him.

Because he knew exactly what he wanted. He wanted Abigail. And Maya. He wanted his little family. Forever. The prospect of a future without them in it was bleak and unbearable.

To distract himself, he turned on the TV and flicked through the news channels, pausing when a familiar item caught his attention. The anchor was holding up a bottle of RevitaYou pills. Griffin stopped chopping vegetables for a salad and turned up the sound.

"The woman, who has not yet been named, died in Grand Rapids Hospital in the early hours of this morning. Her death has been linked to the controversial supplement RevitaYou. Extensive testing on the unregulated vitamins has revealed that the formula is toxic and potentially fatal. Since no one can be sure who will be affected, the public are being advised not take this product and to dispose of any unused pills."

"Oh, no."

Griffin turned to see Abigail standing in the kitchen doorway, holding on to the frame with her good hand as she stared at the TV. Her hair was damp and piled up on top of her head in a loose knot and she wore sweatpants and a T-shirt. He hurried to her side, sliding an arm around her waist to support her. She leaned against him, resting her head on his shoulder.

"I knew it was only a matter of time before someone died." Her voice trembled with emotion. "The ricin in those pills means the people taking them are dicing with death. But now my dad is a killer as well as a con man."

"Will people listen to the warning?" Griffin wondered. "When we put out social media blasts about RevitaYou causing sickness, there were always those who fired back at us about how much they loved the vitamins."

"Let's see what the response to the news of the death has been." Abigail fumbled her cell out of her jeans pocket with her good hand. Griffin looked over her shoulder as she checked the RevitaYou hashtag. "Look at this." She shook her head, her expression disbelieving. "People are still defending RevitaYou, calling it a wonder drug. There are dozens who are claiming it's made them look twenty-nine instead of forty-five."

Griffin pointed out one post. I'd rather die than be an old hag. "I'm sure it's meant as a joke, but it's not exactly good taste on a day like this."

"I don't usually reply, but I can't let that pass." Abigail awkwardly used one hand to hold her phone and type her reply. This is no joke. Someone has died. "And I know more deaths are coming. What will it take to stop people from taking these hateful, poisonous 'vitamins'?"

"The only way I can see this ending is if there *are* more deaths," Griffin said. "People have to take notice if they think they could die as a result of trying to look younger."

"You read some of those posts." Abigail looked seriously worried. "I genuinely think there are some who would take a chance."

"Then we have to keep trying to lure your dad and Landon Street out of hiding. A court case is the only other way to highlight the dangers." He ran a hand through his hair. "But I know how much you hate the idea of being drawn into that."

"I hate the idea of even more people dying."

"Do you think you can eat some lunch?" he asked.

She gave him a weak smile. "Are you asking because the doctor told you to take good care of me?"

"The nurse is coming this afternoon. We have to be able to tell her what a model patient you are."

She huffed out a mock sigh. "In that case, I guess I could manage a little lunch."

"There's a good patient." He guided her toward the dining room. "Oh, and Abigail?"

"Yes, Griffin?"

"I would take good care of you, whether a doctor told me to or not."

"I know you would." He caught a glimmer of tears in her eyes and wanted to lighten the mood. She was right when she said there was a time and a place for the deep conversations. The devastating news about the RevitaYou death had already taken its toll on her emotions. He didn't want any more setbacks.

"I have to." He leaned closer to whisper in her ear. "You promised me that, when you're well again, we get to share a shower."

THE NURSE HAD finished cleaning and dressing Abigail's wound. She had left, giving her strict instructions not to overdo things before she returned the following day. Abigail lay back on her pillows feeling tired, slightly nauseated and tearful. Those emotions had been her companions almost constantly since she'd left the hospital.

What is the matter with me?

She tapped a finger to her chin. *Let me see.*

Could it be the fact that my former friend, not content with having stabbed me, wants to kill me and my little girl? Or that I had surgery yesterday to repair the five-inch wound in my arm? Or that I have to stay hidden away like a fugitive with a patrol car at the gates? Or is it maybe that my dad has finally upgraded from fraudster to killer?

That was before she started on the other things: someone had killed her boss, her professional reputation was in shreds, the fate of the research of which she was so proud hung in the balance, people hated her because of her name…

There were so many reasons for her to feel low, it was impossible to single out just one. And yet, if she was honest, she wasn't sure if any of those were responsible for this weight pressing down on her. Her mood ricocheted between low and lower and she couldn't summon the inner strength on which she'd always relied in times of trouble.

Part of her mind kept dwelling on this house. On the Colton family. And on Griffin. What was she ever going to do when they were no longer part of her life? She gave a soft, bitter laugh.

They? *You mean "he."*

The Coltons were very special people. They'd made

her feel like part of their family. But she was in love with Griffin, not his siblings.

She loved him, and she was certain that he loved her. Could he ever acknowledge that or admit it? His traumatic early life had left him with emotional scars that were so deep he might never recover. When they first met, she'd thought he was cold and distant. Now, she knew better. Behind that facade, there was a scared, shy little boy.

Being ripped out of his home and relocated at such a young age had damaged his sense of identity and had a devastating effect on his ability to form bonds. Added to that, it was clear that he had been unable to fully fit in with his Colton family. No wonder he was afraid of getting too close to another person, scared of letting his craving for love show.

But, whether he liked it or not, they were in a relationship. Despite all the chaos around them, Griffin, Abigail, Maya and a heroic little ferret had become a family. And she was not going to give that up. Not without a fight.

There it was. She'd found her fighting spirit. Almost without noticing, the gloom had lifted from her shoulders a little and, instead of wanting to cry, she felt more like her old self. Ready to square her shoulders—well, maybe to just square one shoulder for the time being—and face the world.

Her cell phone pinged with an incoming text from an unknown number and she frowned as a photograph unfolded on the screen. It was an image of herself, clearly taken at the gym without her knowledge. She recognized the locker room decor behind her, and, in the picture, she was holding a towel against her chest as she emerged from the shower. It felt intrusive and Abigail had no memory of it being taken.

After she'd studied it for a few seconds, a message followed.

I have others. You and the Coltons love social media. Let's see how much you enjoy it when naked pictures of Wes Matthews's daughter start going viral.

There was a knock on the door and her voice shook as she called out, "Come in."

"Ready for some company?" Griffin opened the door and stepped inside. He was carrying Maya, who gave Abigail a beaming smile and held out her arms. He took one look at her face and crossed the room in quick strides. "What's happened?"

Wordlessly, she held out her cell. His face darkened with anger as he read the message. When he finished, he looked up. "Jenna?"

"It has to be. We were members of the same gym. We went together a few times. But I had no idea she was taking pictures of me."

"Forward this to Emmanuel," Griffin said. "I know she's not using her own number, but he may be able to do something."

As they were talking, Maya started squirming to get to Abigail.

"It's okay. Put her on the bed," Abigail said. "I'm not going to let Jenna spoil our time together."

Griffin came to sit next to her and placed Maya between them. The baby curled up contentedly against Abigail's side and she drew her into the crook of her uninjured elbow for a closer snuggle. Griffin placed his arm around Abigail's shoulder, resting his cheek on her hair and they sat that way for long, silent minutes.

"This," Griffin said at last.

"I know."

"Do you?"

She held her breath for a second or two. "I love you, Griffin."

When he didn't answer, she thought she'd blown it. Closing her eyes, she blinked away the tears. Even if he never admitted it she knew he loved her. And she wouldn't regret saying it. He needed to hear it...

"I love you, too." She looked up and saw the raw emotion in his eyes. The wetness on his cheeks. "I was waiting for the right time to tell you."

She turned awkwardly, reaching over Maya's head to touch his cheek. "It's always the right time."

He nodded, leaning closer to kiss her. "Then I'll keep saying it."

Chapter Fifteen

Griffin had the strangest feeling. As if his past, while not exactly floating away into obscurity, had at last been relegated to where it should be. It was behind him. He couldn't change what had happened and he had to move on. He had a future now.

Happiness flowed through him, warming his skin like the rays of the early morning sun. His usual cautious smile had been replaced by a grin so wide it was in danger of splitting his face in two. He would never fear love again, because he had found it. And, after all his years of angst, it had been the most natural, wonderful thing in the world.

Now, we just have to defeat the bad guys, get Maya's adoption back on track, and get on with our lives.

With that in mind, he had checked in with Emmanuel about Jenna's message to Abigail. The detective wasn't hopeful about tracing her from it.

"She's using a burner phone. The likelihood is she'll discard that one and buy another to send the next message. The chances of tracking her down that way are slim, if not nonexistent."

It was frustrating but not unexpected. Emmanuel had continued to assure him that they were doing all they could to find Jenna.

Now, still on the subject of bad guys, the CI team was gathered for another meeting. This time, the focus was on Capital X, the anonymous, underground loan company.

CI had been determined to break open Capital X. But, no matter how hard they tried to get details on the group, it was intricate and underground. Operating out of the dark web, it was as devious as it was dangerous.

The team was joined by Ashanti Silver, their brilliant technical expert.

Occasionally, a burst of laughter from the kitchen reached them and lightened the mood. Charlize was preparing dinner and Abigail had joined her, since she knew nothing about Capital X. Maya was with them and was clearly proving to be a source of entertainment. Griffin was pleased that the two women got along so well and that Maya would soon have someone in the family to play with.

"I don't have any more news for you guys about Capital X," Ashanti said. "Because they use the dark web, they are able to hide their activities well. It's a haven for bad guys."

"Explain to us again how that works," Kiely said.

"Putting it simply, imagine that the internet is a forest and within it there are well-worn paths, the ones that most people use. Those paths are the popular search engines. Away from these paths—or search engines—the trees will mask your vision. Then it becomes almost impossible to find anything, unless you know what you're looking for. This is how the dark web works, and it is essentially the name given to all the hidden places on the internet."

"So you stumble around and get lost?" Sadie said.

"Yes." Ashanti nodded. "Or you need a guide. Just like the forest, the dark web hides things well. It hides actions and it hides identities. The dark web also prevents people from knowing who you are, what you are doing and where you are doing it."

"How do you ever find your way?" Vikki asked.

Ashanti gave a confident grin. "You have to understand the forest better than everyone else."

"If the only way to communicate with Capital X is via the dark web, we have to send them a message that will make them take notice," Pippa said.

She had a reckless look about her that worried Griffin. "What do you have in mind?"

She leaned forward. "Let's take this fight to them. I think one of us should infiltrate Capital X by pretending to be looking for a big loan. They won't be able resist getting hold of another victim."

"I don't like the sound of that." Riley shook his head. "These guys are ruthless."

"Who are you suggesting should be the one to go undercover and get inside Capital X?" Griffin asked. He had a feeling he already knew the answer.

"I'll do it." Pippa tossed her head. "It's my plan, I'll be the one to see it through."

There was a general chorus of dissent, with none of the siblings approving of her suggestion. Each of Pippa's brothers and sisters had their own forceful argument to put forward for why it would be too dangerous. Pippa remained calm in the face of their opposition.

"Putting my neck out is my job. This is what I do," she insisted, when everyone was all talked out. "These low-lifes will take one look at me and think they've got their claws into another vulnerable person. They won't know I can handle myself."

"We can't let you do this," Griffin insisted. "Look at what's happened to Brody. That has to be a warning to anyone thinking of tangling with Capital X and their thugs."

She sighed. "At least let me do some more research before you try and stop me. Then I'll come back to you with a detailed plan. Ashanti, we can work together and use the dark web to find out more, right?"

Ashanti nodded. "Yeah. But stick with me. Your team are right to be nervous. These guys don't mess around."

Pippa grinned. "Nor do I."

ONCE THE MEETING was finished, Charlize served dinner to the team. Ashanti had left, having explained that she was going on a date with the love of her life, her math teacher husband, Jeffrey.

"That's so sweet." Sadie placed a hand over her heart after Ashanti had gone. "I hope Tate and I are still like that after a few years of marriage."

Abigail had noticed before how a curious silence descended whenever Sadie mentioned her fiancé, Tate Greer. It happened again now. No one responded to the comment, and the other siblings suddenly became engrossed in passing around the food and handing out drinks.

Sadie tossed her head. "Since we're all together, it seems like a good time to let you know that Tate and I have decided on a Christmas wedding."

None of the usual outpouring of congratulations followed the announcement. Abigail caught a glimpse of tears in Sadie's eyes and felt sorry for her. She didn't understand what was going on. The Coltons were such a close, caring family. How could they ignore something so important to their sister?

"Could you pass the potatoes, please?" Vikki asked Kiely.

"Don't all rush to congratulate me, will you?" Sadie's lower lip trembled as she looked around at her brothers and sisters.

"All we want is for you to be happy." Griffin reached over and pressed his sister's hand.

"But you don't think that will happen if I marry Tate." Sadie was clearly upset. Getting to her feet, she snatched up her purse with a trembling hand. "I'm sorry, Charlize. I know you've gone to a lot of trouble, but I'm just not hungry."

Pushing back her chair, she ran from the room. Her heels clattered on the kitchen floor and they heard the rear door slam behind her.

"I'll go after her." Riley followed her from the room.

"Why can't she see through this guy instead of getting upset with us?" Griffin asked his other sisters.

"She thinks we have an irrational dislike of him." Vikki, Sadie's twin, shrugged. "She can't see past her own feelings and understand why we're so worried about her."

"You can tell me it's none of my business," Abigail said. "But what is it about this guy that troubles you so much?"

"Firstly, it is your business." Kiely smiled at her. "You and Charlize are part of the family."

"And secondly, Tate Greer is a slick, expensive-suit-wearing businessman who throws his cash around. He claims to be in imports/exports but he has no visible means of making money," Griffin said.

"We've checked him out off the record, and he has no criminal record," Pippa said. "But there's just something about him..."

"I worry that the guy is really a gang boss," Griffin confessed. "Or that he's involved in some other dirty business."

"Is that really possible?" Abigail asked. "Sadie is a CSI for the Grand Rapids PD. Wouldn't she recognize a criminal if she saw one? Particularly if she got to know him well?"

"Sadie is dazzled by him," Vikki said. "She was a late bloomer. Tate is the good-looking bad guy with his tattoos and his Harley. He's swept her off her feet and I don't think she could ever see anything bad in him."

"You know her better than any of us," Griffin said. "Has Sadie ever confided that she has any hesitations or suspicions about Tate?"

Vikki shook her head. "Not to me. The only times she talks about him are to say how much she loves him. I've met him a few more times than the rest of you. He's a charmer but I didn't like him even though I can't say why. There is one thing that strikes me as odd, though."

"What's that?" Griffin asked.

"Why does he want to marry Sadie?" Vikki shrugged. "I mean, we all love her and think she's gorgeous. But I do wonder what a guy like Tate would see in our good-girl sister."

They were quietly pondering the question when Riley returned. "She's calmed down, but she wants to go home." He rubbed a hand along his jawline. "We need to be careful. We can't let our dislike of Tate cause a rift between us an Sadie."

"That won't happen." Griffin's voice was firm. "We won't let it."

"Even so, we should try to lighten up and look like we are accepting him into the family—" Riley held up a hand. "I know. I know. I feel the same way as the rest of you. At the same time, we can keep investigating him without letting Sadie know what we're doing."

"We could find out that Tate is just an obnoxious guy but that there is no harm in him," Pippa said.

"If that's the case, we'll have to welcome him into the family for Sadie's sake." Griffin's gloomy expression was reflected around the table.

"That won't happen," Riley assured him. "Our instincts will be proved right. He's a bad guy and it's just a matter of time before we find out what that means."

"Meanwhile, we have to wait for him to hurt our sister." Glumly, Kiely speared a carrot and glared at it as though she hated it.

"If he does that, he'll regret it." Griffin's words were greeted by nods from his siblings. "Now, can we forget Tate Greer while we finish this delicious meal?"

ABIGAIL WAS SURE that the improvement in her physical health had a lot to do with her emotional well-being. She was happier now than she'd ever been. Not even the threat of Jenna lurking in the background could destroy her newfound joy. Over the following few days, as she basked in the knowledge that Griffin loved her, she grew stronger. At the same time, her worries about getting Maya's adoption back on track remained. Until Jenna was caught, and the true story came out, Abigail's status as a mom was still in doubt.

When the nurse came for her visit, she nodded approvingly. "This wound is healing really well."

"When can I stop wearing the sling?" Abigail

asked. It felt like a big step on the road to recovery. Having two arms again instead of one would make a huge difference, especially when it came to caring for Maya.

"You can take it off for short periods each day," the nurse said. "But if your arm aches, or feels tired, you must start to wear it again. I'll speak to Dr. Reynolds and ask her to arrange your physiotherapy."

"Thank you."

After walking the nurse to the door, Abigail went in search of Griffin. She found him drinking coffee in the kitchen with Emmanuel Iglesias.

"Where's Maya?" she asked.

"Sleeping." He jerked a thumb in the direction of the baby monitor. "She finished her lunch while you were with the nurse, then got a bit cranky, so I took her for a nap."

"Oh, that's good." She smiled. "Dealing with a tired baby when I only have one working arm. Well, it's something I'd rather not do."

"Emmanuel is here to give us an update about Jenna," Griffin said.

Abigail turned hopefully to the detective. "Really?"

He held up a hand. "Please don't get your hopes up. I came to see you because I thought you deserved to know where the investigation was. But that doesn't mean I have anything new to tell you."

Abigail's shoulders slumped. "So you still have no idea where she is?"

"I'm sorry," Emmanuel said. "I do have some news

for you. I put out an alert to all medical facilities in the Grand Rapids area to inform me if a woman sought help for an animal bite to the left wrist. Two days ago, a woman matching Jenna's description attended a private clinic and asked for antibiotics because of an infected injury. The doctor who attended her believed the wound could have been caused by an animal bite. When we showed him pictures, he identified his patient as Jenna Avery."

"Where was this clinic?" Griffin asked.

"In the Roosevelt Park area but the address she gave was a false one."

"Of course it was." Abigail rolled her eyes.

"We've concentrated our search in that general location and the clinic visit tells us two things. One is that Jenna is still in the Grand Rapids area. The second is that she is badly injured. The doctor said the wound was deep and the infection was serious. He told her to come back and see him the following day because she might need hospitalization. She didn't return."

"Do either of those things bring you closer to catching her?" Abigail asked. She knew there was a sharp note in her voice. She also knew the police were doing their best. But their best wasn't good enough right now. She wouldn't feel safe until Jenna was behind bars and that wasn't happening.

"I know it may not look like we're making any progress," Emmanuel said. "But we are doing everything we can to find her. And the injury that your ferret inflicted might just be what brings her in. If she is as ill as the doctor who saw her recently believes, she won't be able to manage much longer without help."

At that precise moment, Abigail's cell pinged with an incoming message. Once again, the number wasn't in her list of contacts.

Hey. How about I shoot Griffin in the head while he's out running? I'd enjoy sharing that video on social media.

Feeling slightly nauseated, she passed her phone to Emmanuel. "Jenna seems to be managing just fine."

The detective's lips tightened as he read the message. "Have you been out running since Abigail was stabbed?" he asked Griffin.

"No. But surely that's not the point?" Griffin frowned as he read the text over Emmanuel's shoulder. "Despite your efforts, Jenna is still out there, and she is feeling confident enough to send harassing messages to Abigail."

"It's not just her confidence in sending messages that worries me. It's her willingness to put her plans into action." Abigail moved her left arm slightly, feeling the pull of her injury. "She stabbed me in a public place. I'm scared that she won't hesitate to come after me and Maya even though we are living here in Riley and Charlize's home."

"I can only stress again that you have to be vigilant and let us do our job," Emmanuel said. "We will catch her."

"But will you be in time?" Abigail asked as he gave her back her phone.

"That's the plan." Emmanuel got to his feet as he spoke.

She watched him as he and Griffin walked to the door. Those words weren't confident enough for her liking. Not when her own, and her little girl's, lives depended on them.

AN HOUR LATER, Abigail picked up the baby monitor and checked the battery warning light. It seemed to be in working order.

"Is something wrong?" Griffin asked.

She returned to the sofa in the den, where they had been snuggled up together enjoying an old movie. "No."

After a few minutes, she sat up straight. "Maya has been awfully quiet. Usually we hear grunts and snuffles but there's been nothing."

He grinned at her. "Just relax and enjoy it."

"I know I should." She returned the smile. "But I think I'll go check on her."

He picked up the remote and paused the movie. "Want me to go?"

She shook her head. "I'm fine. Back in two minutes."

It was foolish she knew, but the situation with Jenna was making her nervous. Of course Maya was fine but she needed to see that for herself.

"Is everything okay?" Charlize was coming out of the kitchen as Abigail headed toward the stairs.

"Yes. I'm just going to Griffin's room to check on Maya."

"But…" Charlize looked confused. "Isn't she with you?"

A tiny slither of dread trickled down Abigail's spine like a raindrop down a windowpane. "No. Griffin put her down for a nap over an hour ago."

"Yes, but then the nurse came to get her. She said you asked her to take Maya to you."

Letting out a cry, Abigail started to run up the stairs. "Get Griffin," she called over her shoulder.

Although she already knew what to expect, her heart dropped to her feet when she saw the empty crib. Her knees buckled and she felt herself falling. Before she hit the floor, a pair of strong arms caught hold of her and pulled her upright.

"What happened?" Griffin held her against his chest. "Where's Maya?"

"I'm sorry." Charlize was in tears as she stood in the doorway. "She told me she was the nurse."

Griffin already had his cell phone in his hand and, within seconds, was telling Emmanuel what had happened.

"What did she look like?" Abigail asked Charlize.

"Small and dark. She was wearing a nurse's uniform, of course."

Abigail shook her head. "The real nurse was tall

and fair. I walked her to the door when our appointment was over."

Griffin ended his call. "Emmanuel is on his way over, but he already has an alert out for Jenna and Maya. I don't understand how, if she's injured, she could have carried the baby down the stairs?"

Charlize hung her head. "She asked me to carry Maya for her. She had a bag in her left hand and she explained that she couldn't hold the baby as well. It was only when we reached the bottom of the stairs that she took Maya from me." She started to cry again. "I asked if she wanted help carrying her to your room, but she said she'd be fine. And now I think about it, I briefly held her bag as she took Maya from me and it felt like it was empty."

"That's because it was a prop to disguise the fact that her left wrist was injured," Griffin said. "It's not your fault, Charlize. You couldn't have known that it was Jenna in disguise."

"Of course it's not your fault. Jenna has been waiting to trick one of us. But how did she get in?" Abigail could feel panic bubbling up inside her and threatening to boil over. "We've been so careful to keep the house secure."

"While we're waiting for Emmanuel, let's take a look and see if we can figure out how she did it," Griffin said.

When they reached the bottom of the stairs, Riley came into the hall from the kitchen and Charlize ran to him with a cry. "Thank goodness you're home."

He looked at her tear-stained face in alarm. "What's been going on?"

Griffin quickly told him what had happened. "Let's split up and check out the downstairs rooms." He tightly clasped Abigail's hand and they headed through to the dining room.

"I can't bear this." She clung to the front of his T-shirt, scared to let go. "What if—?"

"No." He kissed her forehead. "We are not going to do 'what if.' We'll find her and she'll be fine."

She gulped back a sob before looking around the room. "I can't see any way Jenna could have got in here."

They moved on, stepping into the next room. It was little more than a storeroom, but it had a small window.

"There." Griffin pointed. "There is a broken pane and the lock has been tampered with."

"You mean Jenna could have gotten in and out of the house anytime she wanted?" Abigail swallowed hard.

"Well, with a police presence outside, I'm guessing she used the cover of darkness most of the time." Griffin frowned as he looked around the small space. "Today, she must have been concealed in here, waiting for the perfect opportunity. It came when you were busy with the nurse, I was with Emmanuel and Riley had gone out. There was only Charlize to deal with and she tricked her by dressing as a nurse."

Abigail shuddered. "The thought of her hiding out

in this house, watching us, waiting to pounce… Then taking our baby girl…"

He gripped her uninjured arm. "Stay strong. For Maya."

Although she felt sick to her stomach and light-headed, Abigail clung to those words. "For Maya."

A few moments later, they heard Emmanuel's voice. Griffin called him into the storeroom and showed him the window.

"Jenna must have approached the house from the rear." The detective studied the broken window thoughtfully. "We've had a patrol car at the front the whole time."

"Can we save the speculation about the details of *how* she got in for after we have Maya back safe?" Griffin asked. "Right now, I'd rather focus on how we're going to find them."

As he finished speaking, Abigail's cell phone pinged and, with a feeling of dread, she withdrew it from her pocket. A picture of Maya filled the screen.

"My baby," she gasped.

"Forward it to me," Emmanuel said. "I'll send it for instant analysis in case there are any clues in the background."

Another picture followed. It was of a syringe next to a bottle of RevitaYou vitamins.

"What does that mean?" Abigail turned to Griffin in confusion.

"There's a text message coming through." He held the phone so they could read it together.

Your dad put ricin in his pills. He didn't care that the people who took them were dicing with death. Some would live. Some would die. Which group will Maya be in? Guess we'll find out when I inject her with the poisonous vitamins.

Abigail gave a moan and stumbled to her knees. Griffin knelt beside her, wrapping his arms around her. Looking up at Emmanuel, his voice reflected Abigail's own anguish. "We have to find them. Now."

Chapter Sixteen

The next few hours had a nightmarish quality to them. Abigail had retreated behind a wall of silence and she was shivering wildly as though suffering from a terrible illness. Griffin tried to comfort her and, at the same time, liaise with the police and his siblings.

Emmanuel had thrown every resource available to the GRPD into the search but, with no real leads, he was struggling to track Jenna down. Although no one said the words out loud, they all knew they were racing against time. If Jenna carried out her threat to inject Maya with RevitaYou, the consequences would be unthinkable.

The Colton siblings had raced to see what they could do to help. Riley was coordinating the CI team and his sisters had mobilized everyone they knew into a task force. As a result, dozens of people were out on the road, trying to trace where Jenna could have gone after she snatched Maya. Like the police, they were finding it hard to come up with any leads.

"I'll make coffee," Griffin said. "Strong and black

with plenty of sugar. Isn't that meant to be good for shock?"

Abigail didn't answer. Instead, she continued to stare at the blank screen of her cell phone as though willing something to appear on it.

"Come to the kitchen with me." He took her hand and she rose from the sofa, allowing him to lead her. Her movements reminded him of a rag doll, as though her body had no muscle or bone, nothing to give it strength or resistance.

While he prepared the drinks, Griffin kept talking, watching Abigail as he did. It would destroy them both if anything happened to Maya, but she was already crumbling. When her cell phone indicated that there was an incoming message, she almost went into orbit.

"It's her again."

He rushed to her side in time to see another picture of Maya. This time the baby was lying on a table with brightly colored cartoon characters painted on its surface. The bottle of RevitaYou and the syringe had been placed next to her.

It's almost time. Are you ready for the video?

Abigail gave a hoarse cry and covered her mouth with her right hand. She gestured wildly at her phone, but no sound came out of her mouth.

"It'll be okay—"

"No." Finally, she managed to speak. She gripped

his arm so tightly that he winced. "That picture… I know where she is."

"What?"

"The table." She pointed to the image on the screen of her cell. "It's in the laboratory at Danvers University where Jenna and our colleagues worked on the miscarriage project. It's like a baby changing table, but there was a mobile above it to distract the infants when we needed to take blood, or do other tests. If you look closely, you can even see a corner of the university logo in the background."

Griffin already had his own cell phone in his hand. Emmanuel answered immediately. "Jenna is at Danvers University in one of the laboratories. Abigail will be able to guide you to the exact location. We'll meet you there."

"There's still a patrol car at your gate. They'll give you an escort."

Griffin called out to Riley. Partly to let him know what was happening, but also because he needed to get his licensed weapon from the gun safe. Minutes later, they were dashing toward the door. Then they were outside in the warm night air and running toward the car.

"Will we be in time?" Abigail asked as Griffin gunned the engine.

"We have to be."

Secure in the knowledge that he had a police car just behind him, he drove at speed through the familiar streets. It wasn't enough. If his vehicle had been powered by rocket fuel, he'd have wanted more. His daughter needed him.

When they reached the Danvers University entrance, a uniformed cop halted them. "Detective Iglesias is expecting you. He asked that you turn off your lights, then drive to the far side of the parking lot."

Griffin followed his instruction. In the darkened corner of the lot, Emmanuel was waiting for them with a number of other police officers. There was also an ambulance and a couple of paramedics standing by. Griffin and Abigail alighted from the car and Emmanuel beckoned for them to join him under the cover of a group of trees.

"I don't want to alert Jenna to our presence." He held up an electronic tablet. "I have a plan here of this part of the building. Can you show me which room Jenna is in?"

Abigail stepped forward, consulting the plan on the screen. "She's in this laboratory." She pointed to a room. "It's on the first floor and on the opposite side of the building to where we are now."

"You're basing this on a table that was in the picture she sent you. Are you certain she couldn't have moved it to another room?"

"No." Abigail shook her head firmly. "It's fixed to the wall."

"Okay." Emmanuel addressed the officers around him. "The danger in this situation is that if the kidnapper becomes aware that we are here, she may harm the baby. Therefore, I need a circle around the building, with every exit covered. But, when I decide the time is right, I will go in there alone." He looked directly at Griffin. "Is that clear?"

Griffin nodded. "Crystal."

When Emmanuel turned away to give instructions to his officers, Griffin leaned closer to Abigail. "It may be clear, but it's not happening."

AFTER A FEW MINUTES, Emmanuel gave the order for his officers to get into position. Once they'd formed a circle around the laboratory block, he went to the front entrance. He had called ahead and arranged for the building supervisor to meet him there and disarm the security system and unlock the doors. Having removed his weapon from its shoulder holster, he stepped inside the lobby.

Once Emmanuel had disappeared from view, Griffin took Abigail's hand. "He's going to take this too slow. Is there another entrance?"

She nodded. "There's a door close to the laboratory where Jenna is holding Maya. Unless the code has been changed since I left, I should be able to get us in there." She cast a quick glance around. "I want to get Maya out as much as you do, but are you sure we shouldn't leave it to Emmanuel?"

"I'm not going to interfere with the police operation unless I have to, but he's going to play by the rules and Jenna won't. I just want to make sure we're there for Maya when things get messy."

She nodded. "Let's go."

Avoiding the police line, she led him to a smaller entrance on the opposite side of the building. Typing the familiar code into the keypad at the side of the door, she held her breath, half expecting it not to work. Instead, there was a click, and she pushed the door open.

How many times had she entered the building this way, coffee in hand, ready to start a day's work? Now she was here to save Maya's life.

"We need to be careful," Griffin whispered as they stepped inside. "We don't want to meet Emmanuel coming in the opposite direction. He could shoot first and ask questions later."

"The laboratory is two doors down on the right."

"Here's the plan. You grab Maya while I tackle Jenna."

She nodded. "Simple but effective."

With Griffin in the lead, they slowly inched their way along the wall. Although she tried to force herself to stay positive, she couldn't help wondering why Maya wasn't crying. It was hours since the baby had last eaten or had a bottle of formula. She would be confused and missing Abigail and Griffin. Maya was going through a phase in which she was wary of strangers unless she was in her mom's arms. And Abigail couldn't imagine that Jenna had treated her gently. A baby who could scream the place down at the sight of a diaper should not be silent in these circumstances.

Griffin stopped outside the second door and raised

his eyebrows. Abigail nodded. This was it. Their baby girl was on the other side.

She has to be okay...

After pausing to listen carefully, Griffin placed his hand on the door handle and slowly turned it. Abigail's hands shook at her sides, her injured arm ached from being out of the sling for so long, and she jammed her right fist against her lips to mask her noisy, ragged breathing. Her eyes were open so wide that the muscles felt strained, and as the door swung open, she followed Griffin on legs that felt stiff and clumsy.

The room was almost completely dark, the only light coming from a small desk lamp. Maya was still strapped to the table, as she had been in the picture. She was asleep. Or drugged? *Not worse. Please, not worse...*

Jenna was slumped in a chair at her side, from the way her head had dropped forward and her mouth gaped open, she appeared to be sleeping.

As soon as she saw her baby, Abigail gave a soft whimper and made a movement to brush past Griffin to get to her. He reached out an arm to hold her back, pointing to Jenna's hand. In it, she was holding the syringe that had been in the picture she'd sent.

He moved up close, pressing his lips to Abigail's ear. "Startle her and she could use it."

The tight cramps in Abigail's stomach loosened a little. From where they were standing, they couldn't see whether the syringe was empty or full. It was possible that Jenna *hadn't* already injected Maya with the

RevitaYou. Griffin was right. If their girl had a chance, they had to take care.

Griffin signaled for her to move with him across the room. If they could get to the other side without disturbing Jenna, they would be able to approach her from behind. It was a long shot but all they had. Even though ice water seemed to be flowing through her veins and trickling down her spine, Abigail felt curiously calm. They were doing something. Back at the CI headquarters, when everyone else was out searching and she'd been waiting for news, she'd seriously believed her mind might just cave under the pressure.

Now, she and Griffin had taken charge. She was almost in touching distance of her baby girl...

"What?" Jenna grunted and sat up. She appeared dazed as she looked around her.

"Now." Griffin dived forward, toppling her from her chair. Jenna let out a screech of anger and sprang up, clawing at him.

Although she was concerned about Griffin, Abigail had one priority: Maya. Struggling to see in the gloomy light, she grappled with the restraints on the table. As she did, she was relieved to note that Maya was breathing, although she was definitely sleeping too soundly. She'd been drugged. But was it the RevitaYou, or had Jenna given her a sedative?

Finally, she managed to get the straps that were holding Maya in place free. Clutching her baby to her chest, Abigail stepped to one side. She needed to get Maya outside to the paramedics, but Jenna was between her and the door. She switched on the overhead light, anxiously watching what was going on and waiting for a chance to make a run for it.

Jenna was no match for Griffin's size and strength, but she had reached the desk and was hurling everything she could find in his direction. He ducked the flying objects and continued to approach her. When she picked up a pair of scissors, he paused.

"The police are outside, Jenna. It's all over."

Even though Jenna had been on the run and the bite Lucy had given her was infected, the other woman's appearance shocked Abigail. Her skin was deathly pale with brilliant crimson blotches and her eyes were red rimmed. She looked like an extra from a horror movie.

"Over for who?" Throwing the scissors at him, she dived to the floor, snatching up the discarded syringe.

As she rolled toward Griffin, Abigail cried out a warning. At the same time, Emmanuel burst into the room. As Jenna prepared to jab the needle into Griffin's leg, Emmanuel grabbed her and pinned her down. She gave a wail of mingled pain and fury as the action caused her to release the plunger and inject herself in the side.

"This stuff is poisonous. I could die."

She was still screaming as Emmanuel handcuffed her and explained that she was under arrest.

"Don't you see what this means?" Abigail turned to Griffin. "She didn't inject Maya with the RevitaYou."

"Not because I wouldn't have." Jenna spat the word

out. "I just wanted to torture you a little longer. All I gave her was the oral sedation we use for babies who need an MRI scan."

As she spoke, Maya hiccupped and opened her eyes.

"Let's get her checked over by the paramedics," Griffin said.

A few minutes later, they were seated in the back of the ambulance. Maya was drinking water from a sippy cup and playing with a stethoscope.

"Her vital signs are all fine," the paramedic told them. "There can be side effects from oral sedation, but they are minor. Tiredness, irritability, possibly vomiting. If you have any concerns, just call us."

"She's okay." Abigail rested her head on Griffin's shoulder. "We're all okay."

"What part of 'I'm going in there alone' didn't you understand?" Emmanuel joined them in the ambulance.

"She's our baby," Griffin said.

"I guess I'd have done the same in the circumstances." The detective sighed. "If Maya is ready to go home, we're going to need this ambulance. Jenna is screaming about police brutality and forcible ricin poisoning."

"We were there," Griffin said. "We saw what happened."

"Thanks." Emmanuel patted Maya's cheek. "Totally worth it to get this little one back unharmed."

When he'd gone, Griffin lifted Maya into the

crook of one arm and placed the other around Abigail's shoulder. "Let's go and let the rest of the family know we're safe."

THE WHOLE FAMILY had gathered around the dining table to briefly celebrate Maya's homecoming. The baby, who had shown no ill effects following her ordeal, had been delighted to see everyone. Having entertained them with her whole repertoire of clapping, waving and peekaboo, she had finally fallen asleep in Abigail's arms.

Now it was close to midnight and Abigail was still watching over her as she slumbered.

"She's fine and you need to get some sleep." Gently, Griffin steered her away from the side of the baby's crib.

"I know. It's just, after everything that's happened, I almost can't believe we can stop looking over our shoulders at last."

"Why don't we take the baby monitor downstairs. I'll make us a hot drink and we can talk without disturbing Maya," Griffin said.

"I'm not sure…" She gave the monitor a wary look and he knew she was thinking of what had happened the last time they'd left Maya alone. Although her caution was understandable, he was determined to help her overcome it.

"Riley has put new locks on all the first-floor windows and I'll check on Maya regularly." He took her hand. "But Jenna is behind bars."

She nodded. "I know that. I just keep thinking about how close we came to losing her."

"And now we have her back." He led her to the door. "And she's not going anywhere ever again."

They went into the kitchen and, even though the night was warm, Griffin made hot chocolate. Once they were in Abigail's room, they switched on the bedside lamps and sat side by side on the bed.

"This is nice." She rested her head on his shoulder with a contended sigh. "Like something normal people do."

"We could go home tomorrow." He paused for a few seconds. "If you want."

"Oh." She reached across him for her drink and took a sip. "Whose home?"

"That's up to you."

She returned her drink to the bedside table before shifting position to look at his face. "What does that mean?"

"It means I'm asking you—very clumsily—if we can get married and adopt Maya together as husband and wife."

Her beaming smile was the only answer he needed. "I would love to marry you, Griffin."

"I was so scared of love that I never gave myself a chance to try it. I loved my mom with all my heart and when she died my world fell apart. I felt like nothing could be worth that same gut-wrenching pain all over again." He wrapped his arms around her, taking care not to hurt her injured arm. "But, at the same time, I craved love. I was terrified that I would drive other people away with my longing for acceptance. I can see now that was why I backed off from my Colton family. I wanted to be part of the group, but I was scared of losing them. When it came to dating, I would take a few steps, then back off, afraid of getting in too deep or coming on too strong."

She touched his cheek. "I'm so sorry you were scared."

"But that's just it. Because of you, I'm not scared anymore. I fell in love with you during the worst possible time in our lives. Your world had been shaken upside down and I wanted to be the one you could lean on to get through it. I fell in love with you in the darkest most painful days we'd both experienced. But loving you is worth it. Loving you makes me feel alive. And I know now that I deserve to know what it feels like to fall in love. Even better, I deserve to be loved."

"You do." Abigail placed a hand on his face. "And I'm looking forward to spending my whole life loving you. For me, it was a different kind of fear. I knew what happened when you love the wrong person," Abigail said. "I saw my own mom give her heart over and over and get it broken every time. And somehow, because she'd made a commitment to my dad, she was supposed to glue the pieces back together, pin a smile on her face and carry on. I knew from a very early age that I wasn't going to let that happen to me. I would never let someone else be careless with my heart."

She felt the tears on her cheeks and brushed them

away. "But I know I can trust you with my heart, Griffin, just as I trusted you with our baby's life. I'm so glad we didn't let our fears hold us back from finding each other and from something so magical."

He drew her back into his arms, sliding into a half-lying position. "What sort of wedding shall we have?"

"One where Maya can be a flower girl." She answered promptly. "And, if Maya is walking, she can hold Lucy's leash as they walk down the aisle."

"Have you already planned this?"

"I might have given it some thought." She tilted her chin and gave him a mischievous smile. "There's something else I've been thinking about."

He studied her face in fascination. "What's that?"

"Remember that shower we said we'd share…?"

Chapter Seventeen

The next day, Emmanuel came to see them. "Jenna hasn't confessed. Not exactly. But there is so much evidence against her that it doesn't really matter."

"Why did she kill Evan?" Abigail asked.

"Because he was going to fire her. She believed it was over her online adoption scam," Emmanuel said. "When Jenna was working on the miscarriage project, she'd seen an opportunity to make money and had developed the MorningStar baby con. It had worked well for her with no real issues and she made a lot of money from it. When she found out someone was on to her about her fake company, she assumed it was you, Abigail, because she knew you were looking into adoption."

"But it was me," Griffin said. "Liam and Shelby Desmond had asked me to investigate the online scam."

"And the reason why Evan had decided to let her go had nothing to do with her dirty tricks," Emmanuel said. "When we went through his computer, we found her dismissal letter in his files. Jenna was a shoddy worker and she'd been falsifying scientific evidence as part of her research. Dr. Hardin had warned her in the past, although it seems he'd given her chances because of their brief affair. This time he wasn't prepared to give her another chance."

"She killed him for that?" Abigail asked.

"People kill for less," Emmanuel said.

"But she went back and planted the bracelet at the scene," Griffin pointed out. "Are you sure it wasn't her intention to frame Abigail all along?"

"That's a possibility, I guess, but we'll never know the answer. Any half-decent defense lawyer will go for the spur of the moment scenario. Killing her boss in anger because she was devastated at the thought of losing her job sounds better than bashing his head in to frame a coworker she hated."

"But I lost the bracelet six months ago, long before the RevitaYou story broke, or before Griffin started looking into MorningStar." Abigail was confused. "Jenna and I were friends back then. If she picked up my bracelet when I lost it, why didn't she just return it?"

"Jenna's diary will be part of the evidence against her at the trial. It even gives details of how she planted the idea with Ryan Thorne of how you should 'get what was coming to you.' If you're feeling strong enough, I suggest you come and see me and read it before then," Emmanuel said. "But the answer is simple. She was jealous of you. Personally, and professionally, you were everything she wanted to be."

"So she made up the story about taking RevitaYou in order to publicly humiliate me?"

"It was a clumsy attempt. If she'd been serious, she could at least have researched what the pills looked like." Emmanuel smiled. "But I'm glad she didn't. Even though that damn green bottle gives me nightmares, Griffin was able to use it to trick her and spook her into the open."

"Yeah." Abigail rolled her eyes in Griffin's direction as she rubbed her left arm. "Thanks for that."

"Things could have gotten a lot worse," Emmanuel reminded her.

"I know." She leaned against Griffin. "I have a strange way of showing gratitude."

He smiled down at her. "But I like you anyway." He looked back at Emmanuel. "Returning to the serious conversation, do you know where Jenna was hiding out while she was on the run?"

"She was in the basement of an old house down the road."

Abigail gasped. "You thought she was in Roosevelt Park."

Emmanuel looked embarrassed. "I reached that conclusion because she sought medical help at a clinic in the Roosevelt Park area."

"So she was right here, watching us, the whole time?" Abigail shivered. "That's creepy."

"It seems she was reconnoitering the house, studying the entrances and exits, and watching who was coming in and out. We found pictures on her cell phone of the doors and windows, including close-ups of the window she smashed to get in here on the day she abducted Maya."

Abigail had to ask the next question, even though she dreaded the answer. "And the contents of the syringe?"

"Crushed RevitaYou pills mixed with water." Emmanuel grimaced. "Jenna was planning to film herself as she injected Maya with the compound and send the video to you in real time. She was slowed down by her infected wrist and took a nap. You can thank your little ferret buddy that she wasn't feeling strong enough to put her plan into action sooner."

Overtaken by a bad case of the "what-ifs?" Abigail bowed her head. Griffin placed a warm hand on the back of her neck, and, after a few seconds, she looked up again with a smile.

"I'm okay. But Lucy needs some serious treats when we get her home."

THE COLTON FAMILY removal machine was in full flow again. This time the team was moving furniture from Abigail's house into Griffin's apartment and taking other items to be placed in storage. They had decided that they would live at his place for the time being and make some permanent arrangements after the wedding.

"Abigail has her job back at Danvers and she's been completely cleared of all the allegations against her. The adoption process is proceeding as planned, so it feels like life is back on track," Griffin said to Riley. He looked across at where Abigail and Charlize were sitting in the shade and sorting through a box of baby clothes. As soon as they placed anything in a neat pile, Maya, who was trying out a crawl, came over and tossed it aside. "Well, life is a whole lot better than on track. A whole lot better than before."

"And I couldn't be happier. For both of us." Riley gripped his arm.

Pippa carried a tray of lemonade out onto the lawn and everyone gathered around as if she was a rescue dog carrying brandy in a blizzard. As they took a break, Griffin checked the local news on his cell phone. One of the items caught his attention. A homicide victim had been found in Heritage Park. The man, named Robin Olver, had been shot twice at close range.

In the video accompanying the news item, the anchor reported that Olver had invested in RevitaYou, the vitamin that had been in the news lately because of its deadly ricin compound. Anyone with information was encouraged to call the tip line…

"This needs to be checked out." He sent everyone

a link to the news item. "Robin Olver had eight recently broken bones."

"An even number of broken bones?" Riley looked up from his own cell phone when he'd finished reading. "You're thinking Capital X?"

"Has to be," Griffin said. "I'll call Emmanuel."

Emmanuel answered almost immediately. "Tell me you aren't thinking of performing any more heroic acts."

"Tell me you aren't thinking of taking up a new career in comedy."

"I'm too tired to be funny." Griffin could hear background noise as though Emmanuel was in a busy office. "What can I do for you?"

"This case that's being reported on the local news channel. The homicide victim who was found in Heritage Park? He was clearly killed by Capital X."

"What leads you to that conclusion?" Emmanuel asked.

"Aside from the fact that he'd invested in RevitaYou? The guy had eight recently broken bones. You know the Capital X goons break two at a time when their borrowers can't pay up. This Robin Olver must have been one of their victims."

"You could be right," Emmanuel conceded. "It's an angle we need to look at."

Griffin looked over his shoulder at the family group on the lawn. He took a few more steps away, making doubly sure he couldn't be overheard. "My sister, Pippa, is determined to infiltrate Capital X."

"You need to talk her out of that plan. Those guys are loan sharks and they're dangerous."

"We're doing our best to change her mind, but she's pretty stubborn. If she goes ahead with it, can I count on you to take care of her?"

"Griffin, if you sister manages to go undercover and get inside Capital X, you can rest assured that I will be watching her like a hawk."

Griffin thanked him and ended the call. A hand landed on his shoulder and he turned to find Pippa studying his face. "Who were you talking to so seriously?"

He considered the matter and decided it wouldn't hurt to tell her. "Emmanuel Iglesias."

She pulled a face. "Oh. Him."

It wasn't exactly promising. "Yes. I told him about your plans to infiltrate Capital X."

Pippa sucked in a breath. "It's got nothing to do with him."

"Maybe not. But he said he'd look out for you if you go ahead with that strategy."

"That's big of him." Pippa's whole body bristled. "But you can tell Detective Iglesias that the only way I'll work with the enemy will be over my dead body." She flounced away to join the rest of the group.

Bewildered by her reaction, he went to sit on the grass with Abigail and Maya. "Why would Pippa think of Emmanuel as the enemy?" he wondered.

Abigail shrugged. "I'm sure she has her reasons. And we should probably stay out of them."

"Wise words." He grinned. "Hey. You're all moved in."

She nudged his arm. "No getting rid of us now."

Griffin slid one arm around Abigail and the other around Maya. "That's exactly the way I want it."

* * * * *

COMING SOON!

We really hope you enjoyed reading this book. If you're looking for more romance, be sure to head to the shops when new books are available on

Thursday 6th August

To see which titles are coming soon, please visit

millsandboon.co.uk/nextmonth

LET'S TALK
Romance

For exclusive extracts, competitions
and special offers, find us online:

MILLS & BOON

THE HEART OF ROMANCE

A ROMANCE FOR EVERY KIND OF READER

MODERN

Prepare to be swept off your feet by sophisticated, sexy and seductive heroes, in some of the world's most glamourous and romantic locations, where power and passion collide.
8 stories per month.

HISTORICAL

Escape with historical heroes from time gone by. Whether your passion is for wicked Regency Rakes, muscled Vikings or rugged Highlanders, awaken the romance of the past.
6 stories per month.

MEDICAL

Set your pulse racing with dedicated, delectable doctors in the high-pressure world of medicine, where emotions run high, passion, comfort and love are the best medicine.
6 stories per month.

True Love

Celebrate true love with tender stories of heartfelt romance, the rush of falling in love to the joy a new baby can bring, and focus on the emotional heart of a relationship.
8 stories per month.

Desire

Indulge in secrets and scandal, intense drama and plenty of hot action with powerful and passionate heroes who have it all: wealth, status, good looks…everything but the right woman.
6 stories per month.

HEROES

Experience all the excitement of a gripping thriller, with an romance at its heart. Resourceful, true-to-life women and strong, fearless men face danger and desire - a killer combination!
8 stories per month.

DARE

Sensual love stories featuring smart, sassy heroines you'd want as a best friend, and compelling intense heroes who are worthy of them.
4 stories per month.

To see which titles are coming soon, please visit
millsandboon.co.uk/nextmonth

JOIN US ON SOCIAL MEDIA!

Stay up to date with our latest releases, author news and gossip, special offers and discounts, and all the behind-the-scenes action from Mills & Boon...

 millsandboon

 millsandboonuk

 millsandboon

might just be true love...

MILLS & BOON
MODERN
Power and Passion

Prepare to be swept off your feet by sophisticated, sexy and seductive heroes, in some of the world's most glamourous and romantic locations, where power and passion collide.

Julia James

Heiress's
PREGNANCY SCANDAL

MILLS & BOON
Modern

Jennie Lucas

Chosen as the
SHEIKH'S ROYAL BRIDE

MILLS & BOON

Kim Lawrence

A WEDDING
of the
ITALIAN'S DEMAND

MILLS

Sharon Kendrick

The
SHEIKH'S SECRET BABY

MILLS & BOON
MODERN

MILLS & BOON
True Love
Romance from the Heart

Celebrate true love with tender stories of heartfelt romance, from the rush of falling in love to the joy a new baby can bring, and a focus on the emotional heart of a relationship.